THE OTHERS

Also by Jeremy Robinson

Standalone Novels
The Didymus Contingency
Raising The Past
Beneath
Antarktos Rising
Kronos
Xom-B
Refuge
Flood Rising
MirrorWorld
Apocalypse Machine
Unity
The Distance
Forbidden Island
The Divide
The Others

Nemesis Saga Novels
Island 731
Project Nemesis
Project Maigo
Project 731
Project Hyperion
Project Legion

Post-Apocalyptic Sci-Fi
Hunger
Feast
Viking Tomorrow

The Antarktos Saga
The Last Hunter – Descent
The Last Hunter – Pursuit
The Last Hunter – Ascent
The Last Hunter – Lament
The Last Hunter – Onslaught
The Last Hunter – Collected Edition
The Last Valkyrie

SecondWorld Novels
SecondWorld
Nazi Hunter: Atlantis

The Jack Sigler/Chess Team Thrillers
Prime
Pulse
Instinct
Threshold
Ragnarok
Omega
Savage
Cannibal
Empire

Cerberus Group Novels
Herculean
Helios

Jack Sigler Continuum Novels
Guardian
Patriot
Centurion

Chesspocalypse Novellas
Callsign: King
Callsign: Queen
Callsign: Rook
Callsign: King 2 – Underworld
Callsign: Bishop
Callsign: Knight
Callsign: Deep Blue
Callsign: King 3 – Blackout

**Horror Novels
(written as Jeremy Bishop)**
Torment
The Sentinel
The Raven

Short Story Collection
Insomnia

THE OTHERS

JEREMY ROBINSON

BREAKNECK MEDIA

For Frank Robinson,
Who may or may not be from this planet,
but is definitely my father.

PROLOGUE

"You know I don't like coming here, Harry." Sheriff Albert Godin dusted off his hat, despite it being clean. "Especially for something like this. Even more so at this time of night."

Godin's stomach lurched as he looked down at the dead horse, its tongue lolled up atop its snout, as though mocking him from beyond the equine grave. Part of him felt like the creature was staring at him, too, but it had no eyes.

No organs.

No blood.

The cause of death was one or all of those things. There was no evidence about which had occurred first. Aside from the dead animal, and what was missing, there was no evidence at all.

Never was.

No fingerprints, hairs, foreign objects, or DNA. The incident would be written up as a mutilation, but Godin didn't think that was the right word. Mutilation implied something more...savage. Tearing. Rending. Chaos. But the horse had been operated upon. The organs removed. The blood drained. The flesh cauterized. Whoever did this—whoever was doing this—worked with the cool, calculating hands of a surgeon.

Or a Nazi scientist, Godin thought.

He shined his flashlight into the gaping cavity, examining the pink, marbleized flesh, and gleaming white, exposed ribs. He knew he wouldn't find anything, but he wouldn't stand by being accused of not doing his due diligence. "This is what, my fifth time out?"

"Sounds about right," Harry said. "Three cows. Two horses. My stallion's missing too, but we haven't found him. He'll turn up in the morning."

The Arizona horizon flashed pink with heat lightning. For years, Godin had believed the silent flashes of light to be something like magic. The advent of the Internet and instant answers to all of life's questions had taught him it was simply a storm too far away to hear. The knowledge had stolen his appreciation for the sight, but he welcomed the distraction tonight.

"You gonna do something about it this time?" Harry asked. His temper ran hotter than the previous day's hundred degree temperature, and Godin sensed the man was just warming up. "Or you just gonna write another report and leave me with an animal husk to clean up?"

"There's no evidence, Harry. You know that. I'll look for it, same as always, but you and I both know we're not going to find shit."

"Watch your language, Sheriff."

Godin took a breath, watched the lightning, and reminded himself that Colorado City was not the place to start a feud. As a Mohave County Sheriff, he served many communities, but none quite as notorious as the Mormon city where half the population was descended from one man. Kissing cousins wasn't just a cute catchphrase here, it was a reality, and picking a fight with one of them was like picking a fight with the whole damn town.

And since the arrest of Warren Jeffs, their fundamentalist, polygamist leader who most now viewed as a martyr, the general tone toward outside government officials, both state and federal, was cold at best. Godin knew well enough to tread lightly.

"Sorry," he said. "Stuff like this makes me forget myself."

Harry gave a gray-haired nod, and Godin wondered how many wives the man would go home to after they were done.

Lightning lit up the sky to the west. Godin watched the pink roots fan out through the clouds.

A breeze caressed his face, carrying the scent of death with it.

Harry gave his shotgun a pump. "You smell that?"

Godin nodded and crouched. He put his nose down close to the horse's open cavity. Breathed in deeply. The wound was as odorless as it was bloodless. The creature had been dead for hours, but was bone dry, as though it had been lying in the desert for weeks.

Harry headed west, following a slope topped with Palo Verde trees.

Lighting flashed again, this time nearly overhead. Godin squinted in the light, and then froze.

The lightning wasn't on the horizon.

Wasn't from a distant storm.

It should have been tearing through the air with all the fury once attributed to Zeus. Instead, it was silent.

"What the fuck?" Godin whispered.

Harry paused, shotgun in hand. "You say something?"

"The lightning..." Godin pointed his flashlight up toward the sky. "Where's the thunder?"

Harry turned his head up, but saw only starless darkness. "Ain't here to solve the mystery of quiet lightning."

He's right about that, Godin thought, and he followed the man up the hillside. His slacks shushed through the tall, dry grass with each step. If there was anything or anyone atop this hill, they'd have plenty of warning that someone was coming.

Godin tried to suppress a growing sense of dread. Whoever had carved up the horse, not to mention Harry's other horse, his cattle, and thirty more animals in Mohave County since Godin started the job eight years earlier, might still be out here. And if he was, what kind of person would they find?

It's not a he or a she, Godin thought. *It's a them.* Of that he felt sure. Only a team of well-trained people could sneak onto a ranch, complete a complex, bloodless surgery in a field, and get back out without being detected. But what if they hadn't left yet?

What if they were still operating on the missing stallion?

For the first time in Godin's career, he unbuttoned his sidearm.

"Hold up," Godin whispered as Harry pulled ahead. The man was old, but spry, and Godin's spare tire was slowing him down.

The stench of death grew dense.

It clung to his skin, the air humid with it.

A flash of silent lightning lit up the path ahead. Godin saw the bent grass marking Harry's passage. And then Harry himself, shotgun rising toward a figure standing at the hill's crest. The intruder's identity was hidden in shadow, but the size left Godin with no doubt—Harry was about to put a shotgun shell into a child's head.

"Harry, stop!"

Godin drew his sidearm, intending to shoot Harry's trigger hand, or at least try to, but Harry could outwalk and outgun him. The lightning's flash disappeared a moment before Harry's shotgun lit up the night. The exploding shell boomed loud enough to make the lightning envious, and was followed by the hint of a scream.

Godin stormed up the hill as Harry pumped the shotgun. He grabbed the old rancher by his overalls and shook him with a righteous anger he had never before experienced. "That was a child, you goddamned sonuvabitch!"

With a shove, Godin freed Harry from his grasp and scrambled up the hill. He steeled himself for a sight worse than a desiccated horse, unsure if all the preparation in the world would make him able to stomach the sight of a ruined child.

The grass at the top of the hill was flattened, but there was no blood, and no body.

Thank God...

Godin turned his flashlight on the trees, sweeping back and forth, but he saw nothing. Whoever had been here was lucky to be alive, and they had made a wise and hasty retreat.

A breeze fell atop him, carrying the fetid scent of blood, bile, shit, and decay. His stomach heaved, and then spilled its contents into the empty grass. Godin spat, blocked his nose and breathed through his mouth.

Then he turned his head, and the flashlight, up.

"I get 'em?" Harry asked.

When Godin looked at the man, he found the barrel of a shotgun leveled at his gut.

"Harry," Godin said, looking from the man's angry eyes to the shotgun.

The rancher hesitated, and then shifted the weapon to the side.

"No one here," Godin said. "Which is lucky for you."

"How's that?" Harry asked. "I got a right to defend my land."

"I told you to hold your fire, and I'm damn sure you saw the same thing I did."

"Language," Harry grumbled.

"Fuck you," Godin said. "One more word out of you and I'll arrest you for attempted murder, and then I'll arrest any of your inbred family who comes callin' as a result. Also..." He pointed the flashlight up to the branches above, where Harry's stallion, its stomach opened up, its organs decorating the branches beneath it, hung as though caught mid-leap. "I found your fucking horse."

1

"We're about to embark on an odyssey. I'm not sure where we're going, or how we'll get from here to there, but maybe it's not the ending that's important. Maybe it's the journey itself." I look up from page one of the novel Winifred 'gifted' me this morning. "That has to be the most pretentious opening paragraph ever written."

Winifred Finch—Wini to me, and me alone—waddles in from the kitchenette, her plaid skirt too tight for her aging, plump body; not because it's unbecoming, but because she can barely move in the thing. Not that she seems to notice or care. "I had a dream this morning, about men with detachable penises."

When a woman who's barely over five feet tall in heels, wearing thick glasses straight out of the '80s, mentions detachable penises, anything less than a spit-take makes you a stick in the mud. I'm normally not a stick in the mud, but today, I am.

"And that's what they call juxtaposition," I manage to say, trying my hardest to reward her efforts to cheer me up.

Wini stands up straight, eyeing me. "The dream had penises, but no positions. And that book you're holding is a genre-bending science fiction classic that everyone should read."

She holds the steaming mug out to me. "Back to the dream."

I smell the perfectly prepared hazelnut brew, but can't enjoy it.

"I was working in this corporate factory setting," Wini continues, "hanging out in the breakroom with my fellow roughnecks. Salt of the Earth types. Grimy, but good people. The hue was green. Harsh lighting. Had a Ridley Scott vibe to it, honestly."

"I don't know who that is," I say.

"Ridley Scott," she says, enunciating the name with the slow, melting volume typically reserved for people her age and older. "Director of Alien. And Blade Runner. And The Martian. And—"

"You know I don't like science fiction." The reminder is unnecessary. It is the one point of contention in our now five-year relationship.

She frowns at me, and then, "So we're in this break room, yucking it up, when the men—I'm a man in this dream, too, by the way—they start complaining that they can't have their penises attached on the job. Someone holds up a large Ziploc bag full of smaller Ziploc bags, and I swear to God, each one holds a—"

"Penis," I guess.

She snaps her fingers at me. "Right. But not mine. Because I'm intact. And now I'm outraged. So I go to bat for the guys, because that's what roughnecks do for each other."

"I wouldn't know." Before being a private investigator, I was a detective, and I was relatively disliked by my co-workers, mostly for being a standup guy with a pretty wife, a white picket fence, and an impeccable track record.

"Then I'm in this fancy office. Lots of reds and whites. And your classic power suit-wearing, straight black haired boss-lady is staring me down. She's not the kind of woman that's easily intimidated, but I demand that the men be allowed to wear their penises to work."

"And...?" Sensing the dream is winding down to an anticlimactic end, I take a sip of coffee. I know it's good, but I just can't taste it.

"She rips off her blouse and I give her the high hard—"

Coffee becomes a fine mist as it's expelled from my lungs.

Shit, I should have seen that coming.

Wini looks pleased with herself as she hands me a napkin. She found a chink in the emotional armor I put on this morning. And as nice as laughing feels, a chink can become a gaping hole of emotions, and I'm trying hard to feel nothing today.

"She agreed," Wini says.

"What?"

"My boss, in the dream." Wini takes a seat across from me. "She agreed to let the men wear their detachable penises to work."

She sits back in the chair, story finished, sipping her black coffee. 'It's bitter,' she once told me, 'so that I'm not.'

"You must have heard the song," I say.

"What song?"

"Detachable penis."

Her eyebrows make a slow stretch toward her hairline. "There's a song about detachable penises? Who would write trash like that?"

"Probably someone who dreams about them."

She raises her mug in a toast, says, "Someone with impeccable taste," and then she takes a sip.

I lean back in my chair, the mesh back flexing too far. I'm not heavy, but the chair is cheap and old. I could have replaced it. Business is good. But I have a hard time letting things go. And that's the real reason Wini is talking about removable man-meat.

"So?" she says. "What's it mean?"

"You're searching for meaning in a dream about emasculated science-fiction factory workers with severed penises?"

"They weren't severed. They were detached. And by the end of the dream, restored." She smiles. "I think it's a metaphor."

I clasp my hands and wait for her impending explanation.

"I think the penises represented something essential that the workers were missing. And I was one of them." She leans forward, hands wrapped around the mug like she needs to warm up despite the chill in the air being from the air conditioner and all her warm-blooded doing. "The penises represent money. You're the tightwad in the power suit. I just mentally reversed our genders."

"You're asking for a raise?"

"My *subconscious* is asking for a raise," she says with a sly grin.

"Your penis was intact," I point out.

She frowns. "Shit."

"Also, our paychecks are the same."

That catches her off guard. All her forced humor dissolves into earnest surprise. "Are you serious?"

I open my hands. "What can I say? I'm a feminist."

She shakes her head. "A man like you..." She sighs, and I know what's coming. "You're young, handsome, and fun. You shouldn't be alone."

"I have you."

"I'm thirty years your senior," she says, her smile returning. She shimmies in her seat and runs her hands over the lumps of her body. "You couldn't handle all this."

She manages to get a second smile out of me. Before she can capitalize on it, my cellphone plays the sound of chirping birds.

"New ringtone?" Wini asks, as I pluck the phone from my desktop.

"It's peaceful." Caller ID shows *UNKNOWN*. I swipe to answer. "Delgado Investigations. This is Dan Delgado."

If my phone rings, it's not because something happy has happened. The person on the other end is generally distraught. A woman suspects her husband is cheating, or vice versa, and is usually right. A tenant believes his landlord installed cameras in bathroom vents—he did. A teen believes her girlfriend is straight—she wasn't. But I can't tell if the woman on the other end of this call is upset or just loud, because she's speaking Spanish.

Despite having a Puerto Rican grandfather and a half Puerto Rican father, the most Hispanic thing about me is my last name. My grand-parents passed when I was young, and my parents not much later, all of them claimed by a different disease or cancer, long before their time. I was raised in foster homes, which left me with just two things to remember my family by: a last name and a perpetual tan.

I did take three years of Spanish in high school, but I spent most of my afternoons smoking pot and forgetting the day's lessons. High school had a different meaning for me. There are two things I can ask for in Spanish. Cerveza and el baño, which go hand-in-hand and reveal my state of mind at that time of my life, which I generally refer to as B.H.—*Before Her*—in my own personal timeline. The past five years have been A.H.—*After Her*. The seven years between the two... I try not to think about and generally succeed, except for one day each year.

Today.

The day Kailyn died.

It was a car accident in every sense of the term. She veered off the road. Struck a tree. Most likely evading an animal. Happens all the time. No one to blame. No one to be angry at. No one to hate.

I was at the office working a missing persons case, but was mostly waiting for The News. Instead of a phone call, I got an office visit, and instead of my wife's voice, it was my captain's. After hearing, 'She didn't make it,' I have no idea what else was said.

The weeks that followed are a haze.

I don't remember the funeral.

That was the same day I left the job. They never did find the missing woman from my case.

I hold the phone out to Wini. "Español."

Wini speaks fluent Spanish because her grandmother was Mexican, fluent French because who knows why, and enough German to intimidate me.

"Hola," Wini says, "Soy Wini—"

Wini falls silent, listening. After a few minutes, she looks her age. When she speaks, it comes out as a squeaky whisper, "¿Cual es tu direccion?"

She scribbles an address down on a notepad kept hidden in the strap of her bra. Looks like we're going for a drive, which is good news. There's nothing more distracting than a new case.

"Mantenerte fuerte. Llegaremos pronto." Wini hangs up the phone and lets out a long sigh.

"What's the job?"

"Juxtaposition," she says, trying to rediscover her sense of humor. She fails. "Missing child."

"Missing— We don't handle— Has she gone to the police?"

"Marta Ramos, the mother... That was her on the phone. She's illegal. Father's still south of the border. The daughter was born here, but if Marta calls the police—"

"I get it." I ponder the predicament for a moment and wonder if taking the case means breaking the law. I decide I don't care, and am about to say so, but Wini takes my silence as debate.

"You used to work cases like this. Before. You might try to bury the man you once were, but—"

"Wini."

Her mouth clamps shut.

"Get the keys."

"I'm coming?" she asks.

"I no habla Español, remember? Also, you're driving."

"What are *you* going to do?"

I stand from my chair and head for the door, phone in hand. "Research."

I'm a half step through my home office's doorway when I stop and turn around.

I nearly left it behind.

Today of all days.

Wini takes the keys from a hook mounted on the wall behind her desk. Eyes me, and then my desk. "You don't need it."

"Mmm," I say, which could be taken as agreement, or at least mulling it over. It's neither. I hurry back to the desk, snatch up the unopened envelope—one of the few things to survive Kailyn's crash intact—and stuff it into my pocket before leaving.

I hope the kid isn't really missing, but that it will take at least the whole day to find her.

I can already feel the chink widening.

2

Here's what I found out about Marta Ramos and her missing daughter—Isabella—during the two hour drive from San Francisco to Santa Cruz: absolutamente nada.

They're ghosts. There're no criminal records north or south of the border, which means Marta successfully moved between countries with-out being caught. There's no mention of them in any newspapers. No school records for mother or daughter. The father, who Wini says was named Mateo, has been out of the picture since Isabella's conception.

But that doesn't rule him out.

The vast majority of child abductions are committed by parents or close relatives, often times out of a sense of duty or justice. In this case, it could be that Mateo, having finally heard that his Mexican daughter was being raised as an American, decided to take her home. Motivations are simple like that. Most people are driven by refined ideas of right and wrong.

Once you identify a person's ideals, they're easy to predict and track down. If Mateo took his daughter because of national pride, he'd likely return home, secure in the belief that he was doing what was right, that Marta lacked the means to pursue him, and that she would not report the abduction to authorities, who would hurt her case more than help it. If that was the case, Mateo would be mostly correct. Under normal circumstances, he'd have little to worry about beyond getting back across the border.

But these aren't normal circumstances. Marta managed to reach me on a day when I'm more sensitive to the plight of a severed family. I understand her anguish. Her desperation. And by the time we stop, I'm ready to summon Seal Team 6 and descend on Mexico with a holy rage until Mateo—that bastard—is caught.

"You all right?" Wini asks, putting the car into park. "Been staring at your phone for nearly two hours, and you look ready to throttle someone."

"Fine," I say in a way that says I'm not. I look up and I'm surprised to see we're parked in a decent neighborhood. "I thought they were…"

"Poor?" Wini says the word for me.

"Most first generation illegals are." I'm feeling angry *and* defensive now. "It's not exactly easy to get a job or buy a house when any kind of paperwork will flag ICE."

"You're right," she says, "and wrong." Wini leans forward, looking out the window. The house we're parked in front of has a manicured lawn, a bright blue paint job, and what looks like newish construction. Maybe ten years old, tops. She points to the side yard, where an unruly pecan tree commingling with two palms shades an unkempt portion of yard in which sits a small trailer. The tires are flat. Its front end is propped up on cinder blocks. Some kind of moss is growing up the side wall, the white door stained black with some kind of mold. "That's where they're staying."

And now I'm offended. Not for myself. For Marta. It's bad enough that the place is a shithole. Honestly, I expected that. But sitting beside this house, in this neighborhood… I can't imagine how demoralizing it must feel.

"Let's go." I open the door, step out into the summer heat and close the door behind me, a little too hard. The air here smells like flowers, and something earthy. *Manure*, I think. *How much do these people spend on their yards? Does grass really need cow shit to grow?*

Slow down, I tell myself as I charge up the grass-covered slope, heading for the ramshackle trailer. My spiral into self-righteous outrage isn't going to do anyone any good.

By the time I reach the trailer, I'm calm, or at least able to project a less tumultuous state of mind. I knock on the trailer door and note that it's open a crack. "Hello?"

"Hola?" Wini says.

"Pretty sure she understands 'hello' in English," I say.

"Take a tone with me and I'll slap it out of you." Wini grins for just a moment before giving me a stare that makes me wonder if she was serious.

"Hola," I say, and tug open the door, peeking through the gap. "Hola..." I open the door wide and I'm nearly staggered back by what I find. The trailer's interior is...nice. Plush. Modern. Stylish. I give the exterior a onceover and notice that the mold and moss are artificial. This isn't a defunct trailer at all. It's a very nice tiny home in disguise. From the street, no one would give it a second look. Most people in the neighborhood probably pretend it's not there.

Not a bad place to live off the government's radar. And big enough for a mother and daughter.

I take a step inside, noting the handmade decorative pillows, the bright drawings on the small fridge, and the cellphone resting on the kitchenette table.

Movement through the windows draws my eyes. Wini turns to look at me through the glass. "Out here."

I'm once again caught off guard. Hiding behind the trailer is a lush and well-tended garden, a lemon tree, and an orange tree. Even during hard times, Marta might have been able to live off this small plot of land.

"Here," Wini says, pointing to the garden's edge.

A discarded shovel lies atop a pepper plant, which has broken under the garden tool's weight.

"Whoever planted all this would *not* do that," Wini says, and she's right. Given the garden's pristine appearance, whoever tends to it—maybe Marta—would be horrified by the shovel's abuse.

I crouch by the shovel, inspecting its head for signs of anything nefarious, but I see only dirt. The soil at the garden's fringe tells another story. Footprints. Partials. But two distinct sets—one narrow, one broad. Both deep.

"Over here," I say, scooting a few feet further down. When Wini joins me, I position her at the garden's edge. "Stand there."

"Is this normal behavior for you on a case?" she asks, watching me pick up the shovel.

"I'm usually alone," I say, handing her the shovel. I angle the shovel toward the ground and push it in between a pair of tomato plants. "Okay, you're her. Marta."

"What should I—"

"Just stand there." I move up behind her.

"But what do you wa—"

Wini's voice is cut off as I wrap one hand over her mouth and struggle to hold her, as she reacts like anyone would.

"Okay, okay, okay," I coo, letting her go.

"What the hell, Dan?" Wini looks about ready to knock my teeth out, and she probably could.

"Sorry. I had to see. Had to simulate it." I point to the garden's edge. The shovel lies discarded atop a tomato plant. The two sets of footprints at the garden's edge.

When Wini sees the mess we've made, she turns to the mess we found and puts a hand to her mouth. "Someone *took* her?"

I don't want to say it. Nothing is certain—until it is. But that requires more evidence, and sometimes a body. Right now, there are signs that a man came up behind a woman and startled her. Coupled with the open trailer door and left-behind phone, there's enough to raise suspicion, but not nearly enough to make me break Marta's trust and call the police.

Though that is now an option. Better for Marta and Isabella to be alive and deported to Mexico than dead and deported to whatever kind of afterlife might exist. I'm good at finding people. I was a fine detective. But my resources are somewhat limited, and my man-power is...aging and sarcastic.

"Check the house," I say. "If no one answers the door, listen for..."

"People doing the nasty," Wini says. "Got it. Though I doubt a worried mother would be screwing around right now, especially knowing we were on the way."

"When it comes to sex, people are like Jurassic Park dinosaurs. Sex...finds a way."

Wini gives me a set of squinty eyes. "Thought you didn't like science-fiction."

I head back to the trailer. "Dinosaurs aren't science fiction."

"When geneticists bring them back to life in the present day, they are." Wini's words trail off as she walks toward the home's front yard and I step inside the trailer.

Without touching anything, I scour the mini-home for anything unusual. The only thing out of place is the cellphone, and that's only because I'm pretty sure its owner isn't here. I lean out the door and hear Wini's fist knocking on the front door. It's followed by six muffled doorbell rings. "Hey, Wini!"

"I don't think anyone is home," she yells from the front.

"Call Marta's phone."

In the silence that follows I start to worry that whoever snuck up on Marta might still be here, and might have subdued Wini.

When the phone blares the vibrato voice of an opera singer, I flail back and nearly fall from the trailer's door. After composing myself, I note the caller ID number displayed, answer the phone and say, "Thanks," before hanging up.

I take a seat at the small table and tap the phone's home button. "Shit," I grumble when I'm greeted by a six digit passcode screen. I try the three most common numbers—all ones, all nines, and one through six. None work. "Shit, again."

And then, an epiphany of sorts, written out and stuck to the fridge above a drawing of a castle. My eyes linger on the drawing. There's a princess in the tower, her brown hair blowing horizontal in the wind. A prince is on one knee below, arms raised in a proposal. A word bubble extending out from the princess says, 'Necesito orinar.'

From the drawing, my eyes shift to a photo of a woman and a girl, who I identify when I spot the trailer behind them. I pluck the photo from the fridge. Marta is a beauty, wearing a colorful skirt, a dirty tank top, and gardening gloves. Isabella's large brown eyes all but break my heart, not just because she's an adorable ten-, maybe eleven-year-old kid, but because I can feel the love for her mother radiating off the photo.

I pocket the photo and try the six digit, very random code stuck to the fridge. Works on the first try.

I'm greeted by a text message received forty-five minutes ago. The text is simple—yesterday's date, and a set of coordinates. The photo accompanying the text drains the blood from my face. I place the phone beside the photo and compare faces. The phone's image is dark, taken at night, and somewhat blurry, but there's no doubt; they're both Isabella.

The biggest difference between the two images isn't the lighting, or the focus. It's the look on Isabella's face. In the second photo, she's terrified and on the run.

Wini gives the door a gentle knock before opening it. "Anything?"

I wave Wini to enter, and when she sits across from me, I turn the phone around so she can see the text and the photo. When she looks confused, I turn the fridge photo around and tap it. "I think that's Isabella."

"Oh, dear," Wini says, picking up the photo, her hand shaking. Then her eyes snap back to the phone. "This is dated yesterday."

"But was delivered today."

"What does that mean?"

"Could be the kidnappers. But there's no ransom ask, and I doubt she has anything to give."

"Except herself," Wini points out, reminding me how dark the job can get.

Using Marta's phone, I copy and paste the coordinates into Google maps. The location pops up immediately and I double-tap to zoom in, revealing the town's name. "Colorado City. Arizona."

"Do you think that's where she went?" Wini asks. "Or was taken?"

"I'm not—"

The phone chimes in my hand. A fresh text. It's just three words, but they hold my heart hostage for a beat.

WHO. ARE. YOU?

3

I stopped carrying a gun on the day I turned in my badge. I still own a Glock 22, but it's been sitting in my office drawer for five years. My job occasionally leads to confrontations, but most are settled with words and only once with fists—he was drunk.

As I reread the three-word message, some instinctual caveman part of my brain screams 'danger' to which the modern, well-trained peace officer in me responds, 'Where's my gun?'

But maybe it was a coincidence? Maybe whoever sent the photo and coordinates doesn't know Marta is missing, too? If Isabella was kidnapped, this might be my only chance to communicate with her captors.

After turning the phone around for Wini to see, her eyes going wide, I tap out a reply: *Marta. Who is this?*

I'm about to tap the Send button when Wini grasps my wrist. "Spanish!"

The phone drops from my hand, released as though scalding hot. The three-inch fall to the tabletop does no visible damage. *If I had hit Send...*

"Can you?" I ask Wini.

Wini turns the phone around, sliding it across the small table. She's not a technophobe—she's a champ on the Internet—but her cellphone is a Nokia brick and she doesn't text.

"Just type your message and tap the Send button," I tell her.

"I understand the concept of texting." She deletes my near catastrophic message and starts typing in Spanish. I can't read it upside down, but the phone chimes again before she can hit send. A fresh message appears, and I'm able to read it upside-down:

LEAVE. THEY'RE COMING.

"Who's coming?" I ask aloud.

The phone goes black. I take it from Wini's hand and squeeze the power button. Nothing. It's a brick.

The chop of approaching helicopter blades tickles my ears, but doesn't really register until Wini grasps my hand and turns her eyes to the small window beside us. "I think they're already here."

We share a collective 'oh shit' moment and stand together, rushing out the door. A black helicopter thunders overhead, banking hard to swing around.

I assume the chopper belongs to one of the federal law enforcement agencies, though it has no markings or serial numbers. No matter which agency it is, I don't want to be here when they arrive. I've failed to report a missing child, not to mention having knowledge of illegals residing in the U.S. They're not the most grievous of crimes, but they could land us in an interrogation room for the day, and at a later date, in a courtroom.

If we don't boogie, and fast, the worst day of the year is going to get a whole lot more craptastic.

I make it two steps before experience kicks panic in the face and reasserts itself.

"Have the car running when I get there," I shout to Wini, who's shuffling at top speed in her tight skirt.

The incognito tiny-house shakes as I careen back inside. I pick up the phone again, my hand wrapped in a handkerchief I keep on me for moments like this. I wipe down the phone, then the tabletop. The photo of Marta and Isabella goes in my pocket beside the envelope, my fingers lingering on the paper for a moment. Then I wipe down the door handle and step back out into the pecan tree's shade.

A torrent of wind slaps into the branches above as the thunderous pounding of rotor blades thump. The chopper is directly overhead, just a hundred feet up. Leaves peel away from the trees, as dust swirls. Before blocking my eyes, I catch sight of Marta's garden, the plants bowed low in subjugation to the helicopter's power.

They can't land *here*, I think, aghast.

Two ropes unfurl beside the tree.

Aww, shit.

I break out in a run without looking back and pass Wini ten feet from the car. I attempt a classy action-cop hood leap, but two things prevent me from accomplishing the feat in style. First, the car is a black Toyota Prius, bought for stealth, not power. Second, my foot clips the car's side and instead of sliding over the almost non-existent front end, I roll over it and off the far side.

The pavement greets me as pavement does—without mercy—but it fails to slow me. I stand, reach toward Wini and shout, "Keys!"

But Wini is already in the passenger's seat, closing her door.

Beyond the car, back by the trailer, two men dressed in black tactical gear land on the ground. I glance up at the chopper. It's a Black Hawk. Military. With no more information to be gleaned by staring, I climb inside the car and don't bother looking to see if the soldiers spotted us.

I start the car and let the Prius do what I bought it to do, drive silently away.

"What are you waiting for?" Wini asks. "Step on the gas!"

"Trying to not draw attention," I say, nearly whispering, like someone might overhear us.

"Look in the rearview!"

A quick glance is all it takes to register the black SUV racing up behind us. But I still don't hit the gas. The truck is most likely heading for the house. If we don't draw attention, they'll just assume we live—

Nope. The SUV passes the house.

I crush the gas pedal to the floor and the vehicle accelerates like a three year old on a tricycle. The SUV roars up behind us, but it doesn't run us down or make contact. The shrill chirp of an amplified horn moves through me in painful waves. Headlights flash in the rearview. The message is unmistakable. I know it well.

Pull over.

Now.

But since I don't know who these guys are and they're not making any effort to tell me, I'm not legally obligated to obey.

I decide to use the one advantage a Prius has over the hulking behemoth behind us and crank the wheel hard to the right. Tires squeal, but we stick to the road, rounding the corner while the SUV barrels forward.

With a thump and a grinding of metal, the Prius continues to turn, even after I've straightened the wheel. The big vehicle clipped us as it drove by, putting the small car into a spin. We wind up facing the wrong way in the middle of a residential street. A group of kids, standing with their bikes on the sidewalk, look at us like *we're* the bad guys. And then they flinch when Wini starts yelling.

"Those sons-a-bitches are going to get someone killed!"

I throw the car into reverse, speeding away as the SUV performs a similar maneuver on the side street. When I see the black monster lock its brakes and spin its front end toward us, I do the same, putting us in a 180 degree spin, slamming the car back into drive and speeding off again. Though 'speeding' is a gross exaggeration.

The neighborhood is a vast maze crammed with homes. If I can keep making turns, I might be able to get enough ground that the SUV's driver won't be able to track us. That is, until the chopper joins in the hunt.

I lean forward, looking up through the windshield. The chopper is nowhere in sight, but I can still hear it, no doubt still hovering over Marta's trailer.

Tires squeal as I bang a hard left.

I watch the rearview as I speed away, waiting for the SUV to thunder into view.

"Lookout!" Wini screams.

Without looking forward, I mash the brakes, and it's a good thing I do. When we come to a stop, a young boy stands up, eyes as round as the ball he's clutching.

This is *not* the place for a high speed pursuit.

Tears burst from the boy as he retreats back to his house, meeting his irate and foul-mouthed mother along the way. She pursues us into the road as we speed away again and narrowly avoids being mowed down by the SUV, which is once again gaining.

I take the next right, followed quickly by another left, eyes locked on the road ahead.

I need to get out of this residential area.

"Find me a mall, or any place with a lot of people." I hand my phone to Wini. "They know the car, but not our faces. We need to get lost in a sea of people."

"Won't they be able to figure out who we are from the car?" she asks.

Shit. She's right. While we could take the registration with us, if these guys have access to government databases, they'll be able to ID me from the license plates or even the VIN. But that means... "If they can ID from the plates, they already have."

"But maybe they can't?" she asks.

"Maybe," I say, but I think there's an equal chance of Santa Claus being my father. But right now, 'maybe' is our best hope, so I cling to it and turn right.

Midturn, I glance down the street from which we've just come. It's empty. My eyes flick to the rearview as I accelerate again, but all I see is black. It's disorienting for a moment, and then painful.

The SUV smashes into the Prius's rear end, lifting the small vehicle before releasing it and sending us up onto the curb.

"They're trying to kill us!" Wini shouts, as we bounce to a stop just short of a parked Mercedes. She's beet-red angry and digging in her purse.

"Hold on," I tell her, putting the vehicle into reverse.

"Wait!" Her hand emerges from her purse clutching a small revolver. Before I can stop her, she's out the door, leveling the weapon toward the SUV. She unloads all six rounds, holding back whoever's behind the tinted windows, and freeing the air from both front tires.

She climbs back in, closes the door and brushes the gray hair from her face. "Okay."

Dirt sprays from the Prius's reversing front tires, coating the Mercedes. Then we screech from the curb and back onto the street. As we speed away, I watch two men who look like Secret Service agents, climb out of the SUV to inspect the tires.

"We did it!" Wini shouts, matching Dora the Explorer's excitement level. I half expect her to follow it up with "Lo hicimos!" but instead, she shakes the spent cartridges from the weapon and starts reloading, one bullet at a time.

As it occurs to me that I actually know a few more Spanish words than I believed, I glance in the rearview again and realize that, *no...no lo esimo.*

The Black Hawk is closing in.

4

The road curves to the left and I follow the bend, trying to keep a wall of houses between the car and the approaching chopper. It works for a moment, but there's no universe in which a Prius can outrun or outmaneuver a Black Hawk. But we can still outfox the men piloting it.

"We need to ditch the car."

Wini's response confuses me. Instead of looking at the maps app on my phone, or giving me directions, she leans forward and looks past me, through the driver's side window.

The bend continues. Endless. Feels like we're driving through a particle collider. Centrifugal force pulls me to the right as the endless left continues. When we pass a house with a pink door for the second time, I realize the horrible truth—which would be hysterical under other circumstances. We're driving in literal circles.

The neighborhood streets are laid out in a series of rings with straight crossroads leading to the core...which is where Wini's focus lies. I glance left at the next intersection and see a large brown building surrounded by a sea of cars. Looks busy.

"Next left," Wini says. "All the way to the center. I think it will do."

Turning hard left after the endless curve nearly puts me in Wini's lap. The helicopter roars past overhead, unprepared for the sudden change in direction. I lay on the horn as we accelerate toward the building at the neighborhood's core, hoping the noise will warn people out of the street.

When the white steeple and large cross come into view, my question about what the building is has an answer. But there's still something that confuses me. "Why are there so many people here?"

Parked cars line both sides of the road ahead. The church parking lot is loaded. But I don't see any people.

"It's Sunday morning, you heathen," Wini says.

I've been transported to another world, my mind sent reeling by this revelation. "What?"

"It's a church. People go to church on Sunday morning."

"Yeah, but...we don't work on Sunday." Saturdays are big cheating days, so our work week, depending on the case, is typically Tuesday through Saturday. Wini is a church-goer in addition to being a science fiction buff, so even if I put in hours on the 'day of rest,' she doesn't.

"Last night you said, 'See you tomorrow,'" she explains. "I knew what day it was. Figured your subconscious was asking for company, so here I am." She points out an empty spot in the lot.

I can see the blue and white paint of a handicapped space from here, and even under the circumstances I don't feel comfortable taking it. "We can't—"

Wini produces a handicapped placard from her purse. "In case you haven't noticed, I'm an old lady."

"An old lady who can run in a tight skirt," I point out, tires screeching as I brake hard and pull into the lot. The helicopter roars past again, circling the building. When it's behind the steeple, I pull into the handicapped spot, and turn the car off, hoping we'll just blend in with the sea of vehicles.

"First, there aren't many old folks who can't shake a leg for a few minutes when commandos fall from the sky. Second, I'm glad you like the skirt." She gives me a wink and hangs the placard from the rearview mirror. Then we're out and hustling through the heat. When the chopper circles the building, I put my arm around Wini, to slow her down and look casual. Just two people late for church.

"Skirt's making you frisky," Wini says, and I hold the door open for her as the distinct smell of church—of every church—wafts out over us. It stops me in the doorway. Smell is occasionally an important part of my job, both in my investigations, and my clients' stories. So I understand how it works. The technical term for what I'm experiencing is Odor-Evoked Autobiographical Memory. The short version is that life events, either repeated ones like school, or traumatic ones, like the funeral for your wife, can be linked to a specific smell. Catching a whiff of that odor later in life can transport you back in time, where you might not remember the circumstances in detail, but you relive how you felt. In my case, it's the funeral scenario and the somehow universal smell of churches. On most days it would be disconcerting. Today, it nearly undoes me.

Wini tugs me into the foyer as a second black SUV pulls into the parking lot. Impending danger returns me to the present, and I peek through the church doors just before they close, memorizing the faces of four men climbing out of the SUV. It's not hard. They're all big, ugly, and well dressed. A little too hairy to be government agents...unless they're not agents. The Black Hawk suggests military, and the facial hair and muscles suggest Special Ops.

I wrack my mind, trying to think of military branches that might fit the profile and come up with just one: Delta. The anti-terror specialists are allowed to dress down, and have facial hair and styles uncommon in the rest of the military because they often need to *not* look like soldiers. They often don't even acknowledge rank. If these guys are Delta, Wini and I are screwed on so many levels. Not just because we'll be jailed and questioned, but because it means Marta is somehow involved in terrorist activity. And that means we'll be suspected of the same. There's no evidence of it, but our mad flight through the streets, not to mention Wini's quick shooting, would support the accusation.

As we stroll into the vast, half-circle shaped sanctuary mid-prayer, a number of people look at us with disapproving eyes. We should have waited to sit, I realize, but we also need to plant our asses in seats before the men follow us in. The space is larger than expected, seating perhaps five hundred people. The floor slopes down toward the shiny, wooden stage. Every seat in the house has a good view. And there are no old-school wooden pews here. The seats look cushy—not quite movie theater cushy, but close enough. Arched, stained-glass windows line the sidewalls, filling the space with pleasant colors and not too much light. If not for the men chasing us, the atmosphere might even be pleasant. The pastor, a black man with a thick beard, stands behind a podium, head bowed, eyes closed.

"Help us to experience your Word with an open heart today, Lord," the pastor prays, and I tune out the rest. I spot two seats in the middle of a row and start shuffling past the folded hands of annoyed believers.

Wini offers apologies, her kind smile and aging body gaining sympathy from those we're passing. When we reach the clearing, I make a show of helping her sit, and I can see forgiveness in the eyes of those whom we offended. I can also see the four men enter through two different doorways. I sit slowly and keep my eyes forward.

When the prayer ends with an emphatic "Amen," I glance back. The men haven't moved, but they're scanning the sea of heads.

"Just keep your head forward," I whisper to Wini. "Try to look like you're listening."

"That's what people do in church," she says, settling in like she was meant to be there. "And maybe you should actually listen."

She's been trying to get me into a church for years. Says a little faith would go a long way, especially since Kailyn believed in all this, which to me seems as otherworldly and as strange as Wini's science fiction.

The pastor clears his throat behind the podium and starts speaking. I don't hear a word of it. Ten minutes pass, and while several older gentlemen look close to nodding off, I'm in a hyperaware state, tracking the four men acting like beefy doormen. They let people out, let people in, inspecting faces as they do and offering phony smiles.

If they're checking faces, they know what we look like. And if they know what we look like, they know who we are.

I identify the other exits, six in total. The two at the back are blocked, but the two near the front are... A little boy doing the potty-dance exits one of the front doors and bumps into the large man waiting on the far side.

Shit. All the exits are covered.

Working my phone with the sound muted, I open Uber and summon as many drivers as I can. I then put in requests to every taxi company in town, timing their arrival thirty minutes out. If we can get out of the building when the service is over, the commingling storm-fronts of arriving drivers and departing worshipers might give us enough cover to slip away.

If that's what we should do...

I ponder simply turning myself in. Explaining the situation. But that warning from the phone, coupled with my distrust of federal agencies, tells me to not attempt that until I have something concrete to deliver. These guys are brutes, not detectives.

"Brothers and sisters..." The pastor's voice doubles in volume, startling a few old men awake and gaining my full attention. "We do not want you to be uninformed about those who sleep in death, so that you do not grieve like the rest of mankind, who have no hope."

My stomach sours. *What the fuck is this?*

"For we believe that Jesus died and rose again, and so we believe that God will bring with Jesus those who have fallen asleep in him."

The words stir up an anger in me. The only thing keeping me from standing up and delivering a big 'fuck you' coupled with a pair of middle fingers is the fact that I'm being hunted.

I realize the pastor has been quoting scripture because the words are plastered on a big screen hanging behind him crediting 1 Thessalonians 4:13-18. That only makes it slightly less offensive. I don't need a pastor, or a two thousand year old work of fiction telling me how to feel today.

Wini places her hand on mine. Gives me a gentle squeeze. This small sign of affection is a catalyst for an emotional shift that catches me off guard with its suddenness and strength. Before I can think to contain it, a choked sob escapes my mouth.

I shrink down, lowering my head into my hands, my logical mind raging for control as it's swallowed up.

The tears don't stop.

Can't stop.

Five years of pent up sorrow spill out of the chink-turned-floodgate in front of a few hundred worshipers and a handful of people chasing me down. If they hadn't seen me before, they're seeing me now. But are they seeing the man who led them on a bold chase through packed neighborhoods, and the old woman who shot out their tires, or are they seeing a broken man mourning his dead wife?

"Today is the anniversary of his wife's death," Wini whispers to someone. For a moment, I'm horrified that she shared this personal detail with strangers. Then I hear the news sweep through the congre-gation like a wave of static and have no doubt that our pursuers have heard as well. Definitely not the guy they're looking for...unless they've already dug up and studied my history.

In the silence that follows my outburst and the revelation of today's significance, the pastor clears his throat. "I think we will stop there, today. Young man?"

I blink the tears from my eyes and will myself to take control again. *Bury the pain,* I tell myself. *You're good at it.*

"Young man?"

Wini rubs my back and whispers, "He's talking to you."

I look up, keeping my hands on the sides of my head. The pastor is staring at me, his eyes not unkind, his smile merciful. "Would you like to talk?" He motions to a fifth door that I hadn't noticed before because it lacked an Exit sign. It might not be a way out, but I'm sure it leads to one.

I give a nod and stand up, wiping the real tears from my eyes with a fake, face-concealing arm wipe. Wini stands with me, keeping an arm around me as our row clears out for us, making a nice barrier between us and the men at the back of the room. In the aisle, we keep our heads down and head for the stage.

"What are you doing?" Wini asks.

"Improvising," I say. "The exits are being watched. His office could be the only way out."

"Dan, please tell me you didn't fake that outburst." Wini looks up at me with the sincerest eyes I've ever seen.

"Wish I had."

"It was a good thing," she says. "Good for your heart."

With all her sass and colorful language, I sometimes forget that Wini is the closest thing I have to family. With no brothers and sisters and both parents long since in the grave, there are very few people in the world I feel truly care for me, and if I'm honest, who I care for in return.

And there's a bonus to this. Our mutual affection and my outburst is all genuine. A pair of actors couldn't sell it as well. So when we reach the stage and head toward the door at the back, the men guarding the exits are looking everywhere except at us. On the surface, we match who they're looking for, but we definitely don't *feel* right. And honest emotions make people uncomfortable. If I were to look back right now, which I'm not going to do, I'm sure every member of the congregation would divert their eyes. An hour from now, they'll barely remember what I look like. Same with the stooges tracking us.

The pastor starts singing what I recognize as the doxology. "Praise God, from whom all blessings flow..."

The last time I heard it—Kailyn's funeral—the voices were melancholy at best, but here, the people join the pastor and raise their voices as though trying to carry me into the next room.

"Praise him, all creatures here below; Praise him above, ye heav'nly host; Praise Father, Son, and Holy Ghost."

I'm simultaneously moved, and annoyed. I've got bad guys to evade. That's hard to do when your eyes are blurry.

When the door thuds behind me, I turn to thank the pastor for the invite, and then ask to be shown the door. The man's raised arms confound me for a moment.

Is he coming in for a hug?

Then I see the big man behind him, sound suppressed gun in hand, and realize that they'd known exactly where I was the whole time. I also realize, as the weapon rises toward my face, that these men are not Delta operators—though I suppose they might have been once.

They're mercenaries.

Maybe.

I'm not entirely sure.

But I think I'm about to find out.

Or die.

One of the two.

Maybe neither.

Shit, this sucks.

5

"Who are you?" the big man asks, looking over the barrel of his gun. It's a Beretta M9, and with the sound suppressor it will sound less like a gun booming and more like somone dropping heavy books. He could gun down the three of us and no one would know the noises were gunshots until our bodies were found by some congregation member seeking wisdom, or solace, or whatever people meet with pastors about.

"Who am I?" I repeat, "Who are you?"

I don't like failing tests. Asking me a question is like challenging me to a life-and-death game of Jeopardy. But this time, *not* answering is what's going to keep me alive. His question reveals that these guys don't have the endless resources I feared, and confirms that they're not part of the government. If they could have run my plates, they would have, and the question of who I am would be moot.

Of course, not answering could get me shot, so there's that...

"I'm the guy who's going to put a bullet in your head." The man shoves past the pastor and levels the long, tubular sound suppressor at my right eye. "I'm going to put a round through your right eye so that it scrapes along the inside of your skull and comes out the left eye."

I squint at the man. "Won't that shoot you too, then?" I demonstrate the bullet's passage through my head, complete with squishy sound effects, tracing the round's imaginary path out my left eye and into the man's chest.

While the man watches me, I look him over. The Beretta harkens to a military past. The M9 is most well-known for its reliability, and if there's one thing soldiers appreciate more than big booms, it's shit working when it's supposed to. Between the black glove of his stretched out gun hand, and his suit coat, is the bottom half of a tattoo featuring a skull and crossbones atop what I think is a parachute. A banner cuts through the image, the word cut in half by his cuff, but I'm fairly certain it says, 'Airborne.'

This man was a U.S. Army Ranger, which would normally be enough to ensure my respect and gratitude, not to mention a fifteen percent discount on my services, but under the circumstances, he can go sit on a fuck stick. I don't even know what that means, but it's not good.

"Counting to five," he says. "If I don't know who you are by then, you're dead. And then your friends are dead."

"I only just met them."

The man is lethal. I have no doubt about that. In a firefight, I'm sure I'd want him on my side, and by my side, but in a battle of wits, the man is outmatched.

"Doesn't matter," the man says. "Your name."

"Scott Flannagan," I say. He bullied me from third grade through high school. If I manage to get out of this mess and these men go hunting for Scott Flannagan, I'll sleep with a smile on my face tonight. "I'm from San Jose."

The man reaches out his free hand. "Wallet."

Damn.

"It's in the car."

Furrowed eyebrows reveal the man's churning mental gears. He doesn't know whether to believe me or not. From his perspective, I've been fairly forthcoming, and most people would be with a gun to their head. But lying is tricky. Everyone has tells. Mine was smiling a little when I gave him that name.

Damn you, Flannagan.

His trigger finger inches from beside the trigger, to around the trigger. I'm about to find out if this man will follow through on his threats. Though, if he does, I'll be dead before I can think the first syllable of 'Huh, what do you know? He *is* a murdering nut job.'

The man closes the distance between us, keeping the weapon raised and the trigger finger ready. If I twitch, I'm dead, so I don't even consider putting up a fight. He pats down my right pant pocket, plucking out the phone, which has everything he needs to ID me and Wini. Then he pats down the left and takes the photo of Marta and Isabella, along with my envelope.

"Weren't lying about the wallet," he notes, backing off a step.

"I never lie," I say, trying my best not to give the envelope any attention. He's watching me. Gauging my reactions.

"I'm sure you don't, Mr. Flannagan."

He's not as dense as I'd assumed. He's a better actor than me, and in this match of wits, he now has the upper hand. He pockets the phone and looks at the photo of Marta and Isabella. "How do you know them?"

"I don't." It doesn't reveal much, but I think he'll know it's the truth.

"Why were you at their home?"

"Why were you?"

The man sighs, toggles a throat mic I hadn't noticed before, and says, "Targets subdued. Three total. Request evac."

He waits a moment and when he nods to someone who can't see it, I have little doubt that a chopper is now en route to pick us up. And fast. Sounds from the world around us are muffled by the room's thick walls, decorated with a strange combination of religious paintings and DC comics super hero toys, but I can hear the approaching whine of multiple police cruisers.

"Three?" the pastor says. He looks mortified, leaning on his desk to support himself. He all but collapses into his chair. "I've never met these people before."

"So much for Christian solidarity," I grumble, and I notice Wini's hand dipping into her purse...the purse where her revolver sits waiting.

The soldier discards the photo and turns his attention to the envelope. He gives it a once over, but there's nothing to see. It's unlabeled and still sealed. He grips the side, preparing to tear the top open with his teeth.

"Don't," I say.

He pauses. Stares me down.

"Something in here you don't want me to see?"

"Please," I say, the emotion in my voice real. "It's personal."

"After today, nothing in your life will be personal. Every skeleton in your closet will be revealed." He nods to the pastor, still seated behind this desk. "This guy might call it judgment day. And that makes me God, which means I can do whatever the hell I want."

"Please don't..."

Paper tears.

"Put the fucking envelope on the floor or I will fucking erase your God damn head!" The man flinches to a stop at the savage fury booming from Wini's mouth. When he sees the revolver clutched in her steady hands, aimed at his head, he lowers the envelope, but not his gun.

"Do what she fucking told you!" This time, it's the pastor, his voice cracking with emotion. He's clutching an honest to goodness .50 caliber Desert Eagle in his hands. If one of those big rounds even clipped the soldier, it would be a kill shot. .50 cal bullets don't pass through a body without taking a significant chunk along for the ride.

The pastor's weapon and shaking hands make him the most urgent threat. The soldier's aim remains on me, but his eyes shift to the heavily armed man of God.

The soldier opens his hands so that the envelope falls to the floor and his gun swings loose on his index finger. "I'm impressed."

"I'm a Republican," the pastor confesses, and I nearly laugh.

The envelope calls to me from the floor, beckoning me to retrieve it and the potentially precious cargo it contains. But while the man has loosened his grip on the gun, he has not dropped it. If he's as experienced as I think, he can probably still get off a shot before the pastor can squeeze his trigger.

And that puts Wini in danger, because the soldier's second shot will be directed toward her. Two shots. Probably in less than a second. And then I'll be next. Our only hope is to act first, but how can I convey that to the pastor or to Wini—neither of whom really want to take a man's life—without getting them killed?

I can't.

So I charge.

The man's gun swivels back into his hand and turns in my direction. He fires once, the round clipping my shoulder with a tiny fraction of the force my shoulder delivers to his gut. I lift him off the floor with a shout, directing my fury over the envelope's molestation, and I slam him into a bookcase.

The impact is enough to draw a shout of pain from the man, but it sounds more angry than pained. A sharp thud on the hardwood floor tells me I've managed to disarm him, so now we're down to fisticuffs.

In a straight forward fist fight, this guy would take me with little effort. He's a good five inches taller, muscly, and judging by how hard he was to lift, he has a good fifty pounds on me. All that, and he's an ex-Army Ranger. Best of the best.

Here's the difference between us, though. He's probably mastered several martial arts, and that's all well and good, but I don't care about looking good or feeding my ego with superior technique. I want to win, and fast. So while he raises his elbows up to drive them into my back, I go to work on his nuts. I get in three hard shots, working my fists like I'm at a punching bag.

When the elbows strike my back, all the power is gone from them.

"Fucking coward," the man says, his face beet red, all of his strength fighting against the fetal position his body is crying out for. He manages to throw a right hook, which I block with my left arm. Instead of throwing a punch, I thrust my open hand out, catching him in the throat. He's rattled and gagging, but training and probably pride, moves him past it.

His left hook sails over my ducked head, and when his side opens up, I strike with both fists.

Coupled with the nut-shot trio, this strike is enough to double him over and end the fight. But he still doesn't drop. I pick up his gun, then the envelope and Marta's photo, both going back into my pocket. I retrieve the phone next, a mystery man once more.

The man looks ready to vomit when he looks at me again. The trouble is that he's also smiling.

"Now, who are you?" I ask him, leveling the Beretta at his face.

"You're fucked," he says, then he turns his head toward Wini and the pastor. "You're all fucked."

He turns his head slightly, the way people do when they're listening to something. Only in this case, he's the only person hearing it. That's when I notice the earbud in his ear and remember the throat mic he activated, but never shut off.

Reinforcements are en route. Probably about to kick down the door.

"Is there another way out of the building?" I ask the pastor.

He nods and motions to a side door I hadn't noticed. "Leads to an emergency door," he says. "It'll set off the alarms."

"Even better," I say, and then to Wini. "Go. Take the pastor."

"I have nothing to do with this," the pastor protests.

"Until they think otherwise, you do," I tell him. "There are at least seven more of these guys coming this way. Go. Now!"

When Wini and the pastor hustle toward the side door, I take a step back.

The merc matches my pace. "Not going to let you leave."

"Think I don't know that?" I ask, and then I adjust my aim from his head to his leg. "But you're not going to have a choice."

When the guy's eyes go wide with the realization that I'm not bullshitting, I pull the trigger. The weapon kicks and puffs out a round into the man's leg. He takes the abuse like he did the rest—by not falling. When he rushes me, I put a round in his other leg.

Now he drops, teeth grinding in anger.

"I wonder, are your buddies out there more loyal to you, or the mission?"

He says nothing.

"Will they let you bleed out to catch me? And by the way, I'm nobody. I have no idea what's going on and that's the truth. But I'm not about to let you assholes threaten good people. So..." I fire once more, putting a round in the man's side. It's not an instant kill shot, but without treatment, he could bleed out.

He goes down to his side, wisely applying pressure, no more threats on his lips. But he doesn't need to verbalize them. I can hear the footfalls of his 'back up' thundering across the stage. I leap through the side door, swinging it closed behind me just as the office door shatters.

Then, as an alarm blares throughout the massive mega-church, I run. I can't hear the men pursuing me anymore, but I know they're back there, and that they'll cross the twenty foot office before I reach the open door and sunlight at the end of this fifty foot corridor decorated with bright crayon drawings of boats, rainbows, crosses, and shepherds.

6

Running forward while looking back will never be an Olympic sport. It's all but impossible to move in a straight line. Colliding racers would drop in a tangled heap of limbs not far from the starting line...which would be more entertaining, but less of a sport and more of a mosh pit. The corridor's walls repel me, a human pinball, my advance slowed with each impact, but the chaotic course is necessary.

Running forward while looking back is hard. But firing a gun without aiming is harder. Not just because I'd miss the target, but because an innocent bystander could exit one of the many side doors while I'm pulling the trigger. My situation is desperate, but I'll be damned before putting a bullet in someone who doesn't have it coming.

I pull the trigger, sending a sound-suppressed round into the wood beside the pastor's office's opening door. The weapon is impossible to hear over the alarm, but the mercenary pushing the door open understands the shattering wood's message: show your face and catch a bullet.

These kind of guys—built for action, and fighting, and domination—won't be deterred by promises of pain, even with their colleague bleeding out on the pastor's office floor, so I pour on the speed. I fire three more rounds, evenly spaced to hold the mercs back.

Sensing the hallway's end just ahead, I lean forward, ready to careen into the pushbar and burst out into the parking lot.

But there is no impact. I simply fall through a rectangle of light and spill onto hot, hard pavement, skinning my elbow and my side.

Wini looks down at me, holding the door open, caught off guard by my dramatic and clumsy exit. "Should I have not held the door?"

I sit up, aim back down the hall and fire two rounds toward the two mercenaries pushing out of the office, weapons raised. The first shot kills a wall, but the second strikes the lead merc's shoulder, twisting him to the side and slowing his partner. "Close it!"

My voice is hard to hear over the wailing alarm, honking horns, the fleeing congregation's screaming voices, the approaching sirens, and the thumping of helicopter blades, but Wini slams the door shut.

I'm disoriented and unsure about where my car is, but I know one thing for sure: we need to get the hell away from this door. I scramble to my feet, throw a protesting Wini over my shoulder, and run away from the door at an angle, hoping to join the fleeing masses fanning out through the parking lot like a river's delta.

"This way!" It's the pastor, our partner in crime, or at least in flight. He's shepherding us toward a shiny red SUV. It will be easy for our pursuers to track—if they attempt it despite the growing police presence —but it's a beast of a vehicle and will be faster than running.

A boom from directly behind me nearly sprawls me to the ground. My first thought is, 'explosion,' but when it repeats I realize it's Wini firing her revolver from my shoulder. The men chasing us must have exited the building.

"Wini!" I shout.

Boom.

"Stop…"

Boom.

"Firing!"

Boom.

Her shots might deter the men for a moment, but they're also making us an easy target, not to mention putting other people at risk. She stops firing when I lean forward and plant her on the pavement beside the SUV.

"Two down," she announces, and both the pastor and I pause to glance back. Two men lie in the open doorway, both bloodied, but still moving. For now.

I know what it's like to take a life. What it does to your soul. So I step in front of Wini and direct her toward the SUV, hoping to leave the men's fate a mystery.

Just as Wini is about to slide into the back seat, the vehicle is rocked by gunfire. Glass shatters. Tires blow out. I drop to one knee, head ducked, looking for targets, but find nothing.

The bullets are coming from above, the chopper hovering a hundred feet up on the far side of the SUV. Two men in tactical gear, firing assault rifles, stand in the open side door. Rotor wash slaps us down, peppering us with the vehicle's shattered glass.

The mercs are no longer trying to subdue us. They're trying to kill us.

"Still have your weapon?" I shout to the pastor.

He nods and holds the gun up.

"We're going to open fire on that chopper and head for the street," I say. "When they stop to reload."

He looks to the nearby street, flooded with cars and fleeing people. It's our only chance to blend in and escape.

I grasp Wini's shoulder. "Are you good?"

The assault rifles go silent and Wini is the first to raise her pistol and fire, the loud crack kicking off our race to safety. The pastor aims his weapon at the sky, firing blindly. Wini does the same with her last two rounds. Together, they fill the air with the sound of returning gunfire. So it's up to me to be accurate.

Instead of running, I stand my ground behind the SUV's hood and fire the Beretta's remaining sound-suppressed rounds. The first three miss, the fourth strikes one of the mercs, knocking him back. The rest pepper the cockpit glass, letting the holes and spider-webbing glass inform the pilot that they're under fire. The helicopter and the men inside are far from disabled, and our group is out of ammo, but the pilot reacts by veering to the side.

They'll come around for another pass, but it might be enough time for us to disappear. As I sprint to catch up with Wini and the pastor, I spy a nearby house. Congregation members are taking shelter inside, peeking out of windows. I have no doubt we would be welcomed there as well, but I don't want to stick around, and I don't want to try explaining all this to the police. In part because no one will believe us, even with the good pastor's support, but also because it will make Wini and me very easy to locate. I have a feeling these aren't the kind of people who give up easily, especially since we've managed to draw first blood. Being far away when the dust settles is our safest option.

The pastor's, too.

We cross the street as a trio and are honked at by a man trying to transport his family to safety. The man's curses are followed by apologies when he realizes he's just cussed out the pastor. Then we're on a side street, and I'm eyeing the vehicles parked there. I understand the concept of hot wiring a car, but I've never done it.

My eyes move to the cars locked in traffic, slowly moving away from the church. Carjacking one of these vehicles using our guns, empty or not, would be a simple thing. But stranding someone here could be putting them in serious danger, especially if the mercs return and the police end up in a gun battle. Not an option. Carjacking someone at gunpoint would also add law enforcement to the list of people trying to take us down.

A police cruiser skids to a stop across the street, digging troughs in the dry grass of a front yard. Two officers spill out and take up positions behind the vehicle, weapons aimed toward the sky. Right now, they definitely see the mercs as the aggressors. No need to alter their focus.

Before I can come up with a plan that doesn't result in us getting arrested or killed, a voice beckons to me, "Mr. Delgado!"

A young Hispanic man leans out the driver's side window of an orange Dodge Charger—brand new from the looks of it. "Yo, Mr. Delgado. I'm your ride!"

I nearly lift my weapon toward the man's smiling face, but then realize what's happening. This man is one of the many Uber drivers I summoned to the area, and he's recognized me from my profile photo.

I tuck my weapon into the back of my jeans. The heavy gun and large sound suppressor make it an awkward fit, but at least it's out of sight. Wini slides her revolver into her purse, which she's managed to cling on to. The pastor attempts to tuck his weapon into the back of his dress pants, but gives up and opts for his pocket.

"This is some shit, right?" the driver says, watching the fleeing masses, the helicopter twisting around behind the church steeple, and a newly arrived police vehicle that stops beside us. The officers climb out, head for the opening trunk and emerge with assault rifles. "Some real shit, man!"

"Get us out of here," I shout, sliding into the passenger's side front seat, while Wini and the pastor dive into the back.

Despite the moment's chaos, I note the new car smell, the spotless interior, and the odometer, which reads 897.

"Hold on, bitches!" The driver throws the car into reverse and speeds away backward, matching the speed of fleeing vehicles facing the correct direction, on the right side of the road. Then he spins into an empty driveway, before peeling back out into the road and merging with other, far more careful drivers.

The chopper thunders closer.

I brace for their attack.

Shots ring out, but not from the chopper. The police are giving them hell. The chopper roars past overhead before peeling away and retreating, staying low to avoid radar.

A few minutes later, when we pull onto a mostly empty highway, the pastor loosens his silk tie, yanks it off, and with a shrill, cracking shout, asks, "Will one of you please tell me what in the name of shit is going on?"

7

There's a lot going on that makes very little sense to me. The disappearance of Isabella, and then her mother has become the top layer of a larger, far more sinister and dangerous mystery cake that I was not hired to deal with, but am now choking on. On top of that, I'm joined by Wini-turned-Dirty Harry, a foul-mouthed, right-wing, gun-toting pastor, and an Uber driver in a brand new Dodge Charger, who seems unfazed by the chaos.

I'm not comfortable with the large number of unanswered questions, but at least I can get answers to the smaller unknowns.

I turn around to Wini, "Where did you learn to shoot like that?"

"Self-defense classes." She looks a little offended when I raise a skeptical eyebrow. "I wasn't always old and pudgy. A girl has to look after herself."

"Excuse me," the pastor says. "I asked you a damn question."

I crane my head toward the man. "What's your name?"

"Aaron Young, currently a pastor, previously a U.S. Marine chaplain, and I haven't seen action like that since coming home from the Middle East. So I'll repeat my question in kinder terms, what is going on, and who are you people?"

"I'm not done yet," I tell him in my most stern voice. He might have been deployed with Marines and seen some shit, but I still manage to intimidate him with a stare. I turn to the driver. "This car is too nice. Whose is it?"

"You saying I stole this ride?" The driver looks aghast, but I can tell it's a show. "Yo, that's racist." He gives me a watered down version of my own 'shut-the-hell-up' stare, but barely contains his smile. When I don't blink, he takes both hands off the wheel for a moment and says, "Geez, man, you're stone cold! Okay, okay, it's not my car..."

"Good Lord," Wini says.

"But, it's my uncle's. I swear. He's rich. Famous south of the border, know what I'm saying? But he wants me to make my own way, so I become an Uber driver. But I don't have a car, see? So he..."

"Lets you borrow the car," I finish.

"Right."

"But he doesn't know that yet," I guess.

"What he doesn't know, hombre..." He smiles at me. "You know the rest."

I nearly point out that the odometer is going to give him away, but decide our driver's muscle car, youthful naiveté, and willingness to drive are imperative to our next steps.

"Name?" I ask.

"You can call me Lindo," he says with a smile that looks tailor-made to impress the ladies.

Wini snorts from the backseat. "You're not hard on the eyes, honey, but 'Lindo' is pouring it on a little thick."

He flashes that same smile back at Wini. "You know what else is thick, maravillosa?"

I cut off Lindo with a raised hand, not because Wini can't go toe to toe with our driver, but because I've seen and heard enough horrible things for one day, and this is one road I don't want Lindo to take us down. "Let's just stick to business, eh, Lindo? Muy bien?"

He grimaces at my graceless use of Spanish. "In that case, where do you want to go? You've already racked up a decent fare driving..." He looks out at the road. "...wherever we are."

"Mind if we do the rest off the books?" I ask, and then I point to the GPS unit tracking us and calculating how much Uber will charge me. "And off the grid?"

"Oh shit," he says. "You weren't just getting the hell out of dodge. You were part of that, weren't you?"

"A thousand dollars," I say, "and I'll pay for gas, if you can take us where we need to go."

"Damn, man. For a grand, I'll take you wher*ever* you want to go."

"Look, I don't know what you all are mixed up in, but my part in this is ending," Young says.

"I wish it were that easy," I tell him.

"It *is* that easy," he says. "Pull over, let me out, and I'll call for a ride. I don't live far from here."

"Except you were seen with us," I say.

"I don't even know you. I've never seen you before. If anyone asks, that's what I'll tell them. You haven't told me anything yet, so I won't need to lie. They'll see I'm telling the truth."

He's stretching, hoping his words will make sense, but even he knows they don't, because of one glaring problem. "You shot at them," I say.

"Oh shit, really?" Lindo says with a chuckle. "Damn, man, a priest with a gun? What church you at, man? I want to sign up."

"I'm a pastor," Young grumbles. "Priests are Catholic."

Lindo waves him off. "Same thing. You all believe in the same dude, right?"

Young stares at the back of Lindo's seat, lost in thought. He can think all he wants, but there's no way out for him. In the eyes of whoever attacked us, he's the enemy. The trouble is that unlike Wini and me, who are two hours from home, Young's identity will be easy to uncover. I'm sure the church's website has his well-groomed mug on the front page.

When I ask, "You have a family?" he snaps out of his reverie. "Better call them. Tell them to lie low until we know what's going on."

We fall silent as a group while Young calls home. He speaks in hushed tones, but I can tell that whoever is on the receiving end is both angry and concerned. When he finishes the conversation he turns to me, fuming, and says, "Okay, now tell me why I just sent my wife and son to stay with my sister. And in case you can't tell by my tone, they don't like each other. At all."

"First," I say, "phones out the windows."

I put my window down and drop my phone on the blur of pavement. It shatters on impact. Wini does the same without question or complaint. She understands why. Young frowns, but he gets it, too. We've all seen enough movies to know how easily smartphones can be tracked, and I'm still not convinced the people hunting us don't have access to such things.

With three phones out the window, I turn to Lindo, who seems just as pleased with the situation as he was when he picked us up. That is, until he realizes what I'm asking.

"Yo," he says, growing more serious. "Yo..."

"I'm sure your dick pics are saved on the cloud," Wini says from the back.

Struggling to not smile, Lindo adds, "This is a six hundred dollar phone, man."

"Two grand," I tell him.

Business is good, and Kailyn was insured. As a bachelor with few hobbies beyond my work and reading biographies, I don't spend a lot of money. Two grand won't put much of a dent in my net worth.

Without taking his eyes off mine, Lindo puts his window down and casually tosses his phone out the window.

Then I turn my eyes to the GPS unit.

"Uh-uh," he says. "No way. Car is under my uncle's name, man. Uber doesn't even know I'm driving it. Seriously, look at my profile. This is supposed to be a shitty Prius."

I believe him, and the GPS will come in handy for what comes next.

"What kind of asshole drives a Prius?" Wini says, getting a chuckle out of me.

"Hey, man," Lindo says. "It's fuel efficient."

"I'm sorry," Young says, gripping the two front, bucket seats. "I'm glad our driver is having fun with all this, but some of us have people who depend on us, and family to get back to. So if we could cut through all the small talk, yos, mans, and general disregard for anything that makes a lick of sense, could you please tell us what is happening?"

"I was hired to find a missing little girl. The daughter of an illegal immigrant living in Santa Cruz."

"Legit?" Lindo says. "My parents are ill..."

He thinks better of making the confession, but I can see he's a little more invested in what I'm telling him now.

"We went to meet her mother this morning. There were signs of a struggle." I tell them about the small house in disguise, the phone, the mysterious warning text, and the mercs' arrival, taking us up to the moment we met Lindo and drove away.

The story sounds unbelievable as I tell it. There isn't a law enforcement agency in the country that wouldn't have serious doubts with some or all of what I've said. But no one in the car questions it. Young witnessed the most unbelievable bits himself, and Lindo saw enough to cast doubt aside. Plus, I think he likes his role in the narrative.

'Seeing is believing' is a cliché, but like many clichés it exists for a reason. That's why most people can't be convicted of a crime without evidence, though it does happen.

"So..." Young says, "we're doing what, exactly? Hiding?"

"Pssh, haven't you been paying attention?" Wini swats the pastor's shoulder. "We're looking for a missing girl, and now her mother, too."

Lindo pumps his fist. "¡A huevo!"

"Huevo?" Young asks. "Isn't that...eggs?"

"Man, if you're taking it literally, yeah." Lindo looks disappointed.

"Pssh," Wini says, again. "No tiene dos dedos de frente."

I have no idea what she said, and neither does Young, but Lindo cracks up laughing. "Yo chica, you're good people." He puts a fist out to Wini, and she bumps it. Then he turns to me and asks, "So, man, where we headed?"

I erase his smile with three words. "Colorado City. Arizona."

8

What I took for horror over the distance is actually a slow brewing excitement that gurgles into a high-pitched squeal of delight, followed by laughter and a string of Spanish so fast that even Wini looks confused.

"Uhh, have you been?" is all I can think to ask when Lindo's exuberance begins to ebb.

It's Young who answers. "Colorado City is fairly infamous."

My full attention shifts from the front seat to the back. "Why?"

"Mormons," he says. "Well, a sect of them that have stayed true to the teachings of Joseph Smith, the same way Islamic Extremists stay true to—"

"Nope," I say, "don't go there." Wini shakes her head while Lindo says, "Yo. Yo. Yo." with varying degrees of seriousness, and then adds, "Man, *you're* the racist? Out of everyone in this car, I'd expect Ms. Daisy back there to be the one stuck in the past. No offense."

Wini shrugs. None taken.

"Islam isn't a race," Young says, growing defensive.

Whether or not he's right isn't the issue. I normally wouldn't mind the debate. But that hot button topic is going to spiral us into a heated discussion that will do nothing more than cause division and not get me any closer to finding Isabella or Marta. "Let's stick to the Mormons."

Young acquiesces with raised hands. "The only real difference between the Council of Friends—what the town's founders called themselves—and the LDS church is that the Council believed in plural marriage."

"Hell yeah," Lindo says. "Polygamy FT-Dubs."

Young takes a deep breath, clearly not accustomed to having his lessons interrupted. He probably doesn't even know that FT-Dubs is slang for FTW, which is slang for 'For the win'. Slang upon slang, upon slang. But he rolls right past it, sticking with the word he does understand: polygamy. "Which *is* what Joseph Smith taught *and* lived. The man had twenty-eight wives. Brigham Young, Smith's successor—to whom I am *not* related—had *fifty-five* wives."

"Damn, dude," Lindo says, eyes wide. This is all news to him, and not why the town's name got him excited.

"The modern church denies much of this," Young continues, "but no one can refute that the U.S. government forced the Mormons to ban polygamy in 1890. Utah wouldn't have been a state if they hadn't, and the LDS church would have been violently wiped out. All that is to say that there are families who still practice plural marriage in Colorado City, and other small LDS communities, usually run by a charismatic cult leader. There've been more than a few arrests and cult breakups in recent years."

I remember seeing something about that on the news, but I keep it to myself.

"The cults are also responsible for the proliferation of homeless men in Utah. As birth rates of boys and girls are close to equal, the boys must be expelled from the community so that the older men can continue to marry. Hundreds of young men have found themselves on the streets over the years, many of them disappearing and never being heard from again."

"Geez," Lindo says. "All that for a little extra poontang?"

"Fifty-five wives is a *lot* of poontang," Wini says. "But if they're keeping it in the family, so to speak, that can't be healthy."

Lindo drum rolls on the steering wheel. "Oh, shit, is this going to be like a *Hills Have Eyes* sitch?"

"Yes," Young says, "there is a high rate of deformity and developmental disability in the community. Some of the highest in the world, in fact. But no, it's not like *The Hills Have Eyes*."

Lindo is surprised, but not about the facts. "Preach, you've seen that movie?"

Young shrugs. "I like horror."

"And religious history," I point out.

"Part of the job."

I'm quiet for a moment, pondering possibilities. Then I ask, "These LDS cults... They wouldn't kidnap women to keep as wives, would they?"

"They're run by men with a penchant for collecting women," Young says, frowning. "Who's to say what they would do? Adding women from outside the community could certainly help the gene pool, and I doubt there are women from outside the community clambering for a life of sexual servitude to an old man. But, they are also notoriously racist, so I don't think that's the case with your missing Latina."

"Better not be," Lindo says.

"Since all of that was news to you," I say to Lindo, "what do *you* know about the town?"

Lindo's grin returns. "Weird shit, man."

"Weirder than polygamous cults?" Wini asks.

"UFOs."

All hope in learning something useful dissolves. "UFOs..."

"Unidentified Flying Objects? You know."

"I do know," I say, and my voice tells him how unimpressed I am.

"I'm not making this shit up," Lindo says. "Colorado City is in a hot zone for sightings. The county its in—"

"Mohave," Young says.

"Right," Lindo gives a vigorous nod. "They have tons of UFO sightings. Like hundreds every year."

"Every year?" I ask. If hundreds of people are reporting something—anything—hundreds of times per year, there is usually something real behind it. Not little green men, but something.

"Hundreds," Lindo says. "And Colorado City is at the epicenter." I'm about to ask him to explain when he turns his lady-killing smile toward me. "Just like Santa Cruz, man."

Now he's got my attention. "What about Santa Cruz?"

"Same deal, man. Lots of weird shit. UFO sightings, like all the time."

"He's right about that," Young says. "I'm frequently asked about the subject. I think most people in the congregation have seen something."

"Have you?" Wini asks.

"No, and I pray that I don't. UFOs and the like are most likely the visible, or tangible in some cases, manifestation of demonic activity."

Young and Lindo are two very different but equal kinds of wacky. But if there is a connection between Santa Cruz and Colorado City, even if it's batshit crazy, I want to hear it.

"I don't know about that," Lindo says. "Demons aren't really my bag."

"Which is what they want you to think."

Lindo gives me a sidelong grin and an eye roll, like we're on the same page when it comes to who is a nut job and who isn't. Then he says, "Look, man, Santa Cruz and Colorado City are both on the 37th parallel."

He waits for a reaction and when he doesn't get one, he continues. "You know, the lines that go around the Earth? Like on a globe?"

"I know what they are," I say, pretending like I knew what he meant the first time.

"The 37th parallel runs straight through both cities, man. Straight through."

There's some kind of significance here of which I am not aware. "And..."

"It's the UFO highway," Wini says.

"Yo!" Lindo directs his smile back at Wini. "I'm digging you, man."

"What's the UFO highway?" Young asks.

"The majority of UFO sightings, and other weird shit, happen along the 37th. All the way across the country from Santa Cruz to Williamsburg, Virginia. Animal mutilations, alien abductions, crop circles, earthquakes, you name it. All of it running along Highway 37."

"How do they know they're alien?" While I heard everything he said, only one word really stood out, and it fits with something Young said. Could this be my nugget of truth? "The abductions."

"I don't know, man," Lindo says. "If there are lights in the sky and then someone goes missing, ipso facto."

"First," I say, "I'm pretty sure you're not using ipso facto correctly. Second, how many abductions?"

"Beats me, man. But a lot, I think. And that's just the ones being reported."

I'm about to ask who wouldn't report a missing person when I remember the pastor's claims about young men being ejected from the cult. Who would report them missing?

I also know that there are, on average, a hundred thousand people missing in the United States at any given time. Many of them are never found. Some are abductions—by people—or unsolved murders. Some are folks just getting lost, or dying of natural causes someplace where they can't be found. There are a lot of reasons why people disappear, but if there is a large number of people going missing in a narrow geographic location, there could be something larger at play.

Human trafficking is often thought of as being a sin of the past. In truth, there are more people in slavery now than ever before. And it's prevalent in the smallest backwoods towns and the largest cities in the U.S. People are shipped, marketed, and sold right under our noses. The idea of an abduction-and-transportation ring centered around the 37th parallel feels like a stretch, but compared to UFOs, it's not only possible, but quasi-likely.

The moment I find evidence of something on that scale, I'll call the authorities in. Until then, I'll try to keep us rooted in the real world.

"How long until we reach Colorado City?" I ask.

Lindo glances down at the GPS, and I realize I could have done the same.

"Ten hours," he says. "Less if I speed."

"Don't speed," I tell him. "Let's try to avoid the police."

"Story of my life, man. No problema."

Twelve hours later, after several stops for gas, food, and bathrooms, we arrive in Colorado City, which in the dead of night is not much to see. But that doesn't mean it's not interesting. Just two minutes after pulling into town in search of a hotel, motel, inn, or B&B—which isn't easy without a phone for research—I know our arrival hasn't gone unnoticed.

"Turn right," I tell Lindo.

"What? Why?" His confusion is understandable. We're on a main road. There are bright signs ahead. One of them is probably a hotel of some sort. Despite my lack of answer, Lindo takes the next right into a residential neighborhood.

Fifteen seconds later, the car behind us follows.

I watch it in the side mirror, maintaining a steady, non-threatening distance. "We're being followed."

9

"Turn left, up ahead. See it?" I say.

Lindo drives with both hands on the wheel and both eyes on the rearview. I snap my fingers, pulling his attention back to the road. "Yeah, man, but—"

"Once we're out of sight, accelerate, quick as you can, but without screeching the tires."

"And then?" Young asks, his voice tense. Moments ago we had all been somewhat delirious from the long drive. Now everyone is amped up and nervous. As they should be. We just drove nearly seven hundred miles without our phones in a vehicle no one could trace us back to.

Short of our faces being picked up by roadside cameras, or our progress tracked by satellite recon, we should have been invisible. And that makes me a little nervous. If the men chasing us had those kinds of resources, I can only think of one possible source: the NSA. And if that's the case, we're well and truly screwed.

Odds are, we'll just disappear, like the people we're trying to find.

"We'll find a driveway. Pull in. Turn the lights off," I say.

"Hide in plain sight?" Young complains. "That's the plan? In this car?"

I glance around the brand new, super cool car interior. It's not the kind of vehicle you spot on the road and don't look at again. I'm not a car-guy, but I'd double-take this beast out of sheer curiosity. Young might be right.

"So then we don't hide," I say.

Young leans forward, pleased that he shifted our strategy away from something that scared him. "And the alternative to hiding is..."

"Ambush," I say, crushing his concerns with far larger ones. "We'll park and hide. When they stop to look at the car..." I waggle my empty, sound suppressed Beretta M9.

"We've no rounds left," Wini points out.

"They don't know that." I look in the side mirror. The vehicle behind us has maintained its distance. "And maybe we'll get some answers."

"Or get dead," Wini says. "But hell, I've got a foot in the grave already."

"I like the hiding in plain sight idea more," Young says.

"Well, better say your prayers, because that's not the way this is going to happen." I turn to Lindo, who hasn't voiced an opinion. "You good?"

"I'm your driver, man. You tell me where to go, how fast to get there, what music to play, and I'll get it done."

I like Lindo, but I haven't figured out if he's got a strong sense of adventure, or he's four straight lines short of a cube. He's been a god-send, and surprisingly knowledgeable—about weird and possibly insignificant things—but what kind of person agrees to go on a cross country jaunt in his uncle's brand new, very expensive car, with strangers who are being chased by armed gunmen and a helicopter?

As he prepares to take the left turn, I decide I don't care. I'm glad he's part of our haphazard team.

His hands grip the wheel.

Foot to the gas pedal.

Eyes shift to the rearview, and then, surprise. "Yo, they're gone."

I turn around in my seat, scanning the road. It's empty.

"Did they bug out?" he asks. "Know we were on to them?"

I give my head a slow shake. There's no way...just like there's no way we could have been tracked.

People gone missing, guns-blazing mercs, a black, unmarked helicopter; it's all affecting my nerves. Making me paranoid. "I was wrong."

"You said they were following us," Young complains, his anxiety melting from him as sweat. He was a lot braver when his gun was loaded, which I suppose makes sense.

"Coincidence." I shrug. "It happens."

Not often, but it does.

I look in the sidemirror again, expecting to see lights, or the silhouette of a vehicle running with its lights off, but the street is empty.

Over the next fifteen minutes, I direct us through a maze of turns, just to be sure. When our chaotic path is done, we're parked in the lot of the Zion Motel.

The single story, concrete building is utilitarian and very solid looking, which I suppose is a bonus if armed goons track us down. When Lindo turns the car off, I turn around and ask, "Okay, who's got cash?"

Lindo scoffs. "Cash? Man, this is the twenty-first century. Who carries cash?"

"Used what I had on gas," Young says. "I've got three cards, but we can't use them, right?"

Wini digs around through her purse, shuffling through makeup containers I'm not sure she's ever used, pens, keys, and packages of mints. Her hand emerges with a money clip, plump with twenty dollar bills. When she sees the mutual surprise shared by the rest of us, she says, "Anyone as old as me knows it's foolish to depend on technology."

"And makes you a target for criminals," Young says.

"Hence the gun." Wini grins and hands the wad of cash to me. "Besides, it's his money."

I'm stymied. "What?"

"You give me a hundred dollars a week for office expenses," she says. "Do you realize how few office expenses we have?"

How much money does she have? I wonder, and then I do a quick flip through. The twenties disappear after the first few bills. A disguise. The rest are hundreds. I'm holding something just shy of ten thousand dollars.

The strangest thing about the wad of cash in my hands is the lack of reaction from Young and Lindo. Granted, Young is the pastor of a mega-church and judging by the tailored suit, tithing is good. But Lindo, who was excited about two thousand dollars, doesn't so much as flinch when he sees five times that.

Maybe he's thinking about taking it? It's possible. I don't really know him, and he did take his uncle's car. But then, he's not really a stranger to excess.

When I peel out a thousand dollars and hand it to Lindo, his surprise kicks in. "Dude, what's this?"

"Down payment," I tell him. "The rest when we're done." I hand him another five hundred. "This is for gas, expenses, and your room."

He takes the cash, smiling now. "Room service tonight, baby!"

"Pretty sure there isn't room service here," Wini points out. The motel isn't exactly seedy, but if they had a kitchen, I wouldn't use it.

"Also..." I hold my hand out to Lindo. "Keys."

"Seriously?" Lindo looks both offended and amused.

"Two grand serious," I tell him. "I like you, but haven't known you long enough to trust you."

He makes a sound like air escaping a tire, but then slaps the keys down in my hand.

I hand another five hundred to Young. "Same as him. Expenses. Food. Room. Go in separately. You don't know each other. Don't know us."

"What about you two?" Lindo asks.

"Wini's with me."

"Oh, I see how it is." Lindo, having a good laugh, turns around to face Wini. "You robbing the cradle over here, Win? What's your secret? What's my boy into, aside from, you know, the age thing?"

Wini stares at him so long, I think she's not going to reply, and that would be fine by me, but then with a straight face, she says. "Detachable penis."

The car is silent for a moment, and then we collectively vent our pent up anxiety from the day. It's a good moment in an otherwise shitty day. Laughing feels good. Therapeutic. I don't know Young or Lindo, but part of me remembers what it's like to have friends. For the past five years, it's been me and Wini. Kaylie's family tried to stay in touch for the first year, but I avoided them until they gave up. Being part of their family—of *her* family—hurt too much. They look like her. They laugh like her.

"Good stuff, man," Lindo says, and then exits the car, walking into the motel and emerging a few minutes later. He flashes the keycard, letting us know all went well, and then struts off to his room, most likely for a night of pay-per-view porn on my dime.

Ten minutes later, I send in Young. When I see him headed toward a room near the end, I leave Wini in the car and enter the motel alone. I'm not being chivalrous, but I don't need anyone else thinking the way Lindo does, to take note. The last thing I want to do right now is stand out.

When the short man behind the counter sees me and makes a face like the Devil himself passed gas in his face, I know I've somehow failed. I give myself a once over. Maybe there's blood on my clothes? When the man groans as he stands up from behind a TV, I realize he's just otherwise engaged and lazy.

"Busy night?" I ask, trying to be friendly.

"Least you're white," the man says, his blatant racism like a slap in the face. I'm about to say something when he leans in for a closer look. "You *is* white?"

The delay gives me just enough time to reign in my emotions. I'm not here to throw down with the locals, even if he is a bigot. I don't even bother correcting him, as it would require explaining the concept of interracial couples, and I'm sure this guy hasn't seen Jungle Fever.

"I is." I manage to say it with a lopsided grin that convinces the man I'm not mocking him.

"How long?"

I nearly say, 'one night,' but then I realize that Young and Lindo probably did the same. Bubba here has already noted the uptick in customers from none to three. No reason to give him a pattern to notice. "Two."

"How many in the room?"

"Two."

He looks around me like he might have missed someone else entering the small, mildew-scented reception office. "Name?"

I'm pretty sure he doesn't need a name and is really just fishing to see if I'm staying with a man, so I tell him. "My mother. We're visiting family."

He goes all squinty again and I realize I might have stepped in it. Colorado City is basically one big family. If I'm visiting someone here, he's likely to know them, know of them, or maybe even be a direct relative.

"Mind if we move this along?" I ask with my best awkward smile. "Been a long drive, and if she falls asleep in the car, I might need your help carrying her inside."

The man plucks a key card up and slaps it on the counter. "No offense to your mom, but I ain't picking up no old ladies tonight."

"Sure as shit don't blame you," I say, swiping the card up. "What's the damage?"

"Hundred for both nights."

I put a hundred dollar bill on the counter and slide it over. Squinty-eyed fart face picks the bill up. Holds it to the light. "Three C-notes in thirty minutes. What are the odds?"

"Beats the hell outta me," I say, opening the door, which chimes when I exit. The man's voice chases me back out into the clear night. "Enjoy your stay."

Relax, I tell myself. *Just stay calm.* And for a moment, I manage it.

Then I reach the car and find Wini missing.

"Wini?" I spin around, searching for her. "Wini!"

"Here," she says, her voice coming from the parking lot's far side, just around the side of the building. "Come see. Quick!"

My feet crunch over a parking lot in need of a fresh coat of tar. By the time I cross the fifty feet, the day's exhaustion has settled on my shoulders once more. I nearly bump into Wini when I round the corner. "Wini, what—"

Her hand grasps my cheek, tight enough to hurt. Then she shoves my head up, turning my eyes to the sky, and obliterates the weariness from my body, mind, and soul. In an instant, I'm more awake than I ever remember being. And yet, I'm reduced to a state of stupefaction.

I manage a simple question. "What is it?"

To which, Wini gives an obvious answer. "I'm not an expert, but I'm gonna guess a UFO."

10

A triangle of lights in the sky might not normally fuse my feet to the ground and drop my jaw with the comical width and height of a Sesame Street puppet, but it's more than just lights. Where there should be stars between the white spheres, there is only darkness.

Think, I tell myself. *Use Logic. Figure it out.*

What is triangular, dark, and flies? There's only one answer to that riddle: a B-2 Spirit stealth bomber. The billion dollar airplanes are big. Somewhere around a hundred and seventy feet across. I try to see the object in the sky as a B-2, but the theory falls apart.

The triangle meanders through the sky, spinning slowly. The B-2 would plummet to the ground, and they most definitely can't rotate.

But this thing is lit. Like a conventional aircraft.

Or not. The three lights at the triangle's points are steady and white. There're no red flashing lights warning other aircraft of its presence. I get the sense that the lights have more to do with propulsion than they do with safety. And then it proves me wrong. All three lights blink out. For a moment, I think it's gone, but then I note the triangle of sky is still devoid of stars.

I focus on my hearing, listening for the telltale signs of something flying. Unless the craft sounds like buzzing insects, it's silent.

A star winks to life on the triangle's left side. Then another.

It's moving.

Southeast.

I try to calculate the size and distance, but there's not enough to go on. The shape merges with the silhouette of a tall bluff I hadn't noticed in the dark. Stars twinkle to life, marking the object's stealthy passage, and then, nothing. It slips from view like a moray eel backing into its den, calm and unconcerned, and yet full of sinister portent.

I watch the empty sky, the luminous stars now unobstructed, for a full minute. Then I turn to Wini, who is still transfixed.

"What time is it?" she asks.

I reach for my phone and have a moment of panic when I feel the empty pocket. Then I remember the device's fate and simply feel frustrated. "Why?"

"Want to be sure we weren't abducted."

"We weren't," I assure her.

"Wouldn't know if you were," she says.

"The stars haven't moved," I tell her, motioning to the Big Dipper overhead. I hadn't actually looked at the stars, or noted the Dipper's position, but if a white lie will ground us in the realm of plausibility, then I can live with it.

"Mmm," she says, maybe agreeing, or possibly seeing through the lie.

"We should tell the others," she says.

I shake my head. "We don't know what we saw."

She looks at me like I've just pooped out a pterodactyl. "That's pretty much the meaning of 'unidentified.'"

"I'm not going to tell them we saw aliens flying—"

"*Unidentified.*"

"Is that what Lindo will think?" I've never taken the UFO phenomenon seriously. The people involved with their 'study' most often seem like crackpots who like to point out how they're suffering ridicule because of the subject matter, all the while becoming rock stars for true believers. Most appear at UFO conventions. Some get book deals. The lucky ones get movie deals.

It's harsh, I know, to call these people charlatans and liars. Most of them seem to be struggling—emotionally, physically, financially—when they are taken and returned with a story that defies both explanation and belief. But logic is unaffected by empathy. It's a key component to my job as an investigator, and even more so when I was a detective. The truth is what matters, not the sob story distracting from it. And one truth about humanity that is universal and unfaltering is that people lie.

All the time.

Most people lie the way I just did to Wini. White lies prevent pain, and conflict, and whether they're used selfishly or not, they don't have a lasting effect on the world. But then there are people who have perfected the art of spinning falsehoods, and not all of them are sociopaths, though that certainly helps.

I once caught a man in the act of cheating on his wife. He claimed, in all seriousness, to be learning an ancient Chinese form of internal massage. Said that he was learning it to help his marriage. The yurt, incense, candles, copious amounts of oil, and Buddha statues lent credence to the lie, but the fictional word he concocted for the mystical technique—and which I recorded on my phone—'cào nǐ mā' translates to 'fuck your mother,' which was a pretty accurate description of what was happening.

I landed that case three months after starting the PI business. Wini, who was new at the time, called it our Jerry Springer case. In the years since, we've had more than a hundred Springer cases, all dealing with creative lies by normal people. But then there are the abnormal people, who make careers out of lying. Actors entertain us by pretending to be other people. Celebrities pretend to be healthier or better looking than other people, utilizing makeup and Photoshop. Politicians...well, that doesn't even need explaining. Lying is a tool employed by everyone on the planet, and people who tell stories of alien abductions, liquid chairs, and anal probes are just that: liars.

Like everyone else.

Their lies are just easier to see through—unless you don't want to.

At the same time, I acknowledge that I've just seen something beyond explanation. If it had been Lindo and Young out here instead of Wini and me, I wouldn't believe their story in the morning. Which is another reason we can keep this to ourselves. I'm not going to sully my credibility by telling stories that make no sense.

Lies serve a purpose.

That big triangle in the sky, visible for all to see, serves a purpose.

And it's the same purpose all lies serve—to conceal the truth.

When a large number of people go missing in a certain area, which happens to be the same area where Isabella was last seen, the presence of a very visible UFO could come in handy. I have zero theories on how it was done, but I intend to find out.

"Until it is," I say.

"Until it is what?" she asks. "You drifted off there for a minute."

"Identified."

"And who's going to do that?"

"We are...." I raise a finger. "...*if* it turns out to be connected to Isabella's disappearance. Other than interviewing people in town, which we're going to do as well—" I redirect my finger toward the dark bluff. "—that thing, which is traditionally associated with missing people, is our only lead. So we're going to follow—"

The sky beyond the bluff flashes orange with silent heat lightning. Each flash carves the bluff's outline into my retina.

The light show transfixes me once more. If this is a lie, it is expensive and elaborate. Far too much to be misdirecting whoever might be watching from the disappearance of a little girl. Then again, I would have said the same about mercenaries in a black helicopter, too.

The lights flicker one last time and then stop. The night feels heavy and foreboding, like it did on Halloween when I was a kid.

"We've stepped in something big," I say to myself, forgetting that Wini is with me.

"And smelly," she says. "What's the plan?"

"We'll head out there in the morning," I say, eyes on the flashing bluff. "See what there is to see."

"And the others?" she motions to the motel behind us.

"They'll come with."

"You don't trust them," she says. It's not a question.

"I trust you."

"Trust no one," she says. "Is that it? You're a regular Fox Mulder."

"Does that make you my Scully?"

She smiles and elbows me. "Thought you didn't like science fiction?"

"Kailyn loved the show," I say, touching the envelope in my pocket. "You'd have liked her."

"That's been a long-established fact." Wini leans her head on my arm. "FYI, the day has passed."

Wini has watched me struggle on this day for the past five years. In comparison, looking for a missing girl, being attacked by mercs, driving seven hundred miles, and witnessing the impossible, is a good day. I feel pretty good. And now, knowing it is past, the weight is lifted. I lean my head on hers. "You want to buy some clothes in the morning?"

"Please, God, yes." She tugs at the skirt she's been regretting wearing all day. We turn together and head toward the motel's corner. "And just so you know, I'm sleeping in my skivvies tonight. You're bound to get an eyeful."

"I'll try to keep my hands to myself."

We round the corner, arms around each other, as close as family ever could be, and are stumbled to a stop by the wide-eyed gaze of the motel's chubby clerk.

"Said she was your mother," the man states, somehow managing to frown while his mouth is open. Out of context, I understand how our conversation could lead to incorrect assumptions.

I'm about to explain when Wini says, "Hey, when in Colorado City, right?"

The man's blank stare says he's perhaps unaware of the city's reputation, and of the original, 'when in Rome,' source material. But then he shrugs and says, "S'pose so."

Wini and I scurry to the motel room, let ourselves in and collapse into the spring-loaded twin beds, wracked with laughter until we both pass out.

I wake up the following morning feeling more like my old self than I have for exactly five years and one day. That is, until I sit up and find the door wide open—and Wini missing.

11

"Wini?" Blankets explode away from me as I launch for the door. Fists clenched, I step into the morning sun and the day's already dry heat. Fear conjures images of Wini being forced into a van, or dead on the pavement, her killer just waiting for me to emerge.

What I find is a mostly empty parking lot. I look right. The Charger is still there, but it's parked two spaces further to the right. I turn left, and am greeted by a woman in tight skinny jeans, a poufy shirt that assails my eyes with a bright flower print, and insect-eye-like sunglasses. She leans on a cart covered in fresh towels and cleaning supplies, takes a drag from her cigarette, lowers her sunglasses, and gives me a blatant up-and-down stare that's downright hungry.

Twin geysers of smoke stream from her nostrils. "Aren't you just a bowl of peaches."

While I have never heard the expression before, and suspect she's just made it up, I know exactly what she's trying to communicate.

I glance down, remembering that I'm dressed in boxer briefs. Concern for Wini overcomes my embarrassment. "Have you seen an older woman—"

"You're into older women?" She grins, and for the first time I notice the wrinkles lining her tan skin. Her age is hard to peg. She could be in her late sixties, or early fifties and spent too much time in the sun. Either way, she's got a decade or two on me.

"I'm looking for my mother."

She ponders this for a moment. "Saw an older gal go into one of those rooms." She nods down the line of rooms. "The one with the open door."

Near the end of the building, Young's door hangs open just like mine.

"Was with a good looking black fella, though, so you might wanna wait before you go knocking. Seemed like they were in a rush, too. In the meantime, I haven't cleaned this room yet. Nobody's going to mind if we mess it up a little more."

Though my thoughts are something closer to 'it will be a cold day in Beelzebub's BBQ grill before that happens,' I've learned that ingratiating people, even those who repulse you, often greases an investigation's wheels. While I doubt the woman knows anything about my case, she's a local—who else would work here—and her knowledge of the area could come in handy. So I smile and say, "Maybe next time."

She gives me a wink. "Next time."

I retreat back into my room and close the door behind me. I look to the floor, searching for the clothing I shed in the middle of the night when the air conditioning stopped working. I don't see the clothes, but I do spot the clock. It's 10am.

Before I can react to the time, I spot a bright yellow bag lying on the room's small desk. The beacon leads me to a neatly stacked pile of clothing. I riffle through the garments and find a pair of jeans, tan cargo shorts, a white T-shirt and a nice, white button-up. Given the heat already beating down, I opt for the shorts and T-shirt. I would normally wear pants and a nice shirt while on the job, regardless of the weather, but I don't want to stand out. Better to look like a tourist.

The shorts fit just right, no doubt thanks to Wini. I pick up the T-shirt and freeze. Hidden beneath the shirt is the silenced Beretta M9. Resting on the desk beside it is a box of 9mm ammo. I pick up the weapon. The weight of it tells me it's already loaded, but I eject the magazine anyway. After confirming a full load, I rack the slide to make sure there isn't a round in the chamber. It's clean.

Wini was busy this morning. After hearing that Wini was seen with Young, and finding the clothing and ammo, I feel a little bit less worried about her. If she bought ammo for me, she'd have bought it for herself and for Young as well, and even though that's a lot of bullets, no one's going to question little ol' Wini. I unscrew the sound suppressor and slip it in my cargo shorts pocket. The naked Beretta goes in the small of my back. I throw the T-shirt on and head for the door.

The door swings open just before I reach it. The silhouette of a man rushes inside and is greeted by my quick-drawn handgun. It's been a while since I had to draw down on someone. I'm happy to see I'm still pretty quick. Far more happy than Lindo, who's staring down the barrel of my gun, arms raised.

"Yooo, man! It's me." When I don't pull the trigger, Lindo lowers his hands. "Damn, Skippy, you nearly capped my ass."

"Lucky I didn't." I tuck the weapon back into my shorts. "Where's Wini?"

"Sent me to get you. You won't believe the shit that's on TV!" Rather than walking to Young's room, I pick up the remote and turn on the aging television, which is already tuned to a local channel. A reporter in a bright red power suit that's nearly as hard on the eyes as the deluge of news graphics announcing a breaking story, sits behind a desk. She's feeling smug and amused with the report already in progress. "Once again, this was the scene in Colorado City last night."

A framed video of the night sky is displayed. Three bright lights inch across the sky. The video is hazy, from several miles away, and accompanied by a diatribe from what sounds like that double rainbow guy, but with a bottle of Jack in him. The video is captioned with: *Aliens Visit AZ? Again?!* When the lights slide behind the dark bluff, the video cuts away.

The reporter returns, smile widening. The video replays beside her. "Reports of the visitation came in just after midnight, with residents claiming to have spotted the otherworldly lights hovering to the southeast of town. Listen to this eyewitness describe it."

"You see, man?" Lindo says. "Thirty-seventh parallel. I *told* you."

A voice that can only belong to a chain smoking woman booms from the TV, the recording marred by static, snaps, and pops. "I saw it in the sky. Watched it for, God, I don't know, an hour. Was spinning. Doing flips. Slipped out of sight there at the end, but then poof! There was this big flash of white light and it shot up into the sky quicker than I could say ho-lee sh-*eeeep*. Watched it bounce around in the sky for a bit, putting on a right good show. Lost track of it after that."

"That's not what happened," I mumble.

"Wait, what?"

Damn. I forgot Lindo wasn't with me. "Nothing."

"Yo, did *you* see that shit? Are you serious?" Lindo steps back, moving his arms in a way I'm not sure how to describe. It's almost like he's on stage, talking to an audience. "How'd it go down?"

There's no point in lying. I turn off the TV and say, "Not like that, and not where they say. Is Wini with you?"

"She's with the preach."

I notice he's wearing new clothes.

"You went shopping?" I ask.

"We all did, man. Where do you think your new digs came from?"

"Right..." Wini going shopping isn't a big deal, but an old white woman in a store with two men of darker skin tones might raise a few eyebrows.

Lindo must sense my concern because he says, "I waited in the car. Preach did his shopping separate. Said he needed to try shit on. Little high maintenance if you ask me."

"And the bullets?" I ask.

"That was all Win, man. Preach was against it, but looked pretty happy when he loaded those fifty cals. Have to admit though, I'm feeling pretty inadequate without a piece."

"You ever fire a gun?" I ask.

"Have I ever...? Man, look at me. I..." He squeezes his lips together, eyeing me. Knows that I can see right through him. "Naw, man, but still."

"You drive," I tell him. "That's it. Cool?"

His frown says it's not, but he says, "Yeah, man. I'm good."

"Good. Now, go get the others."

"We heading out?" Lindo backs toward the door. "We gonna see some shit?"

"We're going to where that happened," I point to the blank television. "Where that really happened. From there, I'm not sure. We'll go where the trail leads us."

"Sweet." Lindo exits the room, leaving the door wide open and missing the conclusion of my thoughts.

"If there is a trail," I say to myself.

We gather by the car two minutes later, all of us in new clothing, three of us with loaded weapons I hope we won't need. While both Lindo and Wini are dressed for the heat, in shorts and T-shirts, Young is dressed in a suit coat and tie. The outfit screams 'federal agent' and when I'm about to question his choice of clothing, he pulls out a wallet and flips it open. I catch a brief glimpse of a badge and what looks like an NSA ID card. Then he flips it closed. "Aaron Young, NSA. Thought it might get some answers." I stare at him, letting discomfort blossom. "You know, if you can't turn up anything."

I answer by climbing into the car's passenger seat. When everyone is inside, I turn around. "If you flash that to anyone else with a badge, you're screwed. If you flash that to anyone without my say so, you'll be babysitting the car for however long this shit-show lasts. Where'd it come from?"

"Thrift store," Young says. "Same as the suit."

"And the ID card?" I ask.

"Made it at a copy shop. Images are from Google. Added text in MS Paint." The way his voice trails off answers my last question. He's realizing just now that he made a mistake. But I need to hear him say it.

"And your photo?"

"Facebook," he confesses. "But I wasn't logged in. I swear."

That's good news, but not great news. I sit back, give Lindo a nod and close my eyes as the Charger roars to life. AC blasts from the vents, calming me. "Which way, man?"

"Southeast," I say, and point to the stunning, sun drenched bluffs that I haven't looked at in the daylight until this very moment. Colorado City is fairly run down, and not much to look at, but the founders certainly picked a stunning location to start their little polygamist hideaway. "To whatever is on the other side of those cliffs."

12

What was on the other side of those cliffs turned out to be a whole lot of empty space. I'm not sure what I was expecting to find, but it was more than nothing. An hour into our search, with nothing to go on, I suggest we question people in town, and no one disagrees.

We start on the northeast part of town, which is actually Hildale, Utah. The 37th parallel that defines the border of Utah and Arizona cuts straight through the center with some buildings being in both states.

"This place is like a military base," Lindo says, maneuvering the Charger down a neighborhood street. But it's not like any neighborhood I've ever seen. Every single house is surrounded by an eight foot wall, impossible to see past. The residents are either extremely secretive or ready for a war. Given what I know about them, probably both.

"Pull over there." I point to what looks like a normal house on a corner lot, if you ignore the wall. I get out alone and approach the solid gate. I push a small buzzer button and wait. No one answers the first buzz, or my second and third, but I know they're home. I can hear the muffled voices and thumping feet. *Sounds like children*, I think, and as much as I don't want to scare a bunch of kids, they tend to be more honest than adults.

I push the buzzer again and step back with a smile on my face. I'm going for non-threatening and kind, but if the people living here are part of the FLDS church, they've been steeped in mistrust for everyone outside the sect. A scrape of feet on the sidewalk turns me around. A young woman wearing a long, poufy-shouldered, light blue dress, rounds the corner, eyes on the sidewalk, a book clutched in her hands. Her hair is done up in some kind of colonial American schoolmarm style with a tight braid. She can't be more than fifteen, but looks like she's lived twice the years.

She doesn't look up. Doesn't see me. So I stop her with my kindest, "Hello."

Her plain black shoes scuff to a stop. She cranes her head up, eyes widening as though the gears inside that operate neck and eyelids are interconnected. Then she just stares, like she's never seen someone like me before.

"I'm looking for a girl," I say, and when she blinks fast enough to create a breeze, I realize that was probably the worst thing I could have said. "She's gone missing."

Surprise is replaced by fear.

"Would it be alright if I showed you a picture of her?" I ask. "Maybe you could let me know if you've seen her?"

When I slide my hand into my pocket to fetch the photo, the girl takes a step back, ready to retreat. "You're okay," I assure her, taking my hand back out of the pocket. I take a step away from her, unsure of how else to put her at ease. "Those were some crazy lights last night. Did you see them?"

She glances back and forth, turns her head down and mumbles through barely moving lips. "You the fella staying at the motel with your mum, the black man, and the Mexican?"

What. The. Hell?

"How do you know that?"

"Whole town knows it," she says, speaking to the pavement. "You best be on your way. It's not safe."

Instead of feeling concern for my safety, I'm now concerned for hers. "Is it safe for you?"

She says nothing, but makes little fists. "New Zion."

"What?"

"New Zion Ranch. That's where—" The gate buzzes and unlocks, and with a raised voice and head, the girl adds, "Please, mister, let me pass."

In the moment of confusion that follows, I fail to notice the burly man thundering from the open gate. My subconscious brings me up to speed, shouting a warning that's impossible to heed in time. But I see the meaty fist before it connects, and I'm able to turn with the strike, minimizing the damage done.

I sprawl to the ground, mostly for show, and resist the urge to reach for my gun.

The large man, dressed in black slacks and a green button down that might be homemade, stands over me. He's beet red and fuming, but doesn't move to kick me while I'm down.

I'm about to play the fearful mouse when he turns to the girl and says, "Get inside. Now. Ain't no wife of mine gonna be talking to heathens."

Wife? Wife?! Back on my feet and pissed off, the man doesn't look so menacing. My instinct is to deliver a beat down of epic proportions, but I also know that won't solve anything. If the federal government has trouble shutting these assholes down, there isn't much I can do. And I'm not here for the backward Mormon sect, I'm here for Isabella Ramos.

I feel like a coward when the girl slinks through the gate. She gives me an apologetic glance and then disappears behind the wall that I have the sudden urge to tear down. When she's gone, the man turns back to me like he's going to give me a stern warning. Instead, he takes another swing.

This time, I'm on guard and amped. The fist misses as I lean back. "You don't want to do this, buddy."

He steps into another swing, his fighting style—if you could call it that—is all power and no skill. I barely have to move to avoid the second punch, and he's already projecting his third. It will leave him wide open and a single punch to his—

"Freeze!"

Aww, shit.

It's Young. He's behind the big man, gun raised. Then he does the worst thing possible in the middle of a town that loathes the federal government. "Federal agent!"

The big man turns around to find Young's gun and open badge thrust out. Young wisely snaps the badge shut as soon as the man sees it. "Back away."

"You're a Fed?" the man asks. He was menacing before, but he's reached a transcendent level of anger, giving him the calm vibe and voice of a serial killer. He glances up at the second floor windows of the homes on both sides of the street. I follow his eyes and find a small army of men and boys, some of whom are clutching rifles.

Young catches my eye, looking pleased with himself until I give a slow shake of my head and motion to the windows with my eyes. His pride takes a hard hit, but he manages to stay calm, and even improvises, though I can't say I approve of his strategy.

"Yes, sir," Young says. "And I've been pursuing this man all across God's creation." He redirects the .50 caliber Desert Eagle so that it's pointing just to the right of my head. "Hands behind your head."

I obey the command, trying to muster the indignant glare all criminals manage before they realize how long they're going to be in prison.

"What'd he do?" the man asks, not quite buying it yet.

"This...man, if you can call him that, is a child molester." Young delivers the lie with convincing emotion. I even feel a little guilty. "He picks up little girls like that one, and...well, I'm sure you can imagine the rest."

I'm sure he can, too, and I wonder if Young would be so composed if he knew the girl he'd just seen was married to this forty-something year old behemoth.

"Some are never found," Young says. "Now, I'm going to interrogate him, you better believe that, but if he doesn't talk... Have you heard of any local disappearances lately?"

I'm both horrified and impressed by Young. He's selling the story well enough, damning me in the process, but he's also fishing for info and doing a good job of it.

"Girls or boys," Young says. "This perverted slave to the devil has no preference. In fact, he often keeps photos of his recent victims." Young works his way behind me, places the gun against my back and fishes into my pocket. He digs out the photo, looks at it, and shakes his head in dismay. Then he holds the photo out for the man to see. "Don't suppose you've seen her around?"

The man looks at the photo, holds his breath for a fraction of a second, and then shakes his head. He looks Young in the eye and says, "I see you around here again, and we're gonna have words." By words, I'm fairly certain he means shotgun shells. Then he steps aside, allowing Young to head back to the car. As we walk past, I catch a glimpse of him shaking his head, looking at the people in the window. While I won't be able to set foot in this city again, I'm pretty sure Young just saved our lives, though I don't think he's totally aware of that fact yet.

But he's going to be the moment we reach the Dodge Charger and I climb into the front seat. "Put me in the back," I whisper. "And not gently."

"That's the plan," he says, and I notice that neither Wini, nor Lindo are visible.

He opens the back door, and shoves me into the back seat, thumping my head in the process. Then he slams the door shut behind me, gives the big cult member a nod and climbs behind the wheel.

"You so much as scratch my ride, man..." Lindo says, scrunched up on the floor of the front seat.

"Just drive," Wini says. She's seated on the floor beside me. "Old ladies weren't meant to fold up like this."

"Not what you said last night, chica," Lindo jokes.

As we pull away from the curb, I do my very best to not smile at the joke, or in relief that we've survived the surreal encounter. Despite being in the United States, this city feels not just foreign, but unearthly.

"Where to?" Young asks.

"Southeast," I say. "Again. We're looking for New Zion Ranch."

Lindo slides back up into the passenger's seat. "That connected to the hotel or something?"

"Zion, in the Bible, refers to Jerusalem," Young says, making a left turn. "To Mormons it represents the gathering of church members, so any place, or land where God appoints people to gather, can be deemed Zion."

Wini grunts as I help her up, and then asks, "Like a seedy motel?"

"Who do you think stays there most of the time?" Young asks. "How many outsiders do you think vacation here?"

We all pause to look out at the walled-in homes.

"What about the ranch?" Lindo asks. "Isn't that like, a gathering place for cows and shit?"

Young shrugs. "We'll have to ask when we get there."

Finding the ranch isn't hard. The entrance is so close to the border of town that we'd driven past before without giving it a second thought. And since the dirt drive isn't gated, we head straight in. The winding road, framed by electric fencing, heads southeast and wraps around the tall bluffs. This is definitely the right spot. But how would a random girl I met on the street know about it?

If everyone knows about it, I realize, and then I wonder just how fast the FLDS news hotline moves. The girl knew I had stayed at the motel. And knew that Wini, Lindo, and...

Oh, shit.

"Oh, shit," Young says.

The car comes to a sudden stop. We're cloaked in dust for a moment. When it clears, we're faced with two pickup trucks turned sideways in the drive, and four shotgun-wielding men, slacks and button up shirts across the board.

The girl didn't put us on the right path. She sold us out.

13

"I'd take UFOs over cult members, man," Lindo says. "Look at these dudes."

I am, and I don't like what I see. The four men standing in the pick-up beds haven't moved. They're just staring at us, waiting. But for what? If we move will they open fire? Do they want to talk?

We have enough firepower to put up a fight, but I'm not sure how good Wini and Young's aim is, especially under fire, and those four shotguns at close range...well, they're not going to miss. Fighting is not an option.

I roll my window down slowly.

"What are you doing?" Young asks.

"Talking seems like a good place to start," I say.

"They might shoot you." Young's hand reaches for the gear shift. We're still in drive, his foot on the brake holding us in place.

"Just let me try," I say. "We're not going to find answers in town, and we can't really go back to our lives until we know what's going on and separate ourselves from it." *Or tear it to the ground*, I think.

I unlatch the door and push it open, slow and easy, extending my hands out and up before sliding out the door. I emerge from the car like a newborn sloth, smooth and non-threatening. The summertime heat slaps against my skin and sucks it dry. The air smells like desert flowers, but there's something else in the mix...like burned meat. "Hi there."

No response.

"Is this the New Zion Ranch?"

Stupid question. The sign was hard to miss.

"We're..." I'm not sure which story to go with—the missing little girl, or the UFO sighting. "...lost. Well, not really lost, but we're trying to find something...someone..."

As I bumble through an amalgam of sentences, the men's expressions don't shift. Not even a little. By now, they should be thoroughly confused, but I'm not sure they're even hearing me. I con-sider trying to throw in a little improvised sign language, but if the men really are deaf, I think my attempt might just offend them.

"Leave," says the oldest of the four men, his voice emotionless and monotone.

"Go home," says the man beside him. He's a good twenty years younger than the gentleman who spoke first, but his voice has the same dead quality.

"There is nothing here for you." The third man is younger still, and equally creepy.

The fourth man is the youngest of them, perhaps still in his teens. He manages to give his shotgun a pump for effect, but when he speaks, it's the same voice as the others. "The girl you are looking for is not here."

News *does* travel fast. I decide to ignore the statement, wondering if redirection will stumble up the stoic routine, which is both intimidating (as I'm sure it's supposed to be) and comical. "Actually, I was wondering about the UFO spotted last night. I thought it—"

"The aliens." The eldest of them changes facial expressions from nothing to an exaggerated look of disgust. "They visit all the time. See 'em up in the sky. They mutilate our livestock."

"It's no good," says the next man, and then on down the line. "No blood." "Happens all the time."

The strange conversation propels the four men straight from the 'dangerous cult member' category into 'batshit crazy town.'

I glance inside the car. Lindo broadcasts what he's thinking. Probably something like, 'Yo, what the actual fuck?' Wini is even easier to read as she slides her revolver out of her purse. And that's as far as I can take this. I'm not going to put Wini in any more danger if I can avoid it.

I'm about to tell the stalwart sentinels that we're sorry for the trouble and will be on our way when Lindo says, "Hey man, check this out." He turns the GPS screen toward me. A line of text reading 'Stand your ground' covers the map.

What the...

Is this the same mystery man who warned us of the impending mercs?

If so, how the hell did he find us, let alone send a text message via a GPS device not designed to receive them?

And while the first message prevented us from being captured, I don't see how standing my ground against four armed cult members is going to benefit anyone.

The GPS message blinks and updates, displaying, 'Help en route.'

My instinct is to look behind us and search for signs of an approaching vehicle, or even a helicopter. But I suspect we'll be better off if these guys don't know what's what. And since I don't know if they'll actually let us leave, I decide to stall.

"What changed your mind?" the oldest of them asks.

"What do you mean?" I ask.

"You were going to leave," the man beside him says.

And then the next, on down the line, "and now you're not."

The last man asks. "Why?"

Before I can answer, I feel a kind of itch on my forehead. I scratch it, but nails on skin don't help. The itch is on the *inside* of my skull. The intensity flares, making me wince.

Despite my strange behavior, the four men just stare.

As the itch overwhelms me, questions fill my mind.

Why am I here?

Who is with me?

Who else knows we're here?

What is the girl's name?

I know the answers to these questions, but I'm confused by the internal interrogation and I resist answering.

What's in my pocket?

There are several answers, but something instinctual says to not think about the gun. To hide all my secrets. So I focus on my own nagging unanswered question.

What is in the envelope?

The itch becomes painful.

"Yo, you alright?"

I recognize Lindo's voice, but he sounds distant. I open my clutched shut eyes and see a haze. Within the haze is a shadow, its twitchy movements bringing it closer, filling me with a sense of dread.

What's in my...

I have a vague sense that I'm groaning as I force the question to end with *envelope*. It is the solitary question that keeps me up at night, and I'm too terrified to answer it every morning. As long as that envelope stays sealed, two possibilities exist simultaneously, and I'm still not ready to deal with the potential pain.

WHAT IS IN THE—

The screamed question echoes unfinished, interrupted by the sound of tires crunching on rocks.

When the haze and itch fade, I find myself looking into the concerned eyes of Lindo. "You okay? What happened?"

I shake my head. "No idea."

Was that a panic attack? I wonder. I've been in life-and-death situations before, including yesterday, and while I've experienced worry, fear, anxiety, and post-adrenaline shakes, I've never had a panic attack, or anything else similar to what I just experienced. It was like having a conversation with myself. With my very pushy self. "And I'm fine."

"Company behind us," Young says.

A police SUV pulls up behind the Charger, and I'm not sure whether to be worried or relieved. Colorado City has a marshal's office that is operated by locals, most likely members of the Mormon sect. If this is the marshal...

I step back from the car, a little unsteady on my feet. The officer steps from the vehicle, sunglasses hiding his eyes, mustache hiding his lips. With a hand on his sidearm he looks over the four men in the pickup, then the Charger, and then me.

"Mind not moving?" he says.

I stop my slow retreat, lean back, and read the words Mohave County Sheriff. "Sheriff?"

He gives me a nod and addresses the eldest of the four men. "Harry, put those weapons down before I feel threatened."

All four men seem to snap out of a stupor and then lay their shotguns down on the truck beds, out of hand, but not out of reach.

"Folks are trespassing," Harry says.

"You have no private property signs posted," the sheriff says. He's a no-nonsense cop. That's a good thing. "You have no gate at the end of the drive."

"Never needed one before now," Harry says.

"*And* you and I both know you sell enough pies to keep the population of Colorado City just slightly on the portly side. So why the rude welcome?"

"Ten fifty seven." I whisper the code.

He gives me a once-over, then the car and its occupants. Then he steps closer, gun hand ready. When he speaks again, his voice is lowered. "What did you say?"

"Ten. Fifty. Seven." As a detective I occasionally dealt with police forces from other states, as well as the FBI. Knowing the numerical codes for crimes in various states often made communication and paperwork more efficient and less confusing. The three-number code I've just relayed to him is for a missing person.

The sheriff steps closer still. "You're a police officer?"

"Detective," I say, memory guiding my words and forcing me to correct myself. "*Former* detective. I'm a private investigator now."

He gives me a suspicious squint. "You're not here because of..." He points at the sky and whistles two quick notes.

"Yes and no," I say, digging the photo of Isabella from my pocket. "I was hired to find the girl." Given the circumstances, I think being totally upfront with the sheriff is in our best interests. "The mother is illegal. That's why they came to me."

"And you think she's here? Why?"

"Asked in town," I tell him, adjusting my totally upfront policy to mostly upfront. "They sent me here."

"Did they now?"

"These guys were waiting for us," I say. "Knew we were coming."

"In that case, welcome to shit-town. Looks like we've both stepped in it."

"Been wading through it, actually," I say, getting a smile out of the man. I extend my hand. "Dan Delgado."

He gives me a firm handshake and says, "Sheriff Godin. You want to be cut loose, or you ready to get neck deep?"

How much does Godin know? I wonder. He believed my story a little too quickly. "Lead the way."

"Harry," Godin says, turning to face the four men. "These folks are with me, and we'll be—"

"Gun!" Lindo shouts from the front seat, ducking down behind the dash as Harry and the three younger men raise their shotguns in perfect synchronization and pull their triggers.

14

Hitting the ground beneath Godin's two hundred plus pounds hurts—a lot—but it beats being shredded by buckshot. I'm still not sure how I managed to grab the man and pull him down behind the car, but here we are, lying in the dirt like we're posing for a romance novel.

In the silence that follows, I listen. For crying. For groans. For footsteps. But I hear no telltale signs of impending danger, or that someone has been wounded, which could mean that everyone in the car is dead. But I'm only really concerned about one of them. As fond as I've become of both Lindo and Young, it's Wini I want to protect.

The car's glass and Young's body should have shielded Wini, but that was a lot of firepower from multiple angles. If all four fired into the car...

I shove up on Godin, who hasn't moved.

Is he dead? Shot in the back?

"Godin," I whisper, clutching his arms. "Up!"

He blinks, looks me in the eyes, and gives a nod. Moving slow and quiet, doing our best to not draw attention, we rise into crouches, hidden by the Charger's trunk. It takes all of my willpower to not peek into the car. But that would both expose me and redirect their aim toward Wini's seat.

When Godin draws his sidearm, I do the same. He gives me a wary glance, that morphs into outright suspicion when I remove the sound suppressor from my pocket and start screwing it in place. They're not illegal in Utah, or Arizona, but there are not many uses for them that aren't nefarious.

"Sheriff," Harry says. "Got no choice but to show yourself."

"Fuck you, Harry," Godin says. He's rattled, but still in control. "I've put up with your shit for years and this is how you repay me?"

"Ain't you we have a quarrel with," Harry says, "And I've warned you about that ungodly mouth of yours."

"I'm a Mohave County sheriff. Any quarrel you have with anyone outside your family involves me," Godin says, and I respect his resolve, though his straight forward, black-and-white sense of right and wrong could use a little finesse.

"Nobody's hurt," Harry says. I'm not sure if he's telling the truth, but just the possibility of it loosens the invisible fist clutching my chest. "Not yet, at least."

"I can take two of them before they know I'm shooting," I whisper to Godin, motioning to my now sound suppressed handgun.

"Killing these men would start a war," Godin says. "Hundreds would die. Starting with us, and everyone else in my department. By the time help arrived, the whole city would be dug in. You want to be responsible for that?"

Our staring match ends when Godin shouts, "Everyone okay in the car?"

"They shot up my uncle's ride!" Lindo shouts.

"We're fine," Wini says. "And up for however you want to handle this."

The last thing I want is for Wini to go out in a blaze of bloody glory, but I admire her willingness to fight.

"Preach?" I say.

"Car's dead," he says. "We're fine."

"Who the hell do you have in this car?" Godin asks me, voice low.

"A preacher, an Uber driver, and a senior citizen," I say.

"That a joke?"

"Wish it was."

"Don't see that we have much of a choice," Godin says. "As good as you are with that..." He motions to my gun. "We're not shooting our way out of this without taking casualties."

"And that whole war thing you mentioned," I say. "But if we give up our guns..."

"So don't," he says, tapping on the car's rear bumper. Then he speaks up and says, "Harry?"

"Yuh?"

"We're going to come out. My weapon's going to be holstered, but I am *not* handing it over. That'd be something I couldn't look past."

"And you can look past what happened to this fancy car?" Harry asks.

Godin and I share another look. It's an unfathomable thing to agree to, but what other choice is there? I give him a nod and he says, "No charges will be filed against you or your boys."

"You called for backup?" Harry asks.

"I don't have a reason to," Godin replies. "Do I?"

While they're talking, I slip my handgun up inside the vehicle's bumper, lodging it inside. "Wini," I say, quiet as I can.

"Yeah?" Her voice is barely audible.

"Remember the cookie jar?" It's a reference to a case I worked four years ago. A man suspected of cheating on his wife was meticulous in every way. Impossible to catch until I found his storage unit, and the cookie jar it held, with photos of not just one lover hidden inside, but twenty-one. Since then, when Wini and I are talking about finding something elusive, we call it a cookie-jar. In this case I want her to hide something, and I hope she has Young do the same.

"Stand up slow," Harry commands. "You all in the car go ahead'n exit, too. Hands where we can see them."

I feel a little bit like I've got a hood over my head, like someone should be asking me if I want a cigarette or if I have any last words before the firing squad cuts me down. When I'm high enough to look over the Charger's roof, I realize the analogy isn't that far off. Harry and his three younger partners—who look enough like him that they must be his sons—look down the barrels of their shotguns.

And they're not alone.

Young boys and girls along with six middle-aged prairie-dress-wearing women, and one matriarch in an apron, stand in the truck beds with the four men, on the sides of the blockade and in front of it. Each one of them, including the youngest, who must be no older than eight, is armed with an assortment of shotguns, hunting rifles, and handguns.

Godin was right about that war.

These people are ready for it.

My thoughts drift to the GPS message. *Help en route.* Whoever sent that message knew we were in trouble, that Godin was on the way, and that the good sheriff possessed enough understanding of these people to prevent us all from being slain. But who is helping us? And why?

There are too many variables. The mercs. The cult. The UFO. The mystery informant. None of it makes sense and all of it is beyond our ragtag group's ability to handle. If I didn't think going home was dangerous for myself, Wini, and Young, I'd shoulder the guilt of not finding Isabella and call it a day.

"Over there," Harry says, and when he motions to the side, every other member of who I think are his immediate family—children and wives—motions as well, like they're connected.

We follow the man's order, making ourselves a very easy target. If the group decided to unload now, there wouldn't be much left of us. Young looks nervous but has his chin up. Defiant. Wini kind of has a 'just another day at the office,' expression, but I know her well enough to know she's nervous. Lindo looks almost calm, like he's already forgotten that his uncle's new Charger is steaming from the massive holes in its front end.

"What brings you out here today, sheriff?"

"You've seen the news," Godin says. "About the UFO. Seeing as how that's our running theory on your livestock mutilations, I thought I'd come have a look. See if any of your animals went missing. Or if you saw anything last night."

"We were sleeping," Harry says.

"That the case?" Godin says, speaking louder to address the whole group.

Nods all around, aim never wavering.

"Excuse me," I say, stepping toward the group. Godin warns me away with a grunt, but I ignore him. The only place answers reside are on this ranch, and the only way we're getting in is through convincing deception. "I'm an expert on cattle mutilations. I've investigated thou-sands of cases all along the thirty-seventh parallel." I'm laying it on thick, but they've already bought into the whole alien concept, so I might be able to use that to my advantage.

"I'm the one who asked him here," Godin says, adding some credence to my claim.

I give a nod and pat Godin's shoulder like we've already met.
"Before our unfortunate misunderstanding, I was asking about the
UFO last night. I make a habit of checking with local ranchers after
incidents like the one—"

"And the girl you were asking about?" Harry asks.

"Abducted," I say, and point to the sky. "By them. I think. That's
the working theory. And despite what happened here, I'd still love
to take a look around. Inspect your animals."

"I can show him where we found the horse in that tree."

"You found a horse in a tree?" My surprise is real, so I follow it
up with a more thoughtful, "I've never seen *that* before."

"You think it's aliens?" Harry asks.

"Absolutely, and I think I'm close to proving it."

I'm a good liar, but this is stretching the limit of my abilities.
I don't think any rational person would buy what I'm saying, but
these folks are 1) in a cult already, and 2) already believe aliens are
visiting.

Harry lowers his rifle, but no one else wavers. "What group are
you with?"

I'm about to ask what he means when Lindo says, "Mutual UFO
Network." Moving in a slow, nonthreatening manner, he takes out
his wallet, and then an ID card. He steps forward, card held high. He
approaches the truck with uncommon bravery and hands the card
to Harry, who gives it a once over and then hands it back.

"Supposing he's not a Fed," Harry says, motioning to Young, and
then to me, "And you're not a child molester."

"No, sir," I say, noting Godin's glare in the corner of my eye. "We
were...intimidated."

"As you rightly should'a been," Harry says. "Now here's what's
going to happen. You all can come in, have a look at the animals, and
be on your way. I'll arrange for a tow. We'll have it brought to the
motel, and I expect you'll be leaving at first light. I find you speaking
to my children or even looking at the women—"

I divert my eyes away from the matriarch, whose cold gaze has remained locked on me since her dramatic appearance.

"—we're going to have a problem."

"Uh," Young says. "How are we going to—"

"I'll take you," Godin says. He's on edge. Still not sure of how this is going to pan out, but I get the feeling the less we say now, the better.

"Thank you for your kindness," I say to Harry.

The man smiles. It looks unnatural on him.

"And Sheriff, I expect you'll mind your language this time? No matter what you all find, whether it be a horse in a tree or a heifer with no eyes."

Godin nods.

"Say it," Harry says.

"You have my word," Godin says, and he looks at the rest of us. "No one here will speak untowardly. We'll just have a quick look around, let you know what we find, and be out of your hair."

I'm fairly certain the only things keeping us alive right now are our paper-thin fabrication and the fact that the Sheriff's office probably knows exactly where he is.

The large family moves as one, in perfect synchronization, stepping out of the trucks, putting them in neutral, and then pushing them to the sides. Harry motions for us to follow, and we pass through the trucks like ancient warriors being led through the enemy's gate and into the stronghold. Our situation has improved in that we're not dead, but if Harry isn't a man of his word, or if he sees through our ruse, this ranch is going to be where we're buried.

15

A sprawling complex opens up before us as we crest a hill and stroll down into a valley framed by orange bluffs to the east. They rise a thousand feet into the air. The main house is absolutely massive, but I wouldn't call it a mansion. It's not decadent in any way, just an oversized farm house with a footprint the size of a high school gymnasium. There are several other, smaller buildings, whose purposes I can only guess. Three industrial barns house cows, which I only know because I can now hear and smell them. Horses whinny from a smaller, more traditional looking barn. A few dogs mull about, one of which barks incessantly at the empty sky.

If not for the heavily armed, mind-fucked family escorting us, the scene would be picturesque and quintessential Americana at its finest. But it's also not our destination.

"This way," Harry says, opening a gate in the electrified fence on the left side of the drive. We follow him through, into a field of wild grasses that are far greener than anything in this part of the world has any right to be.

Part of me is relieved to not be led into the small village of buildings, any one of which could house a slaughter room or incinerator capable of making us disappear. Then again, maybe the cult keeps a mass grave ready for 'get off my land' scenarios that get out of hand.

While the Stepford wives and younger children continue on their way, Harry and his three eldest, shotgun-wielding sons take us into the field. Harry and the youngest of the brothers take the lead, while the other two close the gate behind us and follow.

We walk through the field like herded cattle, maneuvering around wildflowers and rocks. Through all the shifting, I manage to get Lindo beside me, Young behind me, and Godin and Wini in front. Harry sets a merciful pace, I suspect thanks to Wini's presence, allowing me to have a quiet conversation with Lindo.

"What is the Mutual UFO Network?" I ask. "And why didn't you mention it before?"

I've learned to not trust most people, but Lindo had been warming on me. His involvement in all this had been random at first, and then motivated by a stack of cash. Despite helping put Harry at ease, Lindo's revelation of being part of some kind of UFO investigative group has left me feeling wary.

"MUFON," he says. "For short. It's an organization of UFO investigators, specialists, and enthusiasts pretending to be one of the two."

"Which are you?" I ask.

"Honestly man, they're pretty much all the same," he says. "Just normal people living out their X-Files fantasies. I'm an investigator, though I haven't been on an active investigation in years. That mostly means interviewing witnesses, taking photos and measurements, and if you've got the green to cover the cost, checking the site with a Geiger counter. Nothing ever comes of it. I was called in to help with a few cases involving Spanish speakers, but I don't think they appreciated my style. Know what I'm sayin'?"

I think I do, but don't say so.

"Have you seen one?" I ask. "A UFO?"

"Pssh. I wish. From a distance though. I don't want to screw around with them Grays."

"Grays..."

"Aliens, man. Gray heads. Big black eyes. You know the ones."

He's right. I do. Despite not immersing myself in science fiction, the classic big-headed, black-eyed aliens with diminutive bodies have become iconic beyond the realm of those with aluminum foil hat collections.

"I'm interested in the phenomenon, you know? But I don't want to be part of it. This shit right here?" He motions to Harry with a flick of his finger. "This is beyond weird enough for me."

"Have you ever seen an animal mutilation before?" I ask.

"In books, sure. There's even a chapter in MUFON's blue binder manual about them. They're pretty gnarly, without being gory, if that makes sense. But the really crazy thing about mutilations is that there's been like ten thousand of them since the sixties."

I nearly pause to call bullshit on that, but he anticipates my reaction.

"That's a lot, I know, and you'd think that more people would know about it, but there's a few reasons you don't."

As Lindo delves deeper into the lore surrounding UFOs, aliens, and animal mutilations, his accent slips a little. How much of his 'gangster' personality is a show cultivated to fit in with his friends? I'm working on stereotypes here, but how many people his age are UFO investigators with MUFON? Can't be that many.

"Ranchers don't want people to know," he explains. "How many people you think will be lining up for their meat, or milk, or whatever, if it was public knowledge that some of their cows had been hacked apart and left bloodless in a field? A lot of people hear that shit and think of Satanists. No one is gonna buy food that might be cursed by El Diablo. Right? And then there's this. You investigate people. You find missing people. How many go missing every year and never turn up? Couple thousand?"

I nod. The exact number varies from year to year, but in the U.S. 95% to 98% turn up within forty eight hours. Another 1% to 2% in the weeks that follow. The rest never turn up.

"Let's say two thousand," he says. "So going back to 1960, that's roughly a hundred and sixteen thousand. People. Now, you're a smart dude, so you probably know this. Or have a guess. I actually don't know. How many people have gone missing around the world?"

Globally, the numbers are much more daunting and frightening. "Six hundred and seven a day. Roughly."

"And are never found?"

Another nod, this one more solemn. The conversation isn't exactly boosting my hopes of finding a girl whose presence in this investigation dwindles with every passing hour.

"Damn, man. That's around two hundred twenty one thousand every year." He pauses, doing more mental math faster than I could with a calculator. "Since 1960...that's twelve million, eight hundred eighteen thousand...what?"

"That's impressive," I say. "The math."

He shrugs like it's nothing and continues. "So nearly thirteen million people have gone poof since 1960. How many people know that happy-ass fact? Freak'n nobody. If we're not hearing about all of *them*, why would we hear about ten thousand cows and horses?"

"Over there," Godin says, pointing out into the field. At first I can't see what he's pointing at. Then I realize that what looks like a rough, brown stone rising out of the ground is actually the body of a brown cow.

Harry redirects the group toward the body without a word, unsurprised and unconcerned.

That was fast, I think, and then I ask Harry, "This happen a lot?"

When Harry doesn't answer, Godin does. "Enough to be a pain in my backside."

When we round the cow's back and catch a glimpse of its backside, I pull up short, bumping into Young, Lindo, and Wini, who all see what I do and react with a mixture of revolt and intrigue.

The cow's asshole...is missing.

Where once there would have been a cow-sized sphincter, there is now a perfectly round, clean-cut, blood-free cavity. It's like the thing's anus was apple cored.

Harry, his boys, and Godin stroll around the creature like it's no big deal, and that's when I realize it happens enough that the sight is just part of life on a ranch in this part of the world.

"How many mutilations happen in this area?" I ask Lindo. "I mean, on the parallel?"

"Most," he says. "Within a few hundred miles in either direction. But they're more frequent the closer you get."

"And we're right on top of it," I note.

"What are you talking about?" Godin asks.

"Thirty -seventh parallel," I say. "Latitude. Runs straight through town. Separates Colorado City from Hildale, and Utah from Arizona."

"What's so special about it?" he asks as I round the cow to find another gaping hole, this one in its side. The cut is clean and concise. I wouldn't call the circle perfect, but I suspect it would have been before the cow's insides were removed.

I glance around the body. There're no signs of transportation and no footprints other than ours. Whatever happened to the poor beast, happened right here. And yet there is no sign of blood on the cow, or in the soil and grass surrounding it.

"It's where most of the weird sh—stuff in the U.S. goes down," Lindo says, minding his language. "UFOs, abductions—of the alien variety—and mutilations. A lot of government bases are built on, or close to, the thirty-seventh. Area 51. Dulce. Fort Knox. Then there's the sacred American Indian sites, cave systems, and other well-known locations outside the country, like Fukushima and—"

"Fukushima?" Young asks. "As in the tidal wave and nuclear disaster?"

Crouching down, I look inside the open cavity. No maggots. No rot. No smell. Despite looking like it's been drying in the sun for a week, this cow hasn't been here long.

"The day after," Lindo says. "Yeah. Some people think it helped keep things from getting worse. Like with Chernobyl."

Before anyone can jump down that rabbit hole, which is on the far side of the planet and not on the 37th parallel, I turn to Harry and ask, "Is this fresh?"

He bends down, checks the yellow tag on the cow's ear, and says, "She was up and about last night."

All of this is interesting, but it doesn't get me any closer to finding Isabella or figuring out any of the weirdness that's happened since arriving at her carefully concealed home. I stand up and note the cow's eyes, or rather its lack of eyes. There are now two clean holes burrowed into its face. No brains leaking out. Maybe no brain at all.

I'm about to move the conversation, with a high degree of care, back to the subject of missing people. See if it ruffles Harry's feathers or gets him talking. In the midst of a conversation, especially a stressful one, most people give up information without ever intending to—or even when they're trying to conceal it. But before I can speak, a cellphone chimes.

The sound makes Harry, his three boys, and Godin all flinch.

"The hell is that?" Harry asks. For a moment, I think the family is so backwoods that they haven't experienced cellphones or text messages, but then the old rancher clarifies. "Ain't no signal out here, and you know I don't allow calls."

"Shouldn't be any reception," Godin agrees, digging out his phone. "Never has been, and with all the land you've got, I imagine there never will be."

Godin flicks on the phone and looks down at the screen.

It's subtle, but the micro expression on his face freezes for a second. Whatever he's read, it's not good. But he recovers quickly. "Just the office checking in." He smiles. "They must be worried on account of knowing where I am."

Harry actually smiles at the joke, but not in a way that says, 'that's funny.' The grin is more...pride. "Seen enough?" he asks.

"I think so," Godin says, looking me in the eyes.

"Yes, sir," I say, and motion for Harry to lead the way back.

As we form up and start the trek back to the dirt driveway, where we'll have to pile into the sheriff's SUV, Godin slides up next to me and holds his phone out so I can see it, but no one else can. "This mean anything to you?"

I glance down without tipping my head and read the short text message from UNKNOWN:

Incoming in 5. Evac ASAP.

16

The endless sky stretching to the south and west reveals no incoming threat—by air at least. But that doesn't mean there isn't a fleet of black SUVs roaring up the long dirt drive. The view to the north and east is all cliff, rising up high, blotting out the sky.

"What are you doing?" Godin asks, voice hushed.

"Huh?" I say, and then realize I was whipping my head back and forth like I was sitting center court at a rapid-speed tennis match. I haven't watched any TV or listened to news radio since leaving Santa Cruz, but I'm certain the battle at Young's church is international news by now. "You know what happened in Santa Cruz."

He stares at me. No reaction. "That wasn't a question."

"Doesn't need to be," I say. *Unless he doesn't know.* "The gun battle between armed mercenaries, civilians, and the police? Should have been on the news. Hell, every department in the country should have details on it by now. And the Internet should be crawling with videos captured on smartphones."

He gives his head a slow shake, looking me over with suspicious eyes, reassessing his opinion of me.

"Wini." When she looks back, I wave for her to join us. She slows for a few steps until she's between Godin and me. "What happened in Santa Cruz?"

"A lot," she says.

"Give him the CliffsNotes version," I say.

She looks up at Godin. "A bunch of heavily armed goons dropped out of a helicopter and interrupted our search for Isabella Ramos. They chased us in SUVs. I shot out their tires. Then they followed us into the good pastor's church..." She motions to Young. "...during Sunday morning services no less." Then she motions to me. "He shot one of them. I shot two more. Might all be dead. Might have all lived.

We didn't see, on account of the helicopter's machine gun. Probably wouldn't have escaped if not for Lindo."

"And he is?" Godin asks.

"Our Uber driver," I say, now feeling bad for having Wini bring up the men she shot, and probably killed. She doesn't seem upset by it, though. The fortitude of her spirit never ceases to amaze. Before Godin can verbalize the 'Seriously?' expressed by his twisted eyebrows, I point to Lindo and Young. "Ask either of them. They'll corroborate, starting with when they became involved. But not now. There isn't time. We've already eaten up three of those five minutes."

"Five minutes to what?" Wini asks.

Godin shows her the text.

"Shit's sake," she whispers and then whacks me on the shoulder. "Why did you waste all that time telling him?"

"Because," I tell her, "Right now, he's the only one with a gun."

Godin turns to me, his southwestern tan going a little pale. "And that's important because..."

I'm about to answer when Harry and his three boys snap to a stop, once again perfectly coordinated. I've seen them enough to know when they go all freakshow, bad things are brewing. Harry cocks his head to the side, like he can hear something. With no visual or verbal command, the three boys break and run for the gate ahead. Their strides are stiff and awkward, like they've never run before, but even stranger because they all run the same way and in perfect synch.

Young turns around, flabbergasted by the sight. "I'm ready to go. I think I'd rather face the—"

"What did you bring down on us?" Harry says, turning his wrath, and his shotgun, on me.

I make a show of checking our surroundings once more, and find no signs of approach. "I'm not sure what you're talking about."

"Who are they?" he demands, looking down the shotgun's barrel.

Harry is obviously unhinged and capable of the violence he's threatening. More than that, I'm just as convinced as he is that we're about to have company. The text warnings we've received have all been accurate. I have no reason to doubt them now. And that means this conversation needs to end, ASAP.

I try to respond. To placate. But the itch in my head returns with a suddenness and a fury that drops me to one knee.

Wini is by my side, clutching my arm, speaking my name, but it's all a haze. I can feel myself being drawn from my body, and when Harry's question repeats, I hear it in my thoughts.

WHO ARE THEY?

My response isn't of words, but of memories. The tiny house in disguise. The photo of Isabella and Marta. The mercenaries. The gun fight at the church. The helicopter. The flashes of past events approach the meeting with Lindo and then snap to a stop.

"I got you, bro," Lindo says, his voice in my ear. He's clutching my arm, keeping me upright. There's a sharp pain behind the ear he's speaking into, but it fades as he pulls me back to my feet. My disrupted mental state fades as fast as it arrived. I'm back to myself by the time I'm upright, which also happens to be just in time to see Harry's trigger finger start to pull. I'm torn between wondering what the hell happened to me and if I'm about to die.

Then Harry twitches, lowers the weapon and says, "No time to deal with you now." He turns his gaze to the cliffs above his ranch. "I see any of you all again..." The threat doesn't need to be finished.

Harry breaks into a run, just as awkward as his sons'—even more so since he's too old to be running that fast—and I wonder for a moment if they just learned it from him. If they never participated in sports, or saw them on TV, the simple act of running might have been learned from their father alone. And if that's the case, who taught him?

Useless questions for another day, or not at all.

I start for the gate again, herding the others. "We need to get the hell out of here. How close is your station?"

"Not," is his simple answer.

"Then we'll find cover in t—"

The *whump, whump, whump* of helicopter blades slicing through crisp Arizona air is distant, but slaps into me. My nerves are rattled by it, and I suddenly have to pee. "Move!" I shout, heading after Harry, who has just rounded the open gate and continued his comical sprint for the homestead and his family.

Lindo reaches the gate first, kicking up a cloud of dust behind him as he sprints up the long drive's slope. *Kid is fast.* By the time we reach the dirt road, he's at the top of the hill, but no longer running.

That can't be good, I think, and I have the concern confirmed when he turns tail and runs back toward us. He waves his arms, motioning us to flee, and everyone obeys. The 'oh shit' look on his face is impossible to miss.

Before he catches up, I spot the first problem. The Charger and the sheriff's SUV have been moved into the homestead, parked beside three long, white cargo vans. The second problem is relayed to me by Lindo as he sprints past. "Two SUVs, man! Coming in hot."

Then he's beyond us, heading for the Charger.

"You okay?" I ask Wini, who's chugging along beside me. Free of her tight skirt, her form isn't bad. Young and Godin both seem more winded than she is.

"I use...a treadmill," she says between breaths. "Stop worrying about me."

"You're the only one I'm worried about," I say, getting a smile out of her.

"*Now* you try to get into my pants?" She chuckles. "All those tight skirts, and what turns you on is cargo shorts and a gun fight?"

The drive opens into a large dirt lot holding the five vehicles, which look like our best chance of cover. Beyond the drive, the cult family bustles about, armed with shotguns and rifles, taking up positions in the home's windows, in the various barns, and in and around the smaller outbuildings. Their actions are smooth. Practiced. A well-oiled machine.

I wouldn't wish a battle with these people on anyone in the government, but if the people heading this way are the same ones who chased us in Santa Cruz, I think I'll be rooting for Swiss Family Nut Jobs.

Lindo slides out from beneath the Charger's rear bumper holding my sound-suppressed handgun.

How did he know where it was? I wonder, and then I reach out to catch it when he tosses it to me. Gun in hand, I feel a little more confident, but we're about to become the bologna in a much more heavily armed shit sandwich.

My bologna has a first name, I think, hearing the Oscar Mayer theme song run through my thoughts, *its D-A-N-I-E-L.* One syllable too many, but it doesn't change the fact that a bullet storm is about to reduce us to the consistency of processed lunchmeat.

Lindo dives into the car just before the others arrive, recovering Young's heavy hitting Desert Eagle and Wini's revolver, which he hands to the pair as we arrive. Everyone but Lindo is breathing hard. Wini snaps at the car. "My purse."

Lindo recovers the bag, and when Wini notices all of our confused looks, she opens the purse to reveal our boxes of ammo.

"You folks expecting a war?" Godin says, vacillating back to suspicion.

"Would've had better hardware if I was," I say, holding up the Beretta. "This isn't even my weapon."

The whump of helicopter blades becomes a pounding as two unmarked Black Hawk choppers sweep down over the mesa and drop toward the ranch.

"Speaking of hardware..." Godin holsters his sidearm and hurries to the back of his SUV. He pops the trunk, reaches inside, and emerges with a shotgun. He pops five shells into the magazine loading port and has five more strapped to the stock. He gives the weapon a pump, closes the hatch, and rejoins us.

"Yo," Lindo says, motioning to the sheriff's holstered handgun.

"I make it a habit to not hand over my state-issued sidearm to anyone who asks for it by saying, 'Yo,'" Godin says, "and before you rephrase, the answer is now, and forever, no fucking way."

A flash of mercy sweeps across Godin's face. "But given the circumstances..." He draws a taser from his hip, turns it around and holds it out to Lindo, who rolls his eyes, but accepts the non-lethal weapon.

"What's the plan?" Young asks. "Why aren't we taking off in the sheriff's—"

Two black SUVs roar over the long drive's crest, speeding toward the lot. They come to a stop in different directions, forming a wall that blocks off the drive and kicking up a cloud of dust that conceals the five men who unload from each vehicle and take up positions on the far side. Each one of them is protected by armor and armed with the most sophisticated weaponry available. Harry's family outnumbers them, but they're significantly outclassed, even with our help.

Is that what we're doing? I ask myself. Are we fighting alongside the people who threatened our lives, have been lying since we arrived, seemed to somehow screw with my mind, and who might have had something to do with Isabella's disappearance?

The helicopters round the property and slow to a hover in the sloping field. Four mercenaries slide down ropes, hidden by the hill as they touch down. These are the same guys who took shots at me. Who tried to kill Wini. And who somehow covered it all up so that no one other than eyewitnesses knew any of it even happened.

Definitely fighting with the cult, I decide, and I'm about to strategize our next steps, when the whinnying horses grow louder. Their sharp cries sound off, like the animals are being tortured.

Is Harry going to release a stampede and attack during the confusion?

The helicopters rise again, each one carrying a man standing behind a mounted machine gun. They circle the compound, one on each side. Getting from the vehicles to better cover might be impossible.

"We're here for the people you are harboring." The voice booms from the SUVs, the speakers' volume overcoming the choppers' thumping blades. "Hand them over and we will leave you in peace."

Shit.

Shit, shit, shit.

Harry has no love for us. Why wouldn't he hand us over?

"You all are trespassing," Harry shouts from somewhere in the house. "Leave now, or you'll be facing trouble of your own making."

"Sir," the voice replies, sounding a little incredulous. "We are here for Daniel Delgado, Winifred Finch, Aaron Young, and Steven Cruz."

Wini and I look at each other. *Steven Cruz? Who is...* I turn to Lindo. He looks unconcerned about his real name's revelation, but he should be. Despite the randomness of our meeting, they figured out his identity. Probably through Uber. *Explainable or not, he's now part of the hunted.*

"I don't care what your business is, or who you have it with. You have thirty seconds to vacate my property!" Harry's words reveal his disgust for what appears to be federal authority, far outweighs his displeasure for our ragtag group of UFO researchers and the local sheriff—all of whom he very nearly gunned down, and might have still been intending to kill. "And then we'll unleash hell unto the Earth itself!"

In the silence that follows, I'm sure the mercenaries are discussing their options. If the weapons protruding from the homestead's windows haven't intimidated them, perhaps Harry's rhetoric will?

The problem with that is we've only got one road out of this place, and they can just camp out at the end. I don't picture Harry letting us stay, and there's a good chance he'll still kill us.

The racket kicked up from the horse barn pricks my ears again. What the hell kind of horses are they keeping?

Wini grasps my arm, nails digging U shapes into my skin. "Dan..." She looks into my eyes, afraid...but not for herself. "Do you hear them?"

I focus on the sound and it doesn't take me long to hear what has Wini upset. I wish I couldn't hear it, because it means we're surrounded by enemies. Hell, it might even mean the mercs are the lesser of two evils. There are horses in the barn, but that's not all.

Mixed in with the whinnying, are screams.

Of people.

Of *children.*

I look toward the barn's closed doors, two hundred feet away from our position, and wonder how we can cross the distance without being gunned down by one side or the other.

We can't, I decide, *unless they're already busy with each other.*

Using my sound suppressed Beretta, I lean down below the Charger and take aim. Two nearly silent shots later, a soldier is shouting in pain.

I turn around, aim at the house and fire three rounds into an open window. A half second later, Harry follows through on his threat to unleash hell unto Earth, and the mercenaries reciprocate in kind.

17

I'm not sure what I was expecting when I started a shootout between fanatics and hired guns—honestly, I didn't really think it through—but it wasn't this. The ferocity on display is generally reserved for lifelong rivalries. Historic battles come to mind. Gettysburg. Stalingrad. Cannae. New Zion Ranch. Though something tells me that no matter the outcome, no one will ever know what happens here today.

As the bullets and buckshot fly, it's hard to tell if either side is making progress. I doubt Superman could hear a shout of pain over the thunder of gunfire. On the plus side, none of the gunfire is directed toward us. Yet. As soon as one side gains the advantage, that could change.

"We need to get the hell out of here!" Young shouts.

"Not without getting in that barn," I reply.

Young looks incredulous. He didn't hear the screams, or didn't comprehend their meaning.

"There are children in there!" I shout.

Godin turns toward the barn, looking surprised and then determined. "You're sure?"

I nod, though if I verbalized the answer it would be a less definitive, 'Pretty sure.' I can't be certain about what we'll find behind those red walls, aside from horses, but I won't leave without finding out. My gut twists. The barn is just another envelope, promising relief or pain upon its opening. And yet, even though it might get me killed, looking inside the barn is a much easier decision to make.

My hand rests on my pants pocket, feeling the rigid envelope within. *Should I open it? What if I die without knowing?*

That would be okay, I decide, and I return my attention to the barn.

I can't hear the screaming anymore, but I can't hear much of anything over the gunfight.

"All of you..." I motion to the group. "...in the SUV." Then to Godin. "When those barn doors open, pull in backwards. Fast as you can. When we're ready to run, we'll go off road."

I doubt the sheriff is comfortable taking orders from a stranger, but I think he'd prefer to be behind the wheel of his SUV more than running through the open parking lot.

"We should just go," Young says. "If there're kids in there, they're probably armed and ready to kill."

The pastor's point is cowardly, but valid, so I don't bother scolding him. Different perspectives keep people from making uninformed simple-minded decisions, but in this case, my course is set. An errant stream of bullets chews up the Charger's backside, likely fired by an injured merc. Three feet to the right and we'd have been cut down.

I reach up and open the SUV's driver's side door. Moving slowly, the motion goes unnoticed. Young crawls in first, followed by Godin. I open the back door allowing Wini to climb in. I motion for Lindo to follow, but he shakes his head and pushes the door shut. "I'm with you, man."

I'm stunned by his bravery, or is it loyalty? Before Godin can close his door, I catch it with my hand and reach up. "Shotgun."

He slides it down to me and gently tugs the door closed. With everyone ducked down, the vehicle still looks empty. I turn my Beretta around and hand it to a grateful Lindo, who says, "Let's do this, hombre."

For the first time since taking cover, I do a full sweep of the area, taking in both sides of the confrontation. The two mercenary SUVs are toast. The windows are shot out. The tires are flat. Steam roils from the engines. I don't see any smoke yet, but I do smell gasoline. Six of the eight mercs pop up and down like heavily armed whack-a-moles, firing tight and concise three-round bursts, picking targets and conserving ammo.

More gunfire from the hills in the field, but it's less frenetic. Loud pops and the glint of scopes reveal the presence of several snipers. The assault from the SUVs makes more noise, but I'm guessing those snipers are claiming the lion's share of casualties. At the same time, they're exposed and under constant fire from a barrage of bullets coming from within the massive, solidly built house, and several other buildings.

Firing from deep within the rooms, rather than near the windows, Harry's family can remain unseen until they pull a trigger. As soon as they do, return fire zips toward their positions. There are advantages to both sides, but the mercs have yet to unleash their real firepower. The helicopters continue to circle, but neither machine gunner has opened fire. I'm not sure why they're holding back, but I'm happy for it. Those big guns might end the fight fast, and I need it to continue until we're through the fence, back in town, and out of sight.

A high pitched shriek reaches my ears through the gunfire. A small body wearing a prairie dress dangles from the home's second floor window. There's a lull in the gunfire from the SUVs and I hear a distraught man say, "What the fuck?"

A second says, "We're fighting kids?"

When a pair of hands reaches, takes the girl, and yanks her back inside, a third merc, whose voice sounds like the one that boomed from the loud speaker, shouts, "Doesn't matter. Do your god-damned jobs!"

A rage-filled bellow from the house confirms the worst. The girl is dead, a child soldier molded by sick minds. It's too late for Harry's children, but maybe not for those in the barn.

The gunfire from the house intensifies, all of it directed toward the SUVs, pinning the men behind the vehicles. A spark ignites the spilled gas, setting one of the vehicles ablaze. The heat is intense, but the flames and black smoke help hide the mercs. In their rage, the cult members stop paying attention to the snipers, and I see two more fall before I've seen enough and sense our opening.

I give Lindo's shoulder a backhand smack, say, "Now!" and break from cover. Gunfire from the house buzzes through the air above us, but continues to ping off the SUVs. The mercs, still pinned, never see us move.

We reach the barn without taking fire, and throw ourselves into the doors. Neither budge thanks to the padlocked latch.

"Locked," Lindo says and he steps back to shoot the lock.

A bullet punches into the door, two feet above where Lindo was aiming. We turn toward the house and spot a young man chambering a fresh round into his hunting rifle. Three more family members join him in the room, taking aim at us. Whatever is in this barn, they really don't want us to find it.

I shove Lindo and shout, "Around the back!"

Our sprint around the corner is punctuated by an explosion of wood, shattered by a high caliber round. Glancing at the destroyed plank gives me a good idea of what would have happened had the bullet struck one of our bodies.

It's not pretty.

The hundred-fifty-foot sprint down the side of the barn is unevent-ful, but leaves me winded. Lindo rounds the corner first, weapon raised. His stance and grip look decent. *How many times has he watched* John Wick? I wonder, and then I step out behind him, shotgun raised and ready.

We move to the back door. It's identical to the front, including the thick padlock. Lindo raises his handgun again. I'm about to stop him, unsure that a 9mm packs enough punch to ruin the lock, but before I can speak, Lindo freezes like he's spotted something. I peer at the lock, wondering if he's spotted a booby trap, but then he whispers, "shit," and turns toward the barn's far corner, raising his weapon at a target that doesn't exist.

Until it does.

Two of Harry's eldest sons charge around the corner, weapons raised—sent to intercept us. I start to raise my shotgun, but Lindo is already prepared. He fires two sets of two bullets. Each of the young men is struck center mass, and in the head.

When Lindo turns to face me, an air of 'no big deal' wafting off of him, I shout, "*You* are *not* an Uber driver!"

"Get the lock," he says. "More are coming."

"How the hell do you know that?" It's not that I don't believe him, but I'm not comfortable fighting a battle with someone I'm no longer sure I can trust.

"Satellite imaging," he says, and when he sees the utter disbelief in my eyes, he leans closer, pulls down his eyelid, and opens his eye wide. I'm about to ask what I'm looking for when I see flickers of light from within his pupil. "Embedded retinal display. I'll explain everything—if we survive."

When he turns and raises his weapon to fire, I decide that the little he's given me has to be enough. I take a step back, aim the shotgun at the lock, and blast it off. I shove the door open while Lindo fires sound-suppressed rounds toward the corner, holding whoever is coming at bay.

"We're in," I say, and I slip into the darkness.

Lindo squeezes off two more rounds, and I make a mental note that he's got four left. He slips inside behind me and closes the door behind us. The booming report of gunfire is muffled and mostly drowned out by the sound of horses whinnying and stomping their hooves. The screams I heard from outside have gone silent.

"I don't suppose that thing lets you see in the dark?" I ask.

"Actually," he says, and then lights flicker on around the large barn, revealing two rows of stables and Lindo standing by a light switch. Lindo slides a long plank down across the doors. The old fashioned lock is crude, but it will stand up to a shotgun blast better than the metal padlock.

The barn smells like it's supposed to—horse shit and hay. But there's something off about it. Smells that don't belong. My stomach lurches when I realize the fetid odors are human.

"Hello?" I say, creeping deeper into the barn, shotgun raised. "We're here to help."

When I get no reply, I ask Lindo, "Can you see anyone?"

"It's a satellite, man, not X-ray vision," Lindo says, "But I can tell you that those crazy bastards are sending more people our way. Whatever is in here, they don't want us finding it."

"Or taking it," I add, and I move deeper into the barn. Horses flare their noses at me as I pass, but they seem to calm from the human presence.

The barn's rear door shakes from an impact that makes me jump.

"Little warning next time," I say.

"Three of them back there," he says. "Two more en route."

"Watch the doors," I tell him and hold the shotgun out to him. "You have only—"

"Four rounds left," he says. "I know. And thanks." He takes the shotgun, drops to one knee, and places it on the concrete floor beside him. Then he aims the handgun toward the rear doors and waits. Whoever he is, this isn't the first time he's seen action. Between our crew, the cult, and the mercs, he might be the calmest person on the ranch. It's disconcerting and comforting at the same time, the latter because it means he knows what he's doing, the former because he could turn against us. Here I felt guilty for involving him, and all along, he was playing me.

Obsess over it later, I tell myself, and push onward.

Where I see horses, I continue past. Where I don't, I peek inside. I'm two stalls from the end when I hear whispering.

I slow my approach. "I don't have a weapon. I can take you away."

Both are half-truths and possibly outright lies, but my guilt is diminished by the hopes that I'll find Isabella.

"I'm going to peek in," I say. "I'm not here to hurt anyone. I promise."

I inch my head around the stall's gate, looking through the wrought iron bars. At first, I don't see anyone, but when I step closer and look down, I find six children looking back up at me. Two are girls, both of them white and blonde. There are four boys, young teens, but one of them doesn't look right. His eyes are large, with large black pupils and whites that are closer to a luminous light blue. *Is he wearing custom contacts?* I wonder. He notes my attention and turns his face to the floor. The kids are dressed in gray jumpsuits and are relatively clean and healthy looking. But a bucket in the corner, filled with piss and shit, accentuates the degrading surroundings.

"Daddy won't let you leave," one of the girls says. "We're too important."

"Do you *want* to leave?" I ask.

All six kids nod, including the boy, who I now suspect is one of Harry's unluckier sons.

"Time's almost up," Lindo says. "Five at the back. Shotguns all around. What you got up there?"

"Six kids," I say, opening the stall door to release them. "We need a way out!"

"Already on it," Lindo says a moment before the front door explodes.

18

Godin's SUV reverses through the barn doors, shattering wood with a crack loud enough to make me flinch. The sound of gunfire booms from outside, setting some of the kids to squealing. The vehicle screeches to a stop a few feet short of running me down. I fling the rear door up without missing a beat and motion inside and shout to the kids, "Get in!"

They hesitate.

Shit.

"Running out of time!" Lindo shouts, still watching the door. "They're coming this way!"

"Who?"

"The family. Like all of them."

"You can't beat them," says the kid with big eyes, still looking at the floor.

I take the boy by the shoulders. "We don't need to beat Harry. Just get you away from here."

"I'm not talking about Harry, or the men attacking the farm." The boy looks me in the eyes, and it takes all of my fortitude to not stumble back. In that moment of connection, I can feel his fear, his hopelessness, and his earnest belief in what he's telling me. For a moment, I give in to the surge of emotion, but a lifetime of grit, and the past five years of pushing through pain and loss, keeps me resolved.

And the boy responds to it, standing a bit taller, taking a deep breath. He gives a nod and motions for the others to get in the SUV. All six kids cram into the SUV's rear compartment. I'm about to close the hatch when the strange-eyed boy and Lindo both say, "Too late."

There're two loud booms from the barn's backside. The doors slam open, unleashing a mob of killers into our midst. Lindo has them in his sights, but he doesn't pull the trigger. Harry didn't send his whole family after us—just his kids.

His heavily armed kids.

Lindo dives over the door of a stall as the kids open fire with shotguns. The door is shredded, hanging open and leaving Lindo exposed. Weapons turn in my direction, forcing me into the stall that held the captive children. Buckshot eats up the wood behind me, but not the SUV.

They want the kids alive. It's our only advantage.

The *pfft* of sound-suppressed bullets being fired snaps through the air from Lindo's position. Part of me is horrified that he so quickly changed his policy of not killing kids, but the rest of me is relieved that *I* won't have to do it.

When high pitched screams fill the air, I realize he's not killing them. Just wounding them. I lean out as Lindo fires his final round, winging a ten year old boy's leg, dropping him to the floor. But there're still eight girls and boys, and they're closing on his position. He still has the shotgun, but that's not a weapon for wounding people.

Gunfire from the house intensifies and is met by the resounding hammer-thump of a machine gun. One of the two helicopters opens fire, and as the bullets rain down on targets in other buildings, it's all I can hear.

Then the bark of a shotgun.

Despite the danger I peek out and witness a blur of motion as Lindo surges from the stable, slapping the smoking barrel of a child's shotgun away from his body. The weapon fires again, peppering several stable doors with metal pellets and riling the horses into a frenzy.

Lindo backhands the young boy, sprawling him to the ground. In the same spinning motion, he swipes his shotgun out, connecting with the side of a second boy's head, and performing a sweep kick that drops a girl.

He moves through the group of kids like a Shaolin monk, delivering non-lethal, but quite painful strikes, disarming them as he goes. Harry's family is well-prepared for a shooting war, but none of these kids have been trained in hand-to-hand combat, and Lindo...whatever martial art, or mix of martial arts, he's using, he's a master.

Who is *this guy?*

All I really know is that his name is Steven Cruz, he's *not* an Uber driver, and he's something like a cross between James Bond and Bruce Lee. I also know he's currently fighting for me, and for these kids. And for now, that's enough.

One of the first young men he dropped to the floor pulls himself up behind Lindo, shotgun in hand. He raises the weapon, slips a finger around the trigger—and never gets a chance to fire.

I pull the punch as best I can, but it's still hard enough to send the kid sprawling like a drunk ballet dancer.

With all ten kids disarmed and moaning on the floor, Lindo turns around and flashes me a grin. "Thanks for the assist."

His accent is gone.

I'm at a loss for words about how to respond, so I stand there like a moron for a moment. I'm snapped out of my stupor when Lindo flinches, spins around, draws the taser Godin gave him and fires. The two darts strike a young man in the chest as he rounds the door. Lindo fires the second set of darts at a young woman dressed in a bloodied prairie dress. The pair convulse and fall, their synchronization now unintentional.

Machine gun fire from above grows louder and closer. A stream of bullets cuts through the ceiling, tracing a line between Lindo and me, and leaving a series of sunlit holes.

My first thought is that they're trying to hit us, or the van, but it's also likely that they saw Harry's family rush in the back. And that means they'll be coming around for another pass.

"Help me!" I say, rushing to the nearest stable and yanking open the door. The horse inside whinnies and bucks, but it starts to move out when I step to the next stable and open it. The horses gather in a panicked mass at the center of the barn. When we're done, there are twelve in total. I'm about to give one a smack to get them running when the chopper swings around and unleashes a fresh stream of lead into the barn. One of the horses is struck in the flank. It shrieks and kicks as its blood sprays onto its neighbors. That's all it takes to send the large beasts streaking out of the barn.

Lindo and I fling ourselves into the SUV, slam the doors shut, and I shout "Go!"

We emerge from the barn into the bright Arizona sun just behind the stampede. The horses charge across the lot, kicking up a dust cloud that makes driving difficult, but also helps mask our presence.

I catch a glimpse of the black SUVs as we pass, and the five mercs still taking cover behind them. Then we're beyond them, and the parking lot, racing over the horse-flattened electrified fence and into the field.

The horses stay in a group. I'm not sure where they're going—they probably don't know either—but it's due south and away from the farm. "Stick with the horses as long as you can," I tell Godin.

The SUV careens over the rough terrain, tossing us like popcorn in a hot pan, but compared to the barn, it's almost pleasant.

"How did you know to come?" I ask Godin.

"You sent me a message." He points to the laptop mounted to the dash between us. The black screen shows a simple text message over black: *Have kids. Need you in the barn, now! – Delgado.* "Would like to know how you did that."

I look back at Lindo, seated behind Godin. "I'd like to know, too."

"Had to use your name, man," Lindo says, the accent returning.

"You can cut the act, Cruz," I say. I'm not sure what effect I was hoping for by using his real name, but I get nothing.

"I actually do prefer Lindo," he says. "And the simple answer, in layman's terms, is I've got a computer in my brain."

"That's why you can't hear them," says the boy with strange eyes. He's leaning up over the back seat.

Lindo turns around and sees him for the first time. The look on his face is pure delight. "We haven't met yet," Lindo says, offering his hand. "I'm a friend. My name is—"

"Lindo," the boy says, keeping his hands out of reach. "I heard. I'm Jacob." Then he turns to me and says, "They're coming."

Lindo blinks, gives the kid a squinty stare for a moment, and then says, "He's right."

"No computer needed," Jacob says, tapping his head. Free of the barn, he's becoming a sarcastic little bugger. I like him. When his confidence wavers, I cringe. He seems to have an extra sense of the world around him, so his sudden fear can't be a good thing.

Machine gun fire pounds the air behind us. White hot tracer rounds cut through the horse-driven dust cloud. Ahead of us, there's an explosion of red and a shriek. The struck horse topples. I see its feet upend for a moment and then my head thumps against the ceiling as we drive over the creature's neck.

When the right-side wheels dig into the earth again, we swerve to the left, slipping out of the dust cloud for a moment. That's all it takes for me to see one of the two Black Hawks pursuing us. The chopper is flying sideways, a hundred feet up, a gunner in the side door.

The big gun redirects toward us and I shout, "Back inside the dust!"

"But the horses!" Godin says.

"Screw the horses!" Young shouts from the back seat.

As we swerve back into the dust's fold, a large equine body slams into the SUV's side, spider-webbing the window next to Young.

In the back, Wini unbuckles and turns around, whispering comforting words to the children, who have begun to scream with every turn, thump, and close call.

Tracer rounds burn through the brown grit, striking another horse. It flails and falls away.

They're whittling down our cover. Looking for a clear shot.

"They're not trying to kill us," Godin observes.

"They'll want us alive," Jacob says. "You all, not so much. Not after questioning you." He turns to Lindo. "Well, they might take *you* alive. But not the rest of you."

I think I mistook blunt honesty for sarcasm earlier. Jacob doesn't pull punches.

Another fusillade of .50 caliber bullets tears into another of our escorts, thinning the dust cloud even more. That I can see blue sky ahead means the chopper above can see us, too. It won't be long before one of those big rounds punches a hole in the engine.

"We're out of time." Jacob says, all emotion draining from his face.

"Hard left!" Lindo shouts, even louder. "In three, two—"

19

"Now!" Lindo shouts.

Godin taps the brakes just enough to allow the horse beside us to take the lead. Then he spins the wheel left. The vehicle's eleven occupants slide to the right, crushed against the doors and windows. The chopper soars past, low to the ground, still pursuing the dust cloud. Rotor wash scours the hardpacked earth, kicking up a dust storm of its own and erasing our tire tracks.

We race toward a solid wall of brown stone.

A dead end.

"Lindo..." I say, and I don't need to add anything else. His name is a threat. If he's screwing us over somehow...

"There's a cold spot." Lindo taps the side of his head. "Thermals don't lie." He points. "There!"

I almost miss the gorge's entrance. It's hidden behind a wall of stone that blends perfectly with the wall behind it, creating the illusion of one solid wall.

Godin slows to a careful crawl and makes the sharp turn into the gorge. It's a tight fit. Just two feet of clearance on either side. The walls stretch up several hundred feet. It feels safe, but if the Black Hawk passes overhead, the sheriff's SUV will be easy to spot.

"Keep going," Lindo insists. He looks like he's just staring off into space, but he's seeing things the rest of us can't. "They're coming back around."

Deep inside the gorge, Godin turns on the lights and gooses the engine. We work our way down the winding path, flanked by layers of brown, orange, and maroon strata. And then there's a ceiling.

Darkness melts over us. For a moment, it feels safe.

Then ominous.

"You feel it, too," Jacob whispers to me. "Don't you?"

"How do you do that?" I ask. "Know what people are thinking?"

"I don't know what you're thinking," he says.

"He's an empath," Wini says, her tone suggesting that the conclusion should have been obvious. "Like Deanna Troi."

"I have no idea who that is," I say.

Lindo looks at me like I've just said that I have a computer in my brain. So does Young. And Godin.

"Really?" Godin asks, eyes wide as he steers through the smooth-walled cave. "She was the half-human, half-Betazoid Starfleet officer."

"Next Generation," Young adds.

"Star Trek?" I ask, recognizing the Next Generation reference.

"The comparison isn't entirely inaccurate," Jacob says. "Though Betazoids are fictional."

"Empaths aren't real," Young says, and I'm pretty sure he hasn't gotten a good look at Jacob's face yet, and here, in the dark, he's not going to get a chance. "Perceptive maybe, but—"

"You're afraid," Jacob says.

"We're all afraid," Young says. "We saw mutilated animals, a Mormon cult wants us dead, and a team of mercenaries is hunting us."

"It's more than that," Jacob says, calmer in the dark. "You're afraid... of what people will think of you...because of bad things you did."

After a moment of heavy silence, Young says, "The grace Jesus offers is enough to cover a multitude of—"

"It's not Jesus you're worried about losing, though. It's—"

"Enough," Young says.

"Do the rest of us," Wini says, and while I can't see the other adults in the vehicle, I can feel their tension.

"You're afraid...for him." No one can see who Jacob is looking at, but it's not hard to figure out he's talking about me. "Not that he might lose his life, but...that he'll never get it back..." Jacob sounds confused. "What does that mean?"

"Sometimes," Wini says, "people endure a hurt from which it is nearly impossible to recover."

"You're not talking about physical wounds," Jacob surmises. "The sheriff is afraid for his life, and those of other people he is close to. That his actions today will put them in danger. And it might. I'm sorry."

Godin stops the SUV two hundred feet inside the cave. The twin headlight beams get lost in a larger cavern ahead. "What's that supposed to mean?"

"Only that the men pursuing us felt...ruthless."

"That's putting it lightly," Lindo says, making himself a target for Jacob's keen perceptions.

"*You're* afraid that the others will cast you aside when they learn the truth," Jacob says.

"What truth?" I ask.

"You'd have to ask him," Jacob says. "I can't read minds, just feelings, which are nuanced enough to guess the broad strokes."

Though I'm curious about who Lindo really is, and his agenda, he's helped keep us alive. That earns him a postponement of his interrogation. And Young's scandalous business, whatever it is, can stay his business. "I think we can stop."

"But I haven't done you, yet," Jacob says, his voice calmer than I've heard it. Diving into other people's emotions puts him at ease, or at least lets him know his own fear isn't a solitary condition. Then again, how much of his fear is being fueled by his ability to experience ours? Verbalizing our fears might give him some relief, like venting to a shrink.

I already know what he's going to say, and I'm okay with it. "Go ahead."

"You..." Jacob's voice fades a little. "You're afraid...to be happy? Is that right?"

I'm not sure what to say. It's not what I would have said about myself. Afraid to let go, maybe. Afraid of the envelope. But happy?

"Afraid to be loved," Jacob adds. His words feel like a fresh cut. Hot and harsh. "Because...it could hurt. A lot."

"Yeah," I say to a silent audience. "Sounds about right."

"Is that...a tear on your cheek?" Jacob asks.

His question snaps me out of the emotional quagmire Jacob dropped me into and back into my more comfortable analytic self. "You can see me. In the dark."

Aside from the lit cavern ahead of us, I can't see anything.

"My biology is...adapted to subterranean environments."

"How?" Lindo asks, a little too eager.

"Genetics," Jacob says. His intellect strikes me as being advanced for his age. Probably advanced for my age. "Like Deanna Troi, I am only partly human, though in terms of percentages, I'm closer to seventy percent human, rather than Troi's fifty percent, primarily because I had neither father nor mother."

"Do you remember where you were...born?" Lindo asks.

Three deep breaths and then, "In a place like this." Jacob's own fear surfaces. "But kept at the ranch."

"You've been a prisoner there?" I ask.

"I was unaware of my true status until last night."

He's talking about the UFO.

"What happened?"

"We were brought to the stables," he says. "There were twelve other children. Fully human. They were taken. We were scheduled for tonight. I suppose we still are."

"*None* of you are fully human?" Lindo asks.

"That makes you happy?"

"I'm sorry," Godin says. "But none of this is possible. Empaths? Genetic experiments? UFOs? Cattle mutilations? Aliens? Someone level with me. What the fuck is really going on?"

His doubt is understandable. I've been doing my best to roll with the stream of surreal punches thrown my way, but my willingness to believe what I'm seeing is being stretched to its limits. I think my lack of knowledge regarding science fiction culture insulates me from the ramifications of these things potentially being reality, but it doesn't take a lot of imagination to picture deadly government conspiracies and doomsday scenarios.

"There are no aliens," Jacob says.

"Pssh." Lindo's disbelief about Jacob's lack of belief in the un-believable is borderline angry. "Bullshit. In addition to the long list of phenomena the sheriff just mentioned, there is a well-documented history of alien abduction around the world."

"And crop circles," Jacob adds. "Livestock mutilations. Missing time. Scoop marks. Cybernetic implants—with which you're familiar. It's ingenuine."

"I've seen all of it with my own eyes," Lindo says. "It's real."

"The validity of those phenomena does not prove the reality of extraterrestrial beings, and while some of them are legitimate, many more of them are like the horses let loose into the desert."

"You're losing me," Lindo says, patience still waning.

"A smokescreen," I say.

"A distraction," Jacob adds. "All of it pointing..."

"We can't see you," Wini reminds him, but I'm sure he's pointing up.

The ceiling light snaps on revealing Jacob with one hand on the switch and the other pointed toward the ceiling, and outer space higher above.

Young flinches upon seeing the boy's pale face, large blue eyes, and big black pupils. Jacob glances toward him, registering the pastor's reaction with a subtle frown.

"You're being told a dramatic narrative," Jacob says, "and you're believing it. Don't feel bad. There have been a variety of deceptions told throughout history, all of them pointing away from the truth. Magical fairies and leprechauns. Demigods. Demons. Witches. Not everyone believes them, but those who do often make the truth look like a joke. Aliens are just the most recent incarnation meant to distract humanity from the truth."

"And that is?" Lindo asks.

"They're not from another planet, the future, or another dimension," the boy says. "They're from here."

"From Earth," Lindo says. "You want us to believe another sentient race of beings evolved on Earth? That we've been sharing the planet?"

"I don't claim to have all the answers—only what the man who claimed to be my father taught us, which was also steeped in untruth—but I know enough." Jacob's starting to sound annoyed now, too. I think he's unaccustomed to not being taken seriously.

"I've heard enough," Godin says, opening his door. "I'm going to keep watch. Make sure no one is sneaking up on us."

It's a good idea, so I just nod.

"I'll join you," Young says, tugging on his door's handle. Both of them look ready to bolt, though I don't think they will.

Jacob watches the two men head toward the distant oval of light far behind the vehicle. Then he turns to me. "I'm not sure that's wise."

"Not getting ambushed is—"

Jacob holds up his hand, cutting me short with a surge of worry that I can feel. He doesn't just absorb people's emotions, he also projects his own. I wonder if he knows that.

"You misunderstood me," he says. "When I said *they* were from *here*."

When my gut twists from understanding, Jacob nods.

"What?" Wini asks. While she's not an empath, she's good at reading me.

"They aren't on Earth's surface." I turn forward, looking deeper into the cave. "They're beneath it."

20

Lindo kicks open his door and slides out into the darkness. Like Jacob, he can see in the dark, though for very different reasons. Where Jacob was modified before birth and without a choice, Lindo subjected himself to technological advances that make me squirm.

"Are they here now?" I ask Jacob.

He shrugs. "I'm not able to feel them."

"Because they're protected?" Wini asks.

"Because they have no emotions...I think." Jacob tilts his head, staring at me. Then he turns to Lindo, who's moving deeper into the cave, lit by the SUV's beams. "You're worried about him. But you don't trust him, either. Your emotions are at odds."

"Honey," Wini says, "You just figured out what took me a year to learn."

"Are you his mother?" Jacob asks.

Wini chuckles, but doesn't deny it. I'm not an empath, but I know that's how she feels about me. Wini never had children of her own, and when she found me, broken and wounded, her maternal instincts kicked in and haven't faded. Not sure I would have survived the past five years without her.

"And that pleases you," Jacob says to me.

I reach out and take Wini's hand. She has tears in her eyes.

"I think..." Jacob looks sad. "I think I have not understood the concept of family until now. With some of my brothers and sisters to a degree..." He looks back at the girls and boys huddled behind him. "...but we have learned to not trust those to whom our care has been entrusted."

"Harry," I guess. "Your fath—"

"Not our father," one of the girls says, the same one who spoke up in the barn. She's the youngest of them, and if she's anything like

Jacob—not fully human—I can't see it. Her dark eyes remind me of Isabella.

"What's your name?" Wini asks.

"Hannah," she says and then she glances at her brothers and sisters. "Don't bother with the others. They don't talk."

"Don't," I say, "or—"

"Can't," Jacob confirms. "We don't know what about them isn't... human, but I believe the changes made to them left them without vocal cords. My eyes, for example, allow me to see in the dark, and at great distances, but my vision is monochrome."

"You don't see any color?" Wini asks.

"I see auras," he says, "around people. A visual representation of their emotional state. So I understand what color is, but the world as I see it is in shades of gray."

I want to ask how much of Hannah isn't human, but I suspect that's a question she won't want to answer. And maybe, like the four mute kids, she doesn't know. Of the six, only Jacob shows outward signs of not being human, and that's the only reason I'm buying into this insanity. Conspiracies, mercs, cults—all of that fits into my worldview. Aliens that aren't aliens, hybrids, empaths—not so much. But I tend to believe what I can see, and touch, and hear, and there's no way that Jacob is faking his ability to read people's emotions, and I'm pretty sure he's not wearing makeup or a mask. It's a hard pill to swallow, like choking down an egg, but cases aren't solved by being close-minded.

Jacob looks up, eyes closed. "They're confused. Angry. Distant." He opens his eyes and looks at me. "They're moving on. We have time."

"Time?" Wini asks. "For what?"

"The questions glowing blue around him." His face scrunches up like he's smelled something foul. "Some of the questions. You're not ready for the one I can't answer."

I don't bother asking what he's talking about.

I know damn well.

The photo of Isabella and her mother has taken a beating, but their faces are still visible. When I show it to Jacob, his stare remains blank, showing no recognition. "This is who we're looking for."

Hannah leans forward, scanning the photo. Her eyes widen. She points to Isabella. "She was at the ranch."

"Is she still?" I ask, wondering how wise it would be to attempt a raid. There's no way to know if Harry or any of his gun-toting cult family are still alive.

Hannah shakes her head. "She was with the group they took last night. But she was...different."

"Like you different?" I ask.

Another head shake. "A fighter. She escaped. Nearly reached the sheriff—he was looking into a mutilation, being conditioned to look for the truth in the wrong direction. Harry nearly shot her. They caught her later that night."

"Where is she now?" I ask, feeling hopeful.

"We're a small piece of a much larger picture," Jacob says. "As near as I can tell, the ranch is just one of many waystations for trafficking resources."

"By resources, you mean people," Wini says.

"I do," Jacob says.

I face forward, melt into my seat and let out a long sigh.

"This disturbs you?" Jacob asks.

I don't have an answer for the question, but I'm sure he can see the mixture of rage, sadness, and confusion radiating from me. Human trafficking is hard enough to stop when it's being performed by other humans. But this...this is too much. What can we do against powers that a day ago I would have found laughable?

"You're despairing," Jacob says. He sounds disappointed. "They're not perfect. They're not gods. Or magical. Or even beyond your comprehension. They make mistakes, and their collaborators are human."

It's the last point that gives me the most hope. Human error has toppled empires, computer systems, and governments. It has led to the conclusion of every case I've ever solved. Where there are people, there are flaws. And where there are flaws, there is weakness. "Like Harry."

"Only fools sell out their own species," Jacob says.

"You might be surprised," Wini says.

"Although the man who pretended to be my father was at a disadvantage. By the time he was my age, he was fully indoctrinated in the belief system passed down through generations."

"Mormonism?" Wini asks.

Jacob gives a nod. "The fundamentalist variety. Modern Mormonism has disavowed and forgotten their origins, though the shift was not by choice, and forced when an error in judgment led to the U.S. government's intervention in the Others' plans."

The vehicle goes silent. Wini and I just stare.

"You're waiting for an explanation?" Jacob asks, trying to decipher our reaction.

"No shit," Wini says, causing the mute kids to gasp. Wini twists around to address the children. "You all can speak however you want now. No one will hurt you for it. Not while I'm around."

Hannah smiles, but the rest remain huddled at the fringe of the dome light's reach.

"I don't know the details," Jacob says. "Only what Harry taught the family, and how he felt when he did—superior with a trace of guilt."

"Guilt?" I have trouble picturing a delusional cult leader feeling guilty.

"He knows it's a lie," Jacob says.

I'm pretty sure I know where this is leading, but the political correctness drilled into me by modern society is telling me to block my ears and shout, 'La, la, la, laaa,' like one of those hear-no-evil monkeys. But the truth is the only way I'm going to recover Isabella. "What's a lie?"

"The very foundations of—" Jacob gasps, eyes widening. He's looking through the windshield, eyes on where Lindo had been just moments before.

"Did something happen? Are they here?" Visions of bug-eyed aliens crawling from holes and dragging Lindo away churn in my imagination.

"He found something," Jacob says. "He's...excited."

I don't know what Jacob can see. Maybe Lindo. Maybe just his colorful aura. But he's looking at something. I, on the other hand, can't see shit. I flip the high beams on, which helps illuminate the smooth-walled cave, but Lindo is either beyond the light's reach or my eyes' ability to focus.

"You still have your purse?" I ask Wini.

She hands the heavy, overpacked bag to me. I open it, revealing boxes of ammunition, which I use to refill the Beretta's magazine.

When I slap the magazine back inside the weapon, Jacob flinches.

"Sorry," I tell him. Kid has endured a lot. More than most people in a lifetime.

"It wasn't you," he says, looking up again. "They're coming back. They're...suspicious, but still confused."

The driver's side door whips open and I come very close to shooting Young in the face. Everyone in the car, sans Jacob, who no doubt felt Young's approach, flinches back.

"Sorry," Young says. "We can hear the chopper. They're coming back."

"Already knew," I say, collecting myself.

Young glances back at Jacob, but turns away as though the kid was Medusa. "Right..."

"And next time you approach a vehicle in the dark, with frightened and armed people inside, do yourself a favor and knock." I waggle the gun still pointed toward him.

He blanches at the sight of the weapon.

"Hey!" Lindo's voice echoes from the distance. "Come see this!"

I don't think anyone in a helicopter will be able to hear Lindo's voice, even if it is being amplified by the cave, but I don't want to take the risk. I flash the high beams a few times to acknowledge we've heard him and then turn back to Wini. "You okay here?"

She pats her revolver. "Already reloaded."

I open my door and am halfway out when Jacob says, "I'm coming, too."

"You don't have to," I tell him, trying to hide the fact that I'd rather he didn't. Not because he frightens me, but because I think he should be resting, or processing, or whatever people who were recently freed from a cult's stable normally need to do. I suppose that could include distraction. Hell, I've been doing that for five years.

I wave for him to follow and step out. He's already sliding over the front seat by the time I turn around to close the door.

"Thanks," he says, and slips to the cave floor beside me.

When I close the door, he takes my hand. "Do you mind?"

"Course not," I say. "I hold alien-human hybrid kid hands every day."

When he chuckles, I ask, "What color is sarcasm?"

"Pink," he says as we walk into the SUV's light, our shadows stretching into the distance. "And remember, they're not aliens."

"Right...are they like a sister race?" I ask. "Did they evolve alongside us?"

"Long before us," Jacob says. "Well, before you. Before humans."

"You're human," I tell him. "More human than the man pretending to be your father was."

He grins at that. It's subtle but there. I wonder what color *his* aura would be.

"You're not going to tell us that they're angels?" Young asks, sounding defensive.

"I don't discount the potential existence of a creator..." Jacob's preface is very diplomatic. "...but at times, yes. Whatever narrative helps conceal their true agenda is adopted and promoted. Right now that happens to be aliens in UFOs visiting from other star systems. In fact, before we were interrupted in the car, I was going to tell Mr. Dan about—"

Jacob's hand squeezes mine tight. He's staring into the cave's depths. "Lindo found something else. Something that scares him. A lot."

21

Walking deeper into the cave, I get a sense for how Jacob must feel all the time. The air is heavy with dire potential, pressing on me as though the Earth itself is radiating menace.

I don't want to know what Lindo found.

I don't want to believe that aliens are real, or that they're not aliens at all.

I want to go home. To forget all this. To finally open the envelope in my pocket and move on with my life.

I'm ready for life to be simple again.

But it never will be. Not for me. I know too much. And my conscience won't let me run away. Even when Jacob and his siblings are safe. Even when Isabella is reunited with her mother. As long as there are people being taken against their will, for God knows what, I'll track them down and set them free...if such a thing is even possible.

We're facing forces whose true power is unknown and whose existence has me questioning everything. I'm untethered, grasping for a handhold as I float out into the infinite.

"I have you," Jacob says, squeezing my hand again.

"Huh?" His words shake me out of my thoughts. I heard what he said, but I'm struggling to process what he's really saying.

"You're kind of freaking out," he says.

When it comes to hiding my emotions from people around me, I'm a pro. Literally. I've practiced the skill. Keeps a murderer, or a cheating wife, or a kidnapper from seeing me for what I am—their undoing. But to Jacob, I'm an open book, full of black-and-white pictures with rainbow auras betraying my carefully guarded emotions.

If he wasn't looking up at me with his big, not-really-human, but still innocent looking eyes, I'd probably be furious. Instead, I smile and relax. "I'm supposed to be the one comforting you."

"Why?" he asks. "Because I'm younger than you?"

"Well, yeah."

"I've been steeped in this life since my creation. You're new to it. Take some time to adjust."

"Sure your father isn't Dr. Phil?" I ask.

Young laughs, but Jacob just looks confused.

"He's a TV psychologist," I explain.

"He gives wise advice?"

"Meh," I say. "I was joking. Thought my aura would have given that away."

"You're kind of a mess to look at," Jacob says. "A lot of colors, all the time." He smiles, but I'm not sure he's joking. It's a pretty good description of my emotional state.

Jacob leans forward to look around me, at Young. "Him not so much."

Even I can sense Young's growing apprehension. I'm fairly shaken by what we've encountered in the past two days, and redefining my concepts of reality is challenging. But my belief system isn't nearly as deeply rooted as the pastor's. I have no idea what the existence of a separately evolved race of sentient Earthlings—who sometimes pose as angels—means for him. Maybe nothing. Maybe everything.

I decide conversation might be the best distraction. We're only halfway to Lindo's location. Now that we're deeper into the cave, I can just make him out, two hundred feet ahead, staring at the wall.

"You were going to explain something before," I say to Jacob. "About Harry?"

"Ahh, yes," Jacob says, sounding a little studious. "About the angel."

Shit.

"What angel?" Young asks, already sounding defensive.

Damn it.

"He appeared to Harry's ancestor," Jacob says.

"Moroni?" Young asks.

"Yes!" Jacob smiles at Young. "You know of him?"

"Joseph Smith, the founder of the Mormon religion claimed that Moroni—the guardian of the golden plates—visited him. Smith copied the texts on the golden tablets, which were found underground..." Young gives the cavern a suspicious look. "...in New York. The text became the book of Mormon."

"The subject makes you angry," Jacob observes.

"He was a con-man who fabricated a religion based on an alternative history that science and every shred of historical data disproves, resulting in the world's largest, most powerful cult—and I'm not just talking about the fundamentalists who hide out in this part of the world."

My PC alarm is sounding, but since no one else is here—and because Jacob is nodding—I let it slide. I'm not sure what I'd complain about anyway. I know very little about the faith, and while Young is well educated, Jacob has lived through it.

"You are both right and wrong," Jacob says. "The story is true in that Joseph Smith was contacted by a being identifying itself as the angel Moroni. He was taken underground—" He studies the cave around us. "—to a place like this, and given a seductive message: that we are all gods and can one day rule a planet of our own, to share with the world."

"To what end?" I ask. "What would that accomplish?"

"Livestock," Young says, his voice nearly a whisper. He looks Jacob in the eyes and for the first time, there's compassion in them. "He made a deal, didn't he?"

Jacob gives a nod. "The details of which I have only recently come to fully understand."

I look ahead to Lindo, who's just a hundred feet away now and waving us on. "I'm lost."

"Polygamy," Young says. "Like I told you before. It wasn't just a fundamentalist Latter Day Saints institution. At first, it was mainstream. Smith called it the divine commandment. I've always thought he was just a horny bastard using the future repopulation of their own planets to justify dozens of wives, but that wasn't it at all, was it?"

Jacob looks to the floor, uncomfortable with the answer. "Your allusion to livestock is accurate."

"They were breeding people for the...whatever they are?"

"Genetic material," Jacob says. "Hundreds of undocumented children could be passed on without outside knowledge. And as the religion spread, thousands."

"Until the U.S. government put a stop to it," Young says.

"But they didn't," I say. "Not entirely."

"The pact continues to this day, fulfilled by those loyal to Smith's teachings...and the deal he made."

"A deal with the devil," Young says.

"They are neither angels nor demons," Jacob says.

"They're not human, either," I say.

"But they are flesh and blood. They are fallible. And like all living things, fragile...I believe."

"But you don't know," I say. "Not for sure."

"It's a logical deduction," he says. "If they were truly supernatural, why would they need genetic material? Why would they operate in the shadows, and redirect humanity's attention? While I have never seen them, or sensed them, I'm positive that they, like us, are afraid."

A laugh gurgles up out of my mouth. "I'd like to say that's comforting, but..."

"Yeah," Jacob says. "I know. But you don't need to be afraid of me." Jacob waits for Young to look at him again. "Neither of you do."

Young takes a deep breath, lets it out slowly, and then gives a furtive nod.

Jacob's inexperience with the outside world is more than made up for by his ability to read people. Of course, that raises the question of whether or not he's saying exactly what he needs to manipulate us into trusting him. I've known him for under an hour and already I feel a kind of paternal instinct kicking in.

"Hurry up," Lindo says. There's no need to shout now. We're just twenty feet away. I look at the wall he's been staring at and don't see anything obvious.

"There's something wrong," Jacob whispers. "He looks...off. His color is solid. Perfect contentment."

"What's wrong with that?" I ask, though I recognize that contentment is a strange emotion to be feeling right now.

"There is no such thing," Jacob says. "No one feels any one emotion at a time. There is always a mix. During our short walk, you've experienced a full gamut of emotions, and never once felt totally happy, or sad, or angry. You never have in your life so far, and you never will."

I slow down with Jacob so he can finish his thought. Young pulls ahead, focused on the wall that Lindo is now leaning against, looking at something small. "What does that mean?"

"I don't know how," Jacob says, "but he's projecting false emotions. And he would only need to do that if he needed to hide his true—"

"You're a smart kid," Lindo says. "But you don't know as much as you think." He taps his ear. "I can hear really well, too."

Young convulses and falls to the rock floor, twitching to the sound of a crackling taser. Lindo adjusts his aim and fires a second charge. The prongs punch through Jacob's gray jumpsuit. He yanks his hand from mine a moment before the shock drops him.

I stand stunned for a moment, and then reach for my gun. "You should have shot me second." I pull the weapon from behind my back, intending to wound, not kill. I want answers.

Lindo raises his hands and I hold my fire. As much as I'd like to, I won't shoot someone who's submitting.

"Why?" is all I can think to say.

"I'm sorry about this," he says. "And I appreciate what you've done already. I just can't risk you screwing things up."

I adjust my aim to his leg, reconsidering my stance on not shooting unarmed people. But before I can ask another question, slip my finger inside the trigger guard, or even consider weighing my options, a sharp pain radiates from the side of my head. Burning agony washes down my body, triggering muscles to flex and not let go. I'm locked in place. Unable to balance, I topple back.

I remember hitting the ground, but not being able to feel the pain.

There's a moment of darkness. Just a blink.

And then, as though no time has passed, I wake up somewhere else.

22

The bedroom is white. Glowing. Sunlight slices through the blinds. The room is cool, but the down blankets, heavy with layers, form a comfortable womb around me. Waking up isn't easy.

Until I see her.

She's naked. Mostly. My gun belt, a holdover from my days as a street cop, hangs at an angle from her hip. My wife is petite. Skinny waist. Small breasts. She's barely five feet tall. But her hips are curved like a roller coaster.

Framed by the morning sun, she glows like some kind of celestial being of whom I am completely undeserving. "You can't be real."

She adjusts her stance, straightening those crazy hips. The gun belt thumps to the floor. She crawls onto the bed, the slow stalk of a prowling lion, head low, eyes locked on me.

We've been married for years, but my heart is pounding. Her raw sexuality is alluring and intimidating. We have a great sex life, but this feels next level. Something is different.

I'm good to go long before she peels the comforter away and straddles me, but she senses my apprehension and stops short of lowering herself. At this point, the delay is somewhat agonizing, but then she smiles and I'm undone, at her mercy.

When she says nothing, I return her smile, and say, "How's it going?"

She leans down close to my ear, and whispers, "I'm ovulating," and then she leans back to see my reaction.

"Seriously?" I say.

She nods. "You ready for this?"

The subject of children has been one of constant conversation, but always on the back burner. That is, until a month ago, when she decided her career as a pharmaceutical sales rep was unfulfilling.

In the weeks since her departure, her re-evaluation of her life goals has fueled revelations that we're not as indifferent to the idea of children as we believed.

My response to her question is to slide my hands over those crazy hips and ease her down onto me.

"Yo."

"What?"

Kailyn looks confused, sitting atop me. "Yo," she says, but it's not her voice. "Wake up."

I'm not lying down. Not naked. Not with my wife. The memory turned dream fills me with a deep despair.

Before I open my eyes, I know where I am. The smell of a police cruiser is universal and familiar. But I'm also getting whiffs of Young's cologne, faint, but still present, Wini's perfume, and the earthy odor of six kids who spent the past days living in a horse stable.

"The fuck did you do?" I'm seated in the front seat of Godin's SUV. Lindo is behind the wheel. My head pounds as I crane around to find the rest of our motley crew present, strapped in, and unconscious. "If they're hurt—"

"They're fine," Lindo says. "For now."

"I don't respond well to threats," I say, concern morphing into anger. I've already identified five different ways to subdue Lindo, two of which include taking his life.

Lindo must hear the threat, because he raises Young's Desert Eagle toward my chest, keeping it low on his lap. "Look, man, this isn't how I wanted things to go down. I like you. All of you. But I'm not calling the shots."

"Who is?"

"Time for that later."

I'm about to unleash a little verbal rage and demand answers, when Lindo says, "Have you *looked* out the window yet?"

We're stopped in the middle of an endless stretch of Arizona desert road. There are no signs of civilization or other vehicles aside from the white van parked in front of us. The big vehicle's doors are open, and the windows are rolled down and framing two mercs with assault rifles.

I've got a long string of insults and colorful language locked and loaded, but I reign myself in. Survival has to come before justice, so I turn my ire from Lindo to the men who have been a thorn in my side from the moment I arrived in Santa Cruz. There're only two of them. Both covered in dust and what might be blood. These are survivors from the ranch fight. They hotwired one of the family vans to make their retreat.

Does that mean Harry is dead? I wonder, and then decide I don't care. I feel sorry for his family, especially the kids, but it's hard to feel too bad for a family of human traffickers.

"They want us alive?" I ask.

"Some of us." Lindo points to the sheriff's large glovebox.

I open it and find the beretta inside, the sound suppressor removed. I consider reassembling it, but out here in the middle of nowhere, silence isn't really a concern.

"Brave trusting me with this after what you did," I tell him, chambering a round with slow movements.

"Can't do this without you."

"Hope you remember that when we're done," I say.

He smiles. "I like your confidence."

"How do you want to play it?" The two men haven't moved. I can't see their eyes behind their reflective eyewear, but I'm willing to bet neither have blinked.

Lindo places the Desert Eagle on the seat beside him. "Just follow my lead, I guess." He raises his hands. I tuck the smaller beretta into my pants pocket and assume the same defenseless posture. The message is clear: we give up. But there's no way in hell they're buying it. Not after what we did at Young's church.

Lindo points at his door handle. One of the mercs nods.

Moving slowly, Lindo and I both open our doors and step out. Lindo slides the Desert Eagle to the left side of the chair and raises his hands again. "Who's over there? Luke? Charley?"

"I told you, Cruz," the merc on my side of the van says, "you chose the wrong side of this."

"Hey, Chuck," Lindo says. "Long time."

"Still a chance," Chuck says. "You've proven your worth. Your pal over there is fucked, though. He shot Snyder."

Lindo laughs, glances at me, and offers a wink. "Oh, shit, man. You shot *Snyder?*" His hands come down a bit, relaxing into the conversation, resting on top of the SUV's window frame. "Sounds tempting, but we both know Aeron won't go for it."

For a moment I think they're talking about someone named Aaron. But the pronunciation was air-ron.

It's not a name. Not of a person anyway.

Aeron is a government-contracted aerospace company that supplies the U.S. military with advanced, next-generation weapon systems and vehicles. I don't know much about them, but the name is as well-known as Lockheed Martin and Boeing. But the company is far more secretive. I only know that much because Wini likes her conspiracies.

"Lucky for you," Chuck says, "I'm sure they'll want to interrogate you before killing you. So you get to keep breathing. Your friend, on the other—"

I don't bother waiting for Chuck the merc to finish his threat. I'm three feet to the right of the door, gun in hand, finger pulling the trigger before I hit the ground. Red spits from the merc's left leg as two bullets break through skin, flesh, and bone.

Automatic gunfire bursts from the SUV's far side, punctuated by the Desert Eagle's much louder report. Five shots cut through the air, and then silence.

Chuck's head falls into view. I fire three rounds from my position on the ground. The first strikes Chuck's helmet, twisting it to the side, crushing his eye gear against his face and preventing him from getting a clear look at me. His momentary blindness is a mercy, making the next two 9mm rounds to strike his head a surprise.

Lindo slides over the SUV's hood like an action hero, gun raised. He drops to the ground beside me, rounding the open door until he sees Chuck's body.

"Sorry about Chuck," I say.

"He was kind of a douchebag," Lindo says. He turns around, offering me a hand up, but stops short when he finds my gun pointed at his head. He steps back and lets the Eagle hang from his index finger. "I don't blame you, man. I really don't. But we're still neck-deep in shit."

I climb to my feet and take the heavy handgun from him. "How'd they find us?"

"Dumb luck," he says, but even he doesn't buy that. "Probably tracked the vehicle, same as the sheriff's department. They've got a small army headed toward us right now. Still a ways out, though. I can't track these assholes, though." He motions to Chuck. "But they're chipped, no doubt, and the moment they died, alarms started sounding. Won't be long before those choppers show."

I consider everything he's said and find no fault in his logic. He's still the lesser of two evils. I don't trust him. Not anymore. But if he wanted to kill us, he could have. That we're all alive, and even buckled for safety, says he's a different kind of man than these mercs.

"C'mon, man." Lindo's eyes are on the sky now. Not me. Not the gun. He knows I'm not going to kill him.

"How did you do it?" I ask. "Knock me out?"

"*Seriously?*"

"Answer the question and we'll move."

"Just...stay calm, okay? Let me explain." He hesitates when I give no indication of whether or not I'll shoot him. "There's nanotech in your head. I put it there earlier."

My hand squeezes the handgun a little tighter. "When you picked me up."

"When *you* were hearing voices," he corrects.

"You could hear them?" I'm a little stunned and relieved until he shakes his head.

"I'm protected, too. That's what it's for. Keeps them out of your head."

"Keeps *who* out of your head?"

"Cryptoterrestrials. I call them The Others. Most people just call them aliens."

"But from Earth," I say.

"Right."

"They're real?"

"You've seen Jacob's eyes. What he can do. That's not human, man."

"And these crypto-whatevers. They were there?" I ask. "At the ranch?"

"Yes and no," he says. "That family was like a receiver for them. A conduit."

"For their conscience?" I'm starting to feel doubtful. We're delving deep into the realm of science fiction, and stretching my willingness to suspend my disbelief. "We're talking about mind control, right?"

"It's closer to possession," he says.

"And they were trying to possess me?"

"Trying," he confirms. "But it's not so easy when the host is unwilling."

For fuck's sake, I think. All of this is ridiculous. What's worse is that I can't think of any other explanation. I saw how Harry's family acted. Their synchronized movements and speech. I heard the voice, felt the scratching on the inside of my skull. "And a side effect of the chip is..."

"I can knock you out, yeah."

"If you do it again and *don't* kill me..."

He raises his hands. "I hear you. Just...you're going to have to trust me, and the people I work for, even though you have no good reason to. We're not about killing people." He glances at Chuck. "Nice people."

"And people who aren't fully human?" I ask. "What about them?"

He glances at the SUV. "We've never encountered them before, but we don't deal in biology. That's the kind of shit we're up against."

"What *do* you deal in?"

He taps his head. "Tech, man. Whadayu think?" Lindo goes rigid, eyes on the sky, seeing something that's not there. "Helo is thirty miles out and closing. Time's running out, man."

I open the SUV's side door. "Help me get them out."

"Out? We need to leave. Like now."

"We need to not be tracked." I unbuckle Godin's belt, slide my hands under his armpits, and drag him out of the SUV. "So we're taking the short bus."

23

"The wheels on the bus go round and round." Lindo looks at me, grinning. "Round and round, round and round."

He's in a chipper mood for having narrowly escaped death more than once. And there's still a decent chance I'm going to put a bullet in him the moment he breaks the silkworm thread-thin strand of trust between us. Right now the only reason that trust exists is because he didn't kill any of us when he could have, and the mercs hunting us down have tried to slaughter us on more than one occasion.

"C'mon," he says, "it's funny."

While Lindo isn't a blunt-force killing machine, he is a master of manipulation and can outperform any actor in Hollywood. As I find myself loosening up, I have to remind myself that his motives are not pure, that he might not have our best interests in mind, and that he's serving someone, or some corporation, who I'm sure doesn't see us any differently than I would ants on a sidewalk.

But that doesn't mean I shouldn't play along. Won't be the first time I've worked undercover. "I prefer the wipers going swish, swish, swish."

He stares at me for a moment, and then laughs. I crack a smile, loosening up, but not too much. My participation seems to please him. He settles back into driving, eyes on the endless stretch of desert road before us. We're still in Arizona, and heading west. Other than that, our destination is a mystery.

After a five minute lull, I ask, "How much can you tell me about what's really going on?"

Lindo glances in my direction, but says nothing. His frozen expression reveals nothing.

"Can they hear us?" I ask. "The people you work for?"

When he doesn't answer, I lean forward trying to see his eyes. "Can they *see* us?"

He doesn't answer, but I think that's answer enough. If Lindo can receive data from a satellite, or Wi-Fi, or cell networks, then it stands to reason that he's also transmitting data.

"Just give me a minute, man." When Lindo gets upset, his accent comes back. Tells me he wasn't faking the accent before, but unleashing an accent that he's suppressed. It's not uncommon for people from heavily accented areas to make an effort to lose their accent—for a job or for a girl.

Lindo turns to me, no longer watching the road. "Do you, Daniel Delgado, agree to keep confidential all conversations, revelations, information, and events experienced during the past two days, and any conversations, revelations, information, and encounters you are privy to, now and into the future involving Steven Cruz, his employers, and related phenomena, technology, and identities?"

"Do you agree to watch the road?" I ask.

"I can see the road," he says. "And you."

I'm not sure how his mind could handle seeing me through his actual eyes and the road from a satellite in orbit, but I'm pretty certain that's what's happening. Which makes the strange line of questioning quasi-understandable. "Is this a non-disclosure agreement?"

He nods.

"Can they see me? The people you work for?"

Another nod.

"I know you have reasons to not trust me," he says, "but you also have reason *to* trust me. If it weren't for me, you'd have been caught in Isabella's trailer and locked in a cell."

"*You* sent the texts?"

He nods.

Addressing the people watching me through Lindo's eyes, I say, "You know why I'm involved in this. You know what I want."

"Be specific," Lindo advises.

"I'm looking for Isabella Ramos." I feel stupid stating the obvious. Lindo's very first warning came through Marta's phone, meaning he'd already been in contact with her, which raises a lot of questions that won't get answers until I make a deal with a technological Mephistopheles. "But I am now responsible for the safety of the children we're transporting..."

"And..." Lindo urges.

"And those still lost," I say. "If they're being taken by aliens...by the Others, I'm going to find them. I'm going to set them free, with or without your help or approval."

Lindo smiles a little. It's subtle. Genuine.

He's silent for a good fifteen seconds, and then says, "Your terms are acceptable. Do you agree to our previous terms, knowing that failing to abide by this contract will be considered a breach of the highest order and subject to retribution?"

There's no mention of the law. This contract sounds legal, but isn't binding to any court system. How could they prosecute me for telling the world that aliens live beneath the Earth's surface, that there are people trafficking humans via cults and UFOs, or that there are secretive corporations competing for information and technology garnered from humanity's advanced sister species? They couldn't. No one would believe me anyway. With the lives of Wini, Young, and the children at stake, I have no problem accepting these terms. Not agreeing would probably subject us to 'retribution,' which could be death, or a lifetime in some corporate jail cell.

"I agree."

Lindo looks back to the road and closes his eyes for a moment. When he opens them again, he relaxes.

"They're done watching us?" I ask.

"They can when they want to," he says. "But it limits what I can do, and they trust me, so they generally wait for me to request an audience, which I did to protect you."

"Doesn't feel that way."

"Being a partner is better than being a pawn," he says.

"What about a pawn who thinks he's a partner?"

He frowns, but says nothing.

"And what about them?" I motion to the nine people strapped into the seats behind us. Working together we loaded them into the van in under five minutes. While Lindo drove us away from the scene of carnage, I arranged everyone in their seats, propped them up and buckled them in.

"They'll have to make the same choice when they wake up."

"Which will be when?"

"Few more hours," he says. "Give or take. Depends on the person. Size and metabolism can affect the drug's duration."

"Why did I wake up before them?"

"Didn't drug you," he says.

"Right." I rub my head behind my right ear. I remember the pain when Lindo helped me up, but there's not even a scab. "Do I want to know how it works?"

"Nano-tech," he says. "That's—"

"I know what it means," I say. "And to answer my own question, I really don't want to know how it works. What I want to know is what it's doing to me."

"Besides protecting you?" he says, like the fact that he prevented my mind from being possessed by cryptoterrestrial human traffickers is going to earn him brownie points. It does, but I'm not about to tell him that.

"And knocking me unconscious," I say.

"That's a side effect. And only I can do it," he says.

"Can you remove it?"

"It can be disabled," he says. "But it's in there for good. And before you get all pissy about that, try to remember that they would have had free access to your mind. Everything you know. Everyone you love. Every pain, fear, desire, and sin. If they couldn't control your actions directly, they could have found other ways to reign you in."

"Not sure that's different from what's happening now."

He rolls his eyes. "We might not be after the same things, but our goals aren't in opposition to each other."

"By *our* goals, you mean the goals of the people controlling you." I suspect at least some of Lindo's participation in the events of the past few days, not to mention in the time before we met, have been coerced. Probably not through direct threats, but I have little doubt he once made a similar agreement with his 'employer' to what I just did. "Who are they?"

"The company's public name is Chimera. And no, you haven't heard of them. They don't sell to the public. They develop next-gen tech and sell to the highest bidder. Microsoft. Google. Apple. Amazon. Samsung. Uncle Sam."

"But they don't really *develop* anything do they?" I ask. "Not from scratch."

He shakes his head. "Reverse engineering. It's fueled the U.S. Military and tech sectors since the late 1940s. Stealth. Nano-tech. Microchips. Other shit you haven't heard of yet. Once we knew, and I mean really *knew*, that they existed, we've been hunting them down."

"But not to kill them," I say. "Not to eradicate them?"

"We don't have to do that. They're on the brink, man." He looks at me. "That's what I'm told, anyway."

"But they're taking people," I complain. "A lot of people. Why aren't they treated as an enemy?"

"Because they're a resource," he says. "Until we've matched their tech level. Then it might be open season on the Others."

"Any idea when that will be?" If Chimera is engaged in a kind of corporate espionage with a technologically advanced species, they might pull their punches when it comes to recovering taken people.

He shakes his head. "We've only had direct contact with them on four occasions. You've heard of one of them."

"Roswell," I guess.

"The very first," he says. "The government got that one, but brought outside experts in to analyze what they found. Out of that, both Chimera and Aeron were born. They got to the crash in Kecksburg, Pennsylvania first. Chimera picked up the remains of a UFO in Pinckney, New Hampshire, which wasn't much. And Aeron snagged the most recent, in Needles, California."

"So what you can do...all of that tech...was reverse engineered from the remains of one crashed UFO?"

"Or stolen from Aeron," he says. "Yeah, but—"

Lindo gets a faraway look in his eyes that I now recognize. He's seeing something I can't, and it's not good.

"What is it?"

His foot crushes the gas pedal to the floor and I'm pinned to my seat as the big vehicle accelerates.

"Incoming," he says.

"Aeron?" I ask. "More mercenaries?"

"A missile." He blinks and is fully present once more. "Take the wheel!"

"What?"

He takes his foot off the gas pedal, eyes wide with genuine fear. "Hurry!"

I grasp the steering wheel just as the roar of a missile registers on my ears and the world erupts with bright blue light.

24

A wave of nausea-inducing energy pulses through my body and triggers a brief, but agonizing pain in my head. During the moment I spend clenching my eyes shut against the bright light, the van veers toward the side of the road. The world is cast in hues of green as my eyes slowly adjust to a normal level of light. It's disorienting, but I have no trouble comprehending the situation.

Some kind of unconventional missile detonated not far from the vehicle, apparently designed to impair rather than kill. The mercs might have no trouble killing me, or anyone else fully human, but we've got precious cargo on board. They're not going to simply blow us up.

How they found us isn't really a question. The large white van would be recognizable from the ranch, and as the vehicle in which their two now-dead operatives had left the battle. With very few roads in this part of the world, tracking us down was just a matter of time.

Lindo is unconscious. Possibly dead. His eyes are open and vacant. Very corpse-like. But his chest is still rising and falling. Either way, he's not driving.

I am.

As the vehicle slows, I twist the wheel counter-clockwise and get us back into the middle of the road. Cruising down a subtle grade at a dainty twenty miles-per-hour, I put us on a straight course, let go, and hope the alignment is good.

Unbuckling Lindo is the easy part. Moving his dead weight is the problem. Leaning over his body, I listen for the sound of roaring engines or helicopter blades. I hear nothing, but that doesn't mean they aren't coming. Lindo falls back when I pull the lever to adjust the driver's seat back. My lack of leverage makes moving him difficult, but

I'm able to yank him by his belt and slide him into the back seat, across the laps of Godin, Young, and Wini.

By the time I drop into the driver's seat and put the chair back up we've slowed to a crawl. From all outward appearances, we would appear disabled.

Until I step on the gas.

The speedometer needle climbs higher as the RPMs rise and fall through the gears. We won't be drag racing anytime soon, but once we hit 70mph, I start to feel better.

Briefly.

A glance in the tall rectangular side mirror confirms that my worst fears lacked imagination. There aren't any black SUVs or unmarked helicopters. There's a cloud that isn't a cloud. It's almost gelatinous in appearance. The naïve part of me says it's a storm cloud. That my vision is still being affected by the explosion's bright light. But the rest of the sky is devoid of precipitation, and clouds don't hover twenty feet above the ground and chase vans.

I push the gas pedal harder, but it's already on the floor, and the speedometer is holding steady at 80mph.

Gas pedal has a limiter on it, I realize. The small device is impossible to remove while driving and prevents the van from reaching higher speeds.

Fuck you, Harry.

Even when he's not present, the man is still trying to get me killed.

Unable to change my situation, I maintain my course and speed, and I wait for the cloud's arrival.

A groan turns me around. Despite his deceptions, I hope it's Lindo. If anyone has some insight into what we're about to face, it's him. Two seats back, I see Jacob's head rise up. He's a lot smaller than Young and Godin, but his non-human biology must have metabolized whatever drug Lindo used to knock everyone out. With his brown hair in a tussle and his eyes closed, he looks like any other kid waking up from a nap. Then he opens his eyes and I can actually feel him connecting with my emotions, like there're invisible tendrils extending between us.

He sobers as all the ice bucket of my anxiety, fear, and confusion pours over him. That's when he notices the collection of unconscious bodies around him. "What's happening?"

"Short version is that Lindo kidnapped us, got caught by the goon squad from the ranch, we fought our way free, took their van, got hit by some kind of explosion that knocked him unconscious—"

"He's not unconscious," Jacob says. "Unconscious people don't project emotions so intensely. He's too scared."

I look from Jacob to Lindo and then the rearview. If Lindo's awake, stuck in some kind of aware rigor mortis, then maybe he's still a source of information. "Can you tell me how he feels when I talk?"

Jacob gives a nod. The kid has been through hell and it's pursuing him from the ranch, but he's either numb to it or a stronger person than I am. The perspective his resolve provides strips away layers of denial and reveals my weakness. Before Jacob can comment on what he's no doubt sensing from me, I say, "There's a shimmering cloud closing in on us."

"He feels worse," Jacob says.

"What do we do?" I ask. "Just keep driving?"

Jacob cringes, showing Lindo's emotions.

"Stop and fight?"

Jacob's face sours further.

"Go off road?" Even I know this is a horrible idea. The van is far from an all-terrain vehicle, and the desert, while fairly hard packed in this part of the state, might treat us worse than the cloud.

"He likes that," Jacob says.

Shit.

"Sort of." Jacob unbuckles and moves to the front seat, making no effort to gently step over Lindo. He buckles again and looks in the passenger's side mirror. "That can't be good."

"Pretty sure that's been established?"

He smiles at me. Is he enjoying this? I suppose anything is better than being locked up in a cult's stable. "They're getting closer. They look like flying balls."

He's right.

The cloud resolves as it closes in.

It's composed of hundreds, maybe thousands, of softball-sized spheres, each of them transparent, the interior masked by bright light.

How many UFO sightings are actually something like this? It's not hard to imagine these things flying around at night, bunched together in a sphere, moving in formations that imply a large craft. From what I've heard, Aeron and the Others aren't allies. If they were, the aerospace company wouldn't be racing to collect UFO crashes and human hybrids. But they're not really enemies, either. If the cryptoterrestrials were destroyed, Aeron would lose the opportunity to reverse engineer even more future-tech. In a twisted sort of way, the two species have entered into a kind of symbiotic relationship, with corporations mining cryptos for technology, and cryptos mining humanity for...well, humanity.

A single sphere glides up beside my window. It matches our pace, and within the bright light of its interior, I see something shift in my direction. *They're watching me,* I think. Identifying me. By now they're probably thinking, 'You!', as the man they'd never seen before once again disrupts their operation.

I roll the window down, give whoever's watching a grin, and then reach out and pluck the device from the sky. There's a tug on my arm as it attempts to fly away, but the singular device isn't powerful enough to escape my grasp.

"What are you doing?" Jacob shouts.

"You know something I don't?"

"It's not me who's upset!" he shouts, looking back at Lindo. "Get rid of it!"

I toss the ball to the pavement. It bounces twice and then, ten feet behind the van, it explodes.

Shrapnel slaps into the van's back doors, and shatters my side mirror. It wasn't a very powerful blast, but it could shred a person—or a tire—at close range.

They're flying proximity mines, I think, *or remotely controlled drone bombs operating in a swarm.* Hell, Aeron's resources might be so vast that every explosive drone could have its own operator.

Going off-road really is our only chance. The dust kicked up by the van might help obscure us. But how much time will that really buy us?

Minutes, I decide. *At the most.*

I swerve off the road and nearly tip us as we drop onto the hard packed earth. Dust billows up behind us, but I'm not sure it's doing more than hiding *them* from *me.*

"Look out!" Jacob shouts, looking in the passenger's side mirror.

Trusting the boy's warning, I swerve back up and onto the road just as a dozen spheres explode. Shrapnel peppers the vehicle's broad side, but the tires and windows remain intact. We leave the pavement and crash down onto the road's far side.

My unconscious passengers bounce and slide as we crash back down into the desert. Lindo rolls off his bed of laps and thumps to the floor. Unlike the others, he's fully aware of what's happening, and probably felt that fall, but there's nothing I can do for him right now.

The spheres come in waves, launching like projectiles from the swarm, which thins a little with each salvo. I swerve back and forth as fire and dust erupt all around. The van rocks with each series of explosions. They're still not trying to kill us, but by holding back, they're also increasing the odds that we might actually escape this shit.

A shift of tactics brings a steady string of individual mines spaced further apart. A direct hit dents the back door and spiderwebs the window. Another hit on the side tips us up onto two wheels for a moment.

"You ever fire a shotgun?" I shout to Jacob. Making the kid fight is just about the last thing I want to do, but desperate times...

He shakes his head and I'm a little relieved.

But it also means we're defenseless.

The direct hits increase in frequency, rocking the van back and forth. The side doors dent inward. Windows shatter, coating my passengers with a glittering sprinkle of glass. And then, a loud bang and hiss signifies our demise.

The tire drains fast, and our speed declines as I fight the wheel for control. I crank the wheel hard to the right and surge back onto the road, hoping the smoother surface will be more merciful on the tire.

And then we lose the second rear tire.

Clear of the dust, I watch what's left of the spheres close in. There're only a dozen left, but we're at their mercy. As they pull up on both sides of the van, I cringe. If the dual shockwaves don't kill us, the shrapnel probably will.

"Get down!" I shout, and I grip the lever to drop my seat back.

But then instead of exploding, the spheres launch ahead. I watch them go, as both rear tires shred and peel away. Sparks spray from the grinding wheel rims. Returning to the desert is no longer an option.

A hundred feet out, the spheres stop on a dime and reverse direction. I try to swerve back and forth, but the vehicle fights me. We're an easy target. Rather than plow into the mines at 40mph, I slam on the brakes.

With seconds until impact, I unbuckle Jacob, throw him to the floor on top of Lindo and then cover them both with my body.

I don't see the spheres collide with the van, but I feel it.

In my ears.

In my head.

And even more sharply in my back, as a wave of plastic and shattered glass burrows into my skin.

25

My back feels warm.

Then wet.

And then on fire.

My instinct is to let fly a string of curses, expressing my anger, frustration, and pain. But the scent of a very real fire stings my nostrils. The front end of the van looks like it was struck by a train. The first wisps of black smoke twist out from deep inside. Gasoline fumes burn my eyes. It won't be long before the vehicle looks like it was attacked by a dragon.

My back screams as I shove open the side door. Jacob, still beneath me and on top of Lindo, winces in pain along with me.

"You need to fight it, kid," I tell him. "I need your help."

My resolve seems to support his own. We're up and moving as the first flicker of orange reaches skyward from the engine.

Working together, both of us in different kinds of pain, we drag Lindo out of the van by his arms. He hits the ground hard, but it's better than baking alive. When he's ten feet from the van, eyes still propped open, we head back. Wini isn't next to the door, but I insist on taking her next. With Lindo out of the way, we drag her across the floor and out. Pain lances through my back as I ease her out and lay her beside Lindo. I feel a few shards of something pop out of my skin and fall to the ground. Fresh streams of warm blood flow from my back, already growing tacky as the Arizona heat wicks the moisture away.

By the time we're done moving the kids out, I'm feeling faint. Every part of me, mind and body, says to lie down and close my eyes. Submit to the pain. Embrace unconsciousness. But the van's engine is now an inferno, the flames rising four feet into the air, black acrid smoke billowing as though from a small volcano.

And I still smell gasoline. As bad as the blaze is, it has yet to reach the leaking fuel tank. When that happens, there will be no saving the two men left inside—Young and Godin.

Young goes first. I nearly pass out from the pain of hauling him out of the van. Jacob is helping, but the boy isn't large or strong. As I drag Young to safety, Jacob returns for Godin, tugging the man toward the door, but making little progress.

A whoosh and a sudden temperature rise drags my eyes toward the van's undercarriage. Flames slide beneath the vehicle.

"Jacob!"

Fueled by my fear for his life, Jacob screams and heaves. Godin topples from the van, landing atop Jacob, who's struggling to free himself. Vision tunneling, I grasp them both by the wrist, lean back, and drag them away.

The ball of flame from the igniting gas tank is hotter than it is explosive, and it hurts far less than the holes in my back, but it's enough to draw screams from both Jacob and me.

I lay on my back, face singed, blood oozing from my wounds to the dry earth. The blue sky above is cut in half by a pillar of black smoke, marking our position.

We're going to be easy to find.

How long until helicopter blades kick up a whirlwind of dust?

How long until the SUVs arrive and haul us away?

I'm about to tell Jacob to run and hide when a distortion in the sky above holds my attention. Am I seeing spots? As much as I want to sleep, I don't feel like I'm falling unconscious. The single point of light drops down until it's hovering five feet above me, its identity revealed.

A single sphere, glowing with power. I'm at the mercy of whoever is controlling it.

"Could have avoided most of this by talking to me," I tell the sphere. "Back in Santa Cruz."

"We both know that's not true." The feminine voice from the sphere crackles. "I've studied you, Mr. Delgado. You don't give up. You're resourceful. And you've got nothing to lose." The sphere shifts a little, and I can see that it's looking toward Wini. "Almost nothing."

She, whoever she is, is goading me into a response, trying to find a weakness. So I stay silent and try to keep any emotion aside from pain, out of my face.

"Another time and place, we could have been allies," she says. "Your ability to track down leads is a valuable asset. It brought you from complete ignorance of mankind's true reality to the forefront of the battle for it."

She's overestimating my detective skills. Without Lindo's manipulation, including information about the 37th parallel, Colorado City, the mystery texts, the UFO phenomena, and the photo of Isabella—which he has yet to explain—I would have never made it this far.

"The only side I'm on is the kids'. Let me take them, and you and Chimera can continue your corporate tit for tat."

"We both know you won't stop looking for Isabella Ramos, or the others, and while our tit-for-tat might at times descend into violence, we operate under the unified code of maintaining balance and secrecy. You, on the other hand, do not."

Denying it would be a waste of breath, not just because she's got a good grasp of my character, but because I can't imagine any decent human being sitting on this information and doing nothing about it. And that means Young, Godin, and Wini are just as screwed as me.

"There has to be some kind of deal we can make," I say. "Something that keeps these people alive."

The sphere is silent for a moment, and then offers a question. "Do you know what a chimera is?"

I feel like I should, like it has its roots in some kind of mythology I might have learned about during high school or college, but the word's meaning remains at the fringe of my mind.

"Here's the deal," the woman says. "You find out what that word means, follow the path it takes you on, and do what you think is right. You do that and your friends will keep breathing."

"And the kids?" I ask.

"I'm afraid they're non-negotiable, but if it helps you sleep, they'll be safer with us than they will be with your current company."

Wini once told me that every time we make a decision, an alternate dimension is born where duplicates of us made different choices. Right now, I think I could give birth to about a dozen potential universes, but I like to think that every version of me would use the same logic to come to the one and only choice that makes any kind of sense: fuck them all.

Whoever I'm talking to represents Aeron, whose stakes in all this are clear, and whose methods are deplorable. She'd like me to turn on Chimera, who's a bit more subtle and savvy, but in the end, ruled by the same guiding forces as Aeron. Both corporations know that the human race is being kidnapped, trafficked, and subjugated and neither is doing anything about it. If anything, they're part of the problem, vying for control of the same genetically modified children that the Others want to claim.

The realization that we are, in fact, being hunted by three different factions takes my eyes away from the sphere and turns them to the sky. Maybe it won't be a helicopter that shows up first? Maybe it will be a UFO?

We need to get the hell out of here, I think, but my body isn't cooperating. Even if it was, I couldn't carry everyone to safety.

"Do we have an agreement, Mr. Delgado?" the woman asks.

A loud bang and an explosion of shards draws my hands up over my face. But instead of impaling me, the shards fall beside me. I turn my head to find the device lying beside me, its futuristic insides revealed—and blinking.

Jacob steps over me, grasps what's left of the sphere and pitches it away. Halfway into its arc, it explodes.

Kid saved my life.

He stands over me, smiling, Wini's revolver in his hand. He rubs the gun-wielding arm with his free hand, recovering from the weapon's kick.

"Why are you so happy?" I grumble.

"I can feel your gratitude," he says. "And affection. I have never felt these things before."

"Then how do you know that's what they are?" I try to sit up, but fail with a grunt.

Jacob's smile disappears. "Am I wrong?"

"Just...help me up," I say, reaching a hand up.

He puts the gun on the ground and takes my hand. With his help, I rise into a sitting position, but the motion takes a toll.

"You're in pain," he says.

"Doesn't take an empath to see that," I say, wondering why he's still holding my hand.

"Don't be afraid," he says.

"Of...what?"

Jacob squeezes my hand. A wave of wrongness floods my body, all of my emotions triggering at once. I want to scream, and laugh, and cry, and cheer, all at the same time. The overload paralyzes me for a moment, and then all at once, it fades—along with the pain in my back.

"Did...did you just heal me?"

He shakes his head. "You're still injured. Still bleeding. I just numbed you to it, and the effect will wear off. But for now..." He lets go of my hand, steps back, and motions for me to stand, which I do with a normal amount of effort.

I can still feel the wounds and the now muddy blood sticking my shirt to my skin, but the pain is numbed. Good enough. But we're still at the mercy of whoever arrives first to collect us. I'm about to tell Jacob to leave and hide when an unfamiliar voice calls out, "Hey man, you okay?"

A young hippie—his actual age hidden by his prodigious beard—in loose fitting clothing, looks at me from behind rose-tinted glasses. He gives an awkward wave. "Saw the smoke. You guys need help or something?"

I'm not sure what 'or something' would be, but I'm grateful for the help.

I wave back. "Our engine exploded. People are hurt. We could use a ride to the nearest hospital."

The hippie's eyes widen and he gives a nod that resembles a walking chicken's. As he rushes to the back of his refurbished VW van, Jacob picks up Wini's revolver and puts it in my hand. I pop open the chamber and count five bullets. Then I spot Wini's purse on the ground beside her and realize counting bullets isn't an issue. Had the purse still been in the car when it burned, we'd likely all be dead—cut down by the boxes of ammo held in the bag.

Crunching moccasins on gravel announce the arrival of our long-haired savior. I slip the gun into my waist and cover it with my bloody shirt before he arrives.

The man makes a series of observations as he comes to a stop. "Whoa, man, you're fucked up. Holy shit, is that a cop? I don't know if I can have a cop in my ride, man. Whoa, cool eyes, dude."

"Thanks," Jacob says, and extends his hand. "I'm Jacob."

"Harley, like the motorcycle company." When they shake, Harley relaxes, and then stands straight with a puffed up chest. "Let's do this." He bends down, plucks one of the boys from the ground and hustles to the van. I give Jacob a smile and a nod, which he returns and says, "There it is again."

Then we're dragging, lifting, and laying down bodies like a bunch of battlefield medics, moving our unconscious crew into a third vehicle since fleeing the ranch.

When we close the rear doors, Jacob stiffens. "I feel someone. They're...far away, but really, really angry."

I take a step toward the driver's side door, preparing to comman- deer the van that Harley never turned off, when Jacob takes my hand. I feel his fear before I see it in his big eyes. "And I don't think they're human."

26

The hour-long drive is tense. While Harley is oblivious and grooving to a tune only he can hear, Jacob and I watch the skies. But there are no lights, no saucers, and no helicopters. I'm not sure if it's our unassuming transportation or the actions of unseen forces, but we seem to have escaped the desert without being followed. Jacob's sense of an inhuman anger persisted for a time, but then faded and disappeared. Whoever—or whatever—he sensed is gone.

It's been a while since I was in this part of the world. Vegas holds no interest for me, but a case brought me here three years ago. Another missing person. And while my hotel was smack dab in the middle of the world's most desperate city, I spent most of my time on its outskirts visiting establishments that, while legal in this part of the country, don't get a lot of help from law enforcement.

I pull off the road onto an unassuming driveway that winds around a barren hill and descends into a valley. The house at the drive's end is large and homey. A farmer's porch lined with rocking chairs wraps around three sides. While most visitors take comfort inside the home's many rooms, I spent more than a few nights on that porch, sipping sweet tea, watching the skies, and listening to the desert's creatures.

Although the sky is no longer a source of comfort, seeing the long porch and rocking chairs brings a smile to my face.

"This doesn't look like a hospital," Harley observes. Then his eyes widen. "Wait...is this what I think it is?"

"It is," I tell him. "But we're not here for that. And neither are you."

My tone leaves no wiggle room. He nods and sits back, eyeing my back, which has grown stiff. "How is that not hurting you?"

"It will," Jacob says. "Eventually. But I can help you with that, too."

"Thanks," I say, but I have no intention of keeping Jacob with me as I pursue this mess toward its conclusion. That will either be my death, or the undoing of a human trafficking ring run by non-human entities, supported by cult groups and probably Scientologists. It's also concealed by two secretive and dangerous corporations, and likely older than the United States. Maybe even older than modern humanity's rise from the stone age.

"So, what is this place?" Jacob asks, as I put the car in park beside an assortment of vehicles whose owners are about to have their nights ruined. "Some kind of business? They don't even have a sign."

"Something like that," I say and push open the door. "Both of you stay here. You spot anything, and I mean *anything* unusual, you lay on the horn."

"Uhh," Jacob says, the sound coming out as kind of an uncomfortable laugh. He's smiling wide, and I realize why when he says, "Everything about this place feels unusual." He flinches back and laughs. "And good."

Geez, I think, looking at the two-story farm house. *Note to self, when traveling with an empath in the midst of puberty, avoid brothels.* The sooner I shut down whatever's going on inside, the better. "Just...stay in the car. Try not to draw attention."

Jacob nods, still grinning, and he melts back into his seat.

Shaking my head, I slide out onto the pavement and take a breath of desert air scented with night-blooming jasmine. The smell transports me back to a simpler time, when I found myself here, searching for three missing young women. Amidst all my brooding, I found new friends—and three days later, the missing women, locked in a local man's basement.

My finger hovers over the doorbell ringer. The door here is always locked. Ringing is the only way in, and then the door will only open if you're recognized and expected. While they're definitely not expecting me, I'm not worried about being unwelcome. What I *am* worried about is the wave of shit pursuing me. Last thing I want is for it to crash down on more people who don't deserve to have their world undone. The van full of unconscious people, and my shredded back, urge my finger forward.

Inside, I hear gentle bells chime.

I look up at the camera mounted to the porch's ceiling and try to smile.

Three locks unlatch before the large wooden door swings inward. A smiling woman with long, braided white hair and blue eyes steps onto the porch, arms open wide to embrace me.

"Daniel!"

Sheba—that's not her real name—is dressed in tight jeans and a colorful flannel shirt. She looks more like a farmer than...what she is, but the garb matches her unassuming and caring personality.

Before she reaches me, I hold up my hands, stopping her short and preventing her from wrapping her arms around my tacky, blood-soaked back.

"What's wrong?" she says, eyes already scouring the parking lot for trouble.

"Need your help," I tell her.

"Anything," she says. "You know that."

After a gracious nod, I say, "Clear the building."

She scans the parking lot again, this time spotting the VW van. "This is serious?"

I make a slow turn so she can see my back. "Why I didn't let you hug me."

"Shit, Daniel. Okay. Hold on." She hustles back inside and a moment later, an alarm is blaring. Thumping footsteps resound from different parts of the building. Raised voices. Rising confusion. Several men and a few women in various states of redressing file out of the front door. Some are together, but most of them avoid each other's gaze, and mine. They're all here for the same thing, but that doesn't keep them from feeling shame.

I don't judge them for it. Being alone for five years, I understand the temptation, and that most people are here for the affection rather than pure sex. Sheba once told me that while sex is almost always part of the deal, most of her girls' time is spent talking and cuddling. The clients are sad, lonely people who, for some reason, can't make an intimate connection without paying for it. I don't subscribe to their methods, and I look forward to the day when Sheba decides to close shop, but we've all got our hang-ups. Some people's are just more obvious...and illegal in most of the country.

A man who couldn't be bothered to dress, is the last out the door, holding his clothing, front and back, to conceal himself. He all but dives into an open convertible before speeding off without dressing.

"What did you say to them?" I ask when Sheba returns.

"Only that a private investigator was here asking questions." With a chuckle, she steps toward the door, waving for me to follow.

"Actually," I say. "I could use a hand. Or a few."

She looks back to the VW van, which is now alone in the lot. "What's going on, Daniel? I want to help you, but I need to have some kind of idea of what we're getting involved in. Same way you did when I first approached you."

How do I answer this question? The truth isn't going to put anyone at ease and could put Sheba and her staff in trouble. But I can't lie to her, either. "It's not very different from what I helped you with, except ...it's children."

"You have kids in that van?"

I nod. "And people are still hunting them down. Violent people."

She looks at my back. "They did that to you?"

"Did worse to the kids, and if they find them... Look, if I tell you more than that—"

She holds up a hand, silencing me. "We'll take care of it." Then she moves in close and puts a hand on my chest. "How are you doing, aside from all this? It was two days ago, right?"

I can't help but smile. I haven't spoken to Sheba since the last time I stepped down from this porch, but she still remembers what we talked about. Other than Wini, she's the only person I ever opened up to about Kailyn. That she remembers the date is impressive.

"I'm okay," I tell her. "Better this time around."

"You have friends?"

"New ones," I say. "Maybe. I'm not sure."

She slides her hand from my chest to my hip. It's not seductive at all, but it still makes me uncomfortable. Her fingers push against the envelope tucked inside. "Still there."

I don't need to answer.

"Still closed."

She stares up into my eyes, unflinching. I'm not sure what to say. Any response is going to sting. "We should get them inside. And I could use a patch up before it starts to hurt."

Her disappointment over my inability to let go of the past shifts to astonishment. "It doesn't hurt now?" She looks at my ruddy-brown stained back and shakes her head. "I've got a few clean rooms. And mine. And the lounge. How many are we bringing in?"

"Three of them are conscious..."

Sheba reels back. "How many are unconscious?

"Eight. Four children, four adults. One of them is a sheriff..." I wait, part of me expecting a negative reaction.

"I'm not doing anything illegal," she says, throwing some sass into the statement.

"One of them is Wini."

Sass becomes concern. "Is she okay?"

"I think so, but..." I look to the night sky and see only stars. "We need to get them inside."

Sheba gives a quick nod and heads for the door.

"Sheba," I say, and she hangs back, "just...some of these kids might look a little off."

A single raised eyebrow rebukes me. "You remember where you are, right? 'A little off' pretty much describes our clientele. We'll treat them right." Then she's gone and barking directions at the people inside, who are no doubt slipping into a change of clothes and hiding the non-child friendly décor and accessories.

I realize that to the outside world, this is probably the last place a responsible adult should bring a handful of children rescued from slave-traders, but that's also why it's the perfect place to bring them. Unless we were tracked somehow, no one is going to sleuth their way here.

Twenty minutes later, everyone is inside. The kids are all on the first floor, which has a southwestern vibe, and with the removal of a few art pieces, is actually quite homey. Young, Wini, Godin, and

Lindo are laid out in bedrooms whose décor remains questionable. I'm actually looking forward to Wini waking up in a brothel. Should be fun.

But first, I need to bid our new friend a fond farewell, or attempt to.

"Sure you don't need any more help?" Harley asks, eyeing the brothel from the driver's seat of his van. He's a good guy, but I'm not about to risk another person's life, no matter how much he'd like to spend time getting to know Sheba's girls.

"You can help by not telling anyone about this." When I sense his disappointment, I double down. "The people looking for us are dangerous. If they connect you to us—"

"Then let me stay, man. I can help."

Damn it. I was hoping Harley's mellow personality and willingness to please would make him amenable to moving on, but he's intrigued by the mystery of what's happening...and the brothel.

Before I can think of another tactic to take, Jacob startles me. "Thanks for your help, Mr. Harley."

Our hippie rescuer starts to talk, but Jacob stops him short, placing a hand on the man's bare arm and saying, "You're *relieved* to be leaving because it's *dangerous* with us, and even *more dangerous* to talk about anything you've seen. It's okay to be *afraid*, but it will fade as long as you *don't think about us*. Thanks again for helping, and *drive safe*."

Jacob pulls his hand away and steps back.

Harley's eyes are wide and no longer looking at the brothel with any kind of interest. He offers a frantic nod and puts the van in reverse. "Right on, man. Just..." Harley looks me in the eyes, the fear in his reflecting my own. "...be careful."

We watch Harley drive away into the night. When he's out of sight, I ask, "Does putting emphasis on words help...you know...influence people's emotions?"

"That was for you," Jacob says. "So you'd know what I was doing."

I smile. "Thanks for the—"

A scream cuts me short.

It's Lindo, shrieking the way someone does when they're dying, slowly and horribly. When I charge through the house, crash into his room, and see him twisting on the floor, that's exactly what I think is happening.

27

"Hey!" I drop to my knees, the room's red shag carpet softening the impact. "Lindo!"

He's lost in a frenzy. Teeth gnash. Eyes rolled back. It's like a seizure, but his muscles aren't twitching. He's flailing, clutched by some nightmare he's trying to fight against.

"Wake up!" I shout, but there's no reaching the man.

When the door swings open, I'm surprised to find Jacob. This isn't the kind of scene a normal kid runs toward. But Jacob is far from normal. He's absorbing the mass of emotions roiling from Lindo. I doubt there's anywhere in the house he could hide from them.

Sheba arrives at the door, out of breath, too slow to stop Jacob. "Sorry, I—is he tripping?"

"He's lost," Jacob says. "Terrified."

A shiver runs through Jacob's body. He's dressed in jeans, a T-shirt, and a pair of sandals now, thanks to the collection of clothing Sheba keeps, just in case a client's gets soiled. It's all a little loose on him, but it looks far better than the coveralls the other kids are still wearing.

Jacob falls to his knees beside Lindo's torso while I hold the man's arms down. The kid is so preoccupied with the cascades of emotion that he's oblivious to the room around him, decorated with neon breasts, a rotating bed, and a couch shaped like a part of a woman that I doubt he's seen, or would recognize.

"Hold him still," Jacob says.

I manage to pin Lindo's right arm under my leg and hold his left against the floor. He goes nearly still when Sheba puts her weight on Lindo's legs and kicks the door shut behind her.

Jacob reaches out and clutches the sides of Lindo's head. "Ready?"

I give a nod and Lindo's body reacts to Jacob's emotional manipulation by arching up and nearly pulling free from my grasp.

"What are you doing to him?" Sheba looks about ready to leave her post and tackle Jacob.

"It's okay," I tell her, and after a silent argument with our eyes, she decides to trust me and doubles her efforts.

Jacob sighs.

He's in pain. Starting to shake. "He feels lost."

"Can you help him?" I ask.

"I...think..." Jacob's shaking starts to match Lindo's.

Seeing the kid suffer triggers a reaction with no thought. I reach out and put my hand on his, instantly becoming a conduit for the emotion flowing between the two. On one side I feel the calm Jacob is trying to project. On the other is Lindo's chaos.

My presence in the loop lets me experience it, but does nothing to change it. *Because I'm doing nothing to help,* I decide, and I focus my thoughts. Not on Jacob. Or on Lindo. Or on anything else that I've experienced over the past few days.

I think about Kailyn.

About the day we met.

I was already a police officer. New to the job. Stressed out by it. Not because it was dangerous, but because I was handing out speeding tickets when my ambitions were so much greater.

Kailyn had been going 66 in a 55. Took her five full minutes to pull over. She hadn't seen the lights or heard the siren's whoop because she was on the phone. When she did pull over, I approached her window expecting to find a teenager or a belligerent adult. Instead, I was greeted by a woman in tears that had nothing to do with being pulled over or getting a ticket.

"Ma'am," I said. "Are you okay?"

She exited her car, wrapped her arms around me, and wept into my chest. That was how we met, and despite her broken heart, I felt lighter. I felt whole. When we separated ten minutes later, she smiled up at me, thanked me, and apologized for speeding. She began to explain that her father had been in the hospital, that things had taken a turn for the worse. She was headed to see him when she received the call: her father had passed.

When she began to weep again, I pulled her against me again, infusing her with the calm that she somehow made me feel. We didn't speak. Not during the embrace. And not during the remainder of the day as I escorted her to the hospital, and then to her home. At the day's end, she parted with a final embrace and my card. The following day, she called and asked for my help. I was a stranger to the family, but I helped with the funeral prep, and stood beside Kailyn during the wake, infusing her with all the strength I could muster. Until her own death, we were together every day thereafter.

With my hand on Jacob's, I try to find the same calm and strength that healed Kailyn. I try to do the same for Jacob and the far less deserving Lindo.

Jacob stops shaking first and his own calm starts winning the battle. Thirty seconds later, Lindo's body falls still. When all sense of his mania has faded, Jacob draws his hands back.

He turns to me. The tears in his eyes match mine. "I didn't know that was possible."

I wipe my eyes. "Neither did I."

We both laugh, but Sheba isn't amused. "What the fuck was that?"

"I'm an empath," Jacob answers the same way a plumber might say, 'I'm a plumber.'

Sheba raises a single eyebrow. She's not buying it, but also doesn't press. She nods her head to Lindo and then directs her gaze toward me. "And him? If he's epileptic—"

"We can ask him," Jacob says. "He's waking up."

Lindo groans. His eyes blink open and shift from Jacob to me, and then to Sheba. He looks confused at her presence, but addresses me. "You can let go."

I release his arms and Sheba rolls off his legs. He pushes himself up, rubbing the wrist I had pinned beneath my knee. "Thank you," he says to Jacob. "I don't think I could have come out of that on my own."

Jacob gives a nod and a grin, a trace of pride in his otherworldly eyes.

Lindo turns his attention to me. "You handled yourself well. Thanks for saving me."

"Wasn't just you," I point out, not wanting him to think we're buddies.

"You could have left me behind," he points out, and he's right. Part of me thinks I should have.

"How much did you see?" I ask.

"Enough. But mostly ceilings and floors. I saw what they sent after you, though. They're new to me. Don't think I could have done any better."

"What happened to you?" I ask. It's just the first of many questions in my personal queue, and one I think he'll answer without a filter.

"The missile that missed us..." He glances at Sheba again.

"She's okay," I tell him. "I trust her."

He considers that for a moment and then says, "It was an EMP."

"EM-what?" Sheba asks. "And who was shooting missiles at you?"

"It was just one missile," I say, trying to sound like it was no big deal. "And it missed."

"Clearly," she says.

Lindo leans against the circular bed and seems to notice his surroundings for the first time. His face screws up in confusion, but then he just rolls with it like he's seen stranger before, and I'm fairly certain he has. "Actually, it did exactly what it was designed to. EMP. Electromagnetic pulse. The explosion kicked off a burst of electromagnetic energy powerful enough to knock out electronics."

"Including the stuff in your head," I add.

"And yours," he says, and I understand what he's really telling me: *I am no longer protected from the Others.*

"Why not the van?" I ask. "I thought those things took out vehicles, too."

"In theory, with some models, it's possible," Lindo says. "But most vehicle electronics are surrounded by lots of metal, which acts like a Faraday cage, hardening them from things like EMPs. The human head is far less protected."

"So you no longer have all that..." I swirl my finger around his head. "...stuff going on. No satellite feeds. No night vision. No one listening or watching?"

He touches his right eye. "Can't see out of this side at all."

"Good," I say. "About no one listening. Sorry about the eye."

He studies me for a moment and then says, "You might never be safe again."

"I'm neck deep already," I say, "and we both know I'm not giving up these kids. To you, or to Aeron. I think I've earned some answers."

He gives a nod. "Before the missile, I was telling you about the UFO crashes and reverse engi—"

"Not that," I say. "And not anything else our agreement allowed you to tell me. I want to know what you're *still* not supposed to tell me. What the people you work for have to know, but will do nothing about."

"That's..." Lindo turns to Sheba. "You should leave."

Sheba crosses her arms. "This is my house."

"Sheba," I say, apologetic. "It's for your own safety, and for everyone else who works here." It's twisted to anyone outside Sheba's world, but she really does think of her girls as family. She's protects them, even as she arranges for their bodies to be rented out. It's a strange dichotomy, but it gets her to her feet and the door.

She pauses in the doorway. "Is anyone else going to wake up shrieking?"

"No," I say, and then I offer a more honest, "I don't think so."

She rolls her eyes, leaves the room, and closes the door behind her.

"You, too," I say to Jacob.

"I know you're pretending to want me to leave." When I groan internally at the accuracy with which Jacob has dissected my emotions, he adds, "Sorry."

Accepting Jacob's place in this mess, I give Lindo my most intimidating stare and ask, "Where are they? Where are the Others?"

He pauses, perhaps rethinking whether or not he should answer, maybe for his own protection, maybe even for mine. Then he sighs and says, "Dulce, New Mexico."

28

Lindo stares at me, waiting for a reaction, like I'm a volcano that's a thousand years overdue for an eruption. "That supposed to mean something to me?"

"Dulce. Really? You've never heard of it?" He's so flabbergasted that I want to slap the look off his face. I glance at Jacob. The kid's as clueless as me.

"*I've* heard of it," says a muffled voice from behind the closed door. A slightly dazed-looking Wini enters. "You'd think this place would have thicker doors."

I'm on my feet and wrapping Wini in my arms before realizing the setting might make my affection a little awkward. "You okay?"

Wini returns my squeeze and pats my back. "Takes more than a little bitch with knock out spray to put me down." When we separate, she points her finger at Lindo. "In case you missed the context, you're the little bitch." Then to Jacob, who's smiling. "Excuse the language."

"I've never heard the language before, but I do enjoy the way it made everyone feel," Jacob says. He's been sheltered in a fundamentalist Mormon home. I wouldn't be surprised if 'gee willikers' was considered foul language. "It was an insult, I think, but it made all three of you happy."

Jacob stabs a finger at Lindo. "Little bitch!" When we all start laughing, he lights up. "You see!"

Wini and I take seats on the round bed. She takes in the room around us, her amusement lingering. She leans in close to me and whispers, "I woke up with a dildo in my face."

Part of me wants to apologize, but she's not actually complaining. This is a return to our status quo. A normalization after some truly weird shit, which we're about to be steeped in once more.

"Not the first time," I tell her, gently ribbing her with my elbow.

"What did you just say?" Jacob asks, eyes alight with curiosity.

"Never you mind," Wini says. "You might have an all access pass to how we feel, but not everything we say is for your ears."

"Because you don't trust me," Jacob surmises.

"Because you're a child," Wini says, "and you deserve to have a childhood for as long as you can. If that's even still possible."

Jacob leans back as he absorbs that.

"Dulce," Wini says, putting the conversation back on course. "It's a subterranean military base, right? A secret facility that might or might not be there. I think I read a novel where Nazis had set up shop there."

"Nazis?" Lindo sounds almost offended. "What? No. Who would believe that?"

Wini shrugs. "I remember it being a good read."

"And it's not a base. At least, not in the way we think of them."

"But you don't really know," Jacob says. "You're not confident."

"Well, no," Lindo says. "No one has been inside."

"No one?" Jacob asks.

"No one who's come back out," Lindo says. "It's where Chimera thinks they take the people they collect."

"Why are they collecting people?" I ask.

"Honestly, we're not sure, or the people who *are* sure haven't told me. But I think it's safe to say it has something to do with hybridization." He glances at Jacob, but the kid doesn't miss a thing.

"You think?" Jacob says, rolling his eyes.

"Chimera," I say. "What does it mean?" Something about this conversation is triggering the fragment of a memory.

"It's a merger of different creatures," Lindo says, and then the question seems to sink in. "Or..."

"Or cryptoterrestrials and humans," Jacob says. "Have you really never considered this before?"

"I've always thought it described the merger of human and nanotech. That's how it was described to me. It's been so long that I've stopped thinking about the name." He turns to Jacob. "Even when I found out about people like you."

"Thanks," Jacob says. "For calling me people. Harry never did."

"I'm sorry," Wini says. "But I think I've missed a lot. What's a crypto-whatchamacallit?"

Between Lindo, Jacob, and me, we paint a picture of the day's events that she missed. The EMP, the spheres, and more importantly, the information Lindo revealed about Chimera, the Others, and Aeron.

When we finish, she leans back on the bed. "Well...shit." After staring at the ceiling for a moment, she nudges me with her knee. "I suppose your grand plan is to rush in guns-a-blazing and rescue everyone?"

While I hadn't actually come up with a plan, her assessment isn't too far from how I feel. "Something a little more subtle than guns-a-blazing."

"Subtle or not, we're talking about an advanced non-human civilization, right?" She turns to Lindo. "Right?"

He nods.

"And they've been around how long?"

"Longer than homo sapiens," Lindo says. "Probably longer than our primate ancestors. We don't really know how long. There's no trace of them in the fossil record."

"And you think you can traipse into their subterranean not-really-a-base and waltz back out?" Wini breaks out a collection of verbs when she's really upset. She looks calm on the outside, relaxed even, but traipsing and waltzing reveal her discomfort. I'm sure Jacob senses her true emotions, but he remains silent.

"Of course not," I tell her, "but our options are limited."

"We could take the ones we've saved and not look back," she says.

Lindo puts the kibosh on that plan, saying, "I think you might have misjudged the value of Jacob and his siblings."

"Not really my siblings," Jacob says.

"Aeron isn't going to just stop looking for them." Lindo looks uncomfortable for a moment and then says, "And neither will Chimera. I'm not aware of any genetics program, but I've seen enough to know it's possible, and once they have the kids, probable. But they're not the worst of your problems. The Others deal in people. That's their business. They go to great lengths to collect very specific people, and if their arrangement with the Mormon church traces back to Joseph Smith, we've just interrupted a very long, very successful program."

"You think they'll come for the kids?" I ask.

"And I think they'll be pissed," Lindo says. "Yeah. But we can't just wage war against these things. Wini is right. We've known about the Others since World War II, in the sense that everyone agreed that phenomena like foo fighters were real. Technically we've known about the Others before, but never got past their mythological disguises. The narrative for us, especially after the crash in Roswell, became 'aliens from outer space.' And the U.S. government, along with certain corporations in the know, were happy to let people believe that, relegating the UFO phenomenon to society's fringe. If no one took aliens too seriously, they could deal with the problem on their own terms, which in 1979 meant direct confrontation.

"A mining operation in Dulce ran into trouble when their equipment started malfunctioning and day after day they made no progress. There was also a string of UFO sightings in the area. A team from the FBI, who were clueless about what they were up against, visited the site and disappeared. A second team went looking for them, and—"

"Poof," Wini says. "Idiots."

"Up until this point, the Others had concealed themselves masterfully. In 1961 the UFO abduction of Betty and Barney Hill became known worldwide. And it kicked off a string of UFO abductions, all with the same M.O.: abduction, experimentation, revelations about the Earth, about our species, about the cosmos, and memory loss."

Elbows on my knees, a more complete and frightening image starts to resolve. "You're saying all of those people were—"

"Part of a smokescreen," Lindo says. "Yeah. Aliens became the new narrative, and the Others put on a show that had people pointing to the sky, instead of the Earth, and made it all just ridiculous enough that truly brilliant minds wouldn't give the subject serious scrutiny. By 1979 everyone knew that when UFOs abducted people, they brought them home. Sometimes naked. Sometimes confused. Sometimes with no memory of what happened. But they always brought them back. So when people disappeared and never came back, no one blamed aliens. They weren't idiots, just ignorant. But that changed at Dulce.

"A platoon of Green Berets descended on the mine, catching the Others off guard. A mine worker who witnessed the events described killing two seven-foot-tall grays when they emerged from the caves near the mine. He was later saved by a Green Beret, who later died fighting the Others as they overwhelmed the soldiers using futuristic weapons. Sixty men died during the confrontation. While there were reports of Others being killed, there were no bodies. No traces left behind. Not even blood. And the sixty dead soldiers...they were recovered..."

Lindo is a lot of things that I'm not fond of, but he's not squeamish. But he looks fairly green as he speaks. "They were found naked, and fused together, their bodies arranged in an X."

It's a hard story to believe, but after the things I've seen and experienced, I can't think of a reason to not believe him. And if it's true, the Others' message was clear: come here and die horribly. It was a display of sobering power that has kept interactions with human beings limited to the occasional mishap.

"Isn't there still a town at Dulce?" Wini asks.

"Three thousand people," Lindo says. "And they have no idea who they're living above. The whole thing was covered up. The miner told his story, of course, but without evidence, he's just another crackpot. Even most UFOlogists write him off because—"

"Aliens come from space," Jacob says. "Their manipulation of humanity is impressive."

"Not the word I would use," I say. Jacob isn't really admiring the Others, and he's right, it *is* impressive...in the same way Hitler's conquest of Europe was impressive. It's a power left unchecked that someone needs to stand up against. That someone needs to stop. But how do you stop an ancient civilization that makes the Nazis look as threatening as diaper-wearing baby koalas?

After rubbing my temples, considering our options, and coming up with nothing solid, I ask Lindo, "What can we do? You have re-sources. Access to tech. There's no way Aeron, Chimera, *and* the U.S. government haven't been preparing for a time when confrontation becomes completely unavoidable. There has to be a way we can take the fight to them."

The lights flicker, drawing my eyes to the ceiling for a moment.

Lindo opens his mouth to reply and then stops. Turns his eyes to the lamp. Watching.

The light slowly dims, fading to a dull yellow before strobing and going dark.

"Looks like they're beating you to it," Lindo says from the darkness. "They're bringing the fight to us."

29

"How do you know it's them?" I ask.

Before Lindo can answer, brilliant orange light cuts through the edges of the room's drawn shade.

"I don't feel anything," Jacob says, his eyes on the ceiling, a stripe of orange light dividing his face. "There's no one up there."

"Another drone?" I ask.

"Trust me," Lindo says. "It's not a drone, and it's not Aeron. It's them."

"What do they want?" Wini asks.

Lindo answers by looking at Jacob. "All of them."

I draw Wini's pistol. "That's not going to happen. Hey..." I look Jacob in the eyes. "That's not going to happen."

The look in his eyes reveals he can feel my lack of confidence, but instead of calling me on it, he nods. Gun in hand, I head for the door. "Keep an eye on him," I say to Wini, and then to Jacob, "And you her." Then to Lindo, "You're with me."

After entering the hallway with Lindo, I ease the door shut and hear the door lock behind me.

"That's not going to help much." Lindo motions to the gun.

"They're living creatures, right? That means they can die."

"A platoon of Green Berets got their asses kicked by these guys. The U.S. government is afraid to pick a fight with them. You're just a dude with six shots."

I glance down at the revolver. It's far from my first choice of firearms, but it packs a punch. If my aim is true, I can drop six of these assholes. And I'm not trying to defeat them all or undo hundreds, if not thousands of years of subjugation and manipulation. I just want to open a window through which we can escape.

A nagging voice in the back of my mind asks, *and then what? If they found us here, they can find us anywhere.*

A vibration moves through the large house. Light fills the stairwell from the windows lining the front door.

"Remember, you're not protected from them, but you *can* resist them. Think of something important to you. Lock it in your head. Focus on it as much as you do moving, and no matter what happens, control your fear. They'll use that shit against you. Might even make you use that—" He motions to the gun. "—against me."

A shadow moves into view at the bottom of the stairs. The back of my neck tingles, hair standing on end. My heart thumps against my ribs.

"The hell is going on?" Sheba asks from the bottom step, a shotgun clutched in her arms.

So much for controlling my fear. I nearly shot my friend.

"Get the girls to the shelter," I say. Sheba has a bomb shelter built beneath the brothel. In addition to being a purveyor of questionable services, she's also something of a survivalist. It's capable of surviving a nuclear blast and keeping a dozen occupants alive for a good year.

"Already done," she says. "And they have the kids. Door's locked behind them. No one's getting in there. Now what kind of shit are we expecting?"

I'm about to tell her the truth, which I'm sure she won't believe until she sees it for herself, when the screams of two men billow from the room across the hall. Young and Godin are awake, and it doesn't sound pleasant.

Below, muffled by two floors and a metal bunker, the muffled sounds of six screaming children reach my ears. The house seems to rumble in response to their anguish. They're not waking up. They're being woken up.

Godin stumbles out of the room, stunned and clutching his head with one hand. Then he sees me, gun drawn and terrified, and holds his ground. "What's happening?"

"Safer if you go back in your room, man," Lindo says. "Keep the preach in there, too."

The house shakes as though being subjected to a localized unceasing earthquake. "Feels like the house is coming apart."

"It's just a distraction," Lindo says. "They're coming."

Sheba pumps the shotgun and points it at the front door. "Anyone coming is going to get a face full of buck shot!"

I start down the stairs, handgun raised at the door.

"Yo," Lindo says, fear drawing out old speech patterns. "I feel like this might be a good time to point out that they don't really need doors."

"The fuck you say?" Sheba says, glancing up the stairs.

"They can move through shit," Lindo says, and I notice he's watching the walls around us for the first time.

With widening eyes, I shift my view away from the door and to the lounge's exterior wall. I nearly scream when I see a pair of black eyes peering at me from the wall. The dreamlike image fades out of sight, leaving me bewildered.

"Daniel," Sheba says, her voice a forced calm. She's staring at the same patch of wall as me, her shotgun still pointed at the door. "Was that..."

"An alien," I finish for her, redirecting my aim toward the wall where a pair of neon bra-clad breasts is hung. I'm about to warn her to guard her thoughts when a flash of movement to my right spins me around, too slow.

I catch sight of a large, featureless gray face and black eyes before I'm thrown back. I don't feel any physical contact until I hit the far wall and crash down atop a card table, which gives way under my weight and dumps me onto the floor.

Two shotgun blasts rock the lounge, but each is followed by a "Shit!" and then a shout of pain. When I recover enough to look, I find Sheba on the floor, clutching her head and grinding her teeth, the shotgun dropped beside her.

Above me, I hear thumping and a grunt.

"Lindo!"

No reply.

My body says to stay down, but I push against the pain, recover my dropped handgun, and take two steps toward the stairs.

That's when they get in my head, picking up right where they left off at the ranch.

What's in the envelope?

The question with no answer cripples me.

While every part of me is screaming, *Get up those stairs,* I find myself stumbling back in a kind of stupor, like I'm just a passenger in my own body. *They're doing it,* I think. They're taking control.

Not *taking* control. *In* control.

Fight it, I think, but that's all it is. A thought.

Don't fight it.

It's not worth the trouble.

Wini will be safe.

The others, too.

They're just here for...one?

A moment of confusion washes over me and I wonder where the others are.

These aren't my thoughts, I realize. *They're looking for* all *the kids, but can only find Jacob.*

He has no name, the voice in my thoughts that are not my thoughts says. *Where are they?*

I try to clear my mind. The answer would be so easy to give.

You can end this.

Protect your friends.

That's all you want.

That's everything.

You can't lose anyone else.

Kailyn.

The single-word thought is my own. It stumbles the mental barrage.

You lost her.

She was taken. I couldn't stop it. But I can stop you.

A vibration sifts through my mind and body. I drop to my knees, queasy and unfocused. *You have no choice! The others are dying.*

You are the Others, I think. Rage fills every part of me, pushing out a portion of their control. It's not enough to free me from their grasp or even put up a true fight. But I do manage to move an arm. Muscles twitch as my fingers slide inside my pants pocket and slip back out clutching the envelope. My weakness.

Put it down.

A spasm moves through my arm, but my fingers remain clamped down.

Fuck off.

My body shakes as I reach out with both hands and tear the envelope open.

Stop.

You don't want to know.

The answer will tear you apart.

You won't be able to recover.

Don't, please God, don't do it.

I'm about to tell my mind's invaders to sit and spin when I realize that while the Others might be controlling my body, the thoughts fighting me now are my own.

I'm sorry, I think, willing Kailyn to hear my thoughts. *For being a coward. For not being strong enough to look.*

I reach into the envelope and pull a single, trembling sheet of paper from inside. It's a photo. A print. The white on black image is strange to look at, but the shape is unmistakable.

A baby.

Kailyn was pregnant when she died. She hadn't suffered from any of the usual warning signs and her period had been irregular since puberty thanks to polycystic ovary syndrome. Missing a few months usually meant an incredibly painful period, not pregnancy. In fact, we'd been told she couldn't conceive, so even with warning signs, pregnancy wouldn't have been on our radar.

It was two days of throwing up, and the baby bump that gave it away. And then an over-the-counter pregnancy test. But false positives happen, so she went in for a test. I should have gone. Should have been with her. But I'd been close to cracking a case and went in to work instead. Fucking idiot.

I knew she had the results when she died, and that this envelope contained them, but I was too afraid to look. And now that I have, I finally have no doubt.

I was a father.

I am *a father.*

Text lining the image's bottom draws my attention. The first line reads: Age—18 weeks (est). My eyes shift to the next line: Due date—November 28 (est).

A thanksgiving baby.

My blurring vision focuses on the last two words: Gender—Male.

A son...

I had a son.

A name comes to mind. Kailyn's top pick for a son. "Nathaniel."

My heart shatters.

I'm undone, wilting on the floor, wracked by sobs. I'm not sure how long I'm there before I start thinking clearly again, but as years of raw, contained emotion overwhelms me I become aware of a different sensation.

I'm free.

30

While the voices hold no sway over me now, fended off by the shedding of my weakness, I remain locked down by emotion. My limbs shake as I attempt to pull myself up. Seeing past the tears is all but impossible. I can't stop seeing that small eighteen-week-old body. Can't stop wondering what five-year-old Nathaniel would have looked like. What his hair would have smelled like. If he'd have had his mother's eyes.

My mind's eye tortures me with visions of a child not given the chance to exist. I see him at different ages, toddling toward me, chubby arms reaching, on the ground with a skinned knee, wrestling on the bed, getting angry when I tease him about girls.

God, he would have been beautiful.

A scream cuts through my sorrow, and my mind struggles to identify it. It was high-pitched, like a girl, but not. If the kids are in the bunker below, somehow protected from the Other's mental reach, that leaves...

I look to the ceiling, wiping my eyes.

Jacob.

Clutching the revolver, I shove myself up. The pain over what was lost five years ago is subdued by concern for what might be lost today.

Loud thumps from the second-floor fuel my sprint up the stairs. Lindo attempts to kick the door again, but fails to break through.

Wini shouts in horror from the far side, and it takes all of my experience and self-control to not simply join Lindo's frantic assault. The doors and locks are all solid. I've kicked in my fair share of doors and know when brute force will work, and when a little forethought can speed things up. The lock is a simple push button number, but modified with a deadbolt to help Sheba's clients feel more secure. But that doesn't mean there isn't a simple way around the lock. A toothpick or paperclip would do the trick, but I've got neither. While Lindo takes another kick, I glance at the neighboring doors and find what I need above the frame of the door beside me.

The door cracks under Lindo's next kick, but it doesn't break. He steps back for another kick, but his legs seem to lose contact with his nervous system. He drops to the floor, clutching his head. "They're in my head, man!"

I swipe the 'key'—just a thin metal rod—and hurry for Wini's door as glass shatters on the far side. Orange light glows around the frame as I push the key inside and miss the lock mechanism. It takes three tries before my aim is true and the lock *thunks* open.

I shove against the door, opening it a crack. But that's as far as I make it before a hot burst of air slams against the far side.

Glass shatters.

Wini shouts again, this time angry. She's saying something. I can't make it out, but it sounds desperate.

I shove harder, screaming from the effort. The door opens just six inches, which is enough for me to see the bright orange light flooding the room, and a swirl of debris kicked up by whatever force is holding the door shut.

If not for the events of the past few days, and what Lindo has told me, I'd think the situation hopeless. But the Others aren't gods. They're not even the planet's dominant species. They're fallible, and with enough effort, or thought, they can be defeated. But there's nothing I can do about this door.

Not alone.

The door shudders as it's struck by someone beside me.

"I'm with you!" Young says, now pushing alongside me. He's grunting in pain, probably under mental assault, but resisting it.

The door inches open.

"Wini!" I shout into the swirling chaos. "What's happening?"

"They're taking him!" she screams back, desperate.

The door shakes again as Godin slams into it, adding his muscle and weight to the effort. This time, the door doesn't just open further, it springs open, dropping the three of us to the shag carpet inside the room.

The window is shattered. Large shards of glass cover the floor while smaller pieces swirl through the air. The twinkling debris, cast in orange, is both beautiful and dangerous.

Wini is bleeding from several cuts, but I barely notice the wounds or the blood dripping from them. She's standing by the open window, one foot propped on the sill, her arms and aging muscles twitching from the effort of holding Jacob.

He's halfway out the window, being tugged into the air by an invisible force—a UFO abductee cliché that pop culture, perhaps influenced by outside sources, made sure no one took seriously. Lights in the sky. Levitation. Immaterial beings. The stuff of X-Files and wild-eyed experts proclaiming that the aliens are real. A joke.

But this is no joke, and it's very fucking real.

The hot air buffets me as I crawl forward, hands and knees poked by glass. I reach the window just as Wini loses her grip. I dive forward, clasping onto Jacob's wrists as he's yanked out the window. Young and Godin wrap themselves around me, anchoring me, but they're not strong enough to pull us back inside.

"I got you!" I shout, looking up at Jacob's frightened eyes, and then beyond them.

An honest-to-goodness flying saucer hovers above the house. It's a hundred feet across, metallic, and blazing with orange light from its core. Beyond that, it's featureless. A simple machine, designed to collect people, not navigate the stars or move between dimensions.

Jacob's fear morphs into calm resolution as he looks me in the eyes. It's so sudden and powerful that I'm unnerved by it. He should be terrified. Should be screaming. Instead, he says, "You're different."

"I'm going to pull you in!" I shout.

He shakes his head, fate accepted. "You can't. But you don't need to."

"The hell are you talking about?" I pull with all my strength, muscles pinging in my biceps, but the kid doesn't budge. Eventually, my body will lose this tug of war.

"You'll find me," he says. "They can't stop you now."

"They *are* stopping me now," I shout back.

"They're just delaying the inevitable."

I'm about to attempt another hard pull when a surge of confidence flows into me. "What are you doing?"

"Saving you," he says. "You can't save us if you fall from the window."

I'm not sure how he thinks he's saving me, but I suddenly have no doubts about my ability to track down the Others and rain down justice. "I'll find you," I shout.

"I know," he says.

And then, instead of having Jacob ripped from my grasp...I let go.

Some squelched part of me thinks, *What did you do?!* But my confidence remains, even as Jacob is pulled up into the air. There's no fear in his eyes. In the moment before he becomes a distorted silhouette, he gives me a smile. Then he seems to melt into the light.

The light dulls, but doesn't fade.

Gravity tugs me down. I fold forward and slap against the side of the house, hanging upside down for a moment before Young and Godin manage to reel me back in.

We fall to the floor, the fight over.

Wini looks down at me from the bed, blood framing her face from gashes on both sides. "I'm sorry. I couldn't stop them."

"None of us could," I tell her, "but we're going to."

"How the hell are you—" Godin's reasonable statement of abject disbelief is cut short by a scream from downstairs. It's followed by two shotgun blasts and the sound of thumping feet.

"They're still here," Lindo shouts from the hall, still on the floor, still clutching his head.

The Others are digging through his mind, looking for answers. And if they don't find them with Lindo, who must be known to them, they'll start worming their way through everyone else's minds until they find the answer: that the rest of the kids they're looking for are directly beneath us, shielded by a bunker with metal walls that's acting like a Faraday cage against the Others' telepathy.

The sound of small feet thumping on the floor below us sends a chill down my back. When Sheba screams, I spring into action. My body protests, but I'm fueled by anger and a newfound confidence that these assholes can be defeated.

I'm halfway down the stairs before I realize I've forgotten the revolver. I'm at the bottom by the time I realize I don't care.

Sheba, lying on the floor, her makeup unable to hide her pale complexion, points to a Japanese themed lounge across the foyer. "In there!"

I turn to the lounge, which leads to a kitchen, and the basement door where the entrance to the bunker can be found. If the Others are running around the house, they've given up on searching minds and are scouring the home instead, getting their hands dirty.

They're not the only ones, I think, and I storm into the lounge.

The room is empty, but the door at the back is still moving.

I run for the door, dodging the room's furniture as best I can in the orange light provided by the UFO. Clanging pots reveal the crypto-terrestrial's position. It's still in the kitchen, still seeking out the kids I have yet to fail. Wood cracks as I slam into the door, peeling hinges from the wall. I spill into the kitchen tumbling to the hard floor, grasping a counter, and heaving myself back up.

Light dances around the room, beaming through the long window that normally looks out on the Nevada desert, and reflecting off the hanging pots and pans.

In the ethereal glow, I see it.

And it sees me.

The crypto stands just five feet tall. Its body is thin and clothed in a form-fitting matte gray jumpsuit. It looks almost frail, but the humanoid body of a thin preteen combined with the large, egg-shaped head and sinister, unblinking, black, avocado-sized eyes is unnerving. My instincts are screaming at me to get away, to run away from the monster, and I'm pretty sure some of that fear is genetic, like most people's natural fear of spiders or snakes. History has taught us which creatures to avoid, and though I've never seen a cryptoterrestrial, mind and body shout out together: *Get the fuck out!*

But my soul, and whatever Jacob infused me with, protests.

I'm not backing down.

"Not today, you son-of-a-bitch." I take a step forward, fists clenched, and feel a gentle slapping against my face as the thing levels a menacing glare at me.

It's trying to get in my head.

And it's failing.

"Like I said," I say, stomping forward. "Not to-fucking-day."

There's a moment of surprise in the thing's jet black eyes, and then my right hook collides with the side of its head. There's a satisfying crunch that sends the thing sprawling left, directly into the path of my left swing. I connect hard again. The creature topples back, but I catch it by its soda-can thick neck, and keep it upright.

I look into the black eyes and say, "I'm coming for every last one of you."

My fist cocks back.

"Wait! Stop!" Some part of my mind registers Lindo's warning, but the rest of it thinks, 'Screw off,' and then I throw the punch, putting every ounce of anger, sadness, and retribution burning inside me behind it.

My knuckles connect with the creature's smooth skin, the skeletal structure beneath, and then with a wet slurp, the brain matter contained within.

Realizing what happened, I reel back and let the body fall to the floor, a hole punched into the front of its big head, just above and between its eyes, which look no more dead or alive than before.

I punched through its skull?!

The orange light blinks out.

The dull rumbling falls silent.

I can't see it, but I know the UFO is gone, chased away by the death of one of their own.

Good, I think, and then the lights come back on, revealing Lindo, who's now standing beside me, staring down at the dead cryptoterrestrial.

"Holy shit... Damnit..." He redirects his wide eyes to me and says, "You just started a war."

31

"Wasn't me who started it." Something sluices off my fist and slaps against the floor. My knuckles are coated in what can best be described as purple, crystalized gel. If it wasn't wet and jiggly, it would resemble the crystals of an amethyst geode. A flick of the wrist frees most of it from my skin. The chunky goo strikes a cabinet door and rolls down the vertical surface. It reminds me of one of those kid's toys, the little sticking octopuses that climb down walls.

What it doesn't remind me of is brain matter. I don't care that the Others aren't human. If they evolved on Earth alongside the billions of other species that have come and gone on this planet, some of which I'm assuming they evolved from, then they should have brains.

I crouch by the body, looking into the hole created by my hand. Purple gel and a shard of bone fill the cavity. My fingers push against the flesh around the wound. It's still firm, supported by a skull, but there's a little give to it, like the punch cracked the skull all the way around.

I reach into the cavity.

"Don't do that," Lindo says. He's uncomfortable with this. If I knew everything he does, maybe I would be, too, but I don't, so fuck it.

All I care about is recovering the children I've promised to recover: Isabella, whose role in all this now seems insignificant but still a guiding force, and Jacob, who I've only just met, but I feel connected to. Maybe because he represents the son I never got to have, or because he's manipulated my emotions by projecting his own into me.

Of course, protecting them—really protecting them—means putting a stop to the people and non-people who pose a threat.

I pinch down on the curved section of skull and pull it free.

"Seriously, dude," Lindo says. "Not a good idea. Killing one of them is bad enough. Desecrating one—"

"Desecrating?" I shoot Lindo a gaze that closes his mouth. "How many people have they experimented on? Hundreds? Thousands? Millions? You don't know the answer. You don't *want* to know the answer. Because as soon as you see the truth and then take a good look at yourself, you're going to realize what side you've been fighting for all this time."

I lift the three-inch, triangular bone fragment, give it a quick look-see, and then whack it against a countertop. The fragment shatters, sending chunks, grit and powder falling to the floor.

"Dude..."

"Have you not seen one of these before?"

"Not dead. Tech is the only thing I've ever been able to collect."

"It's not dead," I say.

Lindo looks horrified by my statement, like the crypto might suddenly lunge up and strangle him.

"Help me put it on the island." I grasp the body beneath its arms. When Lindo hesitates, I fill him in. "It's not dead, because it was never alive."

Lindo's expression makes a slow journey from horror, to confusion, to understanding. "These..."

"Aren't the Others," I say.

"Then what are they?"

"Let's find out," I say, and I motion to the thing's feet.

Lindo picks up the feet and we hoist the small body atop the stainless-steel island.

"Oh my God." A wild-eyed Sheba stands in the doorway, shotgun in hand.

"They're gone," I tell her.

She points the shotgun toward the dead creature. "Not all of them."

"Dead," I tell her, not sharing my assessment that it was never alive. "Sheeb, pumping buckshot into this thing isn't going to do any good."

"Might make me feel better." She lowers the shotgun and then motions to the basement door. "Can they come up?"

"Better if we take care of this first," I tell her, and then add, "Once we do, you should send the girls home...those that have homes...but the kids need to stay in the bunker." I turn to Lindo. "They couldn't find them. You know why?"

A slow headshake reveals where his longwinded thought process is leading. "Best guess is that the metal shielded them from whatever frequency is used when they...you know." He taps his head.

"Talk in your head," Sheba says. "That was a new kind of horrible, by the way. I should hate you for bringing this shit down on me and mine..." She heads for the basement door, patting me on the shoulder as she passes. "...but I'm really just glad you're all right." She stops. The pat becomes a squeeze. "No one is better at finding people than you. You'll find him." She pats again and heads down the basement stairs.

"Nice lady," Lindo says. "You come here much?"

When I look at him, he's smiling. "Once. On the clock."

His smile fades when I pluck a butcher's knife from a drawer and test the blade on my thumb.

"Holy shit." Godin stumbles up beside me, gripping the countertop. He's justifiably overwhelmed and a bit weak in the knees. "You got one of them?"

"Lord Jesus, protect us," Young says upon seeing the body. He steps further into the kitchen, trailed by Wini, who has somehow managed to clean the blood from her face and stop the bleeding. Her wounds looked worse than they are, but seeing her injured erases any hesitation I felt about what's going to happen here.

"I'm fine," she says, noting my attention. "Takes more than an alien invasion to put me down."

I'm not really satisfied by her reassurance, but I don't think time is on our side. If not for whatever Jacob did to my psyche, boosting my confidence and steeling my nerves, I'm pretty sure my response would be closer to Young's. But she's alive, and for now that's going to have to be enough. "Anyone uncomfortable with peeling this S.O.B. apart and finding out what makes it tick should leave now."

"You're *dissecting* it?" Young asks, looking like he might take me up on the offer to leave.

"Disassembling it," I say. "Dissection is what you do to previously living creatures. I don't think this thing was ever alive." I motion to the amethyst geode hole in its head.

Young looks ready puke, but Godin sees it. "No brain."

I place the blade against the seam around its neck, preparing to cut away the skin-tight garment. I push the blade forward, expecting a tug as the blade catches on the fabric. But the metal just glides over the seam. I touch my fingers to the neck I'd grasped just minutes ago. This time around, I'm more gentle, sliding my fingertips from the neck to the garment. There's a subtle shift in texture, but it's seamless. "It's not wearing clothing."

The revelation supports my working theory, so I have no qualms about what I do next. Lifting the knife, I stab it into the thing's gut, just below the ribs. My audience reacts with revolt, flinching, squirming, and groaning. I'm beyond caring about whether or not this is sanitary, sacrilegious, or some kind of inter-species war crime.

I want answers, and I want them now.

I cut around the whole abdomen, carving a circle. As the sharp knife slips through the body, I feel no resistance aside from the subtle separation of skin.

When I draw the blade back, Godin says, "I'll do it." He finishes pulling on a pair of bright yellow rubber gloves. "I understand the way you're thinking, but you and I both know there's a right and wrong way to do this. Unless you were lying about who you used to be."

My impatience nearly pushes me to ignore the sheriff, but then I look at my purple stained hands and remember the number of autopsies I've attended. They were nothing like the butcher job I'm doing here. They were methodical. Scientific. And clean.

While the others wait in silence, I head for the sink and scrub my hands. It takes three washes to clear the purple from my hands. The stain that remains will likely stay with me until my skin cells shed away. Still drying my hands, I return to the island and give Godin a nod.

The sheriff slips delicate fingers beneath inhuman skin, pinches, and then slowly lifts. The cleaved epidermis slurps away like a blanched tomato skin. There's no layer of fat or muscle clinging to it. Godin holds the wiggling sheet up and then lays it in the sink.

The exposed innards are what I expected—crystalized purple goo. "Can we all agree that if there aren't organs hiding in there, that this thing isn't a living being?"

No one answers, but I see some subtle nods. "Go ahead," I say to Godin.

The sheriff slides his fingers into the purple, probing. He lifts them out and slips them back in, repeating the process several times. When he encounters no resistance on his fifth pass, he dips his hands further in and scoops out a mound of purple sludge that he deposits on the counter beside the body. Inside is just more purple.

No organs.

"Non-living entities," Lindo whispers, sounding more fascinated than horrified.

"You can call it what it is," I say. "We all know what robots are."

And I know what that means, that the Grays themselves—the beings we believed to be our enemies—are really just autonomous pawns. Part of the extraterrestrial narrative meant to turn our eyes and thoughts toward the stars. Because while they're generally humanoid, they're just different enough that no one would even consider their origins to be local. In that way, they've been perfectly designed.

I lift the creature's arm in my hands. "The bones are closer to ceramic." I prove the point by slamming the forearm against the counter's edge, using moderate force. It breaks and folds at a ninety-degree angle.

Young flinches at the break, and looks ready to run, but hangs in there. "You're sure?"

"Pretty sure," I say, and then I reach a hand out to Godin. "May I?"

Godin peels the too-tight glove from his right hand and holds it out to me. I slip the glove over my hand and move to the thing's head.

"Oh God," Young says, stumbling back to lean against the kitchen counter, a hand to his mouth.

I glance at Wini. She's the only one here whose opinion really matters to me. If this is crossing a line, she'll let me know.

"Do what needs doing," she says. "And we'll get drunk later to forget it."

We share a smile and then I slip my hand through the hole. Purple gunk wells up on the sides of my hand as I push down deep. The top of the head is empty. Just full of more goo. For a moment, I wonder if the sludge itself contains some kind of nano-tech, but when I shift my hand down, just behind the black eyes, I feel something solid.

It's a sphere, but it's not perfect. There are thin strands of something protruding from its surface, like firm tendrils.

And they're feeling me back.

32

I wrap my fingers around the sphere, but I'm not sure it's necessary. The thing is holding on to me just as tightly.

I feel like I'm doing a decent job hiding my concern, but Wini sees through the façade. "What's wrong?"

"Just..." I glance around the kitchen. "Get a pot with a lid."

While Wini hustles away to fulfil my request, I turn to Lindo. "You know what this is?"

He shakes his head, looking both frightened by the possibilities, and excited by them. Too excited.

So I direct my next request to Godin. "Find a thin blade. Like a fillet knife. Or scissors."

"What are you going to do?" Lindo asks, the horror in his voice fueled more by what I might do to our discovery than what it might do to me, or everyone else.

The little tendrils poke against the rubber gloves, twitching around. Impatient. Hungry. "Hurry!"

Wini returns with a chrome pot and lid.

"There," I say to her, dipping my head toward the countertop beside the body's head. "Be ready with the cover.

She places the pot down and holds the cover up, a Spartan warrior peeking over the top of her shield, waiting for action.

Godin returns wielding a pair of heavy-duty kitchen scissors that look tough enough to cut wire.

"Be ready to cut," I tell him.

"Cut what?"

"Wish I knew. On three."

Curiosity pulls Young from the kitchen's far side. He approaches with the same caution one might a case of old dynamite.

"One," I say, "Two..." I take a breath. Let it out. "Three."

My fist moves an inch and then stops. Panic tingles up my arms. Is it holding me in place? I twist my hand and feel no resistance. It's not the sphere holding me tight, it's the gelatinous insides creating a suction around my wrist. I could let go and draw my hand out of the glove, but I want to see this thing. Want to know what we're up against. Because if this is just a piece of tech, something I can wrap my head around, then the overwhelming strangeness of all this will be dulled.

I pull again, this time harder. My hand draws the sphere up through the cranium as the thing inside continues to poke and prod.

A twist and turn of my arm lets me make a bit more progress, but the further I pull the tighter things get. I start tugging in pulses, pulling a little bit further each time, but getting sucked back in a bit.

"Talk about a mind fuck," Wini murmurs. I glance at her as my arm continues its up and down motion. She cracks a slight smile and it's enough to cut through my tension. When I chuckle at her comment and the absurdity of what I'm doing, the tension in the room breaks, my laugh becoming contagious. Just as Young bursts out laughing, the flood gates of his pent up emotions shattering, my hand slurps free of the skull.

Feeling the thing in my hand was bad enough, but seeing it activates some primitive fight-or-flight part of my mind. Instead of holding my hand out for Godin to cut the thing free, I smash the sphere down on the countertop with a shout of fear. I can't see if it took any damage, but the five inch tendrils gripping me, squirm and flail and poke.

"Oh shit!" Lindo says, "Don't let it touch your skin!"

I spot one of the tendrils stretching toward the glove's end, just an inch from my forearm. I slam it on the countertop two more times, but I'm pretty sure, I'm hurting myself more than the sphere.

"Hold it out!" Godin shouts, and I remember the plan. Restraining my panic, I hold my hand out over the pot.

Using his gloved hand, Godin slips the scissor blade beneath one of the tendrils holding on to my wrist and cuts. It snips apart easily enough, but when the blade slides away, the tendril seems to melt back together.

"It's nano-tech," Lindo says. "If it touches you..."

He doesn't need to finish the warning. I remember how easy it was for him to slip his own nano-tech inside my head. If it touches me, it will get inside me, and who the hell knows what would happen then. It could kill me, make me an automaton like the Gray, make me an acolyte like Harry and his family, or maybe just drive me insane. The only thing I know for sure is that it won't be good.

Some of the tendrils latched on to my wrist shrink. Its grip is loosened, but the strand reaching out for my bare arm begins to grow.

"Shit!" I thrust my hand in the pot and slam it back and forth, filling the air with a chaotic gong to couple my string of expletives. I open my hand and let my fingers flop around. The sphere's grip doesn't loosen, but the glove's does. After a few more thrashes, my hand slips back. The tendrils tighten, but it's too late.

"Get ready!" I shout to Wini, and then I send a spasm down my arm that shakes the glove free. It falls into the pot with a thud. Wini is fast with the lid, but not quite fast enough. The sphere clangs against the cover, its little black limbs putting up a fight. Young throws his weight on the lid, shoving it down and severing several of the limbs, which fall to the counter.

"I got it!" Young shouts, wrapping his big hands around both pot and lid.

The thing inside batters the metal cover. Young won't be able to hold it for long. I hurry across the kitchen. "Over here!"

When I yank the microwave open, Young shoves the pot inside.

"What are you doing?" Lindo says.

"Killing the fucking thing." It's not really alive, but the way it moves and acts sure as hell makes it feel like a living thing. And subjecting it to a blast of microwaves will feel satisfying.

Lindo doesn't see it that way. "I could learn so much from it!" When that doesn't stop me from slamming the microwave door shut, he adds, "It could change the world. For the better."

"From what I've seen, the nano-tech you already have only serves one purpose." I punch in ten minutes on the microwave timer. "Yours."

"This is a mistake," Lindo says, but even he knows there's no stopping me.

The pot clangs and bounces inside the microwave. Black tendrils ooze out from under the loosened cover, but there's no room for the sphere to free itself. I push the *Start* button and step back.

As soon as the interior light turns on and the glass plate begins to rotate, a storm of bright blue sparks dances across the pot's surface, and then it hits the tendrils. The streams of nanites spasm and turn to powder.

Not powder, I realize, *just disabled nanites.*

The pot falls still.

The sparks build in intensity. It's going to explode. With no way to know if the nanites are permanently destroyed, or if the sphere is completely disabled, the dust becoming airborne would be a very bad idea. Moving against my instinct to run, I dive for the microwave and hit the *Stop* button.

The microwave and the blue storm within it go dark.

I listen for movement within, but hear nothing. Behind me, Godin starts rummaging through drawers and cabinets. It takes him just a moment to discover a junk drawer with duct tape. He peels off a long strip and then seals the microwave's top seam. He goes to work on the rest, sealing all four seams with an overkill amount of tape, but no one complains. He then locates the microwave's vent and seals it with even more tape. When he's done, the oven looks like it's been wrapped in an alien cocoon.

I stumble back from the microwave, giving my heart a chance to pump a little slower.

"I'm going to be honest," Godin says, "This was the worst god-damn day of my life."

"You're free to go," I tell him. "But I hope you don't." His quick thinking and calm responses kept me from becoming a host to some cryptoterrestrial tech. Well, more of it, anyway.

"I could call in help," he suggests.

"We both know you're more likely to be put on psychiatric leave than have the cavalry come running to help us fight UFOs and aliens. And in the time it takes to convince them..." I shake my head. "We can't wait."

"Okay then," he says, "What's the plan?"

I turn to Wini. "You pick up the revolver?"

She reaches behind her back and retrieves the gun. "You know I wouldn't leave Susie-Q behind."

I take the weapon from her. "You named it?"

"If Jon Hudson can name his truck Betty, then—"

"Who is Jon Hudson?" I ask.

"Sorry," she says. "Fictional character."

"Right..." I check the revolver's chamber, confirming that it's still loaded. Then I aim the weapon at Lindo's leg. "Step one. The truth."

"The hell, man?" Lindo says.

"The accent, the fake accent, and the lingo, *man*, are all fake."

"Pssh."

"Daniel?" Wini asks, probably wondering if I'm a little off my rocker. Lindo is a proven liar and an operative whose endgame might not align with ours, but he's also been an ally who helped keep us from getting killed and mind-controlled. But I can't abide, or trust, someone whose tangled web of deceptions are impossible to untangle.

Right now, there's only one thing regarding Lindo of which I am certain.

"Lindo is lying to us." I pull the gun's hammer back. "And if he doesn't start telling the whole truth and nothing but, I'm going to put a bullet in his leg. And then the other."

33

"You wouldn't," Lindo says, looking a bit defiant, but there's enough doubt for me to capitalize on.

"Would rather not," I say, "but I'm done running away. I know who I am now, and those kids, the kids who were taken already, and are hiding in a bunker below us, they need a protector. If I have to shoot you, I will."

His defiance falters. He believes me, and I think that's because the moment I spoke the words, I realized I meant them. If Jacob was my never-born son, you better believe I'd put a bullet in a man to save him. These kids, many of whom don't have fathers, or were given up by their fathers, deserve to be loved, to be fought for. And right now, the person who can do that for them is me.

"Is your name even Steven Cruz?" Young asks.

When the pastor doesn't voice any concern over the impending violence, Lindo turns to Godin. But the law doesn't come to his rescue either.

"Look, buddy, I don't know you, but I saw what happened here, and at the ranch. If you know something that can save these kids, I suggest you start talking, or I'm going to leave the room." He leans in closer. "Then it will be their word against whatever is left of you."

"Look," Wini says, stepping between the rest of us and Lindo. She takes his hand, gives it a gentle pat. "I like you. You've done some questionable shit, but nothing I can't forgive. Yet. If you don't tell us what you know I'll shank you myself."

She's dead serious, but Lindo smiles. Instead of concerned, he looks pleased.

"Before you became involved, I had no idea who you were." Lindo leans back against a kitchen counter, relaxed and confident that I won't put a bullet in him. "That first text you received from me, on Marta's phone. That was genuine. I had just left with her, and—"

"Left with who?" I ask, ready to slug him if he says Isabella.

"Marta."

I nearly slug him anyway. "*You* have her?"

"She's safe," he says, "and she told me about hiring you. After those texts. But I knew who you were by the time you got in my car. I knew your history, both personal and professional. The people you lost. The people you saved. And the ones you brought to justice. I let you come this far because I thought your determination, experience, and character made you a potential ally, which you proved by saving my life, and the kids, but this..." He motions to the body. "...is too far."

"Fuck it is," I say. "The only reason those kids are still down there is because this son-of-a-bitch has a fist-sized hole in his head. And, the damn thing wasn't even alive."

He points to the body. "That might not have been, but that—" His index finger shifts to the taped up microwave. "—might have been."

I roll my eyes.

"I'm serious," he says.

"I can tell."

"How long do you think it will be before humanity creates a conscious artificial intelligence? Probably within your lifetime. The Others are hundreds of years ahead of us. Life for them might have a very different definition than it does for us."

"If this were a man, I'd have done the same thing," I say. "There isn't a situation in which I would allow any living thing to abduct children under my protection. I couldn't live with myself, and I don't know how you do."

Lindo sighs. "Look, I'm not saying you were morally wrong to kill—or destroy—the Gray. Far from it. And I'm not upset about missing the chance to study the nanite core. The problem is that you have solidified yourself as a threat to them. And probably everyone else in this house. In all my years dealing with the Others, I've never presented myself as an overt threat to their existence. That's why I'm still here, and why Aeron is still operational.

"The Others could have eradicated this house and everyone in it. If they return for the rest of those kids, I'm sure they will. The last people who stood up to them were slaughtered. Your actions might have put a target on your back." He turns to Wini. "And hers." He looks to Godin and Young. "And theirs. And after all this time, mine."

Lindo continues to betray himself. He might know who I am on paper, and what I've accomplished, but he doesn't know how I've done those things. Cases aren't just solved by collecting physical evidence. Every witness questioned, every suspect interrogated, reveals just as much through what they don't say as what they do. I hear the nuances of people's speech like complete sentences. Every 'I,' 'We,' 'Them,' and 'Ours' tells me a lot, and in Lindo's case, presents a theory that, at any other time in my life, I would have discounted as impossible.

"You're afraid of them," I say.

"Hell yes, I'm afraid of them," he says, but he doesn't fully understand.

"Not like I'm afraid of them, or anyone else in this room. Not in a 'holy shit, monsters are real' kind of way. Or even an 'I could have died' kind of way. You're afraid of them in your core. Afraid that they'll see you. Really see you."

His silence is confirmation.

"I'm not following," Godin says. He might be a good cop, but he's no detective.

"He's one of them," Wini says, getting a proud smile from me.

Godin looks from Lindo to the dead Gray, confused.

"Not them." Wini turns to the basement door that leads to the bunker where the children are hidden. "Them."

A long list of questions scrolls through my mind. I put them in a logical order and start with the first, knowing the answer could affect the second. "When?"

Lindo purses his lips.

"When did they take you?"

He shakes his head. "You won't believe me."

"Right now, I'll believe just about anything."

Lindo withers. There's no way out of this for him without full disclosure. "Remember when I told you about Roswell? How the U.S. Government brought in outside experts? That was true, but—"

"It was just Aeron," I guess. And when Lindo nods, it doesn't take a big mental leap to figure out the rest. Lindo *is* Chimera, and is, in some way, like Jacob. "You walked away from the crash."

"Wait," Godin says. "What crash?"

"Roswell," Wini says. "In 1947."

Young leans on the kitchen counter, looking Lindo over as though seeing him for the first time. "You're more than seventy years old?"

"More than eighty," Lindo says. "I'm not really sure. I don't know how old I was at the time."

"You're immortal, then?" Godin asks.

"I can be killed...I think. Mostly, I'm just aging slowly," Lindo says. "The nanites repair flaws in my DNA and keep my telomeres from growing shorter."

"Telom-what?" Young says.

"Telomeres. They separate our chromosomes. As people age, they get shorter, and when chromosomes start encountering each other and bonding, the results are cancer, cell death, and a whole bunch of other age-related ailments."

"Tell me about it," Wini says, stretching her back.

Some more pieces fall into place.

"You're not a tech-genius," I say, "are you?"

Lindo shakes his head. "Slightly above average intelligence, at best."

"But enhanced," I say. "Connected to the world. But not because of anything you did. The Others did it to you. Made you like this. And when the UFO crashed in Roswell..."

"I survived," Lindo says. "Spent ten years homeless, staying off everyone's radar. It took that long for me to realize no one knew I existed. The Feds had no way to know I was there. I'd fled the scene long before anyone arrived. And the Others...they'd have assumed I died. Over time, as computers became part of everyday life, satellites beamed information around the planet, and cell networks sprang to life, I had access to everything. Getting used to the overload of Wi-Fi and the Internet took time, but it's now my most useful tool. You're right about Chimera. It has never been more than me, but I'm able to accomplish more than most companies simply by thinking, and to the powers that be, hundreds of tax paying people work for me, all of them with social security numbers, homes, vehicles, and driver's licenses. None of them exist. I've mostly operated on my own, using what they put in my head to collect information about the Others."

That's why he was so interested in the nanites, I realize. It was a chance to study what had been done to him. If the Others' tech really is hundreds of years beyond our own, their nano-tech probably evolved a lot since Lindo was gifted—or perhaps cursed—with it. "But not anymore," I say. "Not since the EMP."

"A temporary setback," he says. "I feel like I'm missing a limb, but I'll be online soon enough."

I don't ask, but I'm pretty sure that means the nanites protecting me from the Other's telepathy will also come back online. "You said you've been collecting information."

"To expose them. To prove to the world that they exist. That's what it will take to beat them. A unified front. Not running to Dulce, guns blazing. They're too powerful. Even if you manage to kick in the doors, get some video, save the kids, and get people's attention, they're masters at misdirection and stealth. They'll have believers blaming aliens from the stars, and unbelievers more convinced than ever that Grays and the Others are modern fairytales. They've been doing this for a long time."

"Why?" Young asks.

Lindo blinks at the floor, pondering the simple question. "I don't know."

"You don't know?" I find this hard to believe.

"It's not like I can just ask them," he says. "Or sneak into Dulce and steal the information. I'm a regular guy, with a few genetic irregularities, and some cryptoterrestrial tech in his head."

"Well, you're not alone in this fight anymore," I say, "and your days of passive evidence collecting are over."

Lindo slams his fists on the counter, shaking the crystalized jelly inside the Gray's open skull. "We can't beat them!"

I ignore the tantrum and turn to Godin. "Are you with me?"

Godin doesn't look comfortable with his options, but nods. "Evil wins when good men do nothing, right?"

It's a butchery of the famous quote most commonly attributed to Edmund Burke, but the sentiment is accurate. I don't care what kind of justification the Others might have for what they're using humanity for, it's wrong. And we're going to put a stop to it. Going to try to. Because it's the right thing to do.

"I'm coming, too," Young says, catching me off guard. I wasn't even sure if I should ask him, but when storming the gates of an inhuman stronghold, a gun-toting, conservative Republican is a good ally to have.

"If you don't ask me," Wini says, "I'm going to kick you in the nuts."

"I wasn't going to ask you," I say, fueling her ire, and then extinguishing it with, "You go where I go. We're a team. Like Michael Knight and that lady from Murder She Wrote."

Wini raises an eyebrow. "Angela Lansbury?"

"That's her."

She smiles. "Pretty sure they were never a team, but it works for me. We're talking Angela Lansbury circa 1985, right? She's older than this asshole." She hitches her thumb at Lindo.

"Of course," I say, smiling. I'm afraid for Wini and the danger her involvement will put her in, but I'm also not sure I could do this without her.

"So, you want to kick down the front door of an advanced civilization, kick their ass, and just walk out with an untold number of freed prisoners, backed up by a sheriff, a pastor, a secretary—"

Wini flips him off.

"—and me."

"It could be worse," I say. "You could be an actual Uber driver."

Lindo groans.

I lower my aim away from Lindo for the first time, tucking the gun into the small of my back. "And *we're* not going to kick down any doors."

34

"Tell me what you want from me," Lindo says.

We're separated from the rest of our group, sitting in a second-floor bedroom, me on the metal-framed bed, its posts scratched by frequent handcuffing, Lindo on a chaise lounge. After explaining the situation to a distraught, but accommodating Sheba—that she'd be babysitting a group of kids who probably weren't fully human, who were being hunted down by corporate mercenaries *and* UFO flying aliens—she sent most of her girls away and set about making her guests comfortable. The bunker is far nicer than a horse stable's stall, but there're no windows, little décor, and nothing to do. And there's no way to know how long they'll have to stay down there.

"I'll tell you what I want." I lean forward, elbows on knees, trying to not think about what a black light would reveal in this room. "What I *really* want."

"Zigazig ahh?" Lindo says.

"What?"

"Spice Girls? Never mind."

I get the reference, but don't give him an inch. He's trying hard to lighten me up, but Lindo's on my shit list. He's proven himself untrustworthy. At the same time, he's working toward a goal I can get behind, with a shot of nitrous. While he's got a few lifetime's worth of time to build his case against the Others and prove to the world that they exist, the people they've already taken, and will soon take, have no such luxury. "I want to trust you."

"You can."

I raise an eyebrow at him, calling bullshit without uttering a word.

"I'll earn it," he says. "But if you go forward with this...right now, halfcocked..."

"We're all going to die," I say.

"Or worse."

I honestly don't want to know what falls under the perview of what's worse than death when it comes to the Others, so I move on. "You can start by telling me who you are."

"I've told you," he says, growing annoyed.

"Peel back another layer. I don't want to know about anything that happened after 1947. Tell me about your parents. About your family."

Lindo looks at me like I've just asked him to explain the meaning of life to an ant. "I'd rather not."

"They gave you up," I guess. "Your last name is Cruz, but your first name... It's not even Estaban. You're too smart for that."

"You give me too much credit," he says. "Slightly above average intelligence, remember. And I was basically a kid when I started going by Steven."

"And your family?"

He takes a minute to process emotions and memories I suspect he's kept buried for decades. Being abducted by non-human entities and being experimented on isn't something for which you can get therapy without being locked in an institution. "I had three younger brothers. And a younger sister. A mother. My siblings had a father, and he raised me, too, but he wasn't my biological father. I'm pretty sure I didn't have one."

I nod, following the implications. Lindo's mother had made a deal to bear a child, raise him, and eventually give him up.

"She didn't cry when they took me." His eyes tear up, but he blinks the wetness away, trying to control these ancient emotions. It's enough to convince me he's being honest. Lindo's a good actor, but I saw through some of it, even before I knew he wasn't who he claimed to be...twice. This doesn't feel like an act. "Didn't care at all. She just let me go. I think she was relieved. Maybe because the waiting was finally over, or because she knew I wasn't...like her."

"Like her?"

"Human. Not fully, anyway."

I nearly point out that there really isn't any way to tell his genetics aren't 100% human, but I hold my tongue when I remember his mother had likely been impregnated by the Others.

How had *that* happened? Some kind of immaculate conception? Was she taken on a UFO and implanted with a fetus? Did she share any DNA with Lindo, or was she just an incubator and a babysitter until he was old enough to suit their purposes?

"Did Marta make the same deal?"

He nods, trying to hide anger. "She's safe, by the way."

"Where?"

"A safehouse in Santa Cruz."

"You're not her friend, though, are you?"

"She didn't agree to set Isabella free until I confronted her. Told her I knew about what she'd done. Unlike many others, she felt guilty and agreed to defy the Others if I could keep her safe."

I note Marta's concern was just for herself and not for Isabella, but I decide not to address it. "Can you? Keep her safe?"

"I can create new identities for people. Give them new lives. New homes. Anywhere in the world, really just by thinking about it."

"How many times have you done that? Given people new lives?"

He ponders the question for a moment, and says, "Five hundred thirty-two, including Marta, but not Isabella, and not the kids in the bunker. Not yet. I mostly help the children, but sometimes the parents if they cooperate. A few, who actually managed to love their children, stay with them. But most just want whatever the Others have offered them, or are too afraid to defy them."

"So you take the kids?"

"Yeah," he says, not a trace of guilt in his eyes.

"How do you find them?"

"I run illegals across the border." He smiles at my stunned expression. "The Others prefer to make their pick-ups as close to the 37th parallel as possible. The kids come north, probably destined for ranches like the one we found, and they're collected en masse. Anyone traveling with a child gets my undivided attention. It's usually not hard to pick out which parents keep a distance from their kids. Obviously, there are other ways they collect people, but I'm just one man. I do what I can."

If he's telling the truth, my assessment of Lindo has been ill-inform-ed. While I chalked up his unwillingness to confront the Others to cowardice, he's been intercepting trafficked people for decades, setting them free before the Others can alter them further. Of course, that also means those freed people are having normal lives, falling in love, getting married, having children. How many generations will it be before the whole human gene-pool contains cryptoterrestrial DNA?

But the oddly precise number of people he's helped has raised a new question, which I imply with a statement. "You're back online."

"Just a minute ago," he says, looking relieved. "You are, too, by the way."

I don't feel any different than I did a moment ago, but how does one determine whether the nanobots in their head are functioning? Beats the hell out of me. I take a little comfort in knowing the tech will bar the Others from entering my mind again, but I also know I can beat them if the tech fails. "Are we in the clear?"

He closes his eyes for a moment, his mind reaching out through Wi-Fi, cell signals, and satellite data. Then he nods. "No one's talking about us."

"Not even Aeron?"

"They're *definitely* talking about us," he says. "But nowhere I can listen in. And they don't know where we are."

"How do you know?"

"Because they'd be here already." He glances toward the open window and the full moon beyond. "And I'd see them coming."

"What about the Others?" I ask. "Will they come back?"

"Eventually," he says. "Sure. But not now. Not when the chance of exposure is high. For all they know, we've got cameras set up and live feeds blasting to the Net."

"Should we?" I ask. *"Do we?"*

Lindo taps the side of his head, by his eye. "Can if we need to, but I'd rather not advertise our location to Aeron."

"Not yet," I say.

He frowns. "That's your grand plan? The enemy of my enemy is my friend?"

"We need an army. Aeron has one. We just need to convince them that attacking Dulce is their best option. You know them. Could they be motivated to move on the Others?"

"First, I don't know them in the way you're implying. We're not friends. At best, they're competition. That's how they see Chimera. Remember, I'm just part of a rival company to them. To me, they're closer to the enemy. Their motivations are far from pure and have more to do with personal gain than saving people. They're after alien tech, including that which can be derived from people like Jacob. I want to—"

"Uh-huh," I say, only half convinced. "Hop down off your soap box and hear your own words. If they're after tech, I'm sure they've been eyeing Dulce. Probably even have plans worked up on how to do it."

"Without a doubt." Lindo says. "From the beginning. But they also know it's suicide."

"You of all people understand the concept of deception," I say.

"You have an idea?"

"I do," I say with a smile. "But you're not going to like it."

A car horn outside the brothel blasts twice. I get to my feet. "Time to go."

When Lindo stands I put my hand on his shoulder, the tightness of my grip letting him know that what I'm about to say is not a joke. "One more thing."

He waits patiently as I think of the best way to say this. "I want an upgrade."

He looks at the room around us, smiling at the context. "I'm not sure what the going rate is."

"I'm serious," I say. "I want what you have." And when he still looks unsure about what I'm asking, I tap his forehead. "All of it."

35

"You can demand all you want, but I'm telling you it's not possible." Lindo shakes his head, vehement in his denial.

His position hasn't changed since I requested my upgrade. Part of me is relieved. Altering my mind and body so severely isn't something I want to do, but under the circumstances...

"Never mind the fact that we don't know what it would do to your fully human brain, I don't have vats of nanites just lying around, ready to implant in people's heads." He's still shaking his head.

Despite his warnings, I still feel that having Lindo's abilities would give us a tactical advantage.

"Look, everything you believed and I told you about Chimera is a lie. There isn't really a corporation. I'm not doing experiments. There isn't a secret laboratory. It's a smokescreen."

"Like the Others," Wini points out.

"But less nefarious," he says.

Lindo watches the steering wheel in front of him turn as the self-driving Model X Tesla—one of a fleet Lindo has around the country, capable of picking up people in trouble and ferrying them to safety—pulls off route 389 into Fredonia, Arizona, the town where Wini, Lindo, and Young previously bought weapons during our stay in nearby Colorado City. None of us were pleased by the Google-mapped route, but the fastest route from Vegas to Dulce is straight through the cult-run city and the entrance to the New Zion Ranch. The ranch's entrance was blocked by a single Colorado City police cruiser, keeping the investigation—if there is one—under local authority's control. We all ducked a little lower as we passed, but we made it through town without incident.

"I have resources," Lindo says, "but not the kind I let the world—and the Others—believe I have."

"You're just one guy," I say. "You've said that."

"But you put those things in his head already, right?" Wini says from the back seat. She's seated beside Godin, while Young is in the third row. We're three hours into our nine-hour drive to Dulce, staring down the rising sun, and are about to make a pit stop for supplies.

"Not enough," Lindo says. "And only as much as I could spare."

"They can't self-replicate?" she asks.

Lindo shrugs. "Look, I know what science fiction says they should be able to do, but I don't know how they work, or how to make more. They can repair themselves, and me, but I only know that because of experience."

"Why not set up a lab to study them?" Young asks. "You have the money, right? If you can send some into Delgado, why not into a petri dish."

"You don't study nanotech in a petri dish," Wini points out.

"Well, whatever," Young says. "You know what I mean."

"Because making more nanites, and implanting them in people, which would require experimentation on the very people I'm setting free, would make me no different than the Others." Lindo's explanation kills the line of inquiry.

The remaining five minutes until we reach our first stop are silent.

When we pull up to a large, light blue warehouse with 'Guns, Guns, Guns' hand-painted on the side, I'm the only one who seems surprised. "Are you serious?"

"Looks sketchy," Godin says, "but they're legit dealers."

"And they sold me a shit ton of guns, no questions asked," Wini says, which furrows Godin's brow.

"They did what, now?" he asks.

"Not the time to be a cop," I say. "If we're lucky, they'll do the same again." I turn to Wini. "How we doing on cash?"

She pats her purse. "Still enough for a small arsenal."

I open my door and then pause, looking at Lindo and then Young. "Keep your eyes open for trouble."

"Pretty much what I do 24/7, man." Lindo has the air of a profess-ional baseball player who's just been given advice by a little league kid.

The Arizona heat distorts the air above the vast, mostly empty parking lot. I squint against the sun blazing in a cloudless sky.

"How do you live here?" Wini grumbles.

Godin, whose face is raised to the sky, eyes closed, smiles. "If you don't enjoy the sun, this isn't the place for you."

"I'd take the wettest, foggiest day in San Fran over this dry, chafing heat any day." Wini adjusts her stride, separating her inner thighs.

"No one wants to hear about your chafing bits." I push the door open with a chuckle and am met by blessed air conditioning and the odor of metal, oil, and gunpowder.

"Pretty sure there's someone out there who'd be all over my chafing bits." She pats my chest as she struts past the door I'm holding open. "It's a weird world."

"Hello," a young man says, from behind a glass counter where a collection of handguns is on display.

"Like this guy," Wini says, pointing to the kid. "Think you could handle me?"

"H-handle you?"

She leans on the counter, heaving her bosom atop her folded arms. "I've got a few minutes. Just give me a wet nap and a—"

"Win," I say.

She pouts. "It's been a long couple of days."

"You can flirt with teenagers when we're done."

The kid raises a hand. "I-I'm twenty-two."

"You see?" Wini says. "Not even illegal this time."

I nearly lose my composure. All of this is for my benefit. Wini once told me she'd die happy if I was happy, too. She's always gone out of her way to cheer me up, even when the stress of life affects us both.

Godin leans in. "She being serious?"

"Give her a wet-nap and find out," I tell him and then approach the counter, slapping down a list of weapons, ammo, and other gear that Lindo researched via his nanites while the self-driving vehicle brought us here. I read the kid's nametag and say, "That's for you, Randy."

While we don't have a military sized budget, we probably couldn't buy much more without raising some serious red-flags, especially if they remember Wini from her less dramatic visit a few days ago. Randy scans the list, his eyes widening. "Holy shit." He looks at me. "Sorry, but I gotta ask what all this is for."

"Family bunker," Godin says. "Never can be too prepared."

Randy gives a nod like it's the most reasonable thing he's ever heard. I'm not sure who or what in the middle-of-nowhere, Arizona would need a bunker loaded with heavy-hitting guns, but everyone's afraid of something these days.

How much more afraid will they be when they learn the truth?

Every adult and child might stroll around with a gun on the off chance an actual alien might abduct them. Granted, it seems like half the country already lives in that permanent state of fear, but things can always get worse.

Lindo's apprehension about revealing the Others' presence makes a new kind of sense. Not only does he need to make sure there's irrefutable evidence, but that the climate on Earth isn't already volatile. Probably wouldn't take long for people to realize the government has known the truth and maintained the status quo, allowing people to be kidnapped and subjected to experimentation. There could be anarchy and it might result in far more damage than the Others could inflict. Cryptos might be good at subterfuge, stealth, and tech, but when it comes to mass destruction and death, I think humanity still wears the tiara and sash.

"Gonna need a few minutes," Randy says, heading for the back room.

"Take your time," I say, betraying my own sense of let's get the hell out of here. Being this close to Colorado City, not to mention still smack dab on the 37th parallel, feels like hanging out in enemy territory.

Randy returns with an older man who could be his boss, his father, or both. The gray-haired, NRA-ball-cap-wearing man looks over the list, and then over at us. He hands the list back to Randy and sends him off.

"Name's Reg," the old timer says, when he approaches, hands relaxed at his sides, but only a few inches from the handgun holstered on his hip. "Randy says you all are outfitting a bunker? Been thinking about doing that myself. Mind me asking what model you went with?"

"Twenty by eighty Rising Admiral," Godin says. "Room for the whole family."

Reg gives a nod. "That it is. Must have cost a pretty penny."

"Four hundred thousand," Godin says, sounding a bit wounded by the price. "Not counting supplies. And not what we're spending here, today."

Another nod from Reg. "'Preciate the business. And I think I can make a few more recommendations for your home defense needs. And hunting, as the case may be, when things go south."

Reg doesn't strike me as the talkative type, or a salesman. Most days, he probably doesn't come out of that office, and doesn't bother upselling customers. I glance around for Randy and find him pulling a pump action shotgun off the wall and depositing it in a cart filled with some of our other requests. He's doing exactly what he's supposed to be doing, but Reg...he's off. And I don't think he's trying to catch us in a lie either, just keep us engaged.

I look back to Randy, loading shells into the cart, moving a little slow. The kid looks up, makes eye contact for a moment before looking away.

Shit.

In a fair draw, I'm pretty sure a gun enthusiast like Reg, even at his age, might be able to drop me at a hundred paces before I clear leather. But by the time he sees the revolver pointed at his face, it's too late for him to react.

"Don't move," I tell him, keeping my voice down and moving out of Randy's line of sight. "Don't even twitch."

"The hell are you doing?" Godin asks.

I ignore him, slipping around the counter. Reg watches me with a killer's eyes, waiting for me to slip up and give him a chance to prove how quick he can fire from the hip. But I don't give him the opening, and the fight goes out of his eyes when I pull his weapon from its holster and hand it to Godin.

"Delgado," Godin whisper grumbles.

To resolve Godin's confusion, I ask Reg, "Who did you call?"

When Reg responds with a gravelly, "Fuck you," I press the revolver against the back of his head and give him a quick pat down. After locating the cell phone in his right pocket, I retrieve it and power it on. When it asks for a thumb print, I put it on the counter and force Reg's hand on the sensor. Phone unlocked, I swipe down to reveal recent alerts and see my driver's license photo, along with Wini's, Godin's, Lindo's, and Young's. The photos are plastered below an Amber Alert, featuring the names of six children and a phone number to call. Upon checking the recent calls, I confirm that Reg did indeed report us.

"Look," I tell him. "I want to treat you fairly here. You did the right thing. Problem is, we're not the bad guys."

"Fuck you're not."

"Those kids came from the New Zion Ranch," Godin says. "You know it, yeah?"

Reg purses his lips, fighting the urge to cuss us out again, and then says, "Yeah."

Godin digs out his wallet, opens it, and slaps it down, revealing his sheriff's badge and ID. Reg looks it over, his posture going slack.

"Those kids were rescued," Godin says. "Not abducted. This alert..." he taps the phone. "...is from the Colorado City Marshal's office. Now, who do you think controls them?"

Reg deflates. "I didn't know."

"Well, you do now," Godin says. "And unless you're fixing for trouble, I suggest—"

The door thumps open, allowing a stream of blinding sunlight into the shop, along with Young and then Lindo. I'm about to chew them out for leaving their position, and getting Reg riled up again, when I note the fear in their eyes.

"We have incoming!" Lindo says. And the way he's eyeing the guns tells me whoever is coming is nearly here.

"Who?" Godin asks.

"Locals," Lindo says. "I think. But it won't take long for Aeron to notice."

I release Reg, and tell him, "Those kids are safe. They're not even in the state. But if we get caught, and they torture the information out of us..."

Reg gives us each a solid stare, his eyes finishing their tour on Godin's badge. "Any of you are lying, I'll kill you myself."

The sound of approaching sirens sends a wave of tension through the group.

"Not sure any of us will be alive for you to kill," I say, as Godin returns Reg's gun and I lower mine.

"Horseshit," Reg says, before cupping his hands to his mouth. "Randy! Code Red!"

36

Randy barrels to the front of the store, propelling the gun-laden cart like a battering ram-wielding Viking. But instead of wearing the face of a warrior, he looks mortified. "Code red? Are you serious?"

"Have you ever known me to not be serious?"

"Shit," Randy says, backing away. "Damn it." His wild eyes glance to me. "They're not..."

"They're with us," Reg says.

"But the alert—"

"Gonna have to trust me, boy," Reg says, brimming with confidence that fades when Randy scurries off. He turns to me. "You make a liar outta me..."

"I know, you'll kill me." I scan the large warehouse. "Now, how many entrances?"

"Two," he says, motioning to the back of the store with his head. "Back door is an emergency exit. Opens from the inside, not the outside."

"If it's on hinges," Godin says. "It'll open with enough force."

I pluck two shotguns out of the cart and hand one to Wini and one to Young. The pair start loading shells into the weapons. "I want you two at the back. Anything opens that door, plug it and we'll come running."

They strike out for the back, each carrying a shotgun and enough spare shells to ward off a battalion. It's possible that some of the law enforcement gunning for us is legit, but I suspect the local Colorado City P.D. will only bring officers who have been compromised. After all, I don't expect to be read my Miranda rights before being killed. And I doubt that a single page of paperwork will be filed. The only way to keep this under wraps and off the radar is to make sure everyone on their way here, is already under control. As I prepare to defend our group, my conscience is clear.

When they're gone, I note Reg's squinty-eyed stare.

"What?" I ask.

"You said 'anything' and 'it' when talking about who might be storming through my doors." He leans into my comfort zone. "You leave anything out of your story?"

"Depends on how open-minded you are," I tell him.

"Been living here my whole life. I've seen my fair share of shit. Lights in the sky. Them Trancers over in Colorado City. Black helos. Why do you think I'm surrounded by all this?" Reg motions to the vast array of heavy hitting armaments. "I prefer hot lead to tin foil, if you know what I mean."

"You've got the gist," I tell him. I'm not about to get into the nuances of the alien-crypto agenda. I think he's got the general idea, and whether or not some of it's misinformation spewed by the Others, it doesn't matter to me. So long as he's pointing a gun in the right direction, he can believe the Others are sex-crazed goblins from another dimension.

"Trancers?" Lindo asks, curiosity pulling him back from the front door where he's been keeping watch. 'Trancer' must be a new term to him.

"It's when people get this real squirrelly look in their eyes and talk kind of monotone, like someone else is talking through them." Reg gets a distant look in his eyes and does a spot-on impersonation of Harry and his family. "This is not your land. Hunting is not permitted here. Leave now." He snaps out of it. "Happened to me and the boys when we were shooting hares over that way."

"Well, good news and bad news," I say. "That's who we're up against. And maybe worse."

Reg's eyebrows rise up, tugging his eyes toward the ceiling. He points at the roof, indicating the sky above. He asks the question when one eyebrow rises higher than the other.

"Let's hope not," I say, feeling exhausted by the very idea of it.

Reg seems motivated by the possibility of duking it out with otherworldly forces. "Randy!"

"Coming!" Randy shouts from the back room.

Lindo reaches for one of the MP5s lying at the bottom of the carriage. I would have preferred something with a little more punch, but the MP5 is an affordable submachine gun capable of unleashing a barrage of 9mm ammo. "We need to load these magazines."

Before I can tear open a case and start stuffing cartridges into magazines, Reg pushes the cart out of reach. "No need. Rand—!"

The kid comes barreling out of the office clutching five Heckler & Koch HK416 assault rifles. It's the kind of hardware the best special forces outfits in the world, including guys like Aeron, prefer to use. Each weapon is outfitted with ACOG sights for ranged fighting, foregrips, and tactical stocks to reduce recoil, as well as compressors to add a little extra kick to the weapon's 5.56 NATO ammo. While I understand how to use a weapon like this, I've never had the pleasure.

Randy passes the weapons out and then shrugs off a backpack, placing it on the counter with a thump. He unzips the pack and peels it open to reveal a mound of pre-loaded magazines.

"Reg," I say, plucking a magazine from the collection. "I wish I'd met you a week ago."

I slap the magazine in, chamber a round, and give the weapon a once over. There's nothing unfamiliar about it, so I set about stuffing my pockets with magazines. Lindo does the same, before hurrying back to the door, ever-vigilant even though he can see everything from above—or perhaps because of it. But if the door was about to be breached, he'd let us know.

Godin loads his weapon and starts toggling the fire selector with his thumb, switching from semi-automatic to full auto. He pauses, looks at the selector with a mix of relief and disapproval. "Did you auto kit this?"

"Gonna arrest me if I did?" Reg asks.

"More likely to hug you for it," Godin says and chambers a round.

Loud sirens and screeching tires announce our adversaries' arrival.

"I'm counting two police cruisers and three pick-ups," Lindo says. "Five men in the back of each. Two officers in each cruiser. Nineteen targets total. All heavily armed."

"How you seeing all that?" Reg asks, looking to the front door, which is solid and closed.

Lindo ignores him. "Our car is around back, in case we need to fall back."

"There's room for you and Randy," I tell Reg.

"Unnecessary. This place is mine. If it's going down in a blaze of glory, I'll be going with it."

I doubt Randy shares the sentiment. The look on his face says as much. But he heard the offer, same as Reg.

"Sheriff Godin." The words are muffled by the warehouse walls, but the voice is amplified by a speaker. It's also recognizable. Harry has come to collect. "Exit the building now or we will be forced to open fire."

Randy scurries away, and I can't help but feel disappointed in the kid's resolve and loyalty.

"We know you can hear us," Harry's amplified voice says, lacking all emotion. "And that you lack all hope of survival. However, if you return what is ours—*Now*—you will be allowed to leave unharmed."

"Trancers," Reg grumbles. "You see? Fuckin' lifeless. He's talking about them kids?"

"He is," I say, "but that he's asking for them now means they don't know where the rest of them are."

"Rest of them?"

"They tracked us down," I explain, my voice filling with a new kind of darkness. "Took one boy back. Name's Jacob." I motion to the gear Randy had been collecting for us. "All this is to get him back."

Randy returns, depositing two arms full of tactical armor and making me glad I didn't voice my disappointment in him aloud.

"You have ten seconds to comply," Harry says, while we all slip into our armor.

"He serious?" Reg asks.

Thinking of the ranch shootout, I give a quick nod.

"Walls beneath the windows are reinforced," Reg says, moving to the far side of the counter.

"What windows?" Godin asks.

"Go on!" Reg says, waggling his hand down the warehouse.

I spot several gaps in the wall displays and head toward the closest. "Look for the empty spaces!"

While the others take up positions along the fifty-foot-long wall, Harry verbalizes our countdown. "Five...four..."

"Light 'em up!" Reg says with just a touch too much eagerness. He slaps a button mounted on the wall beside him.

"Three..."

A series of three-foot-wide, five-inch-tall panels snap up in front of me, Reg, Lindo, Godin, and Randy. The perfect sniper positions give us a clear view of the parking lot, where the five vehicles are parked. Men line the far sides, their weapons aimed at the front door. A few of them flinch when the panels open, but most remain locked on target.

"Two...?" Harry's eyes turn toward my open panel. For a moment, our eyes connect, and through him I see *them*. Watching. Plotting. Hating. Then I pull my trigger and put a round between those sinister eyes.

Men duck for cover as my compatriots unleash a barrage of ammo.

Reg goes through two magazines of ammo, sending a fully automatic fusillade into the vehicles. I'm not sure if he's got a tactic besides mass chaos and destruction, but he buys the rest of us time to pick our targets. A few men shout in pain as they drop to the pavement. Vehicle tires burst and hiss.

Lindo takes his time, punching holes in the sides of cars. For a moment, I'm confused by his tactic, but then a stream of fluid dripping onto the pavement beneath one of the cruisers explains it. He's probably connected to the Internet right now, researching the locations of each make and model's gas tank, putting holes in them for what will be a grand finale.

I duck to reload and the action saves my life. The men outside start to return fire and as we duck down, one by one, the fifteen men still on their feet send a cascade of metal into the warehouse walls. While sunlight streams through a growing constellation of bullet-sized holes, the panels beneath our foxhole gaps resist. I can hear the bullets and buckshot pinging against the wall, but nothing reaches us.

Guns and gear five feet off the floor ping and fall, as rounds slip through the small windows. Had the wall been weaker, or I'd been standing, I'd be dead. But the men outside either lack discipline, or the Others controlling them aren't skilled in the art of a shootout. As each of the men runs out of ammo and pauses to reload, our chance to turn the tables returns.

As I start to rise, Lindo shouts. "Machine gun!"

My eyes reach the window in time to see a tripod-mounted, belt-fed machine gun in the back of a pickup truck swivel toward Lindo's position. The .50 caliber rounds it fires make what the rest of us are shooting look like BBs in comparison. I try to get a bead on the man standing behind it, but he pulls the trigger before I can, spitting ten rounds per second into—and through—the warehouse's protective panels.

"Down!" Reg screams.

A white-hot tracer round burns through Lindo's position, showing the path of several more rounds. Sparks fly. Weapons are flung from the wall. Debris fills the air as though propelled by oversized party poppers.

And then, as I dive to the floor, a cloud of wet red bursts from Lindo's falling body.

37

"Lindo!" My voice is lost to the thunder of the continuing .50 caliber bullet storm. I try to crawl toward his position, but a rack of hunting jackets topples in my path. Scurrying through the loose layers of desert camo, I'm forced to the floor again as the machine-gunner makes a second pass.

The warehouse wall shudders with every impact. I wonder how much more abuse the building can take before the men outside can drive a truck through it. I flatten myself to the floor, bullets buzzing past, striking the mound of jackets just slightly higher than me. A tracer round strikes the mass, embedding itself in the thick layers of fabric. By the time the stream of bullets has passed my position, a haze of smoke rises from the jackets. Somewhere within, the tracer round is setting the clothing ablaze.

I grip a handful of jackets and yank them away, hoping to free the tracer round and reduce the chance of a full-on fire. But my concern for Lindo outweighs my firefighter's instincts. As the machine gun rounds chew through the wall, headed back toward Reg—who is now sprinting for his office—I scramble on hands and knees, punishing my joints on the concrete floor.

Lindo lies amidst a pile of metal, wood, glass, and paper debris, all of it covered in a fine mist of red.

Shit.

I peel the top layers away, exposing Lindo's arm.

It's not attached to his body.

Feeling ill, I dig deeper, finding the rest of Lindo intact, but he's pale from shock and blood loss. He's conscious, though, blinking up at me, his face speckled with blood and bits of what was probably his shoulder.

"We'll get you some help," I tell him, but even I can hear the lie. With no arm left to tourniquet, no hospital nearby, no way to escape this bullet-laden shit show, and no way to seal the massive wound, he's going to bleed out.

Lindo reaches up with his still intact arm, the effort drawing a grunt. He takes hold of my shoulder and tugs me closer. "All my life I've wanted to fight them. To *really* fight them. But I've been afraid of what that might mean. I feign fear for the world, but I've only really worried about myself."

"You've helped a lot of people," I tell him. "A lot of kids."

"A small fraction of the total," he says. "Those whose freedom risks little."

"It's still something."

"Not enough. Not until now." His smile is bloody. "After all this time, I didn't feel brave enough to face them head on. Until now. Until you. You're the liberator the Taken have needed all along. Like Moses to the Israelites, you'll set them free."

Lack of blood is making him delirious. I'm going to be lucky to survive ten more minutes. But I don't tell him that. Better that he dies with some hope.

"Will you do that?" he asks, his voice fading.

"I will," I tell him, flinching as machine gun fire sweeps past overhead. I can hear the others, spread out through the store, shouting, but not screaming. My eyes drift back. Godin is on the floor, hands on his head. Randy, too.

At the far end of the store, Reg runs out of his office carrying a grenade launcher. He's headed for the nearest open slit, raising the weapon. A good shot could turn the tide of this battle, but not for Lindo.

Just before Reg reaches the gap, a few pellets of buckshot slip through a hole carved by the machine gun, striking him in the leg. He twists around, lands hard, and accidentally pulls the grenade launcher's trigger.

There's enough time for Reg to bark, "Fuck!" and then the ceiling explodes.

Before I can see how much of the ceiling is coming down, or if Reg survived his mistake, Lindo squeezes my arm and pulls me closer.

"Tell them what you want, and they'll do the work. Think of them as intermediaries doing the heavy lifting on your behalf. You don't have to know everything, see everything, or be everywhere. Let them serve you, and maybe it won't be too much. Maybe you'll survive."

The hell is he talking about?

Instead of expressing my confusion, I nod.

His eyes close, and I'm surprised when my tears drop onto his face, carving clean paths through the blood on his cheeks. But he's not gone yet. His hand, latched onto my arm, draws me closer.

Expecting to hear his final parting words, I lean in close, allowing him to press his forehead to mine.

"They're going to breach the back door," he whispers, and before I can react to his revelation, or his imminent passing, I'm clutched by an intense pain. I try to reel back away from it, but there are hooks in my forehead, holding me in place. Something burrows through my eyes, up my nose, seeping through the cracks in my skull, slipping into places that have been unexposed since I was formed in my mother's stomach.

Upon being released, I sprawl onto my back, writhing in pain as pressure builds beneath my skull. The pain surges around my head, throbbing behind my eyes. There are no pain sensors in the brain, but I have a strong sense that something is in there, taking up space that's not available, like a mobile tumor.

My vision narrows, as intense pain moves from between my eyes to behind my nose.

And then the pressure subsides as a heat works its way down my spine, following the path of my nerves, spreading out through my whole body. The sensation is something like an extreme sunburn, and I half expect to find boils rising on my skin, ready to burst hot liquid. But then like the pain in my head, the heat subsides to a gentle warmth, and then nothing.

I feel normal.

But I know I'm not.

I know what Lindo did.

What he put inside me.

A parting gift. Or curse. I don't think he knew which it would be. The nanites now spreading through my mind and body could kill me, or give me the tools I need to see this through.

I'm not even sure how to use them.

His parting advice replays in my head, making a lot more sense. *Tell them what you want, and they'll do the work.*

Show me outside, I think, also remembering his warning about the back door. I haven't seen or heard from Wini or Young. If they're distracted by the chaos at the front of the store—how could they not be—they might not be prepared for a breach.

Nothing happens. With the machine gun fire now focused on the store's far side, where Reg is taking cover after blowing a hole in the ceiling, I start making my way toward the back of the store.

Show me a satellite view of this position, I request, hoping a more specific command will get me somewhere.

Just when I think the nanites aren't capable of functioning inside my fully human physiology, I'm struck by a wave of disorientation. The room spins. A total loss of equilibrium sends me sprawling into a glass cabinet, which shatters and drops me to the floor.

It also saves my life.

A fresh wave of bullets punches through the warehouse wall, and it's not just the machine gun now. Sensing our imminent defeat—probably because we haven't returned fire recently—the whole gang has joined in.

At least I killed Harry, I think, as my mind spirals out of control, and then comes into sudden focus...several thousand feet above. A sudden feeling of falling pries my eyes open. I'm greeted by a dual view of the ruined gun warehouse's interior and the airspace above it.

Something like a brain cramp stabs the space between my eyes, sending them both into spasms. My stomach reacts by heaving the little I've had to eat and drink today onto the floor.

I hear—or maybe feel—something like a crack inside my head. Like a chiropractor's adjustment. Then everything feels aligned again. I open my eyes, seeing the satellite view and the room around me simultaneously with no negative side effects.

There're a thousand things I want to try, but right now, the back door is my sole focus. When I push myself up and look toward the back door, the satellite view zooms in on the same location, letting me see the door from inside, and above, at the same time.

There are three men, all armed, working their way down the warehouse's back wall, heading for the rear door. On the inside, Young and Wini are nowhere to be seen. But neither of them are cowards. They wouldn't leave their positions.

Someone's injured, I think, throwing caution to the wind and running for the door. The aisles are cluttered with debris, slowing my progress, but fueling my anger.

Wini comes into view after I shove a rack of tactical sports bras aside. She's on the floor, bleeding, being tended to by Young. Her shirt is torn open, revealing a half-dozen small holes, each leaking blood. She's been hit by stray buckshot, probably from the front of the store.

"I'm fine," she barks when she sees me, and I think she's telling the truth. At this range, the buckshot wouldn't have penetrated too deep, and the wounds aren't anywhere vital. It's going to hurt like hell getting them out, but she's not in mortal danger.

That's about to come through the back door.

Outside, two men with shotguns take up positions on either side of the door, while another one lines up to kick it in. The Tesla is parked behind them, still waiting to drive us away, but now under my command.

I sprint for the door, reaching my hands out toward Young. "Weapon!"

Young tosses his shotgun to me. I catch it just as twin blasts from outside remove the door's lock. The door springs open just before I arrive and find myself staring down the barrel of a shotgun.

38

A lot happens at once, but I find myself able to process it all, from multiple points of view. Even as I act, and feel, and think, the nanites are reworking my brain, adding connections where there weren't any, and adjusting for the discomfort caused by those changes.

When the shotgun comes up, I dive to the floor, ducking beneath the barrel before the buckshot tears through the space where my head had been a moment before. The boom, at this proximity, is painful, but my ears barely register the sound, not because of the nanites, but because it's par for the course at this point. Between all the gunfire and the grenade misfire, I'm already destined for a life of tinnitus...unless the nanites can take care of that, too.

My roll isn't graceful, but it doesn't need to be. While a soldier might come up under the man, lift the shotgun away and headbutt the man, I don't have to do any of that.

He's already airborne, sailing over me, a look of pain and surprise on his face.

The moment I hit the floor, the whisper quiet Tesla slammed into the men from behind, pinning one of the intruders outside the wall, sending the door kicker flying inside, and staggering the third man back.

As the struck man, who looks like one of Harry's sons, hits the floor behind me, I get to my feet and leap through the door, onto the car's hood.

The uninjured man is already climbing to his feet, swinging his shotgun in my direction.

A second too late.

One shell is all it takes to shred the man and send him back to the pavement. I spin around to face the pinned man—one of the marshals—and hold my fire. He's dropped his weapon, and judging by the agony on his face, he has two broken legs and is likely no longer under the Others' control.

"Don't kill me," he begs, confirming the Others have retreated from his mind now that his body is useless.

With a thought, the nanites connect to the car's electronics once more and pull it back. The marshal drops to the pavement, out of commission, but not completely. Before he sees it coming, I give him a good whack with my shotgun's stock, knocking him unconscious.

When I reenter the warehouse, I'm surprised to see Harry's son climbing back to his feet. His shotgun is just a few steps away. I pump a fresh shell to let him know he's out of options.

His hands inch up as he swivels around to face me, his face an emotionless mask. "You are remade."

"I can arrange the same for you." I aim the weapon at his face, but know the speaker won't be threatened. The young man is currently a Trancer, at the mercy of the Others controlling his mind. That doesn't make him innocent, though. Harry and his family might have inherited their agreement with the Others, but they've maintained it. They're slave traffickers, and if he makes a move, of his own free will or not, he'll finish it without a head.

How far away are they? I wonder. *Are they doing this from Dulce? Are there UFOs and Grays stashed in the mesas nearby?*

"Release the children."

"Not going to happen."

I feel a familiar tickle in my head. It's usually followed by discomfort and a voice in my head. This time, it ends as fast as it begins. I smile at the cryptoterrestrial watching me through the man's eyes, trying to emote more confidence than I feel.

The man looks confused for a moment, and then flashes a smile of his own, revealing that the Others aren't as stoic and emotionless as the Grays and mind-controlled people suggest. They're creatures of emotion, which makes them both dangerously unpredictable, but also capable of being manipulated.

They're not gods, I remind myself. *They might be technologically advanced and ancient, but they're not infallible.*

"He's dead," the man says, almost giddy. "The escapee. After so many years, he is gone." The smile becomes wicked. "Because of you."

I pull the trigger.

It was probably a mistake. He was an unarmed man. But he was desecrating sacred ground. My relationship with Lindo was founded on a bedrock of lies, but in the end, his intentions were noble and he gave his life in defense of ours, and those I hope to rescue. He died my friend.

"Holy shit..."

I turn to find Young staring up at me, eyes wide, holding a bright pink camouflage bandanna over Wini's wounds.

"You murdered that man," Young says.

My eyes drift to Wini's. There's a dose of shock in them, too, but no judgment.

"Lindo?" she asks.

When I nod, Young's disapproval melts away.

Gunfire from the storefront draws my attention. Godin, Randy, and Reg are still putting up a fight, peppering the men outside. From a bird's eye view, I see two men dead, including Harry. That leaves ten heavily armed combatants, one with a machine gun, which he's struggling to reload while under fire.

The Others know where I am. Know that the rear door is open. It won't be long before they send more men this way.

What they don't know is what I'll do next.

I step deeper into the store and find the gun I'm looking for lying in a shattered case. I snatch it up, find its ammo in a box behind the counter, and load a single round. Then I confirm that the machine gun is still being reloaded and that the men haven't left their positions behind the blockade of vehicles.

Outside, the heat assaults me long before I round the warehouse and start making my way toward the front. The sound of gunfire conceals the gentle scuffing of my feet on the rough pavement. Watching from above, I can see that no one has detected my approach or even suspected it.

More proof that the Others are fallible, and not the best military tacticians. Maybe that's why they have always stayed hidden. For all their technology, their abilities to hide and to control human minds, they lack the instincts required to wage a war and win.

Whatever the reason, I'm pleased to see not a single head looking in my direction.

The machine gunner racks the slide, chambering the first round in a fresh belt of bullets that will finish erasing what's left of the 'Guns, Guns, Guns' painted on the exterior wall. He swivels it around, silencing the assault rifles from within as Godin, Randy, and Reg dive for cover.

But before he can pull the trigger, I step out from behind the warehouse wall, gun already raised and aimed at the large puddle beneath the vehicles. At any moment in time before now, I might have begged God for mercy for what I was about to do. But this is war, and horrible things don't just happen, they're necessary.

So I pull the trigger.

The bright pink flare sizzles across the open lot. Most of the men see it coming, and not one of them reacts. They smell the leaking gasoline, of that there's no doubt. But the Others controlling them either don't recognize the danger, or couldn't care less about the ten remaining men losing their lives.

How many more cult members are under their control?

How many are on their way?

Flames whump to life beneath the vehicles, instantly engulfing every man. Screams erupt from the ground as the Others controlling them retreat, perhaps because they can feel the men's pain, or because they're focusing on other people.

The screams are silenced when the inferno reaches the breached fuel tanks and explodes. I twist away from the heat and then fall back toward the back door, hoping the Others haven't taken control of my friends.

"What happened?" Young asks when I step back inside.

Wini's still seated on the ground, still in pain, but her shirt's closed up. "Send them all to hell?"

"Wherever people who collaborate against their own species go," I say. "Yeah."

She gives a curt nod, but then her eyes go wide. She snatches her shotgun off the ground, raising it in my direction.

The Others have found my weakness.

I can't shoot Wini.

Can't even consider it.

So as the weapon comes up, I don't bother moving. At this range, she can't miss.

The weapon barks, and my first thought is, *I hear that.*

By the time the soundwave reached my ears, my head should have been missing for a fraction of a second already.

That's when I notice the barrel is aimed just past me, toward the door behind me. I see the marshal I spared when I turn around, and when I scan the area from above. I should have been more aware. What good is the ability to watch the world from multiple perspectives if you forget to use it?

"Everyone okay?" Godin shouts, working his way toward us, shoving debris out of his way, still clutching his assault weapon.

"We're good," I tell him, now positive that no one from Harry's crew, or the Colorado City marshals are left alive.

"Well, shit," Reg says, emerging from the piles of debris with Randy at his side. "That was..." He looks back at his ruined business. "Think my insurance will cover a war?"

I doubt they will, but I don't voice my fear. Once I get a handle on the nanites, I might be able to reimburse the man's losses with a thought. Before that, I still need his help.

"Glad you're okay," I tell him and pull him aside.

"Sorry about your friend," Reg says.

I glance to the front corner of the store where Lindo's body lies. He should be buried, sent off to his long-awaited afterlife with some respect. But there's no time to deal with the deceased when the living are still at risk.

I haven't spotted any nearby vehicles incoming, but that doesn't mean they're not on the way. And I wouldn't be surprised if Aeron wasn't far behind, or even leading the charge. "You have someplace you can take everyone?"

There's a black, extended-cab pickup parked off to the side of the parking lot, far enough away to be undamaged. I'm assuming it's either Reg's or Randy's.

Reg digs into his pocket and pulls out a set of keys. Tosses them to Randy. "Fire up the truck, ASAP."

Randy bolts out the door. I watch him from above, sprinting across the parking lot to the truck.

I lower my voice. "You get them someplace safe, okay? Fast as you can. Off the grid."

"You're not coming?" he asks, assuming the same quiet tone.

"Have a few things to take care of," I say. "Then I'll catch up with you."

"You don't even know where we're going," he says.

"I'll find you," I say. "But if you don't hear from me after tomorrow..."

"Sometimes the score settles you," he says. It's a strange way to put it, but I know what he's saying.

Screeching tires announce Randy's return. Godin helps me get everyone inside the truck. When the vehicle is loaded, Godin offers me the front seat, but I shake my head. He gives me a steely-eyed gaze. Knows what I'm up to.

"Sure about this?" he asks.

"Can't take her to a hospital," I say. "Not until this is finished. I want you to tend to her wounds."

"Not going to say goodbye?" he asks.

"She'd never let me leave," I say. "And I'm not sure I could if she tried to stop me."

I tear up when Wini smiles at me from inside the truck. She's going to hate me for this, but the moment I saw her buckshot wounds, her part in this ended. I can't put her at risk. Losing Lindo hit me hard. Losing Wini would undo me, and I've spent enough of my life wallowing in the tortures of personal loss.

"Godspeed," Godin says. He climbs into the truck, closes the door, and Reg, in on my subterfuge, hits the gas. At the edge of the parking lot, I catch a trace of Wini's raised voice, but then it's drowned out by the big truck's V8.

I watch their progress from above for a mile, making sure Wini doesn't try something crazy like jumping out. Then I move ahead, spreading my gaze over the roads and the city beyond. Seeing nothing coming, I return my vision to my own eyes and find the view of my feet blurred by tears.

"Goodbye, Wini."

39

A perfectly silent self-driving vehicle has its benefits—like running down an unsuspecting Trancer. But when you're feeling anxious about impending events, concerned about loved ones, and distracted by thoughts of the wife and son that could have been, the monotonous sound of tires on pavement doesn't do much to settle the nerves.

At some point, the white noise lulls me into a dreamless sleep. From my point of view, it was a blink. But when I pass a 'Welcome to New Mexico' sign, I know I've missed a good hundred miles of Arizona's stark and beautiful landscape.

A tall gas station sign triggers my instinct to check the fuel gauge...which I don't find. I'm not sure where to look, so I ask the car, or rather, have the nanites ask the car. The large LED screen to the right of the steering wheel displays an image of the car, revealing a 30% charge and the number of miles that will take us.

Where can I recharge? I ask.

The screen shifts to a maps app, revealing a course, due east, leading to a Tesla Supercharge station in Farmington, New Mexico.

Take us there, I think, and I realize I'm already starting to think of the nanites as a silent partner. Always listening and obeying, but never replying, which is fine with me. I've felt what it's like to have a foreign voice in my head. I didn't enjoy it.

I spend the next two hours monitoring the outside world. Rather than having the information and audio play inside my head, I funnel everything through the car, displaying visuals on the screen and audio through the speaker system.

There's no mention of the shootout at Reg's gun warehouse. Like the battle at New Zion Ranch, it's being concealed, despite the involvement of local law enforcement. As a former detective, a cover-up of that scale offends me, but it also benefits me. I've checked for the Amber-alert. It never went beyond the local communities, and if I have a run-in with the law in New Mexico for some reason, my record will be clean.

Better than clean, if I want it to be. My knowledge of police databases made working my way through the system a snap. I have free access to my records, and those of anyone else. I suspect I could do the same with the FBI, CIA, DOD, and NSA if I wanted to. I haven't attempted it yet, on the off chance that I might be detected. After all, Aeron does sell their reverse-engineered tech to the U.S. government. It's possible they could detect my intrusion and track me down. Or maybe not. Lindo didn't leave me with instructions.

I've avoided altering the records or bank accounts of anyone involved in this mess, though I'm confident I could, just by requesting it. That Lindo kept a low profile and didn't set himself up as the world's richest man, or buy himself a country, is impressive. This kind of power would corrupt most people.

I'm probably not going to live long enough to find out if the ability to do anything turns me into a monster.

The stop in Farmington is mostly uneventful. During the seventy-five minute charge, I manage to fall asleep again, the vehicle's AC—running despite the charge—keeping the heat at bay. This time I dream of Jacob. He's holding a baby in his arms. When I reach out, Jacob runs away, his feet slapping against a long wooden dock surrounded by swamp water.

I try to shout to him, but I don't have a voice. My unheard warning has dire consequences as Jacob trips and plunges into the dark water with the child. I dive in after them, but find myself blinded by the water, and unable to swim. I kick and flail, but make no progress.

I wake to find my arms raised over my head, and the vehicle's display screen suffering from some kind of pixelated seizure. When I calm down, the screen returns to normal. *Note to self, falling asleep while connected to anything outside myself can affect the real world.*

Weary despite falling asleep twice, I have a sudden hankering for coffee, or rather, the caffeine in it. With two hours left in the drive, a dose of awake juice will help me come up with a plan. I'm about to utilize my mind-numbing new abilities to find the nearest source of coffee when I'm struck by an idea. If the nanites can modify my brain...

Wake me up.

My personal recharge takes just seconds. I'm not sure about which chemical or hormone the nanites just kicked into high gear, but the effects are invigorating. I feel alert. And strong. My thoughts become clear. I'll never need a cup of coffee again, which is fine by me, because unless it's got copious amounts of sugar, cream, and some kind of artificial flavoring to boot, it tastes like hot shit, and makes people's breath smell about the same.

Back on the road, I enjoy the scenery for a few minutes. This portion of New Mexico is nearly as barren as Arizona, but the rock formations and mesas are far paler, and the land is speckled with pine trees. Then I turn my attention to the subject matter at the crux of my journey.

Dulce, New Mexico and the cryptoterrestrial base hidden there.

Scouring the Internet brings up millions of hits, most of them from UFO enthusiasts, conspiracy theorists, and hordes of other fringe thinkers who are closer to the truth than anyone would ever believe.

The consensus as to the base's location is the Archuleta Mesa, a massive swath of dangerous, steep, mostly inaccessible terrain. A single trail, far too rugged for the Tesla, leads to the top, where several cell towers stand. But no one builds the entrance to a secret base on top of a mountain.

It will be at the base, I decide, *or even miles away.*

Most conspiracy theories involve a high-speed rail tunnel between Dulce and Los Alamos, the location of the U.S. laboratories most famous for creating the atomic bomb. Given what I know about the Others, this feels closer to the disinformation they use to disguise the truth. A secret base is already on the outer limits of believability. But they do exist. No one doubts that. Seeding details like a hundred-mile-long, underground, high-speed rail along with UFOs, alien abductions, cattle mutilations, and a bevy of wild-eyed first hand witnesses is enough to make most people roll their eyes and dismiss both ridiculousness and truth.

Except in this case, the truth is equally ridiculous. Just a different kind of ridiculous.

Despite all the information available on the Web, local historical records—none of which refer to the scuffle between the Green Berets and the cryptoterrestrials—and a number of satellite images of the area, I'm no closer to discovering an underground base than the kooks who risk their lives searching for it.

I'm so immersed in research that I nearly miss crossing the border into Dulce. Of course, the 'Welcome' sign is a plain green sign simply reading 'Dulce.' I realize it's a sign with a single word, but it has a 'Yeah, this is Dulce, want to make something of it,' kind of vibe. The next sign I pass appears to have some kind of Batman logo on it. White text inside the black bat reads, 'Operation D.W.I.,' and the red text below reads, 'Checkpoints everywhere.'

Message received, Dulce.

"We don't really want you here," I say, doing my impression of a local, who strangely sounds a bit southern, "but if you're going to come through town, we're fucking watching you."

"Drive safe," I tell the Tesla and pat the steering wheel. The vehicle slows a few miles per hour, getting a laugh out of me. When I pass a police cruiser parked behind a stand of trees, my momentary dip into a pool of good humor ends with an increased pulse.

I watch the rearview and play local radio chatter through the speaker system. All silent.

I sit a little lower, but not so low I couldn't drive. No faster way to get the police's attention than for them to see no one behind the wheel. Feeling a little paranoid, I scan local police systems for my name or photo and come up empty. I'm relieved for a moment until I remember that's not how the Others operate. Aeron maybe, but the Others wouldn't want anything on the official record. While the Amber alert hit the local population's phones, it wasn't sent by an official source.

If there are people looking for me in Dulce, they'll probably recognize me, my face programed into their minds. Or something.

As little as I understand how the nanites work, I understand the Others' abilities even less.

Dulce is a small town tucked into a valley, surrounded by mesas, including Archuleta to the north. Bathed in the orange light of the setting sun, the landscape looks a little more like Arizona, but the number of trees, both standing and fallen, change the rocky terrain into something otherworldly. Most of the homes are single-wide trailers surrounded by flat fields and punctuated by the occasional ranch.

There are a few nicer homes in town along with some loosely packed businesses. The distance between buildings gives me time to scrutinize each, and the people hustling from air-conditioned vehicles to air-conditioned businesses. After just a few minutes, it's clear the majority of the population is American Indian, a fact I confirm a moment later via the nanites. Eighty-eight percent of the population are members of the Jicarilla Apache tribe.

Spotting nothing out of the ordinary in town, I start to relax. My eyes drift toward a church building where it looks like the four percent of the population that are Caucasian must be having a potluck dinner. That's when I notice the sign outside. 'Dulce Latter Day Saints Meetinghouse.' What are the odds that there would be a Mormon church smack dab on the 37th parallel, right in the Others' backyard?

Pretty high, actually, if Joseph Smith brokered a deal with the cryptos.

I make a sharp right turn away from the building, taking control of the vehicle from the nanites. After manually driving a few blocks, eyes more on the rearview mirror than the road, I let the nanites continue their course through town while researching a place to hole up for the night. As much as I'm eager to kick down the Other's front door, they seem to be a nocturnal bunch, and I'd rather not have to face off against a UFO. The Tesla pulls into the Wild Horse Casino & Hotel before I've decided that's the place to go. A prepaid reservation confirmation appears on the Tesla's screen, under the name Scott Smith.

"Uhh," I say to no one. "Okay. Thanks...I guess?"

The vehicle parks and the door locks snap open.

Are the nanites intelligent? I wonder, and then I ask, *Are you intelligent?*

No response, which is a relief, because I don't really want a consciousness residing inside me.

I sit in the car for a moment, wondering what story I'll give them to explain why I don't have any ID, when someone knocks on my window. I flinch at the sound, expecting to find a mob of torch-wielding, Others-controlled cult members. Instead, I'm greeted by a tall American Indian wearing a beige Stetson. The window descends before I can push the button or instruct the nanites.

"Are you Scott Smith?" the man asks.

I wonder if the nanites somehow included special instructions along with my prepaid reservation, perhaps basing their actions on my subconscious thoughts and concerns long before they reached the forefront of my mind. Conjuring as much confidence as I can, I say, "Yeah."

He smiles at me like we're old buds, says, "Get out of the damn car," and levels a large handgun at my face.

40

"Next door on the right," my captor says. After removing my firearm, he led me from the car to the casino's interior without raising an eyebrow from the staff or patrons milling about. Anyone who looked in our direction simply smiled or nodded at the big American Indian behind me, somehow not seeing or registering the gun in his hand.

The facility is a sprawling single-story maze decorated in southwestern sensibilities. Lots of horses. Exposed beams. Muted pastels and adobe textures. I wouldn't call it fancy. More homey. In some ways it reminds me of Sheba's brothel, though I'm guessing that the only teats displayed on the bedroom walls come in sets of four and belong to a cow.

"Here," the man says, just in case I didn't understand what 'Next door on the right' meant.

I stop in front of the door, and point to a keycard lock on the door, the indicator light turned red. "It's locked."

"You can open it," he says.

Assuming the lock is for show, or broken, I grasp the solid metal knob and turn it. The lock indicator turns green and the door swings open. "I hope your other rooms are more secure."

The humorless man motions me inside the room with the gun leveled at my midsection. If he did shoot me down, it would be a long, painful, bleeding-out kind of death. But I don't think that's what he's got planned for me. Not yet, anyway.

I pull up short when I see what looks like a typical hotel room suite with a queen-sized bed, a small lounge, and a kitchenette. A single step back takes me far enough out of the room to see that there is no room number on the walls to either side of the door, or on the door itself.

"You're not a perv, are you?"

"In," the man says, pushing the weapon against my side.

Risking my life to disarm the man would put Jacob and Isabella at risk of never being rescued. My odds of finding and liberating them are already slim, but they drop to absolute zero the moment a bullet lodges itself in my gut.

The room is comfortable and clean. Pretty standard. But the décor doesn't match the rest of the hotel. There's more of a modern vibe. The paintings are digital. Lots of sharp lines. Fractals. The TV is a large wall-mounted flat panel. Looks expensive. The fridge is fairly large and new.

"This your personal space?" I ask and cringe on the inside when the door shuts behind me.

"On the bed," the man says.

"Look," I say, turning around, "I don't know what you're into, or who you think I am, but if you take this any further, it won't go well for you."

The moment I speak the words, I remember that I'm not entirely powerless here. I can summon the police—though I'd rather stay under the radar. I can upload the hotel's security footage of the gun-wielding behemoth escorting me into the bedroom to YouTube. But again, there's the radar problem. I can drain the man's bank accounts, or bribe him by filling them.

But what's his name?

"What's your name?" he asks, following the same line of thinking as me. "Your real name."

"Not sure I want to tell you that..." I've got one eye on the man and one viewing the casino's personnel records. I don't find him in the list of employees, each of which has a photo ID. Expanding my search to local media, I find several photos of the man accompanying articles about the casino, most of them very positive humanitarian stories. Seems he's an upstanding member of the community. His name appears under each photo. "...Kuruk Moore."

The fact that I know his name doesn't faze him. "Sit."

This time I obey and am relieved when the big man, whose name the nanites reveal means, 'bear,' pulls the chair out from under the desk and sits opposite me. "Your name."

"Not going to happen," I tell him.

He mulls that over for a moment and then seems to resign himself to not gathering that piece of information. "Where is Dénzhóné?"

"I'm not sure I can even pronounce that," I say, trying to lighten the man's mood. His online profile is not that of a killer. Unless he's really good at covering his tracks, he's a good man. "Wait...what does that name mean?"

"It's not really a name," Kuruk says. "It's Apache for beautiful."

I can't help but smile. While so much of Lindo was a mystery, some of his true self shined through, including his opinion about his good looks. "I knew Denz..."

"Dénzhóné."

"Right. I knew him as 'Lindo.' And Steven Cruz."

While the name Lindo has no effect, Steven Cruz surprises the man and makes him tense. The gun rises toward my head. "Who are you with? Them?" He motions his head in a direction I think is north.

I'm not positive who he's talking about, but I see no danger in laying everything but my identity on the table. The man clearly knew Lindo, and if his reaction isn't phony, cared about him. "Are you talking about Aeron?"

The man's trigger finger slips into position.

"I'm not with them," I blurt. "Or them." I motion in the same direction, which the satellite map provided by the nanites reveals *is* north, and directly toward the Archuleta Mesa. "Lindo...Steven...was my friend."

"I know all of his friends." Gravelly emotion sneaks into his voice.

"Do you know about Marta?" I ask. "About Isabella?"

Kuruk stands, emotion welling. "Where is he?"

Afraid the man will put a bullet in my head, I decide to employ the golden rule of novelists around the world: show, don't tell.

Reg's paranoia works to my benefit. Not only did he have security cameras everywhere, but they also uploaded everything to a server. I point to the TV when it turns on. "Best if you see for yourself."

Kuruk glances at the screen, but doesn't react until the inside of Reg's warehouse is displayed, showing myself and Lindo together.

Suspecting that my host knew Lindo and likely called him a friend, I decide blunt honesty is called for. "The Others tracked us to a gun dealer in Arizona."

"Why?" he asks, sitting again and shifting the chair to face the television.

"We liberated a handful of children," I say, and when that gets his full attention, I leave no wiggle room for what we're talking about. "Hybrids."

"Where are they now?" he asks, his concern shifting from Lindo to the children.

"Safe," I say, not quite ready to trust him.

He gives an understanding nod.

"Most of them," I add. "They took one of them. I'm here to get him back."

"Get him back?" Kuruk nearly falls out of his chair. "There is no coming back when the Others have you."

Before I can answer, the screen shifts to a new camera angle revealing the store's interior as bullets punch through the wall, creating beams of sunlight. Kuruk watches as we put up a fight, as we struggle against the machine gun's might, and as Lindo drops in a cloud of red.

The gun lowers to the floor, and then drops. Kuruk removes his hat and puts a hand to his mouth as tears slip from his eyes. Lindo was more than a friend to this man. The video switches to an exterior view, revealing the collection of men shooting us, and then all of them being enveloped in a ball of fire courtesy of my flare. Back inside, the video shows my return to Lindo, our brief exchange and then the touch of our heads together, Lindo's passing, and my confused, stumbling retreat.

"I'm sorry," I say. "You two were close?"

"Forty years," Kuruk says, wiping his eyes. "That's how long I've been helping him."

Kuruk can't be more than fifty. Why would Lindo partner with a ten-year-old? Unless... "He freed *you*. You're a hybrid."

"There are more of us than you know," he says. "Why did he choose you? To receive them?"

"He was dying," I tell him. "I don't think there was much of a choice."

"The nanites could have survived outside of him," he says. "Could have gone anywhere. To anyone he instructed them to. Including me. So why you?"

I replay the memory in my mind, the nanites making it perfect and just as painful. The TV's view switches, showing the view through my own eyes. *Holy shit,* I think, my gut twisting at the realization that I can watch my memories...*any* memories in perfect clarity. My subconscious hijacks the TV screen, showing Kailyn. It's the first time I saw her. Sundrenched, wearing tight shorts and a white blouse that revealed her shape when the sun struck it just right. She's dancing with friends, entrancing me with the sway of her hips. My eyes linger, and then move up, locking onto her blue eyes as she returns my stare.

And smiles.

At the time, I felt my heart swell like the Grinch's.

Now, it breaks.

Grunting, and clearing my throat, I wipe my eyes and focus my thoughts.

Show Lindo. Show Lindo. At the warehouse.

The image shifts back to Lindo, but is frozen, like I've paused the memory.

"Who was that?" Kuruk asks.

"My wife," I say. "She's..." I can't finish the sentence, but I don't think I need to.

Kuruk puts a meaty hand on my shoulder. "Dénzhóné once told me that memories were part of what made his gift such a burden. I always thought he meant his lack of memory. About his life before. But now...I think this might be what he was talking about. Every memory, good or bad, relived with the same freshness as the day they occurred." He motions to the television. "Even the fondest memories can hurt."

"I'm starting to think Lindo is fond of saps," I joke. We both laugh and wipe our eyes.

"You might be right," he says, and turns to the TV, waiting for the memory to replay.

Lindo, on his deathbed, looks me in the eyes with an intensity I didn't notice at the time. "After all this time, I didn't feel brave enough to face them head on until now. Until you. You're the liberator the Taken have needed all along. Like Moses to the Israelites, you'll set them free. Will you do that?"

"I will," I say in the displayed memory.

"You don't seem the type of man who commits to things of which you're not capable," Kuruk says. He might respect Lindo's decisions, but he still doubts my ability. And rightfully so. I know I should, but whatever tweak Jacob made on my emotional state has yet to fade.

The screen shifts between memories, taking us back to the moment I clung to Jacob's arm as he was being pulled skyward toward a UFO.

"You'll find me," Jacob says. "They can't stop you now."

"They *are* stopping me now," I shout back.

"They're just delaying the inevitable."

I watch the view through my own eyes as I try to pull Jacob in again. "What are you doing?"

"Saving you," Jacob says. "You can't save us if you fall from the window."

"Right here," I tell Kuruk. "I felt something in me change. I felt more confident than I have any right to be."

The memory playback continues. "I'll find you," I shout.

"I know," Jacob says, and then Kuruk and I watch as the boy is pulled up toward the UFO. That's where I kill the TV feed, wary of what else my subconscious will decide to display.

"This is when Lindo decided to help you?" Kuruk asks.

"Not exactly," I say. "Not until after I killed one of them."

"Killed one of *who?*"

I motion my head toward the north, indicating the mesa and the inhuman things that reside within. "One of the Grays. And it won't be the last."

41

When Kuruk lets out a resounding belly laugh, I relax. As close as the big man and Lindo might have been, they clearly didn't share the same opinion when it comes to killing Grays. "I wish I could have seen that."

I instruct the nanites to keep the memory of my fist penetrating the automaton's cranium private, thinking, *Don't you dare.* "It was actually pretty horrible."

He nods, sobering a little. "They don't usually let themselves come into contact with people not under their control. Was this before or after..." He waggles his finger at my head.

"Before, and after. Lindo had given me some protection, but they'd been disabled by an EMP."

"Then you have encountered Aeron."

"A few times," I say.

Kuruk leans back in the chair. "You must have a serious constitution. Resisting telepathy is difficult without the nanites. Most people are lost before they realize someone else is in their head."

How I resisted the Gray's mind invasion isn't something I want to rehash right now, so I redirect the conversation somewhere more useful. "Do you know the way in?"

"The way in?"

"To the mesa," I say. "The Others' base."

"I've been living here for thirty years, right under their noses, watching the skies and observing their movements. They come and go at night, but they just *ffft*—appear in the sky."

"You think they're what, teleporting?"

"Tele— *No.* They're flying dark. And...probably moving through the mountain itself."

"Intangibility," I say. "Yeah, that's way more believable than teleportation."

If I hadn't seen it with my own eyes, my comment would have sounded more like mockery and less like a joke. But it does make sense, both because I know the technology exists, and because despite all the amateur searching over the years, no one has found any outward sign of an entrance. Which I suppose could simply be that those who do, disappear or have their memories wiped clean. Either way, we don't know how to get inside.

Or back out.

"Far as I know," Kuruk says, "the only way in is to make your own door."

"Like the Green Berets attempted in the 1960s."

"And I think you know where that got them." Kuruk lets out a long sigh. "Look, no one knows the resources you now have at your disposal, and understands what you can do, more than me. I've helped ferry more than a hundred children out of this hellhole, most of them being transported by people who made deals with those devils."

"Trancers," I say, and then realize that wasn't Lindo's term, but Reg's. "The people the Others speak through."

He gives a nod and then continues. "I've had my share of close calls, but I've never been caught, because I work in the shadows."

"You sound like Lindo," I say, and before I know what's happening, the TV comes to life again, showing Lindo on his deathbed once more.

"After all this time," Lindo says. "I didn't feel brave enough to face them head on until now. Until you. You're the liberator the Taken have needed all along. Like Moses to the Israelites, you'll set them free. Will you do that?"

When the screen goes black, Kuruk shakes his head. "Don't use him against me."

"Wasn't me," I say, feeling a bit taken aback. "It also wasn't me who made the reservation under the Smith name, or opened the window when you approached."

A phantom itch fills the inside of my head. It doesn't really exist, but I feel like reaching through my skull and scratching the gray matter within. Clutching my head in my hands, I think, *Are you alive? Are you conscious?*

My memory of Lindo replays, "Will you do that?

Again. "Will you do that?"

"Stop," Kuruk says.

"It's not me," I grumble.

"Will you do that?"

"Yes!' I shout at the TV. "You know I will!"

The screen goes black.

Kuruk's eyes are wide. "The nanites are...communicating with you?"

"I think so," I tell him. "But...I don't think they're conscious. I'm not an expert with these things, not even close, but my gut says they're carrying out Lindo's final orders, or desires, with some degree of intelligence, taking steps and directing me along a helpful path."

"Which brought you to me," Kuruk says, glancing at the TV. "I think they're talking to both of us."

"Then maybe you should answer them?"

He takes a moment to think things through and then speaks to the TV. "Yes," he says, turning to me. "Yes. I'll help. But I'm not sure how. There isn't much I can tell you that you can't find out on your own. I don't have any combat gear." He pats his round belly. "And my days of moving fast are long behind me. I'm good at hiding in plain sight, not much more."

"Maybe that's not the kind of help I need," I say. "Lindo obviously relied on you, right? For support. For friendship. Maybe it's that simple?"

Kuruk grins and slaps his hands on his knees. "You think Dénzhóné wants us to be friends?"

"First, can we both call him Lindo? You're confusing me. Second, I wouldn't have made it this far without my friends."

"Those other people in the video? In the warehouse?" he asks.

When I nod, I realize that separating from the group might have been a mistake. I only made it this far with their help, and strength. Then again, I can't fathom the idea of putting Wini in any more danger.

"Where are they now?" Kuruk asks. He looks uncomfortable asking, no doubt suspecting the worst.

"Alive," I say. "And safe. I think. I hope."

Kuruk settles back in his chair. He opens his hands and then plants them on his belly. "So, how are we going to do this? I mean, without a way in, I don't know how good a plan we can come up with."

"Oh, I have a plan," I say. It's been percolating since Sheba's, and now that I have a location, all I really need is sleep. The Tesla is filled with an assortment of weapons and gear collected from Reg's. Along with the nanites, I have everything I think I need.

He leans forward, elbows on knees, eager to hear my madness.

It only takes a few minutes to explain the plan, but when I'm done Kuruk is rubbing his head. "You're serious?"

"Already in motion."

"That's...ambitious."

"Close as I could get to Biblical," I say, recalling Lindo's Moses comparison.

"Generations of Taken will likely regard you with the same admiration as the freed Jews did Moses," Kuruk says.

"If I recall, the Jews spent forty years wandering the desert because they decided worshiping golden cows was a better idea than listening to the guy who helped God rain frogs on Egypt."

"Yeah," he says, "but they didn't have smartphones. You pull this off and everyone on Earth is going to know about it." He chuckles. "Just realized that your insane plan might be the only way to actually accomplish what Lindo wanted all along."

"Exposure," I say. "A united front against the Others."

"Yes, sir. Wouldn't that be a hoot?"

I'm not sure 'hoot' is the word I'd use—the worldwide ramifications Lindo was concerned about are very real—but to make the world a better place, sometimes you need to shake things up. It won't be an easy adjustment, learning that a species older and more technologically advanced has been treating humanity like lab rats, but in the long run, I'm sure everyone will agree that ignorance is not bliss. In this case, it's slavery. I'm about to say a simple 'yeah' in reply, but it comes out as a long yawn. "I haven't slept much in the past few days."

Kuruk pushes himself up out of his seat. "Understood. Going to be a long day tomorrow."

"Or a very short one."

He smiles, tries to come up with something encouraging to say, gives up and says, "Can I get you anything? Cheeseburger? Bourbon?"

I mentally scan through the hotel restaurant's menu. "How about six loaded beef tacos and a tall glass of milk?"

He gives a nod and heads for the door.

Thirty minutes later, after pounding down the promptly delivered food, I lie back in bed with a stuffed belly. For a moment, I consider reliving a memory. Hopped up on calories and experiencing a food buzz, I think it might even be fun. But before I can decide on a memory I all but pass out, sleeping through the night secure in the knowledge that even while I dream, the nanites are carrying out my plan.

I jolt awake to the sound of a ringing phone. The lights have been on all night, so I have no trouble finding the receiver. I pick it up and with a groggy voice say, "Yeah?"

"It's time," Kuruk says, sounding as groggy as I feel.

I glance at the clock. 4am. An hour and a half until the sun starts turning the horizon pink. Until I need to be in position. Until the sound of helicopters fill the sky, and soon after, the screams of men.

42

"You're sure about this?" Kuruk asks. "It's not too late to get the hell out of Dodge."

I look around the mesa, spotted with pine trees growing up and around a network of ancient fallen trees and inhospitable, loose slopes of sandstone scree. It's peaceful and mysterious, but will soon be drenched in chaos, and its mysteries laid bare...I hope.

Kuruk's doubts aren't misplaced, but I don't share them. While my rational mind can weigh out pros and cons for what I'm about to do, and the lists are somewhat balanced, my confidence instilled by Jacob tips the scale toward action rather than passivity.

"Somewhere below us might be hundreds of people...children. Maybe thousands. I can't imagine what they've had to endure, and how many will never be seen again."

That's all it takes to get Kuruk nodding. He gets it, even if he can't join me. Had he offered, I would have declined for the same reason I left Wini and the others behind.

"I was nearly one of them." Kuruk looks to the sky, which is just starting to melt into a purple hue.

We haven't seen any UFO activity, but that doesn't mean they're not out there, or that the Others are unaware of our presence. Kuruk has us in disguise, using his Dulce Alien Base Tour SUV that he operates out of the casino for visiting UFO enthusiasts. He believes the Others tolerate the vehicle's frequent presence and its occupants because it promotes their alien agenda. All the while, he's been using it as a cover to monitor the Others, and he can drive up to their proverbial front door without raising an eyebrow... assuming the Others have eyebrows. There isn't a free man or woman on the planet who knows what they really look like. But that's going to change. Today.

"They're thirty minutes out," I say, tracking a fleet of Black Hawk helicopters flying toward Dulce from the west. They're flying dark and hugging the ground, well below radar level. If I wasn't looking for them, with the nanites' assistance, I'd have never found them. If not for the heat showing up on infrared spectrum, they would be invisible. There are eight choppers, each with a maximum capacity of eleven passengers, plus two pilots and two gunners. Assuming the pilots and gunners remain in the birds, that will put eighty-eight pairs of boots on the ground.

It's not even double the number of Green Berets who lost their lives here in the 1960s, but Aeron has likely been prepping for this since then. That they're coming at all means they believe success is possible.

That they're coming now means they believed my timetable.

In the past day, I have shifted money through Chimera accounts, summoned imaginary security forces rivalling Aeron's, and mobilized equipment that doesn't exist. And I've done it sloppy, as though rushing, allowing Aeron to detect Chimera's apparent operation. I didn't spell out what was happening, but the heavy hitting armaments and mercenaries tell a story. As far as Aeron knows, in three hours, Chimera is going to invade the Archuleta Mesa and abscond with all the technology held within. To prevent that, Aeron is doing the only thing they can do—they're going to raid the mountain first.

Kuruk extends his hand. "I'll be ready on the outside. The buses are on the way."

I knew that already. I've been tracking the small fleet of buses approaching Dulce. I'm sure the drivers aren't thrilled about driving through the early morning hours, but Chimera paid them enough to ease their woes and fill their coffee cups a few thousand times.

I shake Kuruk's hand. "If you don't see me again, I've put the contact information for Winifred Finch on your computer system along with a bank account in her name."

"I'll take care of it," he says, squeezing my hand.

With a nod of thanks, I slip out of the SUV dressed in tactical gear that perfectly matches Aeron's. As soon as they hit the ground, and I emerge from hiding, I'll be just another masked mercenary.

Armed with one of the Heckler & Koch HK416s from Reg's stockpile, I climb up the loose scree, heading for an outcrop partially concealed by a pair of pines. I'm counting on the natural bunker, my dark clothing, and the telepathy-shielding nanites to keep me hidden from Aeron and the Others.

I monitor Kuruk's progress from above as I climb and he drives the steep, stone-laden dirt road down the mesa. He manages the drive with far more ease than I do the climb. Every few steps, sheets of rock slip out from under my feet, clattering down the steep grade.

Slow down, I tell myself. *You have time.*

Picking my handholds and footholds more carefully, I scale the mesa at a turtle's pace, yet I still reach the outcrop with fifteen minutes to spare. After rolling a few large rocks aside, I slip into a shallow cave. Looking at my position through one of the many satellites the U.S. government has in geosynchronous orbit over the sight, I confirm that I'm hidden from view. To spot me, one of the Aeron mercs would have to land right outside, and even then, confusion would give me the upper hand long enough to subdue him and stash the body. Maybe. I hope. I'll see them coming, so I can be up and moving before anyone touches down outside my door. Until then, I'm going to rest.

Surrounded by solid stone, in a north-facing cave, the first rays of morning sunlight fail to reach me. In the absolute silence, the experience is something like a sensory deprivation chamber, without the floating. My mind drifts. Memories surface.

I'm standing above Kailyn, holding her hair, because that's what an awesome husband does when his wife is puking in a toilet. It's already in a ponytail, so I'm really not contributing much, but I'm there, and I think that's what matters. It's the second day of what now appears to be a stomach bug.

"Shit," Kailyn says between spitting the taste out of her mouth. She points to the bathroom closet and snaps her fingers. "Bottom shelf. At the back. Pink and white box."

I follow the order with military precision, knowing that now is not the time or place to question what I'm searching for. Locating the box is easier said than done. The closet is a mess. Layers of shampoos, soaps, band-aid boxes, old prescriptions, lotions, salves, loofas, and Q-tips guard the mystery prize.

I don't find it until Kailyn's impatient "C'mon..." spurs me into what she used to call my gorilla mode. My forearm sweeps through the chaos like a knife scraping away chunky peanut butter, gathering it in a pile and revealing the box.

I pluck my prize from the closet, glance at the box, and for the first time in my life, feel my heartbeat inside my chest. Before that moment, I'd been shot at, stabbed once, and pursued by a serial killer, but none of it affected me the way the two bright pink words in a swirling feminine font did: Pregnancy Test.

"Shit," I say, mirroring Kailyn's thoughts.

We had talked about children a few times, but never planned on them. Mostly because her doctors said she couldn't conceive children. Adoption came up a few times, but being in a line of work that included being shot at, stabbed, and pursued by killers tended to squelch most conversations regarding new and fragile life.

Without brushing her teeth or rinsing her mouth, she dropped trou, sat on the toilet, and peed on the test strip. While I paced, and she freshened up, we waited for the results.

"We can do this," she said. "We can totally do this."

"We don't know that's what's happening," I said.

"It's been three months since my last period."

"But that's happened before, right?"

She calmed a little bit, and said, "Twice. But look..." She stood up, turned sideways, and pulled her T-shirt tight. The swell over her stomach was obvious enough that I wondered how I hadn't spotted it earlier.

Because it happened gradually, I thought, and then I denied it. "You're pushing your stomach out."

"I'm not," she said, and then glanced at the urine-soaked test strip lying beside my toothbrush. "What does a plus mean?"

Positive, I thought, but couldn't say it. Instead, I fumbled with the tightly folded instructions and found the images revealing what I already knew. "Pregnant...holy shit, you're pregnant. Holy damn, we're having a baby!"

By that time, we were both smiling. Both in tears. Holding each other.

Given our lives up until that point, I had never really let myself consider what it might feel like to be a father, to hold the living, breathing result of Kailyn's and my love. But in that moment, I did, and it felt amazing.

"Let's not get our hopes up," she said when we peeled apart. "These things give false positives. It's been in the closet for two years. I'll go see the doctor today. Get this confirmed."

"I'll come with you," I say.

"You and I both know you can't," she says. "You're close, right?"

My nod is unenthusiastic, but accurate.

"How about this?" she said. "I'll come to you with the results. I won't even let them tell me. We'll find out together."

"At a police station..."

"We'll meet out front."

After agreeing to her plan, and feeling strangely renewed about everything, I went to work.

That was the last time I saw her.

The sound of helicopters snaps me from the relived memory. I wipe tears from my eyes in the dark, wondering how the choppers got so close without me registering the sound.

Looking from above, I see lines dropping from the sides of choppers, some higher on the mesa, some lower. Aeron's mercs drop from each Black Hawk in pairs, spreading out across the mesa, taking up positions and giving me the perfect opportunity to rise and stand among them. I scramble from my position, not worried about the sound thanks to the thumping rotor blades, or my tears, thanks to the black facemask.

I stand from my position, weapon at the ready, just like all the other men who have already landed. I start moving upward, as though I was one of the first men on the ground, fanning out.

Then I scan radio frequencies, looking for their chatter, which will allow me to follow orders and blend in as they breach the mesa and reach its insides.

Only, there is no chatter.

I scan other modes of communication—Wi-Fi, satellite, cell networks, Bluetooth—and find nothing but a few early morning locals talking about the choppers they can see and hear from town.

They're either operating in perfect synchronicity while totally radio silent, or...

Shit.

The moment the possibility reaches the forefront of my mind, it is confirmed as eighty-eight soldiers turn toward me from every angle, aim their weapons, and speak in a chorus. "Lower your weapon. All hope is lost."

43

The chorus of male voices, muffled by facemasks and distance, coupled with the 'All hope is lost' message sends a shiver through my extremities. While I know the cryptoterrestrials are flesh and blood, the experience has a supernatural vibe to it that shakes Jacob's gifted confidence for the first time.

I'm going to die here, I think, *but it doesn't have to be for nothing.*

Broadcast this, I instruct the nanites. *Send it everywhere.*

My hope is that the Others will reveal themselves rather than simply having the mercs cut me down. That it will be enough to mobilize the world against them. The pessimist in me surfaces, arguing that people will just look the other way. Despite most Americans still patting themselves on the back over the Civil War's results, slavery is more prevalent than ever. With thirty million slaves worldwide, sixty thousand of whom reside in the U.S., people might just shrug their shoulders and go back to watching *The Bachelor.*

Or they'll revolt against a common enemy. The fact that these slave drivers aren't human, and are taking mostly children, might be enough to shock the world into action. The few science fiction movies I've seen present an alien invasion as the only thing capable of uniting the world. That the aliens have been here longer than us doesn't change the theme: humanity's last hope is each other.

We'll see.

A strange kind of tension fills my body, and I sense that the nanites are as close to frustrated as they're capable of getting. They're trying to reach out to the world beyond the mesa, but something is blocking my signals. I'm still connected to a few satellites, but they're the kind with cameras pointed at the Earth, not the kind that can broadcast a signal. I've been made mute, but not blind. The difference, I think, is that the spy satellites are protected by military encryption and firewalls, while the rest...well, a smart teenager could work their way past that security.

I'm cut off from the world, and even though I've only had the nanites for a day, I feel small and alone.

Probably because I am.

"Weapons down," the chorus of men says, the monotone command far more unnerving than a shouted one. It says, if we have to gun you down, there won't be any emotions, or hesitation.

With no choice, I lower the assault rifle to the ground and follow it up with the handgun on my right hip, and the knives on my left hip, my chest, and leg. When I'm fully disarmed, I raise my hands.

"Now what?" I shout to the men, turning in a slow circle, trying to find a single man who might be in control. But their faces are hidden, and I suspect I'd see the same blank stare in all their eyes.

Even the choppers, moving in a perfect circle overhead, their eight machine guns tracking my position, appear to be under the Others' direct control.

Five mercenaries snap out of their rigid positions and hurry toward me, weapons raised.

"Don't move, don't move, don't move," the lead merc shouts, sounding very human now, repeating his message three times the way a military man does. These mercs have their orders, but are no longer under direct control. I hold still, watching the three men approaching, knowing that any sudden movement on my part will probably result in a well-ventilated death.

The mercs fan out as they approach, flanking me as though I still pose some kind of threat. The bright LED flashlights mounted to their weapons make me squint, even in the early morning light that's growing brighter by the moment.

They're racing the sun, I think. The Others don't like their business seen by the light of day, and that must extend to the acolytes working on their behalf. Granted, the battles at the ranch and the gun shop took place in broad daylight, but there were no witnesses to either event. But here, in clear view of Dulce's three thousand residents, not all of whom have made deals with the Others, the odds of exposure increase with every passing minute. As soon as the sun crests the horizon and bathes the mesa in light, anyone with a camera and a zoom lens will be able to capture video of the eighty eight mercs and their lone adversary—not to mention whatever comes next.

"Hands down and together," the lead merc says.

I follow his instructions, but say, "You don't need to do this."

"Left us with no choice, asshole." He cinches a pair of plastic cuffs over my hands. Pulls my helmet and face mask away. Drops them to the ground and doesn't bother stopping the helmet from clattering down the slope. "You think they were just going to let you waltz in here? Now we're all screwed."

"You're afraid of them," I say.

"Fuckin' A," he says. "You know what they can do. You've seen all these fuckin' zombies. I don't want them in my head. Don't want them pulling the strings. But it's better than a war we can't win."

This guy believes every word of what he's saying. He either has incorrect views about the Others and what they can do, or he knows something that Lindo, Kuruk, and I don't.

I'm about to argue with the man, but he's already chosen a side. A few words from me aren't going to change that, and even though the Others aren't in direct control of him right now, I suspect they can hear everything I say.

"You're right," I say, slathering my words in faux remorse. "I didn't know. Didn't understand. I thought I was helping the kids."

"Those kids. The ones *offered* to them. There ain't no helping them." He gives me a shove. "Now move."

I catch his use of the word 'offered', suggesting that the Others' taking the children has at least some degree of morality attached to it. Complicity on the part of a parent, or some long dead ancestor, does not justify the sale of children into slavery.

"Where are we going?" I ask.

"Up."

Another shove gets me moving.

Scrambling over the loose rock is harder with my hands bound, but I manage.

"What did they offer *you*?" I ask, hoping to gain a little understanding before I die.

"Jack and shit," the man says. "Up until now they've tolerated us. You know that. We clean up their messes and make a profit doing it while keeping the status quo. The moment you showed up in Santa Cruz, things have gone FUBAR. First at the church. Then the ranch. A war with these fuckers benefits no one. We're alive because they allow it. They want a blood sacrifice, so what? We get to exist. We collect you and bring you to them, the rest of the world gets to keep spinning in ignorant bliss."

The merc's point of view reveals he doesn't just know about the church and the ranch, but he was a party to both firefights. As a result, he's more emotionally invested in my demise, especially since he blames me for his current predicament. But that doesn't mean he can't be reasoned with, and since he's the only man talking, I think he's in charge.

"What's your name?" I ask him.

"Last name you, first name fuck."

"You have kids?"

"Why would *I* have kids?"

The way he says it tells me that he has nothing against children, but is against bringing them into a world where they can be sold to non-human entities. He's working with the Others, but detests them.

Screw it, I think. *If the Others are listening, let them hear me. My fate is all but sealed already.*

"They're human," I say, drawing a mocking laugh from the mercenary.

"You have no idea, do you? Up to your nuts in acid, and you think it's orange juice."

"Not literally human," I explain. "Human in the sense that they are flesh and blood, capable of making mistakes. If that wasn't true, there wouldn't be crash sites. Aeron wouldn't exist. There would be nothing to reverse engineer."

He laughs again. "You know, Aeron only exists because of a spelling mistake."

I'm not sure what he's talking about, so I remain silent, trusting in the human instinct to never leave a song, sentence, or thought unfinished.

"It was Aaron," he says. "Let me guess, Cruz told you about how Aeron and Chimera were born out of the Roswell crash. About consulting experts?"

I hadn't thought about his story since then, but I now know it was part of his ruse. Chimera didn't exist until years later, when Lindo first started taking action. If Aeron is really Aaron, then... "There were two kids in the crash."

A tug on my shirt stumbles me to a stop. "Right here."

I scan the loose stone around me, noting nothing of interest. The circle of mercenaries keeps their gaze locked on me, but their weapons lower in unison.

The merc tugs down his mask, revealing the face of an aging man with a white mustache, spliced and perhaps maintained by a collection of electronic implants—in his eyes, and head, and cheeks. I look over his armored body, which shows no outward signs of aging or deterioration. How much of him is still flesh and blood?

"The changes to my body are a little more obvious," the man says.

"You're Aaron," I guess.

"Was a time Cruz and I were like brothers. Then he decided to live the life of a servant, and I wanted...more. Our paths cross on occasion. We fight sometimes. But he never put all of us at risk. Not until you." Aaron gives me a shove. "Tell me where he is. Before I turn you in. And maybe I can talk some sense into him. Talk him out of whatever you've got cooked up."

"You don't know..."

The merc steps to the side, looking over my shoulder. "They're coming."

I spin around, looking for some sign of the Others' approach. There's nothing here but stone and tree husks. No cave. No entrance. No trace of a secret door.

Then I remember that the Others need none of those things to move in and out of the mesa.

"Where is he?" Aaron asks, urgent. Worried. Whatever problems this man has with me, and however much his ideals might conflict with Lindo's, there's a reason the two men have never gone to war. They care about each other. Freed from the Others by chance, they must have survived those horrific early years, on the run from cryptos and the government by leaning on each other.

They're like brothers, I realize, and I decide that even though Aaron has screwed me, every captive below this mesa, and every person living on Earth, he deserves the truth.

"He's dead," I say. "They killed him."

The news staggers the man, but he shakes his head and closes his eyes. His voice fills my head, though he hasn't spoken a word. *Where are you? Tell me you're miles away from this shit.*

Even though he's speaking to me through some preexisting telepathic connection, which I think has more to do with his implanted tech and my nanites than actual telepathy, I can hear his desperation. So it's with a bit of sadness that I say, "What's left of Cruz is right in front of you. He gave them to me before he—"

The sound of shifting rock spins me around.

A shout escapes my mouth as a Gray, its big black eyes burrowing into me, its long spindly arms and fingers reaching, dives out of the cliff and tackles me down the steep grade.

I fall through the first warm beams of morning sun, and then plunge into a chilled, endless darkness.

44

Despite my eyes being open, I'm lost in a frigid black soup that feels like the atheist's vision of death, but without the endless bliss of non-existence. When my head throbs, I know I'm still alive. Lights dance in my vision when I sit up, fading as gravity tugs the blood down and away from the wound on the back of my skull.

Understanding makes me angry.

That Gray asshole tackled me *through* the mesa, plunging us through solid stone and into wherever I am now. The impact, which opened the gash on my head, now stinging and warm with blood, knocked me unconscious.

Can you stitch me up? I ask the nanites. I'm not sure if they can, but it doesn't hurt to ask. The back of my head starts to itch, but that's not unusual for an open wound filled with rocky grit.

How about some night vision? I ask. The question comes without too much thought. If I'd thought about the consequences, I might have thought twice. Unlike getting a satellite feed or data from the Internet projected into whatever part of my brain decodes visual information, seeing in other spectrums requires alterations to the device used to gather light—my eyes. Or in this case, my left eye.

I'm rocked back to the stone floor, clutched by the worst migraine I've ever experienced. I roll to my side and retch as an invisible hand grasps my eyeball and squeezes. The pressure is intense, and I'm pretty sure I feel my eyeball melt away before being reformed, sending out fresh tendrils into my brain.

And then, all at once, the pain subsides.

I can see.

In shades of green.

Please tell me you're intelligent enough to have fully upgraded the eye.

My vision shifts through multiple spectrums. I'm disoriented by it at first, but the nanites go to work on my mind. Viewing the world like I never have before becomes second nature. The shifting of colors and views of the world reminds me of something. A movie, I think. Something Wini made me watch, with a human-hunting alien.

I shift back to night vision and try to embody the spirit of that movie, but in reverse.

I'm in a cave. The path behind me is sealed by a rock fall. A wire hangs from the ceiling, running down the tunnel ahead. Steel-caged lightbulbs hang from the wire every thirty feet.

This is a man-made tunnel. And when I see the first body, I know where I am.

This is where the Green Berets attempted to infiltrate, using the tunnel created by a mining operation that had no idea what they were truly digging toward.

All that's left of the body is a rag-clothed skeleton. I search it for weapons and find none. Whatever equipment the man carried has been removed. Spotting his dog tags, I take hold of the chain and yank. The move doesn't work out quite the way it does in the movies. Instead of snapping free, I decapitate the man.

"Sorry," I whisper and hold the tags up. "Alex Maddern."

I pocket the tags and move a little further into the tunnel. I don't think I'm walking into a trap. They brought me here. If the Others wanted me dead, the Gray that tackled me could have finished the job. My being here, in this place, serves a purpose. And since there's no other direction to go, that purpose lies ahead.

It doesn't take long to find another body. I'm about to remove his tags as well when I spot a dozen more men up ahead. How many men did Lindo say died here?

Sixty.

I leave the man's tags and head intact and tip-toe my way past the fallen bodies and their tangled, dead branch limbs.

The eight foot-wide-and-tall tunnel's smooth walls grow rough as I descend deeper into the mesa. The layers of dead come to an end as the tunnel narrows. *This is as far as they made it,* I think, and then I step past.

A hundred feet further, I find the tunnel's end. It's a small opening, large enough to crawl through. Three bodies dressed in blue coveralls lie around the opening.

The miners who breached the Others' subterranean domain.

I suppose it was only a matter of time before someone dug a hole in the wrong place. These three were unlucky, but I don't think they were the first. Humanity has a long history of mythical creatures and monsters emerging from the underworld. I wouldn't be surprised if these stories—like those that have people looking for aliens in the stars rather than beneath their feet—were created by the Others to keep people away. The tactic is different, but the storytelling and manipulation matches their modus operandi.

The tunnel ahead narrows to a claustrophobic squeeze, but it's short-lived. Sliding through on my stomach, I emerge into a cavern like a baby being born from stone. I drop to an unforgiving floor covered in loose rock that mirrors the mesa's exterior.

The wall behind me is flat and smooth, worn down by millennia of erosion, but decorated at some point in the more recent past. The cave paintings are primitive, but they show lines of people carrying children over their heads. I follow the line of people to a crude mountain framed in beams of light, several bright stars, which I think are probably UFOs, and an image of a spindly biped I take for a Gray.

Joseph Smith wasn't the first Southwesterner to cut a deal with the Others.

The rest of the cavern is a vast open space, leading downward. A foot-worn path winds through the rough stone, marking the way that generations of people followed, delivering children for the Others' needs.

Is this what they want me to see?

Are they trying to show me that this is just the natural order of things?

Do they want me to join them? Serve them? Like Aaron does?

I suppose, as a human connected to the world at large, I might have some perspective to offer them. Perhaps some insight on how to remain hidden in an increasingly technologically advanced world. But they must know who I am, and the path that brought me here. What could they possibly offer me to make me betray humanity?

Then again, maybe Joseph Smith put up a fight?

Maybe the ancient ancestors of the Apache living on this land did as well.

Even Aaron seemed displeased by his new arrangement.

In the end, they all folded.

But I'm not them, I tell myself.

I try not to focus on the idea because it casts a bright light on the fact that I have failed. My mission has shifted from taking the Others down on a grand scale to resisting whatever temptation they're about to throw at me. Resistance won't free Jacob. Won't rescue Isabella from her fate. Won't change a system in place since before the first human civilization emerged from the wild.

Change requires more than resistance.

It requires action.

So I press on, determined to protect my secrets, the people I love, and the masses no one else will fight for. I grin, knowing the surge of confidence comes from Jacob. If not for him and Lindo, I'd be just another terrified person at the mercy of a power beyond comprehension. But now I am more.

I won't just resist.

I'll fight.

And probably die like all those soldiers in the tunnel behind me, but at least I will have tried.

The cavern echoes each footfall, announcing my presence to the beings who already know I'm here, and given the tingling in my forehead, are tracking me even now.

The path leads to another tunnel, this one glass smooth and round, carved into solid rock by a technology foreign to humanity. I step into the cylinder and head for a literal light at the end of the tunnel. By the time I reach the end, I'm prepared for anything the Others might throw at me.

Maybe they'll kill me.

Maybe they'll open my head and pry the nanites out.

Maybe they'll make an offer most men couldn't refuse: wealth, power, immortality.

I step into the large space behind the tunnel like a conquering hero strutting through the gates of a subdued city.

Only there's no one there to witness my bravado. What there are, are UFOs, parked in a line, hovering above the smooth floor without any trace of power flowing through them.

They're showing off again, I decide. Trying to make me feel powerless and small. In human terms, this would be a show of force, like when nations perform military drills, or when men work out in public, grunting with each heave so people can't help but notice. Like a peacock strutting for a mate, they say, 'look how amazing and powerful we are.' But when it comes to people, this kind of behavior reveals insecurity, and is most often a bluff.

Perhaps it's the same with the Others. If it is, what are they hiding?

What are they afraid of?

Spotting a second tunnel on the far side of the domed, football field-sized cavern, I head for it without giving the UFOs any direct attention. There are no open hatches, and they're hovering twelve feet above the floor. Even if I understood how they functioned and wanted to attempt to abscond with one, they're just out of reach.

Feeling bolstered by my psychological evaluations of the path I'm being forced to walk, I move through the second perfectly round tunnel feeling true confidence. Not in the knowledge that I know how to defeat the Others, but in the knowledge that such a possibility exists.

The space beyond is half the size of the hangar behind me, but no less impressive. What looks like a large crystal covered in sharp jutting spires rises from the center of the space. It glows with a dull blue, casting the several dozen Grays in a death-like parlor. The rest of the space is featureless, with smooth and curved walls, carved out of solid rock.

I expected to find some kind of modern facility built inside the mountain. But I realize the need for manmade walls, lighting, décor, and signage is decidedly human. Which the Others are not. While the Others are far more advanced, they also seem to be a bit more in tune with living as part of the Earth, rather than remaking it the way people do.

The circle of Grays stand motionless, their big black eyes on the crystal. But they're not who I want to see.

"I'm here," I say, and feel a little silly. Maybe this is just another stop along my journey? But I'm committed, so I add, "Show yourself."

The Grays shift their gaze to me in unison, unnerving me for a moment.

The Others are watching me through their automatons' eyes.

I'm about to demand an audience when a familiar voice says, "Behind you."

I don't need to turn around to know who's speaking.

And I don't want to.

Because it means the worst has happened.

It means I'll be no different than all the people who have given in to the Others' demands.

"Turn around," Wini says, her voice monotone. "Look at me."

45

I obey. What choice do I have?

The Others have possession of the person I care about most in the world.

Trying to conceal my emotions behind a mask of indifference, I turn around and say, "There you are," addressing the being controlling Wini, rather than Wini herself.

Hiding my surprise becomes nearly impossible when I see Wini. She's stark naked and covered in goosebumps, courtesy of the subterranean sixty-degree temperature.

They're trying to demoralize me. Or make me angry. Stop me from thinking.

And they're succeeding.

Why? I wonder. *Why cloud my mind?*

I'm missing something.

"We've met before," a new voice says. Godin, also naked, steps out of the darkness at the room's fringe. He works his way through the still-staring Grays, showing no discomfort at their proximity, or any emotion at all.

"At the ranch," Young says, slipping between the Grays.

I look for Reg and Randy, but there's no sign of them. The men either escaped, were killed, or were deemed not worth taking because I have no emotional connection to them.

When Wini speaks again, I feel a measure of relief, not because she's herself again, but because they're not also using Jacob against me, though I suspect that will come later. The Others are master strategists. They won't show their entire hand until it's needed.

"At the brothel," she says.

"Guns, guns, guns," Young says, an awkward smile on his face. Do the Others feel humor? Do they understand how silly the name is?

"You are impressive," Godin says. "But men just like you come and go, and all reach an agreement."

"Why?" I ask, my subconscious scratching the back of my head, shouting, *you're missing the obvious!*

"Evolution," Wini says. "As the human race becomes more, new arrangements must be made for the sake of survival."

"Whose?"

"All species," Godin says.

"You want me to believe that your relationship with the humans is codependent?"

"Coevolved," Young says. "Old agreements have become invalid. There is a place for you in the new arrangement."

"Because of what I can do," I say.

Wini, Godin, and Young nod in unison.

"Your predecessor was an unreasonable man," Wini says. "I attempted reason, and allowed him to believe he was helping. But your involvement..."

"The ranch," I guess. "One kid here, one kid there, you can live with that, but at the Ranch, that hurt. Losing..." I stop short of saying his name and revealing my fears. "...those kids. They were important."

All three nod again.

"For what?"

The Grays, along with Wini, Godin, and Young, squint at me. My trio of friends ask as one, "Why are you not afraid?"

It's a good question, and I'm certain it has more to do with Jacob's influence on my nerves than my natural ability to be unfazed by the otherworldly. But I'm not about to reveal that. There's a chance they don't know the full extent of what Jacob can do. "Because fuck you."

Wini shakes her head and says, "Human vulgarities have no—"

"Fuck you," I repeat.

"Your attempt to—"

"Fuck. You."

Wini clamps her mouth shut, and I catch a whiff of exasperation rolling off her. She turns to Godin as he turns to her and reaches out.

What are they—no!

Godin's big hands wrap around Wini's neck and squeeze, the pressure increasing steadily.

"No!" I shout, and I attempt to pry his hands away. But he's indifferent to my efforts and I'm pretty sure he won't feel any pain I inflict. Stopping him would mean killing him, and I will if it comes to that, but it will wound me forever. "Stop!"

Wini's face turns red.

And then, she's returned, gagging and choking, desperate, tear-filled eyes darting toward me.

"Are you ready?" Young asks. "To dialogue? Or would you rather this woman die?"

"I'm ready!" I shout. "I'll do what you want!"

Godin's hands release Wini. She falls to the floor, gasping and coughing. I crouch beside her, hands on her bare back. "I got you," I whisper. "I'm here."

"Every man has a weakness," Godin says. "Even those who believe they have already overcome them."

They're referring to Nathaniel, I realize, whose possible existence nearly allowed them to take over my mind. Lindo said that it was possible for the strong-willed to resist their influence, but I couldn't do it without his help, and that's clearly the case for Godin, Wini, and Young as well.

And while the nanites coupled with my opening the envelope might shield my mind, it does nothing to protect my heart, which at this point in my life is focused on the life of a sixty-five-year-old woman.

"Are you okay?" I ask her.

Her voice is raspy, but hers. "This sucks ass." She clutches my hand. "Kill it, Daniel. Kill it n—" Her face goes slack as her mind is taken over.

Tears in my eyes, I grasp the sides of her head and look into her eyes, hoping she can see me. "There is nothing on this planet, in the stars, or living beneath our feet that would stop me from saving you, understand?"

The briefest twitch of her face is the only indication that I've reached her. But it's enough.

Then her retreating mind is replaced by another's.

By the Others.

No, I think, *that's not right either.*

And then I realize the truth.

It's been hidden in plain sight all along, just like Kuruk, only appearing in the nuances of speech. Like any common criminal or seasoned serial killer, the truth is revealed by what is and isn't said, in this case by those whose minds are being controlled, and now confirmed by Wini.

I replay memories of prior conversations in perfect clarity, noting every word. The term for mankind's enemy, coined by Lindo himself, is incorrect. Our adversary, our enslaver, is not the *Others.*

It's the *Other.*

Single.

Solitary.

The last of its kind.

A species on the brink, clinging to life, desperate to make a deal and hide within the Earth from a truly more powerful species. It might have a small army of Grays and UFOs at its disposal, but if they crash on occasion, I'm sure they can be shot down, too. Hell, a good punch dropped one of the Grays. Had there been more Green Berets with shielded wills, this might have all ended in the '60s.

The real subterfuge of the Other, isn't that the world believes aliens come from the stars, it's that the people who know *that's* not true still believe they are submitting to a superior force.

"I want to know the truth," I say.

"About?" Young asks.

"The children."

Young's body relaxes. It's subtle, but there. The Other is afraid I'll learn what I've already deduced. It's vulnerable. The problem is, it's not here.

"And then?" Godin asks.

"I will agree to whatever you want as long as you do not harm these three...and the boy you took from me." I add Jacob to the mix because he's the reason I came all this way and risked everything. To not ask for his return would be suspicious.

"Follow," Godin, Young, and Wini say together, and then they start across the large room, their bare feet slapping against the stone floor. When I follow after them, the Grays follow me with their vacant eyes, each of them a vessel for the Other's consciousness that, while solitary, is powerful enough to control multiple people and all of these automatons simultaneously.

As vulnerable as it might be, I can't underestimate it.

As I'm led past the twenty-foot-tall luminous crystal, I feel drawn toward it. At first it's like a longing to touch it, and then an almost desperate pull to become part of it.

What the hell?

The feeling fades as I follow the others across the room, but I very nearly embraced it like some long-lost friend. Or wife and son. The only thing that kept me from doing so was the knowledge that it's just a big freaking crystal and not actually someone, or something, that I care about.

Little feet tap the stone floor behind me.

The Grays are following.

While I've agreed to abide by the Other's demands, it doesn't trust me, and rightfully so. I have a history of ruining its plans in explosive ways, and it can't read my mind, which I imagine is disconcerting for a creature accustomed to rummaging through people's thoughts.

I'm led to another tunnel, this one leading down at a sharp angle. When we emerge into a chamber that can only be described as vast and horrifying, I conclude that my deduced nugget of information about the Other's identity isn't going to give me an advantage of any kind.

This is bigger than I can handle alone.

I stop short, staring at the thousands of bodies locked in solid rock, and ask, "Where is he? Which one of them is Jacob?"

46

"Recent arrivals are not kept here," Wini says. "The boy you call 'Jacob' is being...processed."

I sense the intelligence behind Wini's words searching for a non-threatening term for what Jacob is undergoing, but I'm guessing it doesn't have much experience with chicken nuggets. As innocuous as 'processing' can be, in this case I'm leaning on the 'about to be blended' side of things, just to be safe, and to make sure I'm not caught off guard.

Can we take a closer look? I think to the nanites, quickly following it by, *Wait!* Expecting eyeball crushing pain to throw me to the ground and reveal what I'm doing, I try to stop the change. But it's too late.

My vision narrows in on a distant portion of the cavern. Best guess, my vision is at 15X zoom, providing a clear view of people's faces several hundred feet away. There's a moment of disorientation as every heartbeat, breath, and micro-shift of my body's many muscles redirect the view. Then the nanites step in, perhaps adjusting my eye, my brain, or both. The end result is comparable to a steady-cam view. Big movements still affect what I'm seeing, but the jittering comes to a stop.

I focus on an American Indian woman, her skin a dark tan despite being held underground. Her black hair hangs over her naked shoulders. Her weathered face puts her at roughly sixty. "I thought you only took children?"

"All were children," Young says. "In the beginning."

"How long have they been here?" I ask.

"Days," Godin says. "Years. Decades." He looks me in the eyes. His are dead, staring through me. "Millenia."

"Are they..."

"Dead?" Wini says. "Not as you would define it, but they do not exist. For them, there is no time. No world. No fear, nor pain, nor even dreams. They experience nothing. It is a merciful existence compared to life in a fallen world. Would you not agree?"

It's trying to find common ground. That's probably not possible, but I've got to play along until...

I don't know what.

"Being alive isn't always easy," I say, "but the most rewarding aspects of life take the most work. Like a marriage. Or being a parent."

"And we do what we need to for our progeny," Young says.

"Is that not your way?" Godin asks.

"Is that how you see these people?" I scan a line of faces, seeing all races represented along with a complete spectrum of ages from maybe ten to older than a hundred. I pause on a man whose eyes are too large, and whose head is oblong, stretched out in the back like those Peruvian mummies. They're hybrids. All of them. Created in partnership with humanity and sold for a life of eternal non-existence. But these people didn't just go from being a few mindless cells in a womb to a mindless meat stick encased in a stone prison. They had lives. Families. Friends. People they loved and who loved them. Their lives as hybrids were probably difficult, but I doubt a single one of these people would have volunteered for non-existence.

"No," Wini says with a trace of humor. "Humanity is...a resource to be cultivated for a higher purpose. A noble purpose if that helps your conscience."

"It might." It won't. This place is basically a big refrigerator where human beings are stored and sustained, their bodies being used, but for what?

I nearly choke on my own spit when I come across a woman whose arms have been removed. Where there should be shoulders, there are two depressions, the limbs removed and the flesh sealed over the joint. I scan for more physical abnormalities and it doesn't take long to find them. Some people are missing eyes, bits of their faces, and others, judging by the scars, their brains or some portion of them. With all of them encased mostly in what I thought was stone, but now looks like some kind of solidified secretion, there's no way to tell how many are missing limbs or organs.

Were this mass of people set free, how many of them would regain consciousness only to fall down dead a moment later?

A lot, I decide. But just as many, perhaps more, would survive.

Would live again.

Would *exist* again.

I think.

I hope.

I decide to not ask about the missing parts or exactly what they're being used for. There will come a point where my compliance will be hard to believe. The Other knows I care about Wini, and that I'll do nearly anything to save her, but it also knows my character, through our confrontations, and Wini's own memories. If I learn too much, it will know I'm lying.

A sharp poke in my back spins me around. I nearly roundhouse a Gray, but am unnerved by its face and its proximity, along with the thirty plus standing behind it, their emotionless faces somehow still conveying hate.

"If you're collecting people, and can control people, why use these things?" I ask.

"People, even those under my control, are fallible and frail." Wini pinches the chub of her stomach. "Humanity tires, requires sustenance, and constant guidance, and they do nothing to promote my narrative. The 'Grays,' as you call them, are my perfect creations—carrying out my desires without pause, without question, without *all this talking.*"

"Come," Godin says.

We move toward another tunnel. I take a look around, trying to figure out how the people are moved to and from the wall. There are no stairs. No lifts. No visible technology of any kind. For an advanced species, they're not big on showing off their advances. It feels like a simple lack of pride or showmanship, but the Other is the apex showman, deceiving the whole world with a tale of aliens. *But that's not it,* I decide. It's a simple lack of time. I don't know how long the Other has been down here, running its strange empire and human-abduction ring, but between all that and its true purpose, the Other has no time to add flare or grandiosity to its own space.

It's trying to survive, I remind myself, *solely focused on the task and the complicated web it must weave to achieve it.*

The next tunnel is like all the others. Uniform in width, grade, and distance. The next chamber is a hub leading to many more tunnels, some leading up, some down. Up until now, I had memorized how to back-track to where my tour began. Then again, no matter where we go, I can use the nanites to retrace my steps. But it's not like returning to the sealed tunnel will help at all. Without the ability to walk through solid objects, I'm going to need a real door, or the assistance of a Gray, whose will to help or not help does not exist. They, like the people held in the nightmare chamber behind us, do not really exist. Unlike the people, the Grays don't even have the possibility to exist.

The path becomes a confusing maze of turns and non-descript tunnels. They look like lava tubes except for the layers of strata streaking the walls, revealing the region's geological history. The surface is perfectly polished, too. My blurry reflection stares back at me in the low light. Whatever made these tunnels, it wasn't lava.

The only thing I learn from this tour is that the base is vast, filling the majority of the mesa, and likely the earth far below it. Maybe there really are tunnels stretching as far as Los Alamos.

"We're nearly there," Wini says, as though sensing my growing impatience. As intriguing as being led through a subterranean base built by non-humans is, I'm far more interested in Jacob, and once I have him, deciding how to handle what comes next.

I'd be lying if the idea of fleeing this place with the people I care about wasn't tempting.

But what about the rest? All those people?

And Isabella.

Has she been here long enough to be displayed on that wall?

And what about the kids still under Sheba's protection? Will I have to give them up for Jacob?

Could I really do that?

Would any of them forgive me if I did?

"Forgiveness is a human concept," Young says as he exits the tunnel.

"Does the lion ask forgiveness for killing a zebra?" Godin asks. His white body glows orange in the light from the chamber he's just entered.

Wini fake-smiles back at me as she walks into the light at the end of the tunnel. It looks more like a grimace and does a better job representing how I feel than the Other, who has just revealed how screwed I really am. "Does the vine feel remorse for the tree it chokes the life out of as it reaches for the sun?"

Shit.

Damn it.

How did I not realize?

How did I not feel it?

While I've been distracted by my grand tour, the atrocities carried out on humanity, and the possibility of cutting a deal, the Other has been slipping past the nanites' defenses.

The Other is in my head.

"Yes..." Wini says, her grimace-smile twisting into something monstrous. The thought is finished by a voice in my head that is as unfamiliar as it is vile.

...I am.

47

As a child I was something of a chess addict. I played and dominated my friends whenever possible. My parents and grandfather didn't stand a chance, either. When I finally convinced them to pay a hundred-dollar entrance fee for a statewide tournament, I waltzed into the American Legion hall with all the swagger of a rock star. I wore a smile throughout the first ten minutes of my first match, chasing my opponent across the board, knocking out pieces with ruthless tactics.

By the time I realized I was being played, it was too late. Every move I made had been planned by the kid across from me. He wasn't out to collect pieces, or even gloat. He was solely focused on one thing: the win. And he achieved it three moves later.

I never did play chess again, but applied the stinging lesson of that day to the rest of my life.

Until now.

Yes, the voice says inside my head, experiencing the memory at the forefront of my thoughts along with me. *You understand.*

The oblong space beyond the last tunnel is striped across the ceiling with what looks like those orange salt crystal lamps you can buy at the mall, but smooth and flush with the flawless curved ceiling and walls leading to a polished floor.

Wini, Godin, and Young part and usher me into the room with their hands, welcoming the guest of honor to a ball of horrors. Several more crystals rise from the floor, gently pulsing with orange light. On one hand, it all looks natural, but it's all too clean and symmetrical for that.

This is tech, I think. *Some kind of computer.*

Beyond your comprehension, the voice in my head says.

"Can you not do that?" I ask. "It's unnerving."

"You would..." Young says.

"...prefer I speak..." Godin adds.

"...through your friends?" Wini finishes.

"I would prefer you stay out of my head," I say.

"Ahh," Wini continues. "But your head contains what I desire."

For a moment, I think he's talking about knowledge, about what I learned from Lindo, or the other kids' location. But that's not it at all. "You want the nanites."

"The boy was never meant to carry them for so long," Young says. "He was an experiment that exceeded expectations, as did the... nanites."

"But you can't just take them," I realize and say. "Because they're bonded to me."

This is why I'm not lying on a table, having my head cut open. I need to *send* the nanites out. I need to *give* them to the Other. That's why it wants to deal. But that's not the only reason. It's hearing my thoughts. The big ones. On the surface. But it's not in my core. My soul. If it could, I'd be restrained. And while it can speak inside my head, it's not close to wresting control.

"We can give to each other," Jacob says, stepping out from around one of the ten-foot-tall orange crystals. Like the others, he's undressed and exposed. My anger flares, but I breathe through it, reminding myself that the Other is using basic tactics to get under my skin. Jacob looks unharmed—physically—and that's at least something.

"You can even finish the job that brought you to me." The new voice belongs to a young girl. She steps out from behind another crystal, as naked as the rest of them. An incision across her midsection has been sealed, but it's surrounded by a purple bruise. The rest of her appears unharmed, including her face, which I recognize from photos.

"Isabella." She doesn't react to the name. "Let them go."

"In time," Jacob says. His bug eyes twitch. He's still in there, fighting. The Other's telepathy seems more powerful here, boosted by proximity. Were we hundreds of miles away, the boy's strong will could probably break free. But here, this close to the Other, only the nanites seem capable of preventing total loss of control.

"What about the other children?"

"Keep them," Wini says.

Those two words reveal just how desperate the Other is. It has been pursuing and collecting its creations for thousands of years, sometimes with explosive results. They're not insignificant to it. That it wants the nanites more means I have some leverage.

Speak it, the Other says in my head. Even it knows it doesn't have full access to my thoughts. But it senses I have more to ask.

"Show yourself," I say.

"Impossible," Young says.

"I don't make deals with a devil I can't look in the eyes."

"You would not...understand." Godin sounds almost sad when he speaks.

Does it mean I won't be able to comprehend its true form? Or that I will morally object to its appearance?

"Then no deal."

Jacob stands in front of me. "What do you think will happen? Do you think you will leave this place? That your friends will survive? That I have no need for them? Your torture will be long and excruciating, experienced by yourself and those you love most. I will give them their minds back so that they know every agony experienced is a result of your stubborn spirit."

"And you will never have the nanites," I say, sounding far more confident than I feel.

"The process that created the nanites in your body is already being recreated," Isabella says.

That might be true, but it's missing what was probably an essential ingredient—Lindo. How long did it work to create those nanites only to lose them in transit? But the answer to that question doesn't matter. Denying the Other access to the nanites means not only subjecting my friends to torture, but all the people and hybrids it will take to find another nanite host like Lindo. I can't begin to understand how these things work, but I think the relationship between Lindo and the nanites were integral to their development. And since people really are one of a kind...

But if I give the nanites to the Other, what will be the result? How powerful will the cryptoterrestrial become? It already has access to people's minds. What will it do when it has free access to all of human technology? Wipe us out? Enslave us all? Turn us into something not recognizable as human? The Other's endgame, beyond survival, is a mystery.

Before I can decide which is the lesser of two evils, Jacob laughs. "Your vexation amuses me."

"Nice to know you have a sense of humor," I lie. The more human this thing acts, the more I hate it, and that will just cloud my judgment. I'll take my alien overlords inhuman, thank you very much.

"It is less of a joke," Wini says, "and more of an irony. Some of your species would call it a cosmic aligning of fate. Some would call it coincidence."

Young puts his hand on my shoulder like we're pals. "I call it an opportunity."

"For both of us," Godin adds.

"We will both get what we want," Jacob says. "We will part ways equally satisfied."

I don't believe it. The Other has nothing left to offer me. "You're going to kill yourself?"

Jacob grins. "I'm going to give you a gift. And I'm going to let you leave this place with all that I have offered you already."

I don't know if it's tweaking my mind, but I actually believe it.

"Are you going to let everyone go?" I ask. "Head to the stars where you'd like everyone to believe you came from?"

"Sarcasm is the defense of the simple-minded," Isabella says, her big, brown, earnest eyes staring up at me. "You are better than that. You are *more* than that."

I wait in silence. All I've got is more sarcasm.

But then I have a question. "What do you mean, *more* than that?"

"What do you know about your parents?"

Jack and shit, I think, but don't say so, mostly because it already knows what Wini knows—my parents died young and beyond their names and mixed heritages, I don't know anything.

"Your grandfather was conceived here," Godin says. "He was one of thousands to carry genetic alterations. Your father was born with them. As were you."

I take a step back, subconsciously looking for a seat as my legs grow weak. I stop when I bump into the wall of Grays behind me.

Wini smiles at me, and she's getting better at it. "This is not your first visit."

"You were brought here," Young says, "while still in your mother. You were tested, but while you appeared to be a carrier of the genes, they were not active in your body."

"What genes?" I ask.

"Inconsequential," Isabella says. "There are millions of genes important to my..."

"You were returned," Jacob says. "Allowed to live your life. Allowed to breed."

"Don't," I say. It's all I can manage before falling to my knees. "Please."

"As I understand it," Wini says. "...you learned of the child's existence the day before your wife was killed in an accident that left her body mangled beyond recognition, all signs of previous injury or operations eradicated."

"I'll kill you," I growl.

"How unfortunate for you. That must have stung." Wini's voice is cold and very unlike her. "Proof of the child. That is what you held in the envelope."

I can feel it, digging in my head, looking for confirmation of something.

"You know the truth now," Jacob says. "You are a father. You have a son."

My insides cramp up as I hear what is unsaid in the words that *are* said.

Are a father.

Have a son.

"Here is my bargain." Isabella takes my chin in her hands, squeezing my cheeks hard. She lifts my head up to look in my eyes. "The nanites, for your son."

48

Emotion clogs my thoughts, making it hard to contemplate a response.

My son is alive.

My five-year-old son is alive.

Focus.

Think!

What do you know, in your core?

My son—what else!

I'm not human. Not fully.

Like Jacob and Isabella, I am, to some degree, a hybrid. That's why the nanites didn't kill me. Whatever change the Other made to my grandfather filtered down to me, and while the genes they were looking for remain dormant, there's still enough of me that's like Lindo. I think. I'm guessing.

"Where is he?" I croak. "Where's my son?"

"Not here," Wini says. "But that can be arranged if it must be."

"No," I say, realizing this could all be a bluff. But it doesn't matter. My course is set. My resolve is set. "You stay away from him. Just... where is he?"

Young grins. "Not yet. Not until you relinquish the—"

I push myself to my feet. "Tell me how."

Godin approaches the nearest of the tall crystals. Places his hand on its smooth surface. "Just ask them to leave you. I will receive them, just as you did."

"And then you'll just let us leave? You'll tell me where to find my son?"

"Yes," Wini says. The Other has clearly chosen her because I trust her with my life, and vice versa. It probably thinks the answer will sound less like a lie coming from her. But it's an unnecessary effort. I believe it already.

I take one last look around, searching for disapproval in the eyes of my mind-controlled friends. Finding none, I look back at the Grays, watching me with sentinel eyes, all of them controlled by the Other.

The crystal glows brighter at my approach and I feel that same tug inside me. I have a sense that the nanites want to be a part of the crystal, which I've surmised is some kind of advanced computer system, spread out through the facility.

But it's not just a computer.

It's a control center. For the UFOs. For the Grays. For all the people under the Other's thumb. While its transmission of the Other's will is powerful enough to influence people hundreds of miles away, perhaps even on the far side of the globe, it's most powerful in this place, like a point-blank shotgun.

I reach out, hand hovering just six inches from the crystal's surface. My skin tingles. Orange flecks of light twinkle at my fingertips.

I had pictured the nanites as a black, almost sinister entity inside me, like a demonic spirit granting me inhuman powers. But they're luminous, made of the same stuff that powers—if I'm right—the Other's intellect.

"My son, and my friends," I say.

Wini, Young, Godin, Jacob, and Isabella all nod with frantic energy. "Yes," they all say. Desperate. Hungry. As much as I desire my son's safe return, the Other craves what I have even more.

And that is its weakness laid bare.

Because I will *never* give it what it wants.

I will *never* betray my friends' trust, or my own moral code.

I will *never* allow humanity to be enslaved.

Wini grips my outstretched hand, the Other detecting the shift in my emotional state. "What are you doing?"

"The only thing I can do," I say, and then I smile at Wini, who now looks confused.

Turning inward, I address the nanites inside me, anxious to leave. Not because they're drawn by the Other's presence, but out of a craving for vengeance. While they are no longer part of Lindo,

I think he is still a part of them. Over the past days I have felt a kind of consciousness emanating from them. But I don't think it's the nanites themselves, just the parts of Lindo's personality still residing in them. Whether that's a kind of technological residue, or if their eighty-plus years together actually changed the nanites is anyone's guess.

And I don't think the Other's situation is too dissimilar. Had Lindo understood how to send his consciousness along with the nanites, he might now be as alive as the Others, except possessing my body...which I suspect is what the Other really wants.

"You're not alive," I say, "are you?"

Wini's face turns up in a sneer, the kind she makes when *America's Next Top Model* doesn't go the way she thought it should. "How long has it been? Since your species died out? Five thousand years? Ten thousand years? Longer? Was it with the last ice age, or with the dinosaurs?"

Wini's grip tightens, but it's not enough to hurt me. The Other is still limited by her body. "Your son will die."

"I don't think so." I press my hand against the crystal. Its warm surface sends a tingling up my arm.

"Your friends will die," Wini says.

Young and Godin wrap their hands around Jacob's and Isabella's necks.

"Not today," I say, and then I address the nanites tasked to the job at hand. "Kill it. Kill it now!"

My hand turns red hot and a swirling energy flows from my head, down my arm, out my fingertips, and into the crystal. My vision tunnels and fades to black. I feel my equilibrium shift backward as my hearing turns to a kind of rushing wind. And then, the effect fades, leaving me feeling a bit exhausted—and hopeful.

My assassins have been set loose.

But the Other hasn't been stopped, and it has an army of its own assassins.

Godin drops Isabella to the floor and takes a swing at my head that nearly connects. I duck to the side, but it's a momentary solve. Young is approaching from behind, and Wini's nails are now drawing blood on my arm.

Worse, she looks like she's about to bite my neck.

"The world will burn!" Wini shouts, snarling. "All because—"

"Now!" I shout, though the vocalization isn't required. The nanites I slipped into Wini's mind, when I held her up and told her that there was nothing on this planet, in the stars, or living beneath our feet that would stop me from saving her, have been waiting for the signal to free her from the Other's influence.

She shouts in pain, gripping the sides of her head and collapsing to the floor. Breaking the Other's connection to a mind is far more traumatic than easing its way out. I remember the pain she's feeling now, but also know she'll be fighting at my side in just a moment.

Godin takes another swing. He's probably a competent fighter, but under the Other's control, he lacks agility and the fighting instincts of a man who hasn't had his consciousness locked inside a computer system for who knows how long.

The slap of Young's feet betrays him as he approaches. I duck to the side as he swings, overextending himself. Needing to slow the man, but having no desire to injure him, I kick out, striking behind his knee. The joint folds and he topples to the ground, tripping up Godin as he charges again.

"Took you god damn long enough," Wini says, pushing herself up. "Before you get distracted by all this..." she motions to her very naked body, "what do you want to do about them?" She points behind me.

The Grays stalk toward us, hunched forward, fingers curled. They're intimidating as shit, not because their five-foot-tall, slender bodies are imposing, but because if we lose this fight, I think they might tear us apart.

I reach behind my back, dig beneath my body armor and remove the two handguns hidden there. Free of the Other's direct influence, Aaron avoided the area when he patted me down. He didn't know I had weapons hidden there, but he also didn't want to know if I did, because then the Other would know.

He let me come here, and that was before he knew about Lindo's death, which gives me a little hope regarding our odds of escape, which are probably still on the slim-to-none side of things.

I hand one of the weapons to Wini, who frowns. "Where's Susie-Q?"

I smile, despite the circumstances. "Susie-Q holds six rounds." I point to the CZ P-09 handgun in her hands. "Fernando holds twenty, which means if your aim isn't shitty, we can take these assholes."

We both take aim at the approaching Grays.

"You had me at Fernando," Wini says, and squeezes the trigger.

A Gray's head snaps back as the round slips through the front of its head and explodes from the back, spraying chunky purple goo.

"That's my girl," I say with a smile, before picking a target and opening fire.

After the sixth round is fired, and five Grays lie on the floor, the rest break into a desperate sprint. And they're not alone. Godin and Young are back on their feet, thankfully at the back of the group. Isabella and Jacob stand behind the small army, frozen in place, both looking uncomfortable.

And then I see something amazing. Jacob is raising his hand, reaching out for Isabella.

Fight, Jacob! I will him, and pull the trigger again.

A charging Gray spills to the floor leaving a streak of purple gelatin behind it. While two of the little assholes round the fallen body, a third steps in a mound of brain jelly and slips, careening backward while sliding forward, its head slapping the solid stone floor, and cracking like an egg.

The Grays are conduits of the Other's will, and horrifying, but they're not built for battle.

Wini drops two Grays with marksmanship that puts my gunplay to shame. But she's not quick enough to stop the third attacker diving toward her. Instead of shooting, she sidesteps and pistol-whips the thing's head, driving the butt of her gun inside. The skull catches on the weapon, tugging it from her hand.

Four frantic shots drop the two Grays coming at me from the right and left. Worried about Wini, I adjust my aim to the creatures closing in on her, dropping three with five rounds and leaving myself exposed.

The next four shots that ring out are fired by Wini, who has recovered her weapon and returned the favor, dropping two more Grays headed for me.

"We can't keep this up," she says.

She's right. While we're doing a decent job of taking the Grays down in one or two shots, our accuracy and speed isn't quite enough to drop all of them. At some point, this is going to become a fist fight. And while I would bet on me against a lone Gray any time, I'm not sure how Wini, or I, will fare against a group of them, especially when Young and Godin are in the mix.

With only a few rounds left, I consider putting a round into each man's leg. If I can wound them, maybe they'll be out of the fight? Then again, maybe the Other will simply block their pain? Or maybe they'll bleed out before we can escape and get help—if that's even possible.

I'm about to pull the trigger again when the orange crystal flickers and dulls, reminding me that while we're fighting for survival, the Other is, too. We don't need to kill all the Grays, we just need to outlast our true enemy.

I think.

Honestly, I'm not sure what will happen to the Grays when the Other is destroyed. Maybe they'll faceplant, which would be welcome and funny, or maybe they'll carry out the Other's last orders, which could be anything from killing me to destroying the world.

"Behind you!" The voice is Jacob's, so instead of looking for danger, I turn toward the boy, who's holding Isabella's hand. The girl appears to be in pain, but she's free of the Other, thanks to Jacob's support. That *he's* free means the ancient being is losing its grasp. Godin and Young are still charging my position, but they lack Jacob's strong will.

When Jacob points behind me and repeats his warning, I heed it and turn around.

What I find takes the fight out of me. The Grays' reinforcements have arrived. An endless stream of the skinny bastards slips through the solid oval wall, charging toward the last defenders of mankind— myself and a stark naked senior who just ran out of ammunition.

49

Facing numbers that would make King Leonidas of the Spartans piss himself, I hold my fire and slip the gun into the holster on my hip. The two rounds it holds aren't going to change the outcome of this fight. Fists clenched, I glance at Wini, who is now wielding her weapon like a very small club. She might get in a few good whacks, but it won't take long for the Grays to overwhelm her. And I probably won't fare much better.

Turning back to the smaller group setting upon us, I throw myself into the fight, delivering careful, but powerful punches. The Grays rush right into my fists, trying to overcome me with their numbers—which they'll soon do—but for now, I drive my fists against, and sometimes through, every bulbous head I can.

Metallic whacks and a string of curses let me know that Wini is still putting up a fight without having to look.

I'm tackled from behind and driven to the floor. The lone Gray caught me off guard, but its follow-up attack is clumsy. Before it can stand, I grasp the back of its neck and drive its head into the floor three times. The third and final blow, delivered with an angry shout, splits the head.

I roll onto my knees, preparing to stand again, when I see Wini fall beneath three Grays. But they're not from the original group. They're the first arrivals of the new wave still pouring through the walls.

My muscles groan as I stand, pushing myself past limits set by a middle-aged body. Before I make it all the way up, I'm struck by a fist and sent sprawling back to the floor. I push myself onto my hands and knees, but don't make it any further thanks to the stars in my vision. I look up at my attacker.

It's Young, his twitching face framed by dancing lights.

"Fight it," I tell him, hoping his twitching face is a sign of the Other's faltering control.

Young steps closer, fists clenched.

"I'm sorry," I tell him as he draws back to deliver a punch that will likely knock me unconscious. Then I deliver a swift backhand slap to his bare balls. Under control of the Other or not, the attack is enough to crumple Young in on himself. While he curls up into a fetal position, I push myself back up onto unsteady feet.

Jacob and Isabella stand back-to-back, surrounded by Grays.

The orange crystals' luminosity continues to ebb and flow, but nothing else has changed. Hundreds of Grays scurry toward me. Wini is on the floor, held by a wiry-limbed gaggle of Grays, overseen by Godin, who is just starting to turn his attention to me.

Seeing Wini struggling for her life throws me into a rage. With a shriek that scares me a little, I run and dive, knowing full well that the attack will be the last thing I do.

I take two of the emotionless little pricks with me, crushing one beneath my weight and driving my forehead into the face of the second—three times. Warm purple chunks slip down my forehead and fall to the floor when I rise. I yank the third Gray off by grasping the back of its neck and tossing it into Godin, who's closing in.

Wini, whose arms are now free, takes care of the fourth, pistol-whipping it in the head, over and over until it cracks and lies still. I kick the limp body off of her, and help her up.

"Look out!" Jacob shouts, even as he and Isabella are subdued by a Venus flytrap of Gray limbs closing in on them.

I find the impetus for his warning at the far side of the room. A lone Gray wearing some kind of backpack aims a large glowing weapon in my direction. There's a hum, and then a deep *whump*. A basketball-sized sphere of crackling energy launches from the muzzle. It's not nearly as fast as a bullet, sailing through the air, rather than cutting through it. But the weapon's effect is devastating to everything the sphere comes into even the slightest contact with.

A line of Grays are mowed down by the ball of energy, which slides through them, leaving empty space in its wake. Some lose arms, but most are cut in half by the waist-high projectile, which is headed straight toward me. Dodging the shot would have been easy if not for one large, naked problem—to reach me, the glowing sphere will first cut down Godin.

Not wanting to see the good sheriff fold in half after his spine and guts are removed, I dive toward the incoming projectile, tackling Godin by the waist. We topple into an onrushing Gray and fall in a heap. Hot crackling energy slides past, making my hair stand on end, but the rest of my body is intact.

"Thanks," Godin says, his voice raspy and weak. I'm not sure if he's regained full control, but at the very least, he's still in there and fighting.

The hum of more energy weapons powering up shakes the air, but it's unnecessary. The army of Grays is upon us.

I leap to my feet, ready to go down swinging. I bump into Wini's naked back.

"Hey," she says, with just seconds left. "Love you, babe."

I take her hand in mine and lower my fists. "Love you, t—"

Orange light flickers and then cuts to solid black. The darkness lasts just a half second, but when the light returns, everything changes.

The horde of onrushing Grays topple forward, all control lost. Those in the front slap against the unforgiving floor with wet smacks. The thin bodies behind them fall atop each other like the grand finale in a long line of dominoes. A few balls of light launch toward the ceiling as the backpack-wielding Gray crumples to the floor, but they pose no threat.

A smile spreads onto my face when a nearby Gray faceplants into Young's ass crack. "I was right."

"About?" Wini asks.

"That *was* funny." I take stock of our group.

Jacob and Isabella are shoving Gray bodies away. Jacob sees me watching and gives me a happy wave. "We're okay."

Godin pushes himself off the floor with a groan. "Thanks again."

Young flinches back to himself as though violated, clenching his butt and launching away from the Gray burrowed between his cheeks. "Ugh! Shit!" He nearly makes it to his feet before the pain from being slapped in the nuts slows him down.

"What happened?" Godin asks. "I was a backseat driver in my own head. I could see and hear, but I couldn't control myself. Then..." He looks at his hand, clenching and unclenching his fingers, back in control. He turns to the sea of still bodies. "Looks like the same thing happened to them."

"But with no one in the backseat," I say.

"How did you do it?" Young asks, straightening himself out.

"I didn't," I say. "It was Lindo."

Godin's face screws up.

"When he passed the nanites on to me, I think part of him came with them. I sent them into the Other's computer system—" I point to the nearest orange crystal, its light now dull. "—with the order to kill it, but it wasn't really my idea. And they were...eager to do it."

"How could you *kill* the Other inside a computer?" Godin asks.

"Because it's already dead," I say. "In the traditional sense. The Others, as a species, are extinct. I think the last of them transferred its consciousness into this computer system, and has been utilizing the Grays and the UFOs to perform genetic experiments."

"But to what end?" Young asks. "If they're extinct, what could they want from us?"

I'm reading between the lines, but I think I've got a pretty good idea. "Host bodies. For its consciousness, to be transferred by the nanites into a body that shares enough cryptoterrestrial DNA to be compatible. I don't think it was possible until Lindo and his nanites evolved together. Had it succeeded, I think the Other's goal would have shifted from survival to repopulation."

"So without a body, the nanites, and its computer system, it's dead?" Wini asks. "For real dead?"

I'm about to answer in the affirmative when Jacob wraps his arms around me from the side. "I knew you'd come."

"Couldn't have done it without you," I say. "Thanks for the confidence boost." I give the two kids a quick once over. Aside from the scar on Isabella's body, they appear unharmed.

Still in my arms, Jacob goes rigid.

"What is it?" I ask him.

When he doesn't reply, I put a hand on his shoulder and a wave of fear swirls into me from the point of contact.

I turn inward, trying to spur the nanites still inside my head into action. I can feel them, but with their number significantly reduced, I'm unable to reach out beyond myself. Though my vision is still enhanced, I'm now only able to see what is right in front of me.

Jacob gasps out of his fright, sucking in deep breaths. "You're wrong."

"About what?" I ask him.

"The Other." He looks up at me with his big blue eyes, terrified. He coils inward, wrapping his hands around his gut, experiencing intense emotions that the rest of us are oblivious to. When I reach out for him again, he shrugs away. "Don't touch me!"

I raise my hands away from him. "What can I do?"

"Kill it," he says, and when I react with confusion, he adds, "The Other. It's alive. It's...angry. *Really* angry. And it's almost here."

Somewhere far away, an explosion rocks the mesa, rumbling the solid stone beneath our feet. The smooth round tunnels surrounding us cough warm air and dust.

What the hell?

The billowing dust is followed by a dry, husky shriek that carries all the rage Jacob is sensing. And then it arrives, slipping through the wall as though it wasn't there, solidifying before us like a nightmare made real.

The Other has arrived, and it is more hideous than anything I could have imagined if I'd been alive for the past ten thousand years.

50

I stagger away from the thing as its two large, fleshy feet pound against the floor, crushing a half dozen Grays beneath them, popping the bodies like stepped-on ketchup packets. Purple chunks spray away from the Other's mass.

Jacob is right. The Other is *not* dead.

But I wouldn't say it's alive, either, not in the same way it once lived on this planet as part of the dominant species. While the nanites might have provided a way for the Other to live in a more human form, I now know that the cryptoterrestrial species—if the creature before us is an accurate representation of them—was nothing close to human.

The creature that's just emerged through a solid wall is more tyrannosaurus than human.

Or is it? I wonder, noting the weird way its body looks almost fused together.

I use my enhanced eye to take a closer look. What I find stumbles me back even further. I trip on a Gray and fall back, sitting atop its oval head, but never taking my eyes off the Other.

It stands on two powerful legs that end with fleshy mounds, broad enough to support its weight, which must be tons, and wide enough to help maintain balance along with its fifteen-foot-long tail. All of that makes sense. Not much else does.

It takes a moment for me to tease out what I'm really seeing, but once I see it, the truth of what the Other has been doing fills me with nausea. It wasn't just trying to become human, it was sustaining its true form using human—*hybrid*—bodies. I think back to all the frozen hybrids and now know where all their missing body parts went. Their altered genetics made them compatible with whatever the Other used to be. Had my genes been a bit more Other, I might be mounted in its collection, my arms, or legs, or eyes made part of the monster's body.

Harvested and repurposed. While the rudimentary form might still be true to the Other's origins, most of what I'm seeing was once human.

The epidermis is a patchwork of human skins, fused together and layered to create what looks like folds of rhino-like fleshy armor. The Other's two long arms hang over the floor, but could easily be used to help it run. They are tipped not with two large hands, but with what looks like hundreds of human hands, all the fingers wriggling in time like some kind of sea plant warbling in an ocean current. The tail, sweeping back and forth with cat-like agitation is composed of human torsos, each one smaller than the last, from full grown adult tapering down to a newborn. A ridge of small bumps running along the creature's spine from neck to tail tip is composed solely of human noses.

Despite the thing's grotesque appearance, I come to the realization that the cryptoterrestrials weren't a subterranean race. At some point in Earth's history, they lived on the surface, and before becoming civilized and then technologically advanced beyond even present day humanity, they probably hunted and killed creatures far more intimidating than mankind.

It's no wonder the Other has no moral qualms about using people for experimentation. Human scientists are creating their own chimeras out of unrelated animal species, and using pigs to grow human body parts, and basically doing anything we want with creatures of different species. We don't like that the Other is using people for those things, but that's because we're people. While technologically advanced now, for the majority of humanity's evolution, we've been primitive. Like animals. When swine flu, or some other super-virus wipes out the human race and the pigs evolve into the dominant species, perhaps the human race's few survivors will find themselves in a similar position to the Other? How many people would find that outlandish? We already do with pigs as we please and would continue to do so, even after they evolved into a more intelligent, self-aware species.

Of course, right now we're the pigs, so fuck that.

The Other rears its head toward me, zeroing in on the source of its pain. Its twenty eyes—all of them human and varying shades of brown, blue, green, and hazel—glare at me. Its wide mouth turns up in a sneer, revealing long rows of small white teeth I realize are also human. Then it unleashes a dry, husky roar, like it's out of practice. The sound is made even more unnerving by the twin rows of appendages that rise and shake on either side of its spine. I'd missed them at first, taking the lines for skin folds. But I can now see them for what they are: arms. The limbs, connected at the shoulder, spasm in a threat display that instills a deep sense of wrongness in my core.

As much as I'd like to turn tail and run, the Other needs to be stopped. Right here. Now and forever.

Young has other ideas. He breaks from our group and bunny hops the fallen Grays as he retreats toward the nearest tunnel.

More Grays burst as the Other stomps toward me, indifferent to the fate of its mindless acolytes.

I draw the gun on my hip, raising it toward the very large target that is the Other's eye-covered face. As big as it is, two rounds in the brain should put it down.

STOP.

My hands lock in place, the gun's potential now impotent.

DROP THE WEAPON.

I release the gun, unflinching as it clatters to the floor at my feet.

"What are you doing?" Godin asks, his stunned face turning toward me.

He can't hear it. The voice. The Other. It's in my head again.

The crystals might work to broadcast its telepathy, but the effect isn't generated by software. It's biological, and up close and personal, it's even more powerful.

Godin reaches for the weapon, and I try to warn him away, but I can't speak. The Other clenches a hundred fists and drives them into Godin, who's sent spiraling fifteen feet away, where he lands on a bed of immobile Grays.

I try to move, to fight the Other's influence, but not even the nanites can shield me from this assault.

KILL THEM.

No, god damn it.

KILL YOUR FRIENDS.

I turn toward Wini. I try to tell her to run, but I'm locked inside myself. My hand snaps out to clutch her throat. Instead, I grasp hold of a small wrist.

Jacob.

Before I or the Other can comprehend the significance of this, I'm flooded with renewed strength, confidence, and determination. Jacob is once again gifting me with his own strong will.

KILL HIM.

My grip on his wrist tightens enough to make him grimace, but I'm able to resist.

"Fight it!" Jacob says.

Wini must sense what's happening, that the Other is trying to break me and torture me by making me its slave, rather than killing me outright, because she puts her hand on Jacob's shoulder, using him as a conduit for her own emotional reinforcements. Wini's love, commitment, and adoration hits me like nitrous in an engine.

The Other roars, its hot breath coursing over me in waves. I stare up into the human-toothed maw and scream back. Pulses of rage, desperation, and hatred slap into my soul. And still, we resist, pushing back with all of the things that make us a family, that make us human.

Together, we manage to stand up to the Other's psychological assault, but we're still at the monster's mercy.

Its jaws unhinge and open wide enough to engulf me. I flinch as it lunges down, but all the fear and anxiety of being bitten in half is replaced by unflappable bravery. It surges through me, and then out of me, slamming into the Other's still-connected mind like a thrown spear.

When the Other reels back, unleashing a high-pitched roar, I'm freed of its lingering control and able to look back. Isabella has taken hold of Jacob's free hand and lent her own emotional prowess to the effort. She's easily as powerful as Jacob, and perhaps even empathic like him.

But she can't stop what happens next.

None of us can.

Because there is nothing all the fortitude in the world can do to stop a one-ton tail made of human torsos from smearing a person.

"Down!" I shout, wrapping my arms around and shielding Wini, Jacob, and Isabella. My body will do little to cushion the blow, but there's nothing else to do.

I shout when my back is slapped hard from behind, but I don't die.

Don't even move.

Smelling fresh blood, I look up in time to see the severed tail pinwheeling across the room, propelled by the Other's swing. The slap I felt was the creature's blood spraying against my back as the tail was severed and flung.

A ball of blue light slides through the air in the other direction, revealing how the miracle save was pulled off. I trace the energy weapon's path back to its origin and find Young propping up a Gray, struggling to fire off a second shot.

The Other stumbles back, rights itself, and unleashes an eye-bulging roar. At first, I think it's just angry, and wounded, but the Grays around us begin to rise. They twitch and brew with energy, serving the call of their wounded creator and master.

And then, gunfire.

Men—actual men—dressed in black body armor, stream out of a tunnel, weapons raised and blazing. The Grays are cut down in bursts of purple. Standing among the men, his mind freed and face revealed, is Aaron. He gives me a nod and returns to his assault on the rising Grays.

The explosion.

I thought it was the Other rising from whatever depths had kept it hidden, but it was Aaron breaching the base.

While Aaron and his mercenaries are welcome, their distraction has more of an effect on me than the Other. While I'm still turning around, the giant jaws have opened to envelop me once more. I see the back of its throat and then hear two loud pops. Two red flowers blossom at the back of its mouth, the bullets that created them slipping inside the brain beyond and wreaking havoc. I dive to the side as momentum carries the Other forward and down.

I land atop a Gray as the automatons collapse once more, as motionless as their master. Wini stands on the other side of the creature's head, its many eyes now closed. She lowers the literal smoking gun, looks down at the Other and says, "No one eats my boy."

She looks me in the eyes, gives me a relieved smile, and drops the gun. Then she turns to the oncoming mercenaries led by Aaron. "Any of you big hunks have some spare clothes, because its frikken cold in here and my tits are out."

"Thanks," a groggy voice says. I turn to find Godin being helped up by Aaron. He's clutching his arm.

"You okay?"

"It's a small price to pay for saving the world, right?" He smiles and winces. "But I think I'll stick to policing angry Mormons from now on."

While I chuckle in solitude at Godin and Wini's humor, Jacob crouches down by the Other and places a hand on its head. Its muscles relax. I crouch beside him in time to hear him whisper, "Go in peace. Your struggle is over."

The Other shudders and then seems to deflate.

"That was...kind," I tell him. It wasn't just kind, it was an act of mercy I don't think many people would have considered, let alone performed. In the Other's last, and most painful moments, Jacob eased its pain and the knowledge that it had failed its thousands-year-old quest to return its species from the ashes.

"In the end, it was just sad." He stands up and confirms my own theory. "I think, in the same situation, people would do the same thing."

I think about everything I've done since getting involved in this mess. All the men I've shot. All the men I've killed. All of the horrors I've subjected myself to, at first just to find one girl—not to mention all the horrible things I genuinely considered doing once the stakes were raised. The Other was fighting for its entire species. That doesn't excuse its crimes, but it means, "You're probably right."

EPILOGUE

"How are you holding up?" Wini asks. She's sitting beside me, dressed in her usual too tight outfit and looking good. In the past three months she's hit the gym and is a lot more mobile than she used to be. Our encounter with the Other and the Grays left her feeling inadequate, despite the fact that she brought the monster down—not the guy with nanites in his head, or even the army of mercenaries. I'm all for Wini extending her life. I'm not sure how I'd get by without her.

Not that I'm without help.

I've struck a tentative deal with Aaron, allowing him access to Other technologies to be reverse engineered for the betterment of mankind. The moment I get a whiff of weapons development, I'll shut him down. With the nanites inside me back to full strength, he knows I'm capable. While motivated by human desires of wealth and status, Lindo's death seems to have awakened something in Aaron. A kind of responsibility for honoring his brother's passing.

If that's really what happened.

The one lie I've told to Aaron is in regards to Lindo.

His brother died. I watched it happen.

But the funeral we held for him in Dulce was something of a sham, because the casket was empty. After confirming that Reg and Randy were both safe—having been left unconscious with no memory of the Grays abducting Wini, Godin, and Young—we returned to the gun warehouse. The place was still in ruins. There was blood—everywhere.

But Lindo's body was gone.

Godin, returned to his job, led a raid on the New Zion Ranch, uncovering a slew of illegal activities including human trafficking. After digging through documents and interrogating the surviving family members with Jacob's aid, we learned that while they had removed the attackers' bodies at the gun shop, they had not removed Lindo.

I like to think that some remaining nanites patched Lindo up. That he's somewhere in the world, taking a much needed and deserved vacation. Wherever he is, if he's alive, he doesn't want to be found. So I've resisted the temptation to track him down. If he's alive, he'll come back to the fold when he's ready. In the meantime, there are plenty of other people to help.

Aaron's army of mercenaries now work for me, under Kuruk's supervision, scouring the globe for children being raised for the sole purpose of being sold to the Other. In some cases, the children are left with their remorseful, loving parents. In other cases, we take the children and place them with families composed of adults who had previously been freed by Lindo.

A few of the mercs hold a grudge...because I shot them, but Jacob tells me that they are grateful for the new focus. They feel pride in their work, and even if they don't like me, they would protect me if need be.

"Feels good to be out in the field again," I say.

"Really, you're going to give me a bullshit answer?"

"How are *you* feeling?" I ask, hoping to divert the conversation away from my emotions. Jacob, who is sitting on the bench across from me, already knows exactly how I feel, including that I'd rather not talk about our newest rescue mission. He's dressed like an average kid wearing shorts and a T-shirt that reads: 'I have issues.' The irony of his shirt is that Jacob is more resilient than anyone I've met before. When it comes to adapting to our new reality, he has been eager, positive, and a light in the darkness left by the Other.

"I'm good," Wini says. "Have a date tonight. And if he's lucky I might let him give me that d—"

"Wini!" I point to Jacob, who's already chuckling.

"*Dinner*," Wini says. "What's wrong with dinner? What did *you* think I was going to say?" She hitches a thumb at me and says to Jacob, "Your dad's kind of a perv. Just FYI."

"I know," Jacob says, and they have a good laugh.

I'm still getting used to being called, 'Dad,' but it's better than 'Father,' which Jacob used during the first week after I created adoption records, school records, medical records, and everything else he needed to legally be my child. We are joined by Isabella and her mother, whose defiance of The Other has grown deeper since learning the full truth of her child's near fate. We all live in Dulce and 'work' in the mesa. As far as the state knows, the kids are homeschooled and always have been, but their education is like none other on Earth.

Between experimenting with the tech left behind by the Other—including fully intact UFOs and still-functioning Grays, not to mention all of the reverse-engineered tech developed by Aeron—they're going to understand the future before the world knows it has arrived.

"Almost there," Young says, stepping into the cargo hold and taking a seat beside Jacob. The pastor's decision to leave his church and join our cause full-time was a surprise to me—and to his family. They've since moved to Dulce, and while Young has started a new church, he mostly works as a counselor for the people we now call the Liberated.

This is the hardest part of our new job. Once a day, we wake a group of people from the Other's collection. Every person freed is a different case. Most are confused. Some are categorically broken. Those most recently taken are returned to society, joining our families around the world. Those with missing limbs are being assisted by Aaron, whose company is developing cybernetic limbs. Those taken before the advent of computers, or cars, or electricity, remain in the mesa, being reeducated. Some of them are already working alongside us, but I suspect most will spend the rest of their lives trying to understand how they've been unconscious since childhood and have awakened in an adult body, hundreds or thousands of years in a future that makes no sense. There are joys every day, and deep despairs.

The most difficult cases are those who emerge from their Other-induced coma to find that vital organs have been removed. Some survive hours. Others just minutes or seconds. But Jacob, and his siblings returned to me by Sheba, are there to provide comfort and peace as they pass away, lost in confusion.

Only three months have passed, but it feels like years. The mesa is now familiar to me. I can navigate its vast and winding insides by memory. I also have full access to its computer system, allowing me to control both the UFOs and the Grays. It took some work to understand everything, but the nanites make the interface smooth, and allow me access to the system from anywhere on Earth.

It's cool. And useful. But I've lost many hours of sleep debating the morality of becoming, in a sense, the next Other. I now wield the same power. Should I be corrupted by it, the world would be mine to control, overtly or covertly. And if the world's governments decided to end our planet in a torrent of nuclear fire, I could retreat to the mesa, transfer my consciousness into a computer system designed to contain it, and over the next several thousand years, do my best to return humanity to power.

Or I could get in a UFO and explore the universe.

Aaron says they're not designed for that, but I'm pretty sure he's full of shit, mostly because Jacob and I already took one into orbit.

Two Grays enter and I can't help but feel uneasy. Even though they're following the orders given by me and transferred to their AIs by the nanites, I have an inherent distrust of them. Also, they're freakin ugly.

"Hans and Frans!" Wini greets the Grays with a smile and a wave. In an effort to make everyone a little more comfortable around our slender helpers—whose tireless efforts really are indispensable at this point—she named them all and dressed them in Star Trek uniforms.

We don't use them outside the mesa very often, but today is a special case. On occasion, when removing a child from trafficking parents, we utilize the Grays, letting the people involved believe the Other is still alive, well, and not to be disturbed. Despite mankind's oldest enemy now being truly extinct, our job will be easier if people are still looking for aliens in the stars, and the U.S. government maintains its policy of not rocking the boat.

When our transportation comes to a stop, I ask. "Are we ready to do this?"

My human companions look at me with raised eyebrows that ask if *I'm* ready. The two Grays raise their thumbs, a gesture taught to them by Isabella. She's a strong kid, and while Jacob can calm me with a touch, she keeps me grounded in the real world, as concerned about the latest exploits of One Direction as she is the liberation of cryptoterrestrial slaves. She's a good kid, and I'm glad she's part of my life.

But she's not my only child now.

The Grays stare at me with their big, malicious black eyes, waiting for the green light.

"Go ahead," I tell them.

The UFO's floor lights up, and they slip through it, dropping out of sight.

"It's going to be okay." Wini pats my knee, but I can tell that she's nervous now, too. "You'll do fine."

"You're both upset," Jacob says. He holds his hand out. "Do you want me to—"

I shake my head.

"What we're feeling isn't comfortable," Young says, "but it's good."

"They feel sad," Jacob says, but then furrows his brow, "but you're not, are you?"

I see what's happening below, in the home. The terrified husband and wife, paralyzed by the Grays, cast in bright light streaming through the windows. Their terror is tangible, and the Other's power is without question. Hans and Frans move from the parents' bedroom, into a child's room. The only decorations on the walls are cobwebs and stains of who-knows-what. Cardboard boxes strewn about the room are being used as furniture...I think. Upon closer inspection, I see that it's worse than that. They're old, damp, and moldy, covered in trash. An empty air mattress lies on the floor, full of holes. Beside it is a yellow bucket, nearly full to the top with human waste. The Grays find the boy, who has been treated like a caged animal, lying behind a wall of boxes curled up like a mouse in its nest. Making sure the boy remains asleep, they lift him and head for the wall.

Looking at the boy's face through the Grays' eyes, I know, without a doubt, that the work that has consumed most of my personal time for the past months has finally borne fruit. I put my hand on my pants pocket, feeling the photo kept there.

The floor lights up again and the Grays slide up through the floor. Frans holds a nearly six-year-old boy in its arms.

I stand and take the boy from them, ordering them to leave with a thought.

The boy stirs.

His eyes open.

My heart breaks.

It's been five years and three months since I looked into Kailyn's eyes, but I have no trouble seeing her in his eyes, in his cheeks, his nose.

Who are you? he asks, and I nearly sob at the sound of his voice. The voice that no one else heard.

A familiar tickle fills my head. Instead of resisting, I open my mind. I let him see enough to understand.

When he starts to squirm, I put him down. He steps away from us, but then stops. His frightened face calms. Jacob has a hand on his arm, soothing his worries.

The boy looks down at Jacob's hand, and then into Jacob's not-quite-human eyes. "Brother."

Jacob smiles and nods.

The boy turns to Wini. "Grandmother."

Wini wipes away tears and hiccups a "Yes."

When Nathaniel looks into my eyes and says, "F-father?" I can't hold back my tears.

I'm incapable of speaking. Any sound that comes from my mouth will be a sob. So I speak the language every parent and child instinctually knows from the moment of birth—I hold out my arms.

There's a moment of hesitation, and then my son, who should be dead, steps into my embrace and says, one mind to another, *thank you for finding me.*

A NOTE FROM THE AUTHOR

Dear Reader,

I need to start this by apologizing to the Mormon church. I know, I know, I accused you of building secret bunkers in *SecondWorld* (you are... ahem) and made Nephi a really bad dude in *The Last Hunter* series (Nephil *is* the singular form of Nephilim). And yes, I had a kaiju fall atop the Mormon Temple, and identified the angel atop it as the afore-mentioned Nephi rather than Moroni (because I think they're the same—look it up—not an invitation for debate). Despite all that, I had zero intention of including any Mormon-related elements in this story. Here's how it went down.

This whole story began where Delgado's investigation leads early on: the 37th parallel. I decided that the story's course would follow this line and when it was time for them to travel west, I followed the parallel, looking for towns through which it passed. Colorado City was the first I found, and pretty much exactly where I wanted to go.

So I researched the town and found...polygamist Mormon cults. My first thought was, "No way. I can't do this." For each of the offenses listed in the first paragraph, I received a good amount of angry correspondence and I'm not looking forward to more. I was looking for ways out of this conundrum when I came across information about how young boys were expelled from those cults and never seen again. Mentally cursing, I really had no choice at this point. Truth and fiction aligned.

Do I really think Joseph Smith made a deal with cryptoterrestrial 'aliens?' Of course not. They were Nephilim. Okay! Okay! Put the pitchforks away. I'm kidding!

Maybe.

As for the Cryptoterrestrial theory on UFOs and alien visitations, I had also not intended on going in that direction when I started writing. But as I dug into the evidence (in the story), I was led in that direction with the help of a book titled *The Cryptoterrestrials: A Meditation on Indigenous Humanoids and the Aliens Among Us* by Mac Tonnies, pretty much the only text I could find on the subject. In the end, I find the theory as plausible, if not more so, than aliens from the stars or visitors from the future or another dimension. It was also unique (as far as I know) in the genre of UFO fiction, and I like unique. I apologize to any E.T.s this may offend, but you know, you are abducting and probing people, so I think a good ribbing is probably in order.

If you're not Mormon (or maybe a Mormon with a sense of humor), nor an alien (or maybe an alien with a sense of humor, like Alf) and weren't offended by *The Others* or this author's note, shoot on over to Amazon, or Audible, or Goodreads and post a review. Every single one helps a ton, and since I really love writing these crazy books, I'd really appreciate it.

Thanks for reading!

—Jeremy Robinson

ACKNOWLEDGMENTS

Special thanks to Frank Robinson, my father, who helped instill a love of science fiction and fear of Grays in me. From tales of his own sightings, to visits with UFOlogist and family friend, Raymond Fowler, my father's influence shines through in *The Others*. We recently talked about our personal theories on the subject and it turns out that we're on the same page, and that if my father wrote this book, it might have been similar, but with less foul language. And now if people think I'm a freak for writing this book, they know who's really to blame.

Thanks to Kane Gilmour, my editor supreme. Thanks to Dan Delgado (the real one) and Sally Ross, for all the UFO-related reading material. And big thanks to the team of proofreaders, Roger Brodeur, Lyn Askew, Julie Cummings Carter, Liz Cooper, Dan Delgado, Dustin Dreyling, Dee Haddrill, Becki Laurent, Rian Martin, Sharon Ruffy, Jeff Sexton, and Kelly Tyler, for making my writing look cleaner than it is.

As always, thanks to my family for inspiring me and for putting up with my weird theories...even when they give the kids nightmares. Blame papa! Love you guys.

ABOUT THE AUTHOR

Jeremy Robinson is the international bestselling author of sixty novels and novellas, including *Apocalypse Machine, Island 731*, and *SecondWorld*, as well as the Jack Sigler thriller series and *Project Nemesis*, the highest selling, original (non-licensed) kaiju novel of all time. He's known for mixing elements of science, history and mythology, which has earned him the #1 spot in Science Fiction and Action-Adventure, and secured him as the top creature feature author. Many of his novels have been adapted into comic books, optioned for film and TV, and translated into thirteen languages. He lives in New Hampshire with his wife and three children. Visit him at www.bewareofmonsters.com.

www.ingramcontent.com/pod-product-compliance
Lightning Source LLC
Chambersburg PA
CBHW022350020726
47500CB00002B/200